A PYRRHIC HISTORY

VOLUME I

THE SHAPING
OF DESTINY

BY

IAN CROUCH

Eloquent Books

Eloquent Books
An imprint of Strategic Book Group
P.O. Box 333
Durham CT 06422
www.StrategicBookGroup.com

ISBN: 978-1-60911-914-0

Printed in the United States of America

Book Design: Bonita S. Watson

CONTENTS

DRAMATIS PERSONAE

Principal characters and their positions at the commencement of the novel. They are presented in order of their importance with regard to setting the historical and political stage.

PYRRHUS—The young disinherited king of Epirus, who fights with Antigonus and Demetrius at Ipsus, where this tale begins.

ANTIGONUS—One of Alexander's generals. King of Phrygia and related territories. Rules Anatolia, the eastern seaboard of the Mediterranean and part of Greece (with his son Demetrius). Aims to recreate a single empire.

DEMETRIUS—Son of Antigonus. Married to Deidameia, Pyrrhus's sister. Declared as heir and co-king by Antigonus.

CASSANDER —Son of Antipater, Alexander's regent in Macedonia. Hated for executing Olympias, Alexander's mother, together with Roxanne and Alexander IV (Alexander the Great's wife and son). King of Macedonia.

LYSIMACHUS—One of Alexander's generals. King of Thrace.

PTOLEMY—One of Alexander's generals. Pharaoh of Egypt.

BERENICE—Wife of Ptolemy. Empress of Egypt.

ANTIGONE—Daughter of Berenice. Stepdaughter of Ptolemy.

SELEUCUS—One of Alexander's generals. King of Asia (Syria, Mesopotamia, and the eastern territories of Alexander's empire).

MENESTHEUS—Scholar and mercenary captain.

PANTAUCHUS—General of Demetrius.

CINEAS—Athenian politician.

NEOPTOLEMUS—Pyrrhus's cousin, who has seized the throne of Epirus from Pyrrhus.

DEIDAMEIA—Pyrrhus's sister, married to Demetrius.

All of these characters are historical figures, with the exception of Menestheus.

PROLOGUE

The great battle that is known to some as Gaugamela, and to others as Arbela, changed the world forever. Alexander had defeated the army of the Great King of Persia for the third time and had made himself the master of the empire of the Persians. Darius the Third was dead soon after, slain by one of his own officers. True, there was more fighting to come. Alexander had to fight the assassin Bessus, who had killed his king; he had to consolidate the empire he had won; and there was the dream of extending his power to India itself, but the cultural axis of the eastern Mediterranean and beyond was altered irrevocably. The stage had been set for the Hellenization of the East, but Alexander would not live to see his dreams come to fruition.

Alexander died in Babylon in 323 BC, at the age of thirty-two. The following years would be ones of continuing rivalry and warfare among the Macedonian generals, the Successors or Diadochoi, many of whom would die in these struggles. By 301 BC, those years resulted in four great Hellenistic kingdoms, in addition to Macedonia itself.

In this year, they would once again do battle for their survival.

These years were perhaps the greatest period of political and military high adventure that the world had yet known, and there were other great figures from the Greek world who would join in the contest. One of these figures was Pyrrhus, the young, disinherited king of Epirus, who would later be described by Hannibal as the most capable military commander the world had seen, after Alexander himself.

It also fell to Pyrrhus to open the struggle between the Greeks and the Romans for domination of the eastern Mediterranean world and to foresee the great contest between the Romans and the Carthaginians in the west.

CHAPTER I

As Antigonus the One-Eyed sat at his camp desk in his tent, he knew that he had grown irritable over recent months. Others thought that it was because of the heavy responsibilities of kingship, but he knew the real cause lay elsewhere. He had been governing Phrygia for over thirty years, give or take a few years interrupted by the war with Perdiccas, soon after the death of Alexander. The problem was that he was running out of time.

He had reached the age of eighty-one, and for the last twenty-two of these years he had been fighting to keep the empire left by Alexander intact. The result of those years would be decided tomorrow, here in the plains of Ipsus. Ranged against him would be two of the other survivors: Lysimachus, who had brought his army from Thrace, and Seleucus, who had come from Babylon. Ptolemy, the other surviving general who had successfully made himself pharaoh of Egypt, had not joined this coalition against him, as he felt himself secure.

The others feared Antigonus's power, and they believed the empire was too unstable to survive without the guidance of Alexander. It was only a small step, then, for them to become dynasts of various parts of his empire. Were they right? Perhaps so. If he was not to be victorious tomorrow, he would certainly die, and he knew that he was the only one left with the idea of a united Hellenistic empire. Even now, he still felt in awe of the greatness of the vision of Alexander. He had taken an army from Macedonia to cross the Hellespont, still leaving factions and jealousies behind him in Greece, and then conquered the colossus that was the Persian Empire, all the way to India. Yet even that was not his greatest achievement. The crowning glory was his conviction that the known world, with its many peoples, could live in peace under the guidance of a benevolent Greek ruler. Not even Aristotle had dreamed of such a thing. Aristotle had believed that the world was made up of Greeks and barbarians. It was left to Alexander to go a step further, to say that the good man was the true Greek, and the bad man the true barbarian. Aristotle had left it to Alexander to be an even greater man than his friend, Philip of Macedonia, captain-general of all Greece, who had united the Greek city-states (with the exception of Sparta, as always), and created the army with which Alexander would conquer the world in his place.

Antigonus was brought out of his reverie by his son, Demetrius, as he entered his tent unannounced. "Father," Demetrius said, "a messenger has arrived with a letter for you."

"Do you always barge straight in," said Antigonus.

"Almost always" replied Demetrius with his usual irritating cheerfulness and passed the roll of sealed papyrus to his father. Antigonus took the letter, looked at the familiar seal, and opened it. A smile crept over his face. "This is from Pyrrhus. He has sent this ahead of his column. He will be here with the mercenary contingent from Sardis before nightfall."

"That is good news indeed, Father," said Demetrius, "Pyrrhus has done well to get here so soon."

Antigonus looked up and said, "I am going to rest for a while, my son. When Pyrrhus arrives, bring him here, and we will have a meal together." Demetrius nodded, smiled at his father, and left the tent.

Demetrius walked over to the large tent belonging to Xanthippus, who was Antigonus's chief general, or *polemarch*, where the various unit commanders, the *strategoi,* were waiting for him to go over the battle plans laid out for them. As he always thought that a king should never have to knock on anybody's door (or make some sort of noise on a tent flap), he walked straight into the tent and greeted the men seated at the table. Xanthippus stood up and smiled at Demetrius. "Good morning Sire," he said, "we have all your father's plans ready for you."

"Thank you, Xanthippus. Please sit down, gentlemen," Demetrius said, sitting down on a folding camp chair. Demetrius looked about him. He approved of the simple furnishings of the tent, which consisted of a bed, with a single soldier's blanket to keep out the surprising cold of the Phrygian nights, one large table, suitable for the examination of maps and documents, and enough chairs for the king and his commanders to sit while in council.

All of the furniture was lightweight and could be folded for easy transport. The two remaining pieces were a stand for Xanthippus to hang his armor and a small table with a basin he used to wash and to shave. The armor was the only example of decoration to be seen. The shield, helmet, and cuirass were all beautifully wrought in bronze and had been given to Xanthippus by Antigonus eleven years ago, when he had saved Demetrius's life after their army had been severely beaten by Ptolemy's forces near Gaza. The helmet was of the final design of the Corinthian type, beaten by an artisan from a single sheet of bronze, with exquisitely shaped cuttings for the eyes, which led into the margins of the long nosepiece, and the broad cheekpieces, which came around to almost meet in the center. The crest followed the top of the helmet for the breadth of an outstretched hand and held an impressive plume of horsehair, dyed red to match the color of a Spartan hoplite's cloak. This always pleased Xanthippus when he put it on, as he had always admired the Spartans for their military prowess and simplicity of life, despite the fact that they were no longer a great power in the Greek world.

The cuirass was made of two pieces. The back plate was plain but curved to closely follow the body contour. The breastplate was of the muscular design with the shape of the pectoral and abdominal muscles one would see in an athlete at the Olympic Games. The two plates were fastened by short leather straps and were worn over a heavy cloth tunic. The tunic itself had sleeves that went to just above the elbow, and the sleeves were covered with strips of leather, into which were riveted discs of bronze, about the size of a tetradrachm piece. The tunic was plain over the upper body, but where the cuirass finished just below the waist, the tunic continued to just above the knee, this part being pleated for ease of movement, and the pleats were once again covered with strips of leather, with the same bronze discs as on the arms.

The shield was round, and just over two feet in diameter, with a Gorgon's head engraved on it, which was thought to increase the fearful aspect of the soldier carrying it. The last items of armor were thick leather greaves to protect the lower leg and the knee.

Xanthippus realized that he was considered old-fashioned, having bronze armor when fine armor was made of the stronger iron or the tough but light linen, but one does not easily ignore the gift of a king. With his combination of the cuirass and the heavy cloth tunic, he felt he was as well protected as his peers. He was also reluctant to admit that he had reached an age where he struggled with the weight of the armor.

Against the armor stand rested a spear with a shaft that was six feet in length, with a foot-long iron tip and a three-inch sharpened base. Last of all, sitting in its sheath, was a two-foot long Thracian sword, hammered out of the finest iron, which was rumored to be sharp enough to shave with.

While he thought such simplicity was desirable in army commanders who adhered to the philosophy of minimalism that was traditional in the Macedonian army, Demetrius had acquired a taste for the luxuries of the East and always made sure he had some of the comforts of the palace with him while on campaign. While he had drawn the line at bringing his favorite courtesans on such an important campaign, he made sure that his bath, ointments, and silk tunics were brought along.

"If you are ready, Sire, I have the dispositions of the army here to show you," said Xanthippus. The commanders looked at him expectantly. As well as Xanthippus, who had the overall tactical command under Antigonus and Demetrius, and whose specific command was the Macedonian right wing of the infantry phalanx, the veteran companions of the king, there were eight other men seated around the table.

Demetrius himself would have overall command of their cavalry, and he was placed on the extreme right wing of the army.

Archesilaus, commanding the left wing of cavalry.

Pantauchus of Pella, whose command was the left wing of the infantry phalanx.

Thorax of Melissa, who commanded the reserve infantry and the king's bodyguard, the Agema, consisting of 500 elite infantry and 500 cavalry.

Demades, the commander of the hypaspists, the more mobile armored infantry, whose shorter spears made them very adaptable and whose role was to protect the flanks of the phalanx and then attack the flank of the enemy army. Demades's place was to the right of the phalanx. Pyrrhus and the mercenaries from Sardis would take their place to the left of the phalanx.

Menon and Callisthenes, commanders of the light-armed troops, composed of light infantry and archers. These troops would begin the battle as skirmishers and would try and disrupt the order of their opponents' front line.

Lastly, there was Charidemus, who would command the elephant squadron.

"Very well," said Demetrius, "but the first issue is the strength of the enemy. They appear to be making their final encampment, and I would like to know what the scouts have been able to find out."

"The scouts came in a short time ago, Sire," said Xanthippus, "and they have a formidable army, although their numbers of infantry appear to be slightly less than our own, if Pyrrhus arrives from Sardis in time."

"I am able to give you some good news, Xanthippus," said Demetrius. "My father had a message from Pyrrhus a short

time ago, and he will be here before nightfall with the reinforcements from Sardis."

"In that case, Sire, that will give us some advantage with the
strength of the infantry. As for the cavalry, it appears that we are
similarly matched, but there is a very important fact that I must
bring to your attention. In order to bring his forces here, and to
join Lysimachus against us, Seleucus made peace with the Indi-
ans on the eastern border of his territories."

"And what is so important about that, Xanthippus?" asked
Demetrius.

"Our problem, Sire, comes from the terms of the treaty
between Seleucus and Chandragupta. In exchange for the
Indian territory Seleucus relinquished that was never any
use to him anyway, Chandragupta has sworn never to vio-
late the border between their two territories. It means that
Seleucus has been able to transfer his troops from the Indian
border to use against us here, and also he has a squadron of
400 trained war elephants, with their mahouts, given to him
as a pledge of good faith by Chandragupta. This is the one
arm of the army in which he has a clear superiority, as we
have only seventy-five elephants."

Demetrius digested this unpleasant piece of news for a
short time, and then, with his characteristic good humor in a
time of adversity, said, "Well, Xanthippus, we will just have to
deal with them, won't we?"

This response disturbed Xanthippus greatly, as he was not
at all sure that Demetrius had understood the fact that his
army could be placed at a great tactical disadvantage if the
elephant corps of their adversaries was well handled. As a
result of this, he felt he must try and continue this briefing
in such a way that Demetrius understood all the fundamental
elements of the battle plan set down by Antigonus. Demetrius
was a brave man and a good commander in many ways, but
he showed much greater ability in the forefront of the army
than in making tactical decisions.

DISPOSITION OF THE ARMY OF ANTIGONUS AND DEMETRIUS.

Total Numbers: Infantry   70,000
                      Cavalry   10,000
                      Elephants   75

Cavalry	Light armed	Light armed	Cavalry
(Archesilaus)	Infantry	Infantry	(Demetrius)
----------------	(Menon)	(Callisthenes)	-------------
	-------------	----------------	

Hypaspists	Phalanx	Phalanx	Hypaspists
(Pyrrhus)	(Pantauchus)	(Xanthippus)	(Demades)
-------------	-------------	----------------	-------------

                  Left Wing   Right Wing

                              Agema &

                              Reserve
Elephants   Infantry   Elephants
------------   (Thorax)   ------------
    (35)   (40)

                                                        (Charidemus)

"As you will see, Sire," said Xanthippus, "your father has followed his usual plans. The phalangites and the hypaspists will hold the enemy in front. The right wing of the phalanx will be strengthened and will try to break the left of the enemy's front line, which will have been subjected to our archers beforehand. We will not be able to depend on that entirely though, as our strength in infantry is only marginally superior. Also, with our small number of elephants, we can only keep them in reserve in case an opportunity to use them presents itself. The critical element will be your cavalry.

"It is imperative that your squadron of cavalry attacks and disperses the enemy cavalry and then returns to attack the flank of the enemy's left wing. This must be done before the enemy does the same to us. Your father believes that Seleucus will make the same mistake that he has made before and use his elephants against our infantry rather than the cavalry.

"You will recall, Sire, that elephants tend to shy away from a phalanx if it is able to keep its close order and form an unbroken line of pikes. Our soldiers are familiar with elephants and can be relied upon to stand firm. If our cavalry can close on their flank before they can bring the elephants to upset our horses, it will give us the opportunity for an early victory. Once the formation of their phalanx is broken they will withdraw and enter peace negotiations. There is no need to base our tactics on uninterrupted slaughter of infantry."

"Excellent," said Demetrius, who was very pleased with the important role he would play in the battle. "If there is nothing else to add, gentlemen, I suggest we adjourn to speak to our various unit commanders. After that, I will take a bath, and I will speak to Pyrrhus when he arrives."

Demetrius stood up and made his way out of the tent. He was in excellent spirits, partly because of having the position of honor in tomorrow's battle, but also because of the fact that he was looking forward to seeing Pyrrhus.

Pyrrhus had joined Antigonus's entourage the previous year, when, at the age of seventeen and apparently secure in his position as king of Epirus, he had been displaced by a bloodless coup while attending a wedding in neighboring Illyria. The usurper was a certain Neoptolemus, a distant cousin from another line of the royal family. As Demetrius had married Pyrrhus' sister, Deidameia, two years ago, there was a family tie that made it easy for Pyrrhus to join Antigonus. In fact, Antigonus would probably have been offended if Pyrrhus had not joined him, as the guest and host relationship among the Greeks was as important now as it was in the time of Pyrrhus's ancestor Achilles.

Although there was a large difference in their ages—Demetrius was now thirty-six—they were both gregarious men, and the two of them had become good friends despite the fact that they both thrived on a half-serious prickling of the other.

Now, on the eve of a great battle, Demetrius hoped that Pyrrhus's arrival would be something of a tonic for his father, who was uncharacteristically withdrawn and brooding. Since he had joined them, Pyrrhus had shown energy and initiative and, as a result, had become a useful member of the group of unit commanders. He resisted the temptation to brood over his misfortunes and had come to regard the goals of Antigonus and Demetrius as his own.

There had been a furious level of activity over the last few months. Lysimachus's arrival in Phrygia had come as a surprise to Antigonus, and they had an almost impossible task of making themselves ready to meet the invading army. They *were* ready, but the arrival of Pyrrhus's troops at the last minute showed the urgency of the preparations.

There was no doubt that tomorrow would be a day that would shape history, for themselves as individuals, as well as the kingdoms represented by their armies, but, until now, Antigonus had never allowed great events to shake his confidence. Demetrius did not dwell on insoluble questions about his father, or on the magnitude of the political issues that would hinge on tomorrow's battle, and set out to find his subordinate cavalry officers.

He walked out of the central area of the camp where the tents of the king and the generals were pitched and walked toward the eastern end of the camp where the cavalrymen were quartered, next to the temporary stables. He picked out his two squadron commanders, Lycoon and Glaucon, who were about to supervise the horses' feeding.

These two men had been in Antigonus's service for many years and were familiar with his ways. Demetrius called to them and they walked with him to a clear area just in front of the stables. After describing the basic disposition of the army, Demetrius took his dagger out of a scabbard on his belt and drew a sketch in the sand to show them the movements that would be required in the battle. Demetrius impressed on them the importance of watching for his signals, which he would make just after his bugler sounded his trumpet. They both felt the plans were satisfactory, and Demetrius left them to continue with their duties and walked back to his tent, impatient for his overdue bath.

CHAPTER II

Demetrius was asleep in his tent, coming to the end of a nightmare, when Xanthippus shook his shoulder, trying to wake him. "Sire, wake up!" Demetrius groaned and then sat bolt upright, almost knocking Xanthippus over as he was bending over him.

"Oh, it's you, Xanthippus. I am glad you are here. I have just had the most disturbing dream."

"I came to get you, Demetrius. Your father wants to see you in private, before you meet him with Pyrrhus."

"That's odd. He never does that before a battle."

"I know, Sire, but then again, he has been acting oddly in many ways lately," said Xanthippus.

"Yes," said Demetrius absentmindedly, "but before I see Antigonus, I must tell you about this dream I just had. I know that one should not worry about such things, but there are some who take them seriously, and I would like your opinion. In my dream, I saw Alexander standing in front of me, in his beautiful shining armor. He greeted me by name, in a friendly way, and then asked me what was our watchword for the battle. I replied, 'Zeus and victory.' He then became very angry and said that he had expected Antigonus to choose, 'Alexander and victory.' He told me he would go and join our adversaries, as they would certainly receive him."

"I would not fret, Sire," said Xanthippus, "it was surely just a dream, and you have had more than enough on your mind lately to unsettle your sleep. I am not so sure what your father would think, though. It may be best not to mention it to him."

Although he had not said so, Xanthippus was appalled by this dream. He was not an overtly religious man, but deep inside of him, he had as much superstition as was usual for the age in which he lived. He believed the gods probably did exist, and, that being the case, why would they not be able to meddle in the affairs of men?

"I am sure you are right. I will not mention it to him. Hand me my tunic, would you Xanthippus?" said Demetrius, "I had better rush, as he will not be in a mood to be kept waiting."

There were still two hours of daylight left as Pyrrhus and his column were nearing Antigonus's camp. The march had been free of incidents, and the small troop of cavalry he was able to use as scouts had not encountered any of the enemy's forces. He and his men were all in excellent spirits, and they were sure that when they arrived in Antigonus's camp, they would be allowed to rest and be provided with a good supper. It would make a very welcome change from the wheat and barley meal that was their staple diet, along with stale bread and dried figs. They had heard from others who had served with Antigonus before that he was always generous in his provisions for his soldiers. He made a point of making sure there was plenty of roasted meat, bread, and wine on the eve of a battle, thinking it was a good investment in the loyalty of his men. This was particularly relevant in these complicated times when both sides in a battle were commanded by Macedonians or Greeks, and the armies themselves were composed of a mixture of Macedonians, Greeks, and barbarians.

This contingent of mercenaries was a large one and had been stationed in a semi-permanent camp outside Sardis for several months. It was composed of 5,000 men and had been commanded by Diomedes of Argos for twelve months, after it had been recruited in Greece by Demetrius. When Pyrrhus had been sent to Sardis to bring the regiment to Ipsus, the men had been very impressed that a king, albeit one without a kingdom, would lead them in their march and then in the battle that was to come. They had heard that, despite his youth, he was a good leader, and a ferocious fighter.

Pyrrhus and Diomedes rode side by side at the front of the column, and they fell into conversation, covering many topics as a pleasant way of passing the time. "Tell me, Sire," said Diomedes, "how was it that this Neoptolemus was able to displace you and take your seat on the throne of Epirus?"

"That is really the galling part of the whole episode, Diomedes," replied Pyrrhus. "When a thing has been done once, no matter how hard it may be, it is always easier the second time. When I was a child, a babe in arms in fact, my father Aeacides was treacherously murdered, and his cousin, also called Neoptolemus, made himself king. I escaped, thanks to two loyal servants and three of my father's squires, who carried me away from the palace. We only just managed to keep ahead of the soldiers who were sent to search for me. After almost drowning when we crossed a river, they finally took me to the palace of Glaucias, who at that time was king of the Illyrians. Glaucias was not at all sure what to do, as I learned when I was old enough to hear the story from his queen, Euridice. It seems that he was afraid of Cassander, the king of Macedonia, who had been my father's enemy, and who was quite glad that my father had been killed. It was not until I crawled over and grasped his leg and pulled myself up that his heart softened. He took me into his household, and I grew up as if I was one of his sons. A short time later, when Cassander found out I was living with Glaucias's family in Illyria, he sent a messenger with an offer of 200 talents if he surrendered me to him. Fortunately for me, this was refused, and at the time, Cassander was not in a position to do any more about it.

"This good man, Glaucias, when I was twelve years old, invaded Epirus at the head of an army, deposed the usurper who had by then made himself very unpopular, and restored me as king of Epirus. In his wisdom, he left one of his own ministers to guide me until I was old enough to rule in my own right.

"I believed that the kingdom was stable and secure, and, a year ago, when I was seventeen years of age, I traveled to Illyria to attend the wedding of one of Glaucias's sons, and it was then that this second Neoptolemus usurped the throne."

"That is an outrageous story, Sire," said Diomedes. "How was he able to do it so easily?"

"It seems he had been plotting the deed for some months," Pyrrhus explained, "and he was waiting for the right moment. It just shows the strength that some people are able to get from their name, as the legendary ancestor of the kings of Epirus was Neoptolemus, the son of Achilles. The fact that Achilles's son was known as Pyrrhus as a youth seems to have escaped the notice of the man in the street."

"I can well understand that, Sire," said Diomedes, "as I have had to deal with the problems of my own name all my life."

"But you have a very fine name," replied Pyrrhus, "one that is steeped in glory from Homer's great poem."

"That is the problem, Sire," said Diomedes. "I have had my doings compared with my namesake all my life. My mother was born in Argos, and she was brought up on the *Iliad* by her father, who deeply loved the poem. He had set her the task of learning the *Iliad* by heart, and she was still trying years later when she met and married my father."

Diomedes's mother had become so obsessed with the *Iliad* that by the time she was old enough to make her own decisions, she had become an enthusiast herself, and continued with it. So much so that she felt she must name her only son after Diomedes, the great king of Argos, who was one of the most valiant and powerful of the Achaean warriors at the siege of Troy. Our Diomedes had found his name something of a handicap, as he was perpetually encouraged to live up to the exploits of his namesake. His mother had almost passed out when he told her, last year, that as a result of his taking command of a contingent of mercenaries to serve with Antigonus and Demetrius, he would be marching to Phrygia and Lydia, and would actually walk past the tomb of Achilles and visit Troy.

While Pyrrhus and Diomedes were chatting so pleasantly, they had ridden up to the crest of a hill and were able to see a group of light cavalry riding toward them from the adjacent hilltop. Half of their troop had remained at their lookout post, and the other six riders were galloping over to them. When they reached them, their leader approached Pyrrhus with a broad smile on his face. "Welcome to the camp, Sire," said the young man, "we had been told to expect you. Have you had a good journey?"

"It has been a very pleasant ride in the countryside, Simonides," said Pyrrhus. "We have not been disturbed at all by our adversaries, and Diomedes and I have had plenty of time to become better acquainted."

"That is good, Sire. If you will follow me, I will lead you into the camp. We have prepared an area where you and your men will be quartered, so they will be able to rest after their long march."

"I told you that Antigonus was a good host, Diomedes," said Pyrrhus. "Let us push on, and then we can quench our thirst and get the dust out of our throats."

An hour later, the contingent had reached the camp, and the soldiers had greeted their friends, attended to their kit, and were about to start their much anticipated meal. Pyrrhus and Demetrius spoke briefly and arranged to meet after Pyrrhus had had a chance to wash and change out of his armor into a tunic.

As Pyrrhus walked over to Demetrius's tent, he felt a thrill of anticipation as he looked around him at this encampment of such a great army. The tents of the infantry were laid out in a regular pattern, as if they fronted onto regularly ordered streets. Three great blocks of tents formed three sides of a square, leaving a central area, the large marketplace of our imaginary town planner, where the troops could be marshaled, and where the king and the generals had their tents. The remaining eastern side of the camp was where the cavalrymen were quartered, next to the stables for the horses. The elephants and their mahouts were stabled outside the perimeter of the camp on the western side, so that the great beasts would be as far as possible from the horses.

Outside the perimeter of the camp were the posts for the sentries, and squadrons of cavalry were sent to all areas of high ground at some distance from the camp to give warning of the approach of any hostile forces that may try to effect a surprise attack. Although Antigonus always allocated strong forces for this guard duty, Pyrrhus would have preferred that he had formally fortified his camp. This, however, was not a matter where an eighteen-year-old could give advice to an old and experienced king.

When he reached Demetrius's tent, he opened the tent flap and called out to Demetrius, who walked over to Pyrrhus and shook his hand. "Welcome, my friend. Come in and sit down. We will have time for a glass of wine before we meet my father for dinner."

The two men sat down and stretched out on large cushions, which were richly covered in red silk and decorated in exquisite floral patterns. Pyrrhus looked around the tent while Demetrius's servant poured the excellent wine that Demetrius had sent to him from Chios. The tent was large, and in contrast to the simplicity evident in the others, this had been decorated with tapestries and furnished elegantly with cushions, fine wooden chairs with a matching table, and a floor with rugs and furs. Pyrrhus took a sip of the wine and said to his friend with a smile, "It is sad to see you having to live so roughly, Demetrius."

"What is the point of being a king if one can't have a few comforts," said Demetrius with a laugh. "Three wagons are all I need to bring the tent and the furnishings with me, and, naturally, another one with personal effects."

"When I finally get back to Epirus, I shall have to take some lessons from you. My single packhorse with my kit seems rather humble," replied Pyrrhus. "Tell me though, how are the preparations proceeding with the army, and how is your father?"

"On the surface of it, everything seems to be going well. We have a strong army, and the battle plans appear as good as one could wish. You and I will be able to go over them later. What has been worrying me has been my father's moodiness over the last few weeks. He is normally so forthright and confident that the possibility of defeat would seem a ridiculous idea. My feeling is that he was caught by surprise when Lysimachus crossed into Phrygia, and he has been forced to respond to this threat rather than being the one in control of the situation. The loss of the initiative does not seem to sit well with him.

"Whatever the cause, he is not his normal self. Two extraordinary things have happened while you were away. Last week, soon after the camp was established, he told me to be ready to meet him the next morning dressed in full armor. When that time came, he presented me to the army and formally named me as his successor and that he wished all of his subjects to regard me as king, together with him.

"After that, when I thought that nothing could surprise me, there was this business this morning. He actually called me over to his tent to go over the battle plans with me. Normally he would never condescend to do that. Many years ago, when I first went with him on a campaign, I asked him one evening at what time the army would be marching on the following morning. He growled at me impatiently and said, 'Why? Are you afraid that you will be the only man who does not hear the bugle?' I have been rather circumspect since then." Demetrius paused for a moment, thinking that he had been too loquacious, but it was a great relief to be able to speak to someone whom he could trust about the concerns that had been troubling him greatly. He looked at Pyrrhus, who had been listening to him intently. "So, my friend," said Demetrius, "that brings you up to date with events in the camp."

"Truly never a dull moment," said Pyrrhus. "It may be a natural thing for an old man to get his affairs in order before a great battle, but whatever the cause, all we can do is our best, and after that we are all in the hands of the gods. On a lighter note, Demetrius, the contingent of mercenaries seem to be a fine body of men. You did well to find them."

"I am glad you think so," said Demetrius. "They are armed and trained as Hypaspists, and, if you are agreeable, our battle plans call for you to be stationed with them on the left of the phalanx. I felt that I had to give Demades the right wing of the Hypaspists, as he has been a trusted friend of my father's for many years, and would probably be offended if I did not give him the post of honor."

"That is very wise," replied Pyrrhus. "I will be perfectly content with the left wing."

"In that case, it is time we joined my father for dinner. His cook has prepared a fine meal for us, and I have saved my best wine for this occasion."

The two men rose and walked out of the tent over to that of Antigonus. Xanthippus was waiting for them outside the tent, greeted them, and took them inside, where Antigonus was finishing a letter. "Come in and sit down, Demetrius," he said. "Pyrrhus, it is good to see you. You had a good journey, I trust?"

"Yes, Sire," said Pyrrhus. "I was just telling Demetrius that the mercenaries from Sardis appear to be good soldiers."

"Excellent," said Antigonus, standing up and walking over to the table that had been set for dinner. "Demetrius has supplied the wine and the lamb for us today, so that we all may eat like kings this afternoon."

Antigonus beckoned Pyrrhus to sit on his right, and Xanthippus to his left. Demetrius took the other chair, sitting opposite his father. The younger men were pleased to see Antigonus in good spirits on this occasion. He was obviously happy the contingent of mercenaries from Sardis had arrived in good time, and he had enjoyed writing a letter to his wife. The thought of her always lifted his spirits, and he was determined to enjoy his dinner today, with the good company of these young men. Antigonus's servant came in just as they were sitting down and poured a cup of wine for each of the men. Antigonus lifted his cup and said to the others, "Demetrius has promised me that this is his best wine, that he has been keeping for a special occasion. At this time, I offer a prayer to Father Zeus." Antigonus stood up, as did the other men. "May he help us in our endeavor and allow us to be victorious tomorrow." The four men said, "Father Zeus," softly in unison, and poured part of their wine on the floor as a libation to the great god. The prayer having been offered, they sat down again, raised their cups, and drank to each other's health.

"May I say, Sire," said Pyrrhus, "Demetrius has excelled himself today with this wine. I cannot recall drinking a better one."

"That is one of my son's great talents," said Antigonus. "He has a gift for organization. As well as furnishing a few luxuries for ourselves, I am able to leave all the details of provisioning the army to him, as well as making arrangements for the equipment of all kinds that an army needs. When we get back to Sardis, you may be able to see some of the extraordinary machines he has had built for the siege-train. They are so impressive, sometimes the very sight of them is enough for the people of a city to capitulate on terms."

"Demetrius the Beseiger," said Xanthippus. "It does have a certain ring to it!"

"And now, my friends, our dinner has arrived," said Antigonus. "Pyrrhus, perhaps you would be good enough to carve the lamb, and we can all help ourselves to the bread and the fruit."

The meal was an unqualified success. The food and the wine were outstanding, and the good humor of Antigonus was quite a relief for the younger men. After they had finished eating and were savoring the wine, with a little prompting, Antigonus told his companions of his days with Alexander, when they made their way from Greece toward the great kingdom of Persia. He gave a vivid account of the battle of the Granicus, the first battle they fought against the Persians, using wine goblets and walnut shells on the table to illustrate the various movements in the battle. When he had finished his tale, Antigonus was pleased to see the looks of fascination and admiration on the others' faces, and said to them, "These were the good days of my life, boys. They were times when we were able to take part in the great deeds of Alexander, and we fought the barbarians to take revenge for the invasions of Greece, and to spread

Greek culture through the world. It was better to fight the Persians than to fight each other, as we do now."

There was a danger that the conversation would quickly become morose, but Demetrius came to the rescue when he turned to Pyrrhus and asked him to explain to them that thing he did with chickens. Pyrrhus burst out laughing, as did the others. When he could speak coherently, he said to Demetrius, "It is not so much a case of doing things with chickens, Demetrius, but the sacrifice of a chicken does take place at the beginning of my treatment. When I was living in Illyria with Glaucias and his family, Glaucias's physician taught me how to cure people who were suffering from diseases of the spleen. I have had the good fortune to be able to help quite a number of people over the years. When a patient was brought to me with this complaint, his relatives would bring a white cock, which served as the sacrifice to Apollo. I would then lay the man on his back—for some reason all of these sufferers were men—and place my right foot on his abdomen over the spleen, and then press gently on the area. After a short time, I would take my foot away, and when the man stood up again, he found that his disease had been cured. After the treatment, it has been customary for the family to give me the cock that had been sacrificed, and I accept it as my fee."

"An excellent story, Pyrrhus," said Antigonus. "I am sure that we will all feel more comfortable with such a physician in our party."

With Pyrrhus's story having saved the conversation from disaster, the four men turned to practical military matters. For Pyrrhus's benefit, Xanthippus went over the battle plans again.

When they had covered these matters to everyone's satisfaction, the younger men took their leave of Antigonus, thanking him for his hospitality. After they had left the king's tent, Xanthippus went to do his rounds of the camp, while Pyrrhus and Demetrius visited their men and then retired to their tents, hoping to sleep.

Chapter III

It was a day for rising early. The soldiers whose fear made them sleep uneasily were glad to see the dawn, as the company of their fellows made their minds dwell less on the battle the day would bring. By the time the sun was above the horizon, all the men had checked their weapons and put on their armor. All the horses had been fed and the grooms had put their harnesses on.

Having made their preparations, the soldiers ate the breakfast that the small army of camp attendants had prepared. There had been bread and meat left over from their dinner yesterday, as well as the usual wheat and barley meal. Each man had also been provided with a goblet of wine to help his courage. Having satisfied their hunger, the men found that some of their fears were soothed, and they began to experience the exhilaration of anticipation. In this area, the history of the world had been changed several times. The great Croesus of Lydia, in ancient times, had been defeated by Cyrus the Persian two days ride from where they were, and their king Alexander cut the Gordian knot in the same country only thirty-two years before.

Xanthippus had breakfasted before dawn and left his tent to make his rounds to speak to the men under his command.

He wanted to encourage them personally and to try to lift their spirits. He was pleased that many of them appeared cheerful and were happy to exchange lighthearted banter among themselves. Having spoken to his men, he walked back to the central area of the camp, as he wished to seek out Pyrrhus before meeting with Antigonus and Demetrius. Not for the first time, his heart warmed to Pyrrhus. Xanthippus came across him returning to his tent, having just made a visit to his men with the same object of settling them and assuring them that he knew they would all fight bravely this day.

"Good morning, Xanthippus," said Pyrrhus, "you are an early bird this morning."

"There is much to do today, my friend," replied Xanthippus. "If you are ready, we should make our way to see Antigonus."

"Let me grab my shield and spear, and I am with you."

Pyrrhus and Xanthippus walked over to Pyrrhus's tent, where he collected his weapons, and they made their way over to the king's tent. At their hail, Antigonus bade them enter, and they found Demetrius sitting with his father as they finished their breakfast.

"Good morning Sire," Xanthippus said to Antigonus. The king looked up and smiled at the two men. "I see you have both been busy this morning, Xanthippus. Please sit down, both of you. How are the men this morning?"

"In good spirits, Sire. I was a little concerned last night that the danger was preying on their minds, but now they are cheerful and have an impressive sense of occasion regarding today's battle."

"That is good, Xanthippus," replied Antigonus. "We will need all our strength today. Have you and Pyrrhus eaten this morning? My cook has been very generous with his portions."

"I must recommend these pastries to you, Xanthippus," said Demetrius, with a broad grin that took in both of these newly arrived friends. "The cook made them especially for me."

"In that case, Sire, I believe I could be tempted," said Xanthippus. He took one for himself and passed the plate to Pyrrhus, who also took one. As they ate, Xanthippus and Pyrrhus looked with some concern at the old man's face, which was worn with

worry. He appeared to be very tired and had obviously slept badly last night. Demetrius, at least, seemed to be in fine spirits, and
in a state of excitement. He was clearly relishing the prospect of
the day's battle.

"If you gentlemen are ready now," said Antigonus, "I believe that it is time to make a start, and we should address the
men before making our dispositions."

The others were all in agreement with this. They had all been
agonizing over the preparations for these months past, and in
some ways it was a relief to have arrived at the time when the
issue would be settled, and all they had to do was to fight, rather
than make decisions and try and anticipate the needs of the moments yet to come. The younger men waited while Antigonus
collected his sword and put his helmet on, and then followed
him out of the tent. As Antigonus stepped out of his tent, he
stopped and looked about him. He saw that all was in readiness,
and a rather fatalistic look settled on his face. He started to walk
toward the center of the camp and suddenly stumbled on a rock
that was sticking through the soil, falling flat on his face. Demetrius and Xanthippus hurried to help him and, taking an arm each,
helped the old man up. He had blood streaming from his nose
and had grazed the skin of his chin and his hands. As he stood
up, he raised his hands toward the sky and suddenly called out,
"O Father Zeus and you gods above, give me victory this day, or,
if that is not my fate and I am doomed to defeat, then I pray you
to give me a painless death, to let me depart this life gracefully."
The other men were appalled by this exclamation and looked
around to see who else was close enough to have heard it. Fortunately, with the amount of activity going on around them, the
only men who could have heard the king's outburst were the two
sentries who always stood guard outside the tent.

Xanthippus looked at Pyrrhus and said, "Quickly, Pyrrhus,
those two men must say nothing to anyone about this!" Pyrrhus
took the two worried looking soldiers inside the king's tent.
Looking fixedly at them, with a frighteningly earnest look on his
face, he said to them, "This episode must never reach the ears of

the army. I know you two men are veterans and love your king. Keep your silence this day and I will remember you as loyal friends. Tell the story, and I will seek you out and tear your heads from your bodies!"

"There is no need to threaten us, Sire," said the older of the two men. "We have both been with Antigonus in better times, and we would not dishonor his memory by telling a story which we know reflects his greatly troubled mind."

"That is good. I knew I could count on two old soldiers to support their king. Go now and resume your places."

Pyrrhus walked out of the tent and rejoined the others. By this time, Antigonus had regained his composure and had been able to clean the blood off his face and his hands. Xanthippus and Demetrius were standing next to him, in case he lost his balance again. With the practiced skill of the true statesman, Antigonus looked up at Pyrrhus as he joined the little group. "Pyrrhus, I am glad you have joined us again. I must apologize to you boys for my outburst. I fear that my worries overcame me. That it behind us now, and we must look at making our preparations."

After a slight prompting from Pyrrhus, Xanthippus turned to Antigonus and said, "Sire, perhaps it would be better if Demetrius addressed the army now. You will take some time to recover from your fall."

Antigonus looked at him sadly and replied, "Yes, perhaps that would be a good thing. The soldiers think of Demetrius as one of them. Yes, let it be so."

The four men walked to the center of the camp, where most of the commanders and many hundreds of the soldiers were assembled, expecting the king to speak to them. When Demetrius stood on the central mound rather than his father, some murmuring between them showed their surprise, but they all fell silent when Demetrius raised his hand.

"Soldiers! My father has strained his voice this morning," he said, looking for a plausible explanation for this unexpected change in plan, "and so, he has asked me to address you in his place. We are to fight in a great battle today, and I ask you to remember all of the other battles that Antigonus has fought. Armies under his command have never known defeat, and we face adversaries we have fought before. We have been victorious on the other occasions, and we shall be so again. I will remind you of the importance of this battle. When they are defeated again, our enemies will be so disheartened that they will seek a permanent peace and beg us for mercy. We will be firm but merciful, knowing that they will not have the stomach to fight us again. Think of it! The greatest general of our time, carrying on the work of Alexander, and this time we will have come to the end of our hard road, and we will enjoy the fruits of our labors, if only your courage is as strong as your king believes!"

There was a great shout of support from the soldiers. Demetrius had discerned their mood perfectly. His use of the collective "we" included the men in the glory of the victory that was to come, as well as the benefits that the following peace would bring. When quiet had returned, Demetrius said to the men, "I have spoken to our priests, and they have told me that the sacrifices have been favorable, so we will have the gods above on our side.

"And now," continued Demetrius, "it is time for us to get ready to fight. Remember our watchword for the battle—'Zeus and victory.'" Demetrius winced inside, remembering his dream, but he was too excited to dwell on this. He loved battle, and this one promised to be momentous. There was another cheer from the soldiers, and the group broke up, with the officers quickly organizing the men into their respective units.

Demetrius walked over to join his father and the others. "Well done, my son. Thorax will be here in a moment, and then I will ride over to my position on that rise and watch the deployment of the army. Off you go, all of you, and get your men organized." At this command, the younger men left Antigonus in the care of Thorax, whom they could see walking toward the king, and set about their duties.

The next hour was spent marshaling the men on the plain. The sun was shining brightly, and the weather was perfect, warm but not too hot, with a gentle breeze blowing. Antigonus, with his bodyguard and the reserve infantry, took his place on the hill that overlooked the whole plain, and was about 500 paces from the camp. From there, Antigonus watched as the soldiers marched past him onto the plain and were marshaled into their formations by the officers. Looking further out, Antigonus could see the enemy formed up in the distance. They had begun to march toward him. The battle would soon begin, and it was only a matter of hours before it would be decided who was to rule Anatolia.

From his vantage point, Antigonus could see all the units of his army. He was pleased to see that they had all taken up their positions as he had instructed and were waiting patiently, watching the advance of the enemy forces. The time had come for Demetrius to lead out the cavalry. Antigonus turned to Thorax and indicated his command. The trumpeter blew a high piercing note, and Thorax waved to Demetrius and Archesilaus. They acknowledged the command, and both wings of cavalry advanced at a walk toward the enemy, where their cavalry was leading the army toward them. Demetrius placed himself at the front of his formation and was already showing exhilaration and excitement on his face.

When he had brought his men to within 300 paces of the enemy, Demetrius raised his lance, waved it in the air, and shouted, "This is our moment, men; remember our battle cry, 'Zeus and victory.'" He dug his heels into his horse's sides and began to gallop toward the enemy. His cavalrymen had been anticipating the command, and they all set off at the same moment, all vying with each other to be at the front with their king.

Demetrius and Archesilaus remembered their instructions. They were to ignore the enemy infantry for the time being and to concentrate on dispersing the enemy cavalry. They led their respective wings to the left and right of the enemy front, finding that the enemy had been surprised at the speed of their approach and were only beginning to gallop toward them. Demetrius was at the front of his column with twenty or so of his men who were able to keep up with him. He picked out his man, and after riding straight for him, lowered his lance, and aiming just below the bottom of the man's shield, thrust it into the man's lower belly.

The blow pushed the man right out of his saddle, and he hit the ground with such force that his scream stopped the instant he fell. Leaving his lance where it was, Demetrius drew his sword and attacked nearby enemy riders. He made passes at three of them, inflicting wounds on the neck or arm of all of them, then he rode into an area of clear ground.

All of his men who first engaged the enemy inflicted similar damage, and the slower riders were now entering the fray, all screaming like demons. As he looked to his right, Demetrius saw Seleucus's son, Antiochus, fighting with two riders. One of them was withdrawing after receiving a wound on his arm, the other raised his arm to strike Antiochus, but the young prince was too quick and thrust his spear into the other man's unprotected armpit. Demetrius shouted for his two bodyguards to follow him and spurred his horse to gallop toward Antiochus. The young man saw Demetrius coming toward him and only just managed to get his balance and draw his sword in time. Demetrius slashed at Antiochus, but his blade was parried away. The two men settled their horses and rode at each other time and again, each failing to wound his man. Demetrius swore at himself and rode toward Antiochus again, this time approaching from the left, shielded side. Antiochus had fought well, but now fatigue was slowing his reflexes. Demetrius steeled his aching muscles and put all of his strength into a final sword thrust. Antiochus put his shield up to take the blow but he could not bring it up quickly enough. Demetrius's sword cut through the edge of Antiochus's shield, and it continued in its murderous sweep to inflict a deep cut on the top of his leg. With a cry, Antiochus looked for a way to disengage from this fight that he knew now he could not win. Behind him was a gap in the melee, and realizing that this was his only hope, he spun his horse around and galloped away from the fighting.

The fighting had been short but violent. Demetrius's men inflicted many casualties on their enemies, and Antiochus's men knew they were being overcome. With doubt and fear creeping into their minds, when they saw Antiochus withdrawing, they were seized with panic and galloped off after him. Seeing their enemy fleeing, Demetrius, who had become intoxicated with the fighting, again waved his sword in the air, shouted for his trumpeter to sound the charge, and set off in pursuit of the enemy cavalry.

After the cavalry rode off, the infantry columns of the two armies started marching toward each other. By the time the cavalry battle had begun, the space between the two armies was reduced to 300 paces. Archers and slingers from both armies were ready to do their mischief, and when the range had reduced a little more, they all sent their missiles flying, trying to disrupt the front line of the enemy's phalanx.

Many men were hit by these missiles, but both armies were made up of seasoned fighters, and neither front line was broken. Their brief time for fighting having come to an end, the archers and slingers withdrew through the files of the phalanx, and the armored spearmen prepared to do their work, holding their shields close to them, and leveling their spears.

Pyrrhus placed himself at the left front of his contingent of hypaspists, together with Diomedes. He wanted to show an example of courage to his men, and having his second in command with him would give him the option of moving from place to place, if it was required, to make tactical decisions or to encourage other units of the army. He had chosen his armor with care, months ago. It was easily recognizable from a distance, and he wore it as often as he could, so that all the men would be familiar with it and would know that he was fighting with them. He wore a linen corslet that extended from his neck to just above the knee. Riveted to the linen were front and back plates of iron and two side plates. In addition, the shoulder flaps of the cuirass were reinforced with rounded iron plates. The rest of the corslet was covered with small scales of iron. The part of the corslet below the waist was pleated, and, as above, the linen was covered in iron scales.

This gave him maximum protection consistent with comfort and flexibility. He also wore greaves on his legs made out of thick leather.

Pyrrhus made sure that his armor was colorful and distinctive, but the most recognizable element by far was his helmet.

This resembled the old-style, enclosing Corinthian helmet, but it was made of iron, and had hinged cheek pieces he tied in front with leather thongs. These could be opened if he had difficulty making himself heard to his officers and men. The helmet was always brightly polished, and on the top was a large crest with a red horsehair plume, and on each side was attached a goat's horn. He realized that with such distinctive armor, he made himself a target for enemy soldiers, but he felt that the benefits justified the risk.

The combination of Pyrrhus's physique and his distinctive armor made him appear more like a god than a man. Although of only middle height, his body was as strong and fit as an athlete at the Olympic Games. His black hair was allowed to grow long and fell in ringlets over his ears and collar. His face still showed some features of the handsome youth, but already one could see the lean hardness that indicated both his royal descent and the underlying strength of his emerging manhood. Below the eyes, which showed a grim determination, his strong aquiline nose once again proclaimed the aristocrat.

Armed then in this fearsome panoply, Pyrrhus led his men forward. The distance between the two armies was now only fifty paces. Pyrrhus lifted his spear and shouted for the men to charge. Keeping close order, as a result of the many hours of drill under their officers, the men of the phalanx and the hypaspists charged the enemy at a run. As they came up to the opposing line, the spears of the first three ranks of the phalanx bristled in front of the soldiers of the first rank. These spears were the fearful sarissas, twelve cubits in length. The hypaspists with their shorter spears had only their own spears in front of them, but they had a great advantage in the flexibility of their movement. When the two opposing front lines came into contact the din was almost deafening. There were the noises of spears hitting shields, and shields hitting shields, but louder again were the war cries of the men, and the screams of the wounded and dying.

Pyrrhus himself had been confronted by two men who singled him out by his armor. In the first contact, he had not been able to wound his opponents, his spear having been deflected by the shield of the man closest to him. He jumped forward and pushed one man back with his shield. The man was now off balance, and Pyrrhus struck at him with his spear, striking him in the neck. As the doomed soldier fell to the ground, his friend drew his sword and struck at Pyrrhus. Turning, Pyrrhus knew he did not have the time to bring his shield up. Using his spear more as a stick, he swept it across in front of him and parried the blow. His spear was now useless, having been cut in two by the savage sword cut of his opponent. More blows came from the man in front of him, who had been enraged by the death of his friend. Pyrrhus brought his shield up to take the first two of the blows. When the third blow was aimed at him, he had been able to get his sword out of its sheath and was able to parry with it. Armed now with his sword as well as his shield, Pyrrhus was able to feel comfortable with his balance, and now it was his adversary's turn to be attacked. Pyrrhus was a fearsome opponent in a battle and the fury of his attack caught the other man by surprise. Pyrrhus thrust and feinted with his sword, looking for an opening in the other's defense. After several ineffectual strikes, Pyrrhus sent three furious blows with his sword at the enemy's neck and shoulder, which were taken on the shield, but his man was stepping backward and off balance. With the feint of another blow to the neck, Pyrrhus slipped his sword under the other man's shield and powerfully thrust it into his abdomen, the point cutting its way through a gap between the scales of his armor. With a scream, he dropped to his knees, and knowing he would die within minutes, looked Pyrrhus in the eye with such a look of hatred that he would dream of this moment again and again.

Exhausted by this duel, Pyrrhus found that he had some respite from the fighting. The space immediately around him was taken up by his own men. He looked down the front line of his soldiers and saw that they were fighting furiously and were overcoming their adversaries, whose front line was beginning to crack and whose rear ranks were starting to panic and trying to withdraw. His own front line had advanced some ten paces, but the cost had been terrible. The ground of the battlefield was littered with the dead and dying from both sides. Looking to his right, Pyrrhus felt a sudden premonition of impending disaster, despite the fact that his men were winning their battle on the left wing.

The elephants of Seleucus's army, which so far had not taken part in the battle, were taking up a position in a great line to the right of Antigonus's army. Where was Demetrius? If he pursued the enemy cavalry too far, these elephants would block his return, and the army would be extremely vulnerable. Pyrrhus looked about him trying to find Diomedes. Thankfully, he saw him, apparently unharmed, just behind the front rank of his soldiers, encouraging his men to stand their ground and keep the pressure on their weakening enemy. Pyrrhus made his way over to him and made him withdraw from the front line sufficiently that they could hear each other speak. Opening the face plates of his helmet, Pyrrhus leaned over to speak into Diomedes's ear. "I fear we are undone, my friend. Seleucus has been able to send all his elephants to the right of our army. When that idiot Demetrius finally decides to return to the battle, he will not be able to get past them, and Seleucus can do what he will with our army."

As if he had been introducing a bard to recite a poem, the ground between their army and the corps of Seleucus's elephants was rapidly filling up with enemy cavalry, who had obviously been able to outpace Demetrius and had the foresight to return to the battle as soon as they were able. All Greek armies were potentially vulnerable on their right, unshielded side. If the men were held in front by enemy infantry, so that they were not able to turn, all the men in the right side of the ranks were unprotected by shields, which were always carried on the left arm. Seleucus clearly observed that Antigonus's cavalry had not returned to protect the flanks of his army and acted quickly. The elephants would stop Demetrius from rejoining the battle, and he sent all of his cavalry who had returned to take up this position.

Seleucus now demonstrated the mastery of tactics that one would expect from a pupil of Alexander. He ordered his cavalry not to attack the exposed right wing but to ride up and down and continually threaten it. Antigonus's men were overcome by fear, trapped by the enemy on two sides. Feeling themselves lost, the right wing of the phalanx and the hypaspists disengaged themselves from the fighting and raised their spears, the customary signal of surrender.

Pyrrhus and Diomedes were of the one mind. They must keep their force intact, keeping their men under control, so that if an opportunity presented itself, the day could still be saved by a determined counterattack. Diomedes called the bugler over to him, telling him to blow the usual signal for withdrawal. The two men went to the front line, telling the men time and again to withdraw in good order, facing the enemy, and that their courage alone would save their lives. The withdrawal was successful. Hoping that all of their opponents would surrender, Seleucus's men who were facing Pyrrhus did not pursue the withdrawal. In any case, they were so shaken by their own impending slaughter that they were glad the fighting was broken off.

Pyrrhus's next thought was for Antigonus, and he looked back at the hillock where the king took up his position. Antigonus sat on his horse watching the battle unfold. Thorax, also mounted, turned to the king and said, "I fear we have lost the battle, Sire."

"Do not worry, Thorax, Demetrius will be here shortly with the cavalry, and we will be able to counterattack."

"Look over there, Sire. There is a column of infantry coming toward us with a powerful cavalry escort. It looks as if they are making for you, Sire!"

"Yes, what other object could they have? But Demetrius will be here soon and save us."

The powerful enemy contingent was nearing Antigonus now. They pushed aside the wings of Antigonus's phalanx and the right wing of the hypaspists who surrendered and lowered their spears to renew the fight. There were a thousand men in Antigonus's Agema, and 2,000 more in the reserve infantry. The reserve infantry, believing their position hopeless, raised their spears and withdrew from Antigonus. The Agema, however, were all veterans and remembered their oath of loyalty to their king. Under instruction from Thorax, the men were deployed in a phalanx eight shields deep in front of Antigonus, the cavalrymen having dismounted and joined the ranks of the infantry.

There they waited and watched as the enemy approached, knowing that they would all die. Seleucus and Lysimachus would not take any chances that Antigonus could live to escape and raise another army to fight them. First to engage were the enemy archers and slingers who wreaked their havoc time and again. While this murder was being done, regiments of the enemy phalanx took up positions on all sides of Antigonus and his men. Antigonus's men did what they could to meet this tactic and changed their formation from a line to that of a hollow square, with the king at their center, but they all understood they were doomed.

When a large proportion of Antigonus's soldiers had been killed or wounded, the enemy archers withdrew and their phalanx advanced, using shorter spears suitable for the individual combat that would ensue, intent on the death of these men and their king. After an hour of heavy fighting, it was all done. Seleucus and Lysimachus could now carve up Anatolia and add the pieces to their own territories.

Watching this tragedy from the other side of the battlefield, Pyrrhus and Diomedes wheeled their small army around, and twice tried to break through to help Antigonus but were beaten back both times by the stronger enemy. Realizing that they could not succeed, Pyrrhus planned their retreat. Having made his decision in a matter of moments, Pyrrhus led his men back to the camp, wanting to stop only long enough to get what provisions were still unpacked in wagons. Fortunately, many stores had been left there, and the men were able to quickly gather enough food to amply feed them for a week or more.

Pyrrhus formed his men into a marching column, with his best troops at the front and the rear, with the wagons and camp followers sheltered in the middle. Before he could give the order to begin their march, he saw Pantauchus running towards them with several hundred men from his left wing of the phalanx. "Pyrrhus," Pantauchus called out. "I am glad I caught you.

When we had lost any chance of getting to Antigonus, I tried to get as many men away from the battle as I could."

"We had the same experience, Pantauchus," replied Pyrrhus. "I am glad you at least are safe. Could you see what happened to Xanthippus?"

"No," said Pantauchus, "I could not make him out in the throng, but it looked as if all the men on the right wing who did not surrender were killed."

"That is what I feared," said Pyrrhus. "Now that the battle is irretrievably lost, I believe our only hope is to arrive in Ephesus before Seleucus. If you agree, I will ask your men to join the rear guard, and we will leave straightaway."

Pantauchus nodded his approval and acknowledged the young king's right to command their remaining forces. He quickly organized his men into marching order and fell in behind the hypaspists who were stationed at the rear of the column.

They then set off westward in a forced march. Their survival depended on keeping ahead of the enemy, who would soon begin their pursuit, and try to reach Ephesus, where Antigonus and Demetrius left their fleet.

CHAPTER IV

By the time the sun was low in the sky, Pyrrhus and his men had marched twelve miles. After the exertions of the battle, the brisk march in full armor had spent the remainder of the strength of the soldiers, and Pyrrhus called a halt. The remaining daylight would be used to fortify the campsite to the extent that was possible with their few resources.

Some basic materials were carried in the wagons along with the provisions. The wagons themselves would be used to form part of the perimeter, the remainder would have to be made in a makeshift way using resources of the countryside. Branches of trees, bushes, and stones were gathered by the men, and by the time darkness fell the work was complete. The encampment was made next to a stream, so water would be readily available, and it would also contribute to the makeshift fortified barrier around the camp. While most of the men had been at work on the perimeter of the camp, others had been detailed to light campfires and to prepare food for the evening meal. This would perhaps be the only bright spot in this disastrous day, as two of the wagons were loaded with wine and delicacies Demetrius brought to Ipsus so he would be well prepared for the victory dinner that he hoped to have with his father and the officers.

After setting a strong watch, Pyrrhus directed the men to choose places where they could leave their equipment and return to later to sleep. After stripping off their armor and tunics, they all went to the stream in their turn to drink the sweet water and to wash the sweat and blood from their bodies. Having overseen the setting up of the camp, Pyrrhus went the rounds of the guard posts and instructed the men who were taking the first watch. He encouraged them and told them he had seen their brave deeds today, and promised they would be relieved and given their dinner in an hour's time, when sufficient men were fed and ready to take their places.

Having done what was necessary, Pyrrhus was able to take his mind off his immediate duties. In that moment, he was aware of his desperate tiredness, but even more aware of the crushing disappointment and sadness that threatened to overwhelm him. All the noble and far-sighted aims of Antigonus were destroyed in today's battle, and the great man himself was dead. He was on the verge of weeping when Diomedes approached and put his hand on his shoulder. "Come, Sire, let us wash in the stream and join the others in the evening meal. We can at least make sure that Demetrius's provisions do not go to waste."

Feeling that he had been saved from a waking nightmare, Pyrrhus smiled at his captain, grateful for his company. The two men took their armor off, cleaned it as well as their weapons, and after placing these effects where they could easily retrieve them if the need arose, they gratefully washed themselves in the stream. Refreshed, Pyrrhus and Diomedes dressed themselves in their tunics and walked over to the center of the camp where the soldiers who were entrusted with preparing the meal had set apart an area where Pyrrhus and the officers could eat and discuss their plans. A blanket had been placed on the ground, and Pyrrhus and Diomedes sat down. One of the junior infantry commanders, whose intelligence and resourcefulness had already become ap-parent to Pyrrhus, took charge of the domestic arrangements, and he walked over to speak to Pyrrhus as soon as he had seen him sit down. "I am glad to see you taking some rest at last, Sire. If you are ready, I will bring you some food and wine."

"That would be very good, Menestheus. I am glad to see that you have taken on this independent command. I will make sure that you have many more opportunities."

"I am sure of that, Sire", said Menestheus, and he walked over to the main campfire where the food was being prepared and returned with a platter that Pyrrhus and Diomedes would share, two goblets, and a wine jug that had been filled with the best wine from the wagons, mixed with water from the stream.

After eating a meal that was far better than he expected, Pyrrhus sent Diomedes to bring the other officers over so that he could discuss his plans with them. They had just made themselves comfortable when the sound of approaching horsemen made them all reach for their weapons, and they followed Pyrrhus to the eastern side of the camp where the sentries were challenging the approaching riders.

Two riders approached the camp ahead of their companions, so the sentries would not panic when confronted by a large number of unidentified horsemen. They approached slowly, and one of the men called out, "I am Demetrius, son of Antigonus. I am a friend." Pyrrhus walked out in front of his men and called on the two riders to approach so that they could be identified in the light. He gripped his sword tightly, prepared to defend himself in case of treachery, but as the two horsemen approached, he saw that it was indeed Demetrius. Pyrrhus turned and called out to his men to stand down, that their king was returning.

"Welcome to our camp, Demetrius. Thank God you are safe." Pyrrhus approached Demetrius as he dismounted from his horse, and shook hands with his friend. "You have had a bad day, Demetrius. Come inside the camp. I will send Diomedes to your men, and he will find them an area to stable their horses, and we can find something for them to eat."

Diomedes nodded to Pyrrhus, walked over to the nearest fire, and found a suitable torch, and then walked out to bring Demetrius's cavalry to the camp.

Pyrrhus took Demetrius through the camp and settled him on the rug that he and Diomedes sat on to have their dinner. The other officers left the two of them alone until Pyrrhus signaled that he was ready for them to join him again. The ever-vigilant Menestheus brought another plate of food and some wine for Demetrius. "I did not know that anyone could feel as wretched as I do now, Pyrrhus," said Demetrius. "I feel that I am entirely responsible for the disaster today. When I set off in pursuit of Antiochus and the enemy cavalry, I was intoxicated with the fighting, and all I could think of was the glory of taking him prisoner and scattering the enemy horsemen. As it turned out, the enemy broke up into five or six groups, all of them going in different directions, and we ended up only being able to catch a small group of them. When we were disarming them and taking them prisoner, I began to think more clearly, and I realized that I left the army without cavalry support.

"A terrible shiver ran through my spine, and at that moment I wished that I was dead. The whole dreadful scene ran through my mind as a terrible premonition. Anyway, as quickly as I could, I reformed our cavalry, and we returned to the battle at the gallop. The first thing that was obvious was that Seleucus had done exactly as Xanthippus had feared and placed all his elephants in our path so we could not rejoin the battle. Whenever we tried to force our way through them the horses panicked, and dozens of my men were thrown off their mounts."

Demetrius paused as he looked again at the battle scene in his mind's eye, and he took a long drink of his wine. "Then, as you know, things went from bad to worse. By this time, Antiochus and his men had returned. They cut their way through my men and the mahouts opened a gap in the line of elephants to let them pass. The rest I imagine you saw as well as I did."

"Yes," said Pyrrhus, "we tried to get to Antigonus and take him away from the battle, but after the right wing surrendered, there were just too many of the enemy."

"You saw him killed?" said Demetrius.

"Yes, I am afraid I did," replied Pyrrhus. "He was where he placed himself at the beginning of the battle, with Thorax and his bodyguard. All of these men remained loyal, and they all died with your father. I don't know whether you will be able to gain comfort from this or not, but Seleucus is not a barbarian. He will give your father a royal burial and provide a fine tomb for his ashes to rest."

"Yes, I am sure you are right. Tell me, though, after all was lost and you were able to withdraw, were you attacked on your march away from Ipsus?"

"No," said Pyrrhus. "We stopped in the camp only long enough to collect some provisions, and then marched as far as we could in the remaining daylight."

"We came across some of them," said Demetrius. "Many of them would have ignored their officers and wasted time plundering our camp. When it was clear that all was lost, we had to ride round the battlefield and then we were able to get onto this road to Ephesus. We came up behind a large squadron of cavalry that set out to pursue you, presumably. That at least was able to give me a taste of revenge. They were quite surprised to see us suddenly appearing to their rear, and, naturally, in these circumstances, we did not leave one of them alive."

Demetrius leaned back onto one elbow and picked at the food that had been brought for him some time ago. "I am glad you found the wagons with the provisions for the victory celebrations in them." This was the last straw for Demetrius, and he hid his face in his hands and wept. Pyrrhus was too drained and tired to join his friend in tears but sat there quietly until Demetrius recovered himself.

"We must make our plans now, Demetrius. You and I have obviously had the same thought, that we must get to Ephesus and collect our fleet, but I am not sure where we will go after that."

"Our outlook is not as bleak as you may think, Pyrrhus," said Demetrius, recovering some of his composure. "The fleet is at Ephesus, and it is fully manned with seamen, and we have enough transports to embark all of our remaining men and the horses. Many cities in Greece are still loyal to us, and, particularly, Athens will receive us. They were quite vocal in support of our cause when I left. Deidameia is still there, and a considerable amount of money has been kept there as well as the other squadron of ships. Also, I believe that Tyre and Sidon will remain with us. They are well garrisoned and well able to withstand a siege."

"That is well then," said Pyrrhus. "But now it is time for sleep, my friend. Let me get you some blankets. Lie down here and rest, and I will speak to the other officers so we will all know what we have to do tomorrow."

Pyrrhus left Demetrius to his troubled sleep and walked over to the fire around which his officers gathered, and who had been joined by the commanders who escaped with Demetrius. All the men had been provided with a meal and were quietly talking among themselves to determine who had lived and who had died this day.

As Pyrrhus approached, Diomedes took him to where he and Pantauchus were sitting with Archesilaus and Menestheus, cleared a space for him, and brought him a goblet of wine. "Thank you, Diomedes. You make an excellent host. I left Demetrius to sleep, but we need to make some plans tonight so we can tell him what his decisions are in the morning!"

Even a weak joke is welcome to people when they are despondent, and it was good to see smiles on the others' faces. "Have you had a chance to find out how many men we have with us? I think we must have about 4,000 men left out of our hypaspists, and possibly several hundred from the left wing of the phalanx."

"Slightly more than that, Sire," said Diomedes. "Pantauchus was telling me that another group joined us just after you began the march. There are about 1,000 men from the phalanx, which brings our infantry strength to about 5,000. As far as the cavalry goes, about 3,000 men from Demetrius's right wing are with us, and Archesilaus was able to save 1,000 from the left wing. So our cavalry strength is almost 4,000."

"That is better than I expected," said Pyrrhus. "We should be able to defend ourselves on our march with this many men. Seleucus will send more men in pursuit, but if we can keep up a brisk pace, we will only have to deal with the relatively small numbers who can keep up with us. What I want to do is to send a squadron of cavalry ahead of us, to get to Ephesus as quickly as they can, so the fleet can make their preparations for sailing, and to make sure the garrison takes control of the city gates, so the Ephesians do not lock us out to curry favor with Seleucus. We are not strong enough to hold Ephesus, and, when we sail, we will embark the garrison, and we will take them to Greece with us."

Pyrrhus leaned back and looking at the others, said, "That is what I will suggest to Demetrius in the morning, gentlemen. If I have omitted anything, I would be grateful for any suggestions."

They were all in agreement with Pyrrhus. Pantauchus added that he would make sure that the advance guard was accompanied by men who knew the countryside well enough to make sure they took the quickest possible route. "The only remaining thing is who will command the advance cavalry," said Pyrrhus. "We will need to send someone who will be known to both our men and the Ephesians and who has enough authority to enforce his commands, if necessary. Archesilaus, you will have to do it, if you are agreeable, and I will give you 1,000 cavalry."

"Yes, Sire," said Archesilaus, "that should be an ample force. We will leave at first light, and we should be able to get there comfortably in three days."

Having made their plans to his satisfaction, Pyrrhus leaned back, desperate to shut his eyes for just a few moments. He was surprised to find the sun shining when Diomedes shook his shoulder to wake him.

CHAPTER V

"Good morning, Sire," said Diomedes. "I hope you slept well."

"I must have, Diomedes," replied Pyrrhus. "I have no recollection of anything after we finished talking last night."

"The advance party left for Ephesus a short time ago with Archesilaus," said Diomedes. "The rest of the army will be ready to march in half an hour, which will give you time to wash and have some breakfast. Archesilaus chose a horse for you before he left, and he assures me it is a spirited one."

"Excellent," said Pyrrhus. "I must leave you in charge of our affairs more often, Diomedes. Have you had a chance to speak to Demetrius?"

"He certainly has, Pyrrhus," said Demetrius, as he walked over to join them. "Diomedes told me about your discussions last night, and I don't think I could have done better myself. I left your orders as they stand, and I must say that you showed remarkable presence of mind to not allow the Ephesians to back out of their allegiance. They will be able to deal peacefully with Seleucus and Lysimachus after we leave."

"Thank you, Sire," said Pyrrhus. "If you will excuse me, I will go now and have a quick wash in the stream to wake myself up." As he bathed, Pyrrhus was pleased to reflect on Demetrius's improved spirits. The man was obviously not one to dwell on his misfortunes, and he accepted the fact that he was now the sole king, following the death of Antigonus. The question that now remained was, king of what?

Refreshed, and now more or less awake, Pyrrhus dressed in his armor. It was a task for two men to accomplish, with the various buckles and flaps to be dealt with. He was glad Menestheus took it upon himself to assist him with it, before attending to his own. He also prepared Pyrrhus's breakfast. The young man clearly felt that he could regard Pyrrhus's cause as similar to his own, and that not being of noble birth himself, he could do worse than to attach himself to a young king. Pyrrhus turned his head to speak to Menestheus, who was busy with the rear fastenings of Pyrrhus's armor, and said to him, "Menestheus, it is true that I am a king in name, but I have been displaced from my kingdom in Epirus, and I cannot give any guarantees that I will be able to return there. I dearly hope that will be the case, but it is possible that my life will only be one of a soldier of fortune. You have been very kind and attentive over recent days, and I would be grateful to have a loyal friend to help me in these difficult times. I do not insist, but if you would choose to be my personal lieutenant, I will be happy to share my fortunes, whatever they may be."

Menestheus finished fastening Pyrrhus's armor and walked around him so that they could talk face to face. "I was hoping you might ask me that, Sire. I will be happy to accept your offer, the only condition being that you would help me with my armor!"

"Let us regard the matter settled then. My ancestor Achilles had Patroclus as a companion, and I am happy to find as good a man for mine. Come then. I will help you with your armor, and then I hope we will be ready to begin our march. Do you have a horse, or should I choose one for you?"

"I have one already, Sire. I asked Archesilaus to pick one for me after he had chosen yours."

"Excellent," said Pyrrhus. "Now that we are dressed for the occasion, let us join the others." Pyrrhus and Menestheus put their helmets under their arms and walked over to join Demetrius and the other commanders as they were finishing their preparations.

As they approached, Demetrius called out to Pyrrhus, "There you are, Pyrrhus. I hope you are feeling refreshed after your bath. I have just finished making our dispositions for the march."

"I feel ready for anything, Demetrius. I hope you were able to sleep last night," said Pyrrhus.

"More than I expected," Demetrius replied. "With our march today, I have kept your column of infantry as you had it yesterday. I have divided the cavalry into three groups. One is naturally the advance guard who left with Archesilaus, one group will ride at the front of the column, and the third group will bring up the rear." Pyrrhus nodded his approval, while Demetrius continued his orders for the disposition of the marching order. "We lost many good officers yesterday, but fortunately we have excellent men still with us. Lycoon and Glaucon are here, and I will ask Lycoon to command the cavalry leading the column. I will ride with him, and Glaucon can command the cavalry bringing up the rear. I don't need to belabor the point to you, Glaucon, that you will need to be the eyes of the army with regard to giving us early warning of enemy columns pursuing us. Please make sure that you have strong patrols following us at some distance, looking out for any pursuers. Lycoon, you will send a strong troop of cavalry ahead of us to act as scouts ahead of the column.

"Diomedes will command 2,000 of the hypaspists from Sardis. He will detail enough men to form a single file on each side of the noncombatants in the center of the column, and he will march in front of the noncombatants with the remaining men. Pyrrhus, I will ask you to lead the remaining hypaspists and to march behind the noncombatants. Behind you, Pantauchus will command the 1,000 phalangites, followed up by the remainder of the cavalry under Glaucon."

All the men who had been given a command by Demetrius took some minutes to contemplate the army's disposition as explained to them. It was as good a formation as one could wish for. Powerful squadrons of cavalry would give early warning of the approach of enemy forces, and would be able to deploy rapidly. As the rear of the army would be the part that would be most likely to bear the brunt of any attack, the phalangites would be able to deploy with their line of pikes and could deal with any direct attack, while the more mobile hypaspists would protect the flanks of the phalanx. They all acknowledged both their understanding of their roles and their approval of the disposition.

Cavalry Scouts.
Cavalry—1,000. Lycoon and Demetrius
Hypaspists—2,000. Diomedes
Camp followers and wagons
Hypaspists—2,000. Pyrrhus
Phalangites—1,000. Pantauchus
Cavalry—2,000. Glaucon

"If we are all agreed, gentlemen," said Demetrius, "please assemble your men and be ready to begin the march in ten minutes." The various commanders went off to marshal their men, who had finished all of their preparations and were awaiting the order to march.

Shortly before Demetrius's ten minutes were up, the army began the day's march. The men had been able to rest well last night and were able to set a brisk pace. It had not escaped the attention of the soldiers that keeping ahead of the enemy was a highly desirable thing, and that although marching was tedious, it had some advantages over having to fight another battle. The ever-present threat of being overtaken by the enemy on the march motivated the men to reach Ephesus as soon as possible. They had to fight off two squadrons of enemy cavalry, but they were able to do this with only small losses. On the night of the tenth day after leaving Ipsus, the army encamped five miles from Ephesus. They made contact with cavalry scouts sent out from Ephesus during that afternoon, and Demetrius sent the scouts back to the city to inform Archesilaus of their approach.

When the camp had been fortified, the sentries set, the rounds of the camp made, and the men settled, Pyrrhus and Demetrius sat down on their well-traveled blankets with the other officers to have their dinner and discuss their plans for the following day. The dinner itself was not an exciting prospect, as it would consist of plain wheat and barley meal and some dried figs, Demetrius's private stores having been already consumed. Archesilaus brightened their day, however, when he arrived from Ephesus with a small troop of cavalry. After settling his men and the horses, Archesilaus walked over to join Demetrius and Pyrrhus. He and several of his men were carrying bulging bags, and after greeting the king and his officers, Archesilaus said to Demetrius, "I am glad you have not started your dinner yet, Sire. I have brought some fresh bread, fruit and wine."

"What a good fellow you are, Archesilaus," replied Demetrius, "a meal without wine is always a disappointment. Menestheus, perhaps you would pour the wine, and then I will ask Archesilaus to tell us how things stand in Ephesus." Menestheus poured wine for them all while the servants brought out the platters of food. When Menestheus rejoined them, Archesilaus turned to Demetrius. "Everything is in readiness, Sire. I have made it clear to the council that their city is in no danger, and they have realized that it is in their interests to do all in their power to help us embark and leave Ephesus as quickly as possible, so there will be no need for any fighting when Lysimachus and Seleucus arrive to claim the city. As far as the fleet goes, all the ships are provisioned and ready to sail as soon as we can get all the men and the horses aboard."

"That is good news indeed, Archesilaus," said Demetrius. "I would think that it will take us the best part of two days for the embarkation. We will need to start loading as soon as possible after we arrive in Ephesus, and we will aim to put to sea at dawn two days from now. Pyrrhus, I believe you have never been to Ephesus?"

"That is correct, Sire," said Pyrrhus, "but I am told it a wonderful city."

"It is that," said Demetrius. "I will leave Archesilaus to supervise the embarkation tomorrow, and you and I and Menestheus will see the city leaders and take a walk around the city. The temple of Artemis is a wonder to behold."

"I would like that very much, Demetrius," said Pyrrhus. "And I am sure I can persuade Menestheus to accompany us." Menestheus nodded his cheerful approval. Everyone in the Greek world knew of the wonders of Ephesus, and all who could do so, did visit the city.

"There is another reason for us to make haste leaving Ephesus," said Demetrius. "As well as the fact that I believe that our best plan is to return to Greece rather than to try and hold Ephesus with the small forces at our disposal, I do not want to take any risks that our soldiers would plunder the city. If we start our embarkation immediately and keep the soldiers busy, then we can avert a catastrophe, and I for one do not want to be remembered as a savage."

This sobering thought brought the larger picture home to all of them, and their own immediate problems seemed to be less pressing. After a moment's contemplation, Demetrius continued, "These thoughts remind me of a letter I received from King Ptolemy years ago. He invaded Syria from his base in Cyprus and was trying to compel the coastal cities there to transfer their allegiance from my father to him. I was twenty-five years of age at this time, and my father gave me the command of an army and sent me to meet Ptolemy and to force him to withdraw from Syria. I thought it was the greatest moment of my life, and when I marched out to meet Ptolemy, all I could think of was the glory of returning home victorious. Anyway, our armies met in the great plain near Gaza, and to my cost I was reminded that Ptolemy was not just an effete king of Egypt, he had also been one of the most capable of Alexander's generals. He inflicted a terrible defeat on my army. Five thousand of my men were killed, 8,000 were taken prisoner, and he captured my camp. All my personal possessions were lost. We retreated as quickly as we could to try and find safety. Shortly after I returned home, and my father was organizing another expedition so the loyalty of the Syrian cities would not waver, a letter arrived from Ptolemy, addressed to me. In it, he said that all commanders will know defeat at some stage, and that he and I, with my father, were not engaged in a struggle for life and death, but only for honor and power. He went on to say that he gave our dead an honorable funeral, and he was sending the prisoners of war home without ransom, as well as returning all my personal effects.

"Ptolemy made me understand that there will always be such struggles as long as there are ambitious men, and there will be a cost where men die, but to destroy the world around us as part of these struggles is a mark of insanity and barbarism." Demetrius looked at the men around him and he saw that they understood that war must not be allowed to be completely uncontrolled. "And so, gentlemen, that is why I will not risk a sacking of Ephesus."

"I am sure that Plato would have approved of your sentiments, Demetrius," said Pyrrhus. "Perhaps we will have a philosopher king after all."

"Only if we get away from Anatolia alive," said Demetrius with a smile. "And now, gentlemen, it is time to lighten our spirits. I propose to challenge you all to a game of dice, and I will keep a tally of the amount of money you will all owe me tonight." They played for an hour or so, and Demetrius earned a total of one hundred Attic drachmas by the time Archesilaus returned to Ephesus and they retired to sleep.

CHAPTER VI

When Demetrius and his army began their march the next day, excitement and anticipation were affecting all the men, from the kings down to the most humble of the camp followers. To reach Ephesus and sail for Greece would mean they survived the disastrous defeat suffered by Antigonus's army, and they would be out of reach of their enemies, at least for the time being. Also, they were all looking forward to arriving in Athens, the great cultural leader of the Greek world. Demetrius had been regarded as a great benefactor of Athens over the last few years, and the city was most vocal in its gratitude for its favored treatment. At one time, when Demetrius returned to Athens after campaigning to oust the Macedonian garrisons in various cities in central Greece, which had been left there by Cassander, the Athenians gave Demetrius the rear part of the Parthenon as his quarters. It could not be said, however, that the parties that were thrown by Demetrius were entirely consistent with the dignity of the great temple of Athena.

The march began shortly after dawn so Demetrius could reach Ephesus as early in the day as possible, as there was much to do today. They were first able to see the city when they entered the far side of the plain on which Ephesus sits, at a distance of a little over two miles from its walls. As a result, there was plenty of time to appreciate the magnificence of the architecture as they slowly approached. The walls of the city gleamed white in the morning sunshine, and at the central gate there were two great towers, each of which had an enormous sculpture of a sitting lion in front of it. Through the open gates could be seen a wide central avenue lined by gracious buildings made of stone and faced with marble.

Demetrius, Pyrrhus, and Menestheus rode at the front of the column today, and Demetrius called a halt when they were about 500 paces from the gates. "Pyrrhus, look through the gates and you will see the temple of Artemis at the end of the central avenue. The building to the right of it is the Hall of Assembly, where we will meet with the ruling council this afternoon. But now we must take this other road which will take us down to the harbor."

"You were right about Ephesus, Demetrius," said Pyrrhus. "It is truly a magnificent sight."

Demetrius then signaled the change of direction to the column, and they made their way along the side road for several miles to the harbor. After spending so long inland, the smell of the sea was stimulating and full of promise. The harbor complex had its own walls on the landward side, and the harbor itself was enclosed by tall breakwaters, which were defensible. The breakwaters had walls and ramparts facing the sea, the whole length of which could be manned, and at regular intervals there were towers that could provide an elevated platform for archers and spearmen, and each tower housed a catapult that could throw burning missiles at attacking ships. Entry to the harbor was through a gap in the breakwaters, which was flanked by the two biggest towers.

Entering the harbor, they marched through a set of gates only slightly less grand than the main gates to the city. Once inside, each unit of the army was assigned an area where they could temporarily encamp until their time for embarkation came. After Demetrius gave his orders for settling the men and the horses, he and the others dismounted and handed the reins of their horses to the servants. Demetrius turned to Pyrrhus and Menestheus and asked them to come with him to see Archesilaus, who was walking toward him from the harbor master's office. Four other men were with him, two of whom were familiar to Demetrius. One of these was Antimachus, who was the admiral of Demetrius's fleet and a childhood friend of his father. The other was the harbor master, a grizzled retired seaman named Callistratus. As Archesilaus approached Demetrius, he called out to him, "Welcome, Sire, you have made good time this morning."

"Good morning, Archesilaus," replied Demetrius, smiling at him and then turning toward the other men, "it is good to see you all, especially you, Antimachus, my old friend." Demetrius shook the admiral by the hand and with a sad voice Antimachus said to him, "I cannot tell you how sorry I am, Demetrius."

"I know, my friend, I know," said Demetrius, "but we must leave our sorrows behind us today; there is much to do. Are all the preparations ready?"

"Yes, Sire," said Archesilaus. "The fleet is all prepared. We have fifty warships, all triremes, which will be our escort, and 300 transport vessels, which will comfortably accommodate our men. We will be able to put a hundred men in each vessel, and each of the horse transports will take twenty horses. All are provisioned and ready to sail, as promised."

"Excellent," said Demetrius. "First of all, I would like the army to have their midday meal. We have enough provisions to take care of that ourselves, and men are always easier to handle when they are not hungry. As soon as they have eaten something, we will begin the embarkation. I wish to sail at dawn, the day after tomorrow. I propose that we all have a glass of wine and something to eat, and then I will leave you gentlemen to supervise the loading while Pyrrhus and I will go into the city to meet the council. Antimachus, perhaps you could send a messenger to the city and inform the council that I wish to meet with them in two hours' time."

Antimachus turned to one of the men whom Demetrius did not recognize, who was obviously one of the harbor master's assistants. "Sthenelus, off you go to find Prothous in the city. Ask him to assemble the other councilors and be ready to receive King Demetrius in two hours in the Hall of Assembly." The young man rushed off to deliver his message, rather relieved to leave such a lofty group of individuals and to not have been put under scrutiny for any of his shortcomings.

Demetrius led the others to the harbor master's office. He walked into the large room, which had a number of chairs and a huge desk covered with maps and documents relating to the ships that had recently entered the harbor. Callistratus cleared away the desk so he could find all the documents again, and the others sat around the table. Food and wine had been brought in earlier in anticipation of this meeting. Demetrius dismissed the servants who laid out the meal and asked Callistratus's other assistant to return to his duties until he was needed. After they left the room, he said to the others, "Gentlemen, help yourselves to the food, and we can talk while we eat." All were hungry after their exertions this morning, and eagerly served themselves and began to eat.

"Antimachus," said Demetrius, as he was busy trying to keep the olives from falling off his piece of bread, "I imagine Archesilaus has told you that we will withdraw our garrison from Ephesus?"

"Yes, Sire," replied Antimachus.

"I do not want this fact to be generally known until the last minute. The garrison will remain at their posts until just before we set sail, and then we will bring them down to the port and get them on the last transports."

Pyrrhus had been a spectator of these conversations since arriving at the city, but he felt it was his duty to scrutinize the proceedings and make any suggestions that could improve the situation. Until now, he had not felt that comments from him were necessary. Demetrius was at his best when dealing with the preparations for great undertakings, but Pyrrhus felt he may get lost in detail as the day went on. Looking up at him, Pyrrhus said, "Demetrius, there is one matter I would like to raise with you, if I may."

"Of course, Pyrrhus. What is it?"

"As we propose to sail the day after tomorrow, would it be prudent to send a fast ship ahead of us to warn the Athenians to expect us? The unexpected arrival of a large fleet can unsettle the calmest mind."

"An excellent idea," replied Demetrius. "Why don't you go yourself? I will get Antimachus to get two triremes ready, with a good pilot, and you could sail this afternoon after we meet the council and have a look around Ephesus."

Pyrrhus was pleased to be given this important undertaking, which promised to be far more entertaining than the tedious business of trying to load frightened horses into the ships.

The practical discussion of the work that was ahead of them occupied most of the next hour, and when the details had been settled to everyone's satisfaction, Demetrius was happy to delegate the execution. Once their horses had been brought, he set out for his meeting, taking Pyrrhus and Menestheus with him, in addition to his usual bodyguard of twenty lancers.

They trotted back up the road to Ephesus and found that they were able to notice much more of the countryside around them than they had previously. All of the plain was under cultivation, the rich soil seemingly suitable for all kinds of produce. There were many small areas planted with vines and olive groves. In the distance were larger plantings of wheat and barley, and, no doubt, if they had time to look more closely, they would find vegetable gardens and fruit trees. This was truly the land of plenty, and it grieved Demetrius to accept the fact that he would have to give it all up. Still, all was not lost. He would be able to retrieve his fortunes in Greece, and he was in no doubt that Tyre and Sidon would remain loyal to him. It took Alexander himself five months to take Tyre by siege, and he was sure that Lysimachus and Seleucus had other matters too pressing to allow them to devote all their resources to these two cities. By the time that his mental ramblings brought him to a more optimistic outlook, they were nearing the gates of the city, and, as before, its grandeur demanded all of their attention. When they reached the gates, they were saluted by the guards on duty, and, leaving their horses in the charge of two of the lancers, they walked through the gates into the city.

Ephesus was a striking place from a distance, but once they passed through the gates and began walking down the central avenue, Pyrrhus and Menestheus were almost speechless in admiration. Demetrius, who knew the city well, was happy to act as their guide. "These buildings along here are the offices and homes of the important merchants and the leading men of the aristocracy. But I must tell you about the Temple of Artemis. It was built long ago by Croesus, who wanted to make it the greatest temple in the world. He dedicated it to the worship of Artemis, because he felt that she was his own patron goddess. It is said that Artemis delights in the cities of just men, and Croesus felt that her protection would make his dynasty last forever. You gentlemen will recall the sticky end that Croesus came to. Obviously not even a goddess is perfect.

"About fifty years ago, the temple was burned down by a madman named Herostatus, who had been a priest of Artemis, until his unsavory conduct led him to be cast out of the priesthood. He took his revenge by firing the temple. However, the temple was rebuilt, faithfully maintaining the original design, and for twenty years the finest artisans from Greece and Lydia worked on it. It is said by the older men that the temple as it stands now is just as fine as the original one. As well as the temple itself, the other great artifact is the statue of the goddess herself. It does not strike one as the work of a Greek but more so the work of an Egyptian. We are very much at a crossroad of different civilizations here, and I will leave you to form your own opinions when you see it."

They arrived at the end of the avenue and were now standing in front of the temple. The size and majesty of the building was enough for them all to stand in wonder that the skill of men could build such things. After a short time, Demetrius said to them, "Come, my friends, we will have a closer look later. It is time to see the council now."

They walked over to the assembly building, left the guards at the bottom of the stairs, and walked up the two flights to the entrance of the chambers. The seven members of the council were waiting there for Demetrius, and all greeted him on his approach. Prothous, the senior member of the council, shook hands with Demetrius and said to him, "Welcome, Sire. All of Ephesus grieves for your father. We offered prayers for him on behalf of the city when we heard the news."

"Thank you, Prothous, your prayers are always welcome. My consolation is found in your friendship."

"Come in, Sire, we will find some privacy in the reception room."

The men followed Prothous into the building, down a corridor and through a door into a large room furnished in such a way that the council and their guests could deliberate on matters of state in comfort. Before they sat down, Demetrius introduced Pyrrhus and Menestheus to the council members. The formalities taken care of, they all made themselves comfortable, and servants brought in refreshments. After the servants left, Demetrius turned to Prothous and informed him of their need to evacuate their garrison from Ephesus, and the plan to return to Greece. Prothous contemplated this for a moment, and then said to Demetrius, "It is what I expected you would have to do, Sire. But I must say that it brings me no joy to hear it. Your father's protection has always been of the greatest benefit to Ephesus. I can only say that we wish you well, and we all hope that your fortunes will improve in the coming days." Prothous paused for a moment before continuing. "There is another matter that I know you will find difficult to bring up, so it may be fitting for me to do so. Your father kept some of his treasure here, on which the people of Ephesus have no claim. There is a sum of 500 talents in gold in this building, and I would ask you to take this money with you with our blessing."

Demetrius did not know of this money, and it was an enormous relief to know that he was not destitute. The problem of paying his men was beginning to prey on his mind, although he was working on the assumption that there were funds being held in Athens. He thought to himself, *How many more surprises does the old dog have in store for me? I wonder.*

"That is very gracious of you, Prothous, and you have my sincere thanks. I must add one more thing, which was pointed out to me by Pyrrhus the other day. Seleucus and Lysimachus are not uncivilized men. They have no animosity toward your city and your people. I formally absolve you of remaining politically loyal to us, and with us gone, you should deal with the victors in a way that will give your city the greatest benefit."

Having spoken of such matters, there was no need to tarry, and Demetrius and his friends took their leave of the councilors. Prothous promised to send the money to the port under a strong guard that afternoon. All that remained was for Demetrius to say farewell, and the three men walked out of the council building into the bright sunshine. Once back in the avenue, Demetrius cleared his throat and said to Pyrrhus, "And now for the temple. Let us spend some time there, and then we will ride back to the port." They walked up the stairs at the front entrance and entered the atrium, which led to the main chamber of the temple. Once their eyes again became accustomed to the interior light, they could see the statue of Artemis at the rear of the main chamber. They continued until they were well inside the great room. Demetrius was well known to the priests, and they bowed as he entered. Pyrrhus thought nothing could surprise him after the happenings of the last few days, but he was quite unprepared for this great work of art. The statue of Artemis sat on a broad pedestal at the rear of the temple chamber, and in height reached two-thirds of the way to the roof.

As Demetrius told them earlier, it was a work unlike anything else he had seen in a Greek temple. The figure was one of a standing goddess, in a stiff and formal attitude. Both her arms were held straight out in front of her. From her waist down, she was clothed in a garment that was decorated with reliefs of animals and hunting scenes. Her torso was otherwise naked, with eight breasts pointing in a variety of directions. Her face was beautiful and serene, and her head was adorned with a high headdress, decorated with many jewels. The statue appeared to be made from a variety of materials, including gold, black stone, and ebony, all beautifully finished so that the transition from one material to another was not sharp or distinct, but blended from one to another in a perfection of color and design, a work that truly deserved the admiration of the world for all time.

"Demetrius, you have exhausted me today," said Pyrrhus. "I can find no more words to describe the marvels of Ephesus."

"I understand what you mean," said Demetrius, "there is only so much that a mere man can absorb in one day. I think it is time to return to the port and deal with simple worldly things for a while."

They collected their guardsmen and made their way back to the port, each of them contemplating their experiences in the city. Demetrius was of a sanguine temperament, and he felt emotionally drained after his meeting with Prothous, which came on top of that with Antimachus. Both of these men loved his father, and he felt as if he could not stand any more sympathy today. He felt as if he desperately needed a diversion. Almost any of his favorite pastimes would do, the thrill of a hunt, or the loving embrace of a woman. Even a battle would help, but all that was on offer was the task of getting his fleet ready for sea. Perhaps there would be some amusing moments when the loading of the horses began. For a moment, he was almost angry with Pyrrhus for leaving for Athens today, but he knew that the young man only acted in their best interests.

When the three men entered the enclosure of the port, Demetrius was glad to see that the process of getting the army on board the ships had begun in earnest. Ten ships at a time could be brought against the wharf. The first group of ships were in place and the officers were busy directing the men to board. Antimachus and Callistratus had a great deal of experience transporting armies by sea, and they made it look like a straight-forward exercise. When each group of ships completed their embarkation, they would move off together to anchor out of the way on the far side of the harbor, and the next group of ten ships would be brought to the wharf. The horse transports would be the last to load, with the exception of the garrison. It was desirable to have the horses on board the ships for as short a time as possible, to reduce the risk of injury and loss of condition, as they did not tolerate well the enclosure of the crowded stalls or the motion of the ships.

Separate to the loading area of the wharf, the two triremes that were to take Pyrrhus to Athens were moored at the far end. Demetrius and his companions rode to the harbor master's office, left their horses with a page, and entered the office where Antimachus was looking out at the wharf, watching out for any problems that may develop.

"There you are, Antimachus," said Demetrius, "all seems to be in hand."

"Yes, Sire. So far, all is going well," replied Antimachus. "If no unexpected problems arise, we will be ready in good time to sail as planned. Archesilaus and Callistratus are down on the wharf supervising the men. Also, the two triremes are ready whenever Pyrrhus wishes to leave. The pilot is aboard the ship with the red pendant. That would be the vessel to use as the flagship."

"Excellent," said Demetrius. "Pyrrhus, if you and Menestheus could get your kit ready, I will write a letter to the Athenians. You should be able to sail in an hour or so, but before you go, I must warn you that when you get to Athens, you will find that you will meet a mixed group of people. The Archons, the chief magistrates, are usually sensible, worldly men. There are, however, some who are unlikeable politicians who will plead any cause if it brings them some advantage. Stratocles is the worst of these. He persuaded the council and the assembly to vote the most absurd honors to be conferred on my father and myself, and I am sure he would be equally prepared to speak against us if it suited him.

"There is one man whom you must meet, however, who has been a good friend to us. His name is Cineas, and although he is still a young man, my father always said he was one of the few who understood that our actions were for the benefit of all Greece. He was a student of Demosthenes and is said to be as fine an orator as his teacher."

"I will be sure to seek him out," said Pyrrhus, "an eloquent ally is always welcome. I will say good-bye now, Demetrius," said Pyrrhus as he shook the king's hand. "Menestheus and I will make our way to the ship and tell the captain we are ready to leave as soon as you send your letter aboard."

Pyrrhus and Menestheus collected their saddlebags and their weapons and walked down the wharf to where the two warships were tied up. Antimachus had obviously been keen to make a good impression on the Athenians, as the boats he chose for Pyrrhus's diplomatic mission were the two handsomest in the fleet. They were new boats, decorated with gold leaf on the prows, the remainder of the hulls bright with immaculate paint work. The ship they were to travel on flew the broad commodore's pendant, a large red flag with Antigonus's emblem in the center, that of a golden lion in a crouching pose, ready to strike.

"It seems we are to travel in style, Menestheus," said Pyrrhus, as they approached the boarding ramp. "Yes, Sire," replied Menestheus, "and I would be surprised if the captain does not give us his cabin for the journey."

They made their way up the boarding ramp, where the captain and the pilot were waiting for them. "Good afternoon, Sire," the captain said to Pyrrhus. "My name is Marsyas. I am the captain of this ship. I would like to present Theophrastus, the pilot."

"Good day to you both, gentlemen," said Pyrrhus, "it is a pleasure to be aboard such a fine vessel. I would like to introduce you to my lieutenant, Menestheus. Perhaps you could show us where we can leave our luggage and then we could discuss your plans for the voyage. Demetrius will have a letter of introduction to the Athenians delivered shortly, and we could sail as soon as possible after that."

"Certainly, Sire. I will show you to my cabin, which will be at your disposal for the journey. My charts are there, and I can show you the course that Theophrastus recommended."

Marsyas led the way to the rear of the ship and into the cabin. Pyrrhus and Menestheus took their armor off and left it with their small pile of belongings in a corner of the cabin. The cabin was reasonably roomy for such a vessel. There was space for an extra bunk, despite the large chart table in the center of the cabin. Now that they were all comfortable, Marsyas brought out the charts and invited Theophrasus to go over the plans they had formulated. "We will only have a few hours of daylight left by the time we sail, Sire," said Theophrastus. "What I would recommend is that we aim to anchor in the lee of Samos this evening. As we are not in a desperate rush, I believe the best course from there would be to go to Ikaria, then to Delos and Cynthos. We will have good protected harbors to anchor in at night. From Cynthos we would sail directly to the Piraeus. The weather has been kind to us so far. If it continues to be fair, we should have no trouble reaching the Piraeus in four days."

"That will be very satisfactory, Theophrastus," said Pyrrhus. "A restful cruise will be very welcome after the goings-on over the last few weeks." A knock on the door preceded the entrance of the first mate of the ship, who brought Diomedes with him. "Good afternoon, Sire," said Diomedes. "I have brought the letter which Demetrius has written to the Athenians. He also asked me to give you this parcel, which has several new tunics in it for both you and Menestheus. He was sure that you would want to look your best when you visit Athens. He also sends these two purses to cover your costs while you are in Athens."

"Thank you, Diomedes," said Pyrrhus. "Please give Demetrius my warmest thanks. Come, let me walk out with you, and I will look forward to seeing you in Athens next week."

After Pyrrhus had seen Diomedes on his way, the captain unmoored the ship, carefully maneuvered away from the dock, and the galley was rowed out of the harbor. Once through the gap in the breakwater, Marsyas was able to set the sail and take advantage of the steady easterly breeze. No doubt the oarsmen would have plenty of work to do before they reached Athens, and the captain was happy to conserve their strength while he could.

Pyrrhus enjoyed being on a ship, and, once in the open water, he was happy to stand on the deck chatting with Menestheus and Marsysas. The weather was glorious and the sea calm. The wind dropped away after an hour or so, and the rowers took over for the remainder of the journey to Samos. From Pyrrhus's point of view, this was even better, as he felt that triremes were at their most beautiful when being rowed. He liked looking down at the action of the oars of his own ship, but even more so to watch the other warship behind them. The slender and sleek trireme had been the pinnacle of naval design for 200 years, and watching the rhythmic rise and fall of the three banks of oars was almost hypnotic.

Late in the afternoon, the two ships entered the small harbor of a fishing village on the northwest side of Samos. Theophrastus went ashore briefly to see the harbor master. After he returned, the four of them stayed on deck to watch a particularly lovely Mediterranean sunset and then adjourned to the main cabin for an excellent meal, which brought their very full day to an end.

CHAPTER VII

As planned, the two triremes glided into the Piraeus four days after leaving Ephesus. The voyage had not been totally uneventful, however. Two days into the trip; while on their way to Delos, they had been caught in a storm, and had to seek refuge in the lee of one of the small islands that are scattered through the Cyclades. The squall, though intense, had been short, and after two nervous hours they were able to resume sailing.

The two ships anchored in the harbor while Theophrastus went ashore to present the ships' documents and declarations of freedom of infectious diseases, and on his return they were allocated docking space on the main wharf. Pyrrhus was pleased to learn from Theophrastus that news of Antigonus's defeat had not reached Athens, which would enable him to argue his point of view from a more advantageous position. He instructed Menestheus to go into the town and purchase horses for the two of them and the six men who would accompany them as an escort.

When he and his men were suitably mounted, they set off for Athens. Pyrrhus had been impressed by the activity and affluence that was evident in the Piraeus. He had seen twenty triremes anchored in the harbor that were in excellent condition and obviously kept continuously ready for sea. There were dozens of trading vessels, some bringing goods to Athens and others taking Athenian exports to their markets in Greece, Crete, and Italy. Although individual city-states no longer had the resources to be politically dominant, it was clear that Athens had not lost all its vigor.

The favorable impression that Pyrrhus gained at the Piraeus was confirmed as they made their way to the city. All of the available land was under cultivation with well laid out and well-tended crops. They passed a variety of shrines by the side of the road that were intended to provide shelter for travelers as well as to placate the gods.

It was toward the end of the afternoon when they approached Athens, and from a distance they could admire the graceful city. Looking over the walls of the city, they saw the Parthenon proudly standing on the Acropolis, gleaming white in the bright sunshine. It was probably the most famous and admired building in Greece and had been built by Pericles during the great years of Athens, when she created a maritime empire after the victories in the Persian wars. Just as the empire of Croesus was brought low by Cyrus, that of Athens would be dealt a death blow when she was defeated by Sparta in the terrible second Peloponnesian War. Though her arms would no longer conquer after this defeat, the intellect of the great Athenian philosophers still carried the name of Athens to the corners of the world. It was over twenty years since Aristotle died, but his pupils continued to educate the Greek world, and it would not be long before Romans would travel to Athens to study at the Academy. Athens gave laws to the Roman republic after the expulsion of the Etruscan kings, and thereby had been held in admiration by the Romans for generations.

As they neared the gates, Pyrrhus and his men rode down a short side road that took them to a large stable that catered to people visiting the city. The horses taken care of, Pyrrhus and the others walked into the city. As they walked, Pyrrhus said to Menestheus, "I believe you have spent some time in Athens, Menestheus."

"Yes, Sire. I spent two years at the Academy before my family's fortunes changed."

"That is excellent. I am sure you can recommend an inn where we can stay."

"There is one I had in mind, Sire," said Menestheus. "It will be quite comfortable, and it is only a short walk from the Areopagus where the council meets."

"Let us make our way there then. Once we are settled, I will send a message to the council and request an audience in the morning."

They made their way through the crowded streets into the central area of the city and found the inn that Menestheus recommended. Leaving their escort outside, Pyrrhus and Menestheus went inside, Menestheus automatically assuming that a king should not have to do such a mundane thing as to deal with an innkeeper. The innkeeper was suitably impressed that his new guest was no less than a king acting as the representative of Demetrius. His extreme nervousness seemed excessive, however, and the man wilted when Pyrrhus turned his gaze on him and inquired about the current political situation. As an answer was not forthcoming, Pyrrhus smiled at the man and said, "There is no need to be afraid, my friend. Neither I nor King Demetrius wage war on innkeepers, nor on Athens herself."

Summoning up his courage, the innkeeper finally found his tongue, "There is bad news for Demetrius, your honor. His garrison was expelled two months ago."

Trying very hard not to show his complete surprise on his face, Pyrrhus stared at the unfortunate man and then turned to Menestheus and said, "Well then, it appears we will have more to discuss tomorrow that I thought. Tell the men to come inside. Keep two of them here in the front of the inn at all times, and the others can stay in their rooms until they are needed. You can tell them that if they wander off and get drunk, they will be thrown overboard after we return to the ship.

"Now, innkeeper, you can show us to our rooms. We will eat dinner here in two hours time."

Pyrrhus handed the man a handful of gold coins, "This will cover our expenses for two or three days." Relieved to end the conversation with his head still on his shoulders, the innkeeper led Pyrrhus and Menestheus to their rooms, promising to have a fine banquet ready for them at the appointed time. Menestheus dropped his saddlebags and Demetrius's parcels in his room and returned to the front of the inn to organize the men. He set a schedule of watch keeping and left the innkeeper to show them where they would sleep. Having settled the men, Menestheus returned to Pyrrhus's room, knocked on the door and entered. "The men are organized, Sire. I have posted the first pair on watch, and they will be relieved at two-hour intervals."

"That is good, Menestheus," said Pyrrhus. "I must see the council as soon as possible. The situation here has obviously deteriorated markedly, and I will have to find out exactly what is going on and let Demetrius know. Go now, if you will, to the Areopagus, and ask the councilors for an audience early tomorrow morning."

Menestheus nodded and said, "Why don't you get some rest, Sire? I will knock on your door when the meal is ready, and I will bring a fresh tunic." He then left on his way to arrange the meeting with the councilors.

Pyrrhus undressed and lay down on the cot, wondering what other surprises were in store for him. Foremost in his mind was the whereabouts of his sister, Deidameia. Was she still in Athens? Had she been forced to go elsewhere? What had happened in the other cities that Demetrius assumed remained loyal? He would find these things out tomorrow. For now, he might as well indulge himself in an afternoon nap.

The knocking at the door woke Pyrrhus some time later, Menestheus entering the room after a decent interval. Pyrrhus sat up in his cot, still a little stupid from his sleep. "How did you get on, Menestheus?"

"The meeting is set for mid-morning tomorrow, Sire. I arranged for the innkeeper to bring hot water and towels, and I will lay your clean tunics over the chair here. Dinner will be ready when you come down, and I will be able to give you the details then."

"Very good," said Pyrrhus. Menestheus let himself out, and the hot water arrived. Pyrrhus washed and shaved, and after he dressed himself in a fine silk tunic, he felt refreshed and was looking forward to dinner. He made his way out to the dining room, where Menestheus and the men were waiting for him. Pyrrhus smiled at them and sat down at the table that was laid out for himself and Menestheus. The others would sit at a larger table on the other side of the room so that Pyrrhus and Menestheus could have some privacy for their conversation. The innkeeper brought wine to the tables and said the food would be served in ten minutes time. The man was much calmer than he had been earlier. If he survived the telling of bad news earlier in the day, then he could be reasonably confident of living through the next couple of days.

"So, Menestheus," said Pyrrhus, "tell me what you were able to learn today."

"I was able to speak to one of the councilors this afternoon, Sire. As we were told earlier, the council decided a couple of months ago to expel Demetrius's garrison. They felt that Antigonus and Demetrius would be too preoccupied with the war in Anatolia to take too much notice of what happened in Athens. The decision was by no means unanimous though . . . "

Menestheus was interrupted by the entrance of a man who walked straight to their table. "Excuse me, gentlemen. My name is Cineas. I was hoping to find King Pyrrhus here."

"You have found him, sir," said Pyrrhus. "We have just sat down to have our dinner, and we would be very pleased if you would join us."

"Thank you, Sire." Cineas sat down, and Pyrrhus introduced Menestheus, then called for another wine goblet. "I heard of your arrival from the councilor who spoke to Menestheus this afternoon, and I felt that I should acquaint you with the situation here before you meet with the council tomorrow."

"That would be welcome, Cineas," said Pyrrhus. "I was taken by surprise this afternoon when we learned that the garrison had been expelled."

"I fear it was a poor decision, Sire," said Cineas. "There are some on the council who are unrealistic in their outlook but manage to convince others that their plans are workable. It has always been a matter of some sadness that Athens, with her great history, should be controlled by an outside power, and that we have to live with the soldiers of that power stationed here to keep the city under control. However, it is difficult to avoid in these times, and apart from the element of pride, the fact is that Antigonus and Demetrius have been great benefactors of Athens. If we cast them out, we leave ourselves open to being taken over by Cassander, who would be a far less generous master."

"I am glad to hear there is still some support for Demetrius here, Cineas," said Pyrrhus. "I should also say that Demetrius told me I should seek you out after I arrived in Athens and that you have been a loyal friend to him and his father. There is some news that I must acquaint you with. Antigonus was defeated by Lysimachus and Seleucus three weeks ago. Antigonus himself was killed, and Demetrius is on his way here by sea with the remnants of the army, 5,000 infantry and 4,000 cavalry."

Cineas looked startled, as if someone had slapped him across the face. He leaned back in his chair, and, when he composed himself, he offered his sympathies but remained lost in thought. "So you see, Cineas," said Pyrrhus, "the world has been turned from one direction to another, and we must all find a way to live in it."

At this moment, the innkeeper and his daughters brought the meal out. The man had done well and brought several joints of roasted lamb, baked vegetables, bread, and fruit. Pyrrhus attended to the carving, and the meal continued for some time in silence. After giving Cineas some time to recollect himself, Pyrrhus pressed him for information about the situation in the other cities, and if he had news of his sister.

"As far as your sister is concerned, Sire," said Cineas, "there is no need to worry. She was escorted to Megara with royal honors and a powerful escort. I have had news from her, and she is safe and comfortable, although naturally uncertain about the political climate.

"With regard to the situation in other cities, I know that Corinth in particular has remained loyal. The Corinthians have several admirable qualities. They have always been extremely loyal to their friends, and they are apt to be less swayed by demagogues than we are here in Athens. Megara, obviously, has remained loyal, but Antigonus's garrisons have been expelled from a number of other cities, most importantly from Thebes and Argos."

"So, it seems we only have these two cities whose loyalty we can rely on," said Pyrrhus. "What I propose, gentlemen, is that we meet with the council tomorrow morning, and then Menestheus and I will join the ships and sail to intercept Demetrius at sea. I am afraid that all we will be able to accomplish with the council is to make a protest on behalf of Demetrius."

Turning to Cineas, Pyrrhus continued, "Cineas, I wonder if I could impose on you to travel to Megara. I would like to let my sister know that her husband and brother are safe and will join her soon."

"I would be happy to do that, Sire," said Cineas.

"I would like you to take two of my men with you for your protection, as well as this purse, which should comfortably cover your expenses for the journey. If you could remain at Megara for the time being, I will join you there after I have spoken to Demetrius. I do not know what he will do in these circumstances, but it would be best if we are all able to meet again after I speak to him."

The innkeeper returned to their table, and after inquiring about whether the gentlemen enjoyed the meal, poured a fresh glass of wine for each of them, cleared the used plates and the meat, and brought cheese and figs. After he left again, Cineas said to Pyrrhus, "There is some good news to balance the bad, Sire. Antigonus left a squadron of his navy at Athens. When the garrison was expelled, the ships and their crews were allowed to leave. They are currently also in port at Megara. There is also a considerable amount of money kept at Athens that belonged to Antigonus. I am sure the Athenians will return this to Demetrius."

"That will ease Demetrius's pain somewhat, I am sure," said Pyrrhus. "I will send two of the men back to the Piraeus first thing tomorrow morning to let the captains know to be ready to sail tomorrow."

Cineas nodded and then stood up. "If you will excuse me, Sire, I will leave you now. I will ride to Megara tomorrow and see Deidameia. If you are agreeable, I will call here at dawn to collect my escort and leave directly after that. I wish you a good journey tomorrow." Cineas bowed to Pyrrhus and Menestheus, and then made his way out of the inn, leaving the two men to talk over their wine.

"I have had quite enough surprises for one day, Menestheus," said Pyrrhus, staring at the wine in his goblet. After a moment's contemplation, he continued. "Despite our many problems, it is extremely fortunate that Corinth and Megara have remained loyal. Corinth has a strong garrison and is a well fortified city. Megara has its own garrison and has in effect been reinforced by the men who were bundled out of Athens, as well as the squadron of ships. Altogether, there is a considerable force, but we do remain at quite a disadvantage, as with the exception of Megara, we do not have any remaining allies north of the Isthmus of Corinth, and we do not yet know about the Peloponnese, apart from the defection of Argos."

"What do you think Demetrius will do, Sire?" asked Menestheus.

"I do not know, my friend," replied Pyrrhus. "He is reasonably secure for the time being, but his enemies will find it easy to isolate him and trap him here if our fortunes do not improve in some way. One thing is certain, however, and that is that he will be extremely disappointed by the actions of the Athenians. Despite his rather unruly behavior while he was here, he, like his father, genuinely believed he was acting for the benefit of the Greek world, and he has always held the Athenians in high regard. Like it or not, we must sail as soon as possible after our meeting at the Areopagus and try and intercept him at sea."

Menestheus acquired many of the virtues of a philosopher in the two years he spent in Athens, studying at the Academy. His natural qualities of intelligence and insight had been nurtured and refined under the guidance of his teachers. It was clear to him now that he and Pyrrhus had reached a point where further discussion of the dilemmas facing Demetrius and themselves would be fruitless. Also, as such discussion would involve dwelling on the lack of loyalty shown by Athens and other cities, there would be a danger of them taking a more belligerent and hostile stance toward these cities. The philosopher in Menestheus was sure that an emotive stance was undesirable in high politics, where all decisions should be made in a logical and contemplative manner. He therefore led Pyrrhus to different considerations and asked him about how his sister, Deidameia, met Demetrius, and how she adjusted her life to accommodate a man who was embroiled in the stormy politics of their times. Pyrrhus seemed grateful to put their problems aside for the time being. He explained the curious side of politics in his native Epirus. How the appearance of usurpers had shaped the lives of both his father and himself, and how he had been displaced from his throne by the most recent Neoptolemus. The curious thing was that as the women in his family were excluded from the offices of power by their sex, they were also excluded from the struggles for that power. His mother was permitted to live comfortably in Epirus after his father had been killed, and Deidameia also continued to live in Epirus after he had been forced into exile. The circle of the ruling families of the Hellenistic world was a small one, and it was natural for Antigonus and Demetrius to know of the beautiful princess in Epirus. Several years ago, Deidameia had been invited to spend a summer in Argos with friends of their father. Deidameia was desperate to go, and Pyrrhus gave his permission because it would be a good thing for his sister to spend time in a city that was one of the greatest and most ancient in Greek history. It was at a state dinner for Demetrius where the two had met. The man who was Deidameia's guardian in Argos was hosting the dinner and naturally introduced her to Demetrius. Demetrius was so taken with Deidameia that for the first, and possibly only, time in his life, he resisted his impulse to force his attentions on her and observed the niceties of courtship. He spent as much time in Argos as he could during Deidameia's visit to the city, and they periodically met there after she returned to Epirus. After something of a fairytale courtship, they were married in Argos the following year. Since the marriage, Deidameia accompanied Demetrius in all of his travels with the exception of the recent and fateful expedition to Anatolia. She proved to be a fine companion, as competent in the discussion of political matters as she was in running their domestic affairs. She had also shown herself to be extremely broad minded. Demetrius was not a man to whom monogamy was a virtue, but Deidameia believed that if she was the wife who held the greatest part of her husband's love, then she would accept that as her just portion.

After dwelling for some time on the subject of his sister and his family, Pyrrhus said to Menestheus, "And what about you, my friend? How is it that an accomplished philosopher becomes a captain in a regiment of mercenaries?"

"A simple matter of economics, Sire," said Menestheus with a smile. "My father was a merchant, and we lived in a village just outside the Piraeus. He worked for many years for a wealthy man who imported spices and artwork from Lydia and Phrygia. Eventually he became sufficiently wealthy to buy two ships of his own. His previous employer became a close friend and helped him in many different ways to start his own business. He provided introductions to a number of Lydian merchants, and between them they found a means for my father to act as a solo merchant, dealing in such items as would complement the trade of his old employer. Initially, fortune favored my father, and his business prospered. It was in this prosperous phase of my father's fortunes that I turned twenty years of age, and the question arose whether I would join my father's business or continue with my studies in Athens. I pleaded my case with my father, whom I knew hoped that I would join him as a merchant. I wanted above all things to stay in Athens and study at the Academy. I already had a chance to speak to Crates about joining his school, and he assured me of a place, if I could get my father's permission. When I spoke to my father, and I shall always honor him for this, he said that everyone must follow their own path. He gave me his blessing to continue my studies, and his promise of support to pay the fees at the Academy.

"I spent two wonderful years at the Academy, and I began to dream that I might become sufficiently learned to teach at the Academy myself one day. It was then that my father's business collapsed. He borrowed heavily to purchase gold and silver ware from Lydia, which he was sure he could sell for a handsome profit in Sicily and Italy. His two ships were sent to Lydia to collect the merchandise, and they were duly loaded and set sail for their destinations. What happened to them after that is a mystery. Whether they sank in a storm or were taken by pirates, nobody knows. Whatever was the cause of their disappearance, my father was ruined. He had to sell everything he owned to pay his creditors. After he paid all his debts, he had almost nothing left, and with all his hopes destroyed he could not live with his disappointment. He wrote a letter addressed to my mother and myself, asking for our forgiveness, and threw himself off a cliff. Suddenly, I found myself in a position where I had to support my mother and myself."

Menestheus paused for a moment of sad reflection, then looked up at Pyrrhus, and, smiling, said, "It was then that I acted more like a traveling sophist than a philosopher at the Academy. I have always tried to keep fit, and at the gymnasium I got to know a group of men who used to visit the same training area in Athens. These men were army officers, and as well as the usual athletic exercises, I spent some time with them performing fencing and javelin exercises. Added to that, I studied military theory as a part of historical study at the Academy. With these two modest qualifications, I was able to convince Demetrius's officers that I was an infantry commander of some experience when he was recruiting men in Greece last year."

Pyrrhus burst out laughing and slapped his thigh. "That is a marvelous story, Menestheus. I am extremely sorry to hear your tale of sadness about your father and that you had to leave the Academy early, but I am sure that the Academy's loss is my gain. I shall try to make sure your talents do not go to waste."

CHAPTER VIII

There was a great deal of activity at the inn at dawn on the following morning. Pyrrhus and Menestheus washed and shaved by candlelight before the sun had risen and made their way to the front room to await the arrival of Cineas. True to his word, Cineas arrived at first light, collected his small escort, and made his way out of the city. He informed Pyrrhus of the name of the man who was Deidameia's host in Megara, and where his house was. Menestheus knew Megara well and was sure the directions were adequate. The innkeeper brought out breakfast for the party, and, once physical needs had been satisfied, Pyrrhus sent two of his men off to return to the Piraeus. They carried a letter informing the captains of his intention of sailing this afternoon. After a good breakfast, Pyrrhus sat back comfortably in his chair and said to Menestheus, "We have two or three hours before we are due to meet the council, Menestheus. I would like to walk around Athens and see the Parthenon if we have time."

"I am sure we could do that, Sire," replied Menestheus. "What I would suggest is that we start by walking up to the Acropolis, spend as much time as we want walking around the

Parthenon and the other buildings, and then walk slowly to the
Areopagus in time for our meeting."

"That sounds like an admirable plan. Let us collect our things
and meet here again in a few minutes and then depart."

Pyrrhus and Menestheus dressed in their finest tunics for
their meeting at the Areopagus, then made something of a contrast with their floppy hats and walking staves. Pyrrhus directed
their two remaining men to stay at the inn until his return. He
and Menestheus walked directly to the Acropolis, and, during
the time it took to get there, the city awoke around them, with
the bustle of a prosperous people in a prosperous city. Although
the Parthenon was the object of their outing, Pyrrhus was glad to
see the beauty of the public buildings and the monuments to the
great men and deeds in the city's history. As they reached the top
of the stairs that approached the Acropolis, they caught sight of a
dignified procession approaching the Parthenon. Pyrrhus turned
to Menestheus and said, "Do you know the significance of this
gathering, Menestheus?"

"Yes, Sire," replied Menestheus, "and you may find that it
allows you to have a greater regard for the loyalty of the Athenians. Today is the first day of the new month, Hecatombaion. It
is the custom, on the first day of each quadrennium, such as today, for the council and city elders to offer prayers to Athena for
her continued protection of the city and its prosperity. It is 190
years since the battle of Marathon, where the Athenians defeated
the army of Darius the First, during the first Persian invasion
of Greece. The only city to send help to Athens, that arrived in
time for the battle, was Plataea. It is only a small city, but they
sent 1,000 hoplites, virtually every able-bodied man in the city.
Since then, on every occasion where the Athenians have offered
prayers for their own city, they have asked for the divine protection to be extended to the Plataeans as well. They are aware of
another debt of gratitude as well. Plataea was Athens' ally during
the fateful Peloponnesian War, and it was destroyed by the Spartans after it was taken at the end of a siege. After the war ended,
the well-being of the Plataeans was one of the prime concerns

of the Athenians. Athens was not in a position at that stage to rebuild the city, but they took the people into Athens and looked after them until Plataea was finally rebuilt by Philip and Alexander as a tribute to their courage during the Persian Wars."

"It does give one a sense of proportion, my friend," said Pyrrhus. "Athens can truly claim the greatest of pedigrees. Tell me, if you will, about the building of the Parthenon. It is quite wonderful."

"It was the product of the maritime empire of Athens, Sire," said Menestheus. "All of the cities and island states that were part of the newly formed Delian League were given the option of supplying either men and ships or contributing a certain amount of money. The league was formed after the victories over Persia during the great invasion of Xerxes. The aim of the league was to protect Greece from Persia, to liberate the Greek cities on the Ionian coast and the islands in the Aegean Sea, and to consider other means of fighting the Persians. All this was under the leadership of Athens. Sparta, the other great force in the victories in these wars, chose not to belong to the league.

"As time went by, almost all of the members of the league chose to contribute money, and to leave to Athens the military role. Over the course of years, the nature of the league changed so that the end result was that Athens had a powerful navy of 300 ships and came to regard the contributions of others as tribute from subjects, rather than offerings from political equals. These greatest days of Athens were tied to the fortunes of one man, Pericles. He led Athens by the force of his personality and wisdom, and it was he who commissioned the Parthenon and engaged the finest architects and artisans in Greece. It was built at enormous cost over sixteen years and was paid for by the tributes of the empire. His critics were not pleased at this use of the money, but he argued that as long as Athens fulfilled her role as the military and naval leader and ensured their collective freedom from Persia, she could use the funds at her own discretion. Pericles died in the second year of the Great Peloponnesian War, his death being the worst of all the tragedies that befell Athens in that terrible conflict. Instead of his wisdom guiding Athens, the leadership of the city fell to men who were inadequate to the task, and Athens eventually suffered a total and catastrophic defeat and surrendered to the Spartans twenty-seven years after the war began."

Menestheus paused, and with some difficulty avoided being emotionally overcome by the recollection of these events. Pyrrhus was affected as well, and, to regain their composure, the two walked in silence around the great temple. Despite the changes in fortune suffered by the Athenians over the centuries, the greatness of their past achievements would always be proclaimed to the world by this wonderful building, even if nothing else survived.

They walked to the far side of the Acropolis and sat down on a bench from which they could look over the city. Eventually, Pyrrhus stood up and said to Menestheus, "Come, my friend, it is time we made our way to the Areopagus."

"Yes, Sire," replied Menestheus. "Forgive me, I find I tend to be somewhat sentimental at times. As a matter of interest, all the men in Athens at some time had to play their part in their city's fortunes. The great Socrates fought in the phalanx as a hoplite when he was a younger man, as did Aeschylus, the tragic poet. Cynegirus, the brother of Aeschylus, was killed at Marathon while he was trying to board one of the Persian ships."

Pyrrhus nodded and the pair kept walking. Their visit to the Acropolis did indeed allow him to revise his attitude to the Athenians. Why would such a people not resent being pawns in the struggles of the current crop of powerful kings? He would speak in a more balanced fashion to the councilors at their meeting this morning as a result of their visit to the Acropolis.

The two men said little as they made their way into the city and approached the Areopagus, but their spirits improved as they walked, and they even chatted lightheartedly while they consumed some crusty bread and a glass of wine they purchased from a street vendor near the council chambers.

After their refreshment, they walked the short remaining distance to the Areopagus and presented themselves to the officer at the entrance. "The councilors are ready to receive you, Sire," the officer said. "They have just returned from the temple. Please follow me."

The officer took them into the chambers and into a large office that was comfortably furnished. "If you could wait here, Sire, I will let the councilors know you are here." Pyrrhus and Menestheus seated themselves and waited quietly until three men entered the room.

A tall and distinguished man of about fifty years was the first to speak. "Good morning, Sire," said the man, "my name is Hippoclus, and my two colleagues are Ismenias and Androcleides." Pyrrhus nodded to each in turn and introduced Menestheus.

Hippoclus invited Pyrrhus and Menestheus to resume their seats, while he and the others brought chairs over so that they could easily converse while seated.

"I am pleased to make your acquaintance, gentlemen," said Pyrrhus, "although I must say I was surprised to learn of the changes that have occurred at Athens while Demetrius has been away in Anatolia."

"I am sure you were, Sire," said Hippoclus. "The three of us were chosen to speak to you, because, with Cineas, we are the ones most favorably attached to Demetrius. We have presented you with unfavorable news, and I hope that you will be able to understand the position of Athens in this matter."

"Please continue, Hippoclus," Pyrrhus said.

"We have known some turbulent times in recent years, and what we hope to achieve is a position of neutrality for Athens. I will not insult you with the rhetoric of Stratocles. Even when he makes the correct decision, it is always for the wrong reasons. We in Athens are not ungrateful for the favor and protection shown to us by Antigonus and Demetrius. However, we find it intolerable to be a pawn in the incessant conflicts between the kings who followed Alexander. As such, we wish to continue to be regarded as friends by Antigonus and his son, but to remain politically neutral, the enemy of no one."

"I understand your position clearly, Hippoclus," said Pyrrhus, "and I appreciate your frankness. However, I should point out some difficulties of your position. Despite your desire to remain neutral, there are powerful forces at work in Greece which may make that impossible. I know that Demetrius and Antigonus will be extremely disappointed in what they will see as a breach of the loyalty which they feel they have earned in their dealings with the Athenians. I would also point out that there are worse things than allying yourselves with the Antigonids, who have a genuine admiration for your city. In particular, if Cassander were to increase his power base in central Greece, it would result in far less generous treatment of your city. He acts with a ruthlessness that would make you think of your previous situation as a golden age."

"I take your point, Sire," said Hippoclus. "In fact, it is similar to the argument that I used myself when I tried to convince the other councilors not to expel Demetrius's garrison. Be that as it may, the decision has been made, and I am not able to reverse it. I can only ask that you pass on our decision to Demetrius and his father in such a way that our interests are considered in his further actions."

"You may have a chance to do so yourself, Hippoclus," said Pyrrhus. "Demetrius is on his way here with a powerful fleet as we speak. I was sent ahead to warn you of his approach, as he did not want to alarm you with the unexpected arrival of a large force."

"In that case, Sire, I will have to try and meet Demetrius at sea, before he arrives here. I am sure that the other councilors will request that Demetrius not land at the Piraeus and will refuse him permission to set foot in Attica."

"Very well, Hippoclus. I can do no more to press Demetrius's case. There are two other matters to consider. Firstly, I know that my sister, Deidameia, was escorted to Megara, and I thank you for your courteous treatment of her. I will be traveling to Megara to see her as soon as I can. There is also the matter of the funds that Demetrius left here in your care. It is only just that this money is given up to Demetrius. It would certainly add credence to the idea that the Athenians are a people who try to act honorably."

"I can assure you that these funds will be returned at the earliest convenient moment, Sire," said Hippoclus. "If you wish, I can have the money loaded on a trireme, and I will convey it to pass on to Demetrius when I seek him out at sea."

"That would be ideal," replied Pyrrhus. "I planned to sail from the Piraeus this afternoon. However, that would be unlikely to give you enough time for your preparations. What I suggest is that you send the money and travel down yourself this afternoon to the Piraeus, and you travel in company with my two triremes tomorrow. We should be able to intercept Demetrius at sea somewhere in the region of Delos."

"Very well, Sire," said Hippoclus. "I will give the orders to that effect, and my ship will be ready to sail at dawn tomorrow."

Having reached this conclusion, Pyrrhus and Menestheus took their leave, shaking hands with the councilors to confirm the agreed upon arrangements. Once they were out in the street, they walked in the direction of their inn. In response to an inquisitive glance from Menestheus, Pyrrhus said to him, "Sometimes one is required to tell something less than the full truth, Menestheus. Demetrius's circumstances are extremely difficult, and the money that Antigonus left here could, quite possibly, be the difference between survival and death. By not revealing the defeat we have suffered, we maintained a stronger position to bargain from. It is entirely possible that they would have handed over the money anyway, as they certainly appeared to be honorable men, but, as it is, even with some concealment of the truth, we are not asking them to return anything that does not belong to us. Also, it may soften Demetrius's reaction to being shut out of Attica."

When they arrived at the inn, to the immense relief of the innkeeper, Pyrrhus announced that they would be leaving as soon as they collected their belongings. Pyrrhus asked the innkeeper to prepare some food to take with them, and no request seemed too much trouble for the unfortunate landlord. He duly prepared a variety of cold foods, pieces of lamb, cheese, bread and wine for them to take on their way.

Having made their way out of the city, and collected their horses, Pyrrhus, Menestheus, and the two remaining guards made their way toward the Piraeus. Pyrrhus chuckled to himself, and said to Menestheus, "Perhaps we should terrorize innkeepers more often. I seemed that our host could not get rid of us quickly enough!"

"You can understand his predicament, Sire. I think that the fellow was frightened out of his wits from the minute we arrived."

They traveled on in silence after that, both men being lost in their thoughts, considering their position, and what would be the next step in their complicated lives. Halfway to the Piraeus they stopped by the side of the road, ate their lunch under the shade of a tree, and resumed their journey as soon as they finished. After contemplating their position for a time, Pyrrhus was able to temporarily put aside his thoughts on their political fortunes and was happy to chat with Menestheus while they rode in the country. As they approached the Piraeus, Pyrrhus was glad to see that the gates were closed and his few men were manning the ramparts on the walls. The gates were opened for them, and Pyrrhus made his way to the harbor master's office and summoned the captains and pilot. The preparations for sailing were already being made following the message that Pyrrhus sent to the Piraeus, so leaving at dawn tomorrow presented no difficulties.

Toward the end of the afternoon, Hippoclus arrived, riding a fine black horse, and with him was a large covered wagon drawn by four horses and an escort of ten fully-armed cavalrymen. Hippoclus instructed his men to dismount and leave their horses in the care of the port attendants and to unload the wagon on the main wharf and then sought out Pyrrhus at the harbor master's office. Pyrrhus had dealt with all the matters of business that required his attention and was indulging himself in the rare luxury of reading. He found a comfortable chair, a flask of excellent wine from Thasos, courtesy of the harbor master's cellar, and was deep in a volume of Aeschylus's play, *The Persians*. It seemed a good choice for one embroiled in Attic politics. When Hippoclus entered the office, Pyrrhus rose to greet him, "Come in my friend. You have made good time in your journey from Athens."

"I wanted to make sure of arriving before dark, Sire. I didn't want to be traveling at night with a treasure such as this in my hands."

"I am sure you are right," said Pyrrhus, who was in an excellent mood after his brief period of relaxation. He also formed a good opinion of Hippoclus in his short dealings with him. "Have you had a chance to get your ship prepared?"

"Yes, Sire. I sent some men ahead of me to let the captain of one of our triremes know to get ready for sea and to bring the ship to the main wharf as soon as possible. It should not be long before it arrives. We keep a number of ships ready to sail at short notice."

"So it appeared to me when we arrived yesterday. Athens still has a formidable navy, then, Hippoclus?"

"You might say so, Sire," said Hippoclus. "We have fifty triremes on the water and another fifty in storage in dry dock. It is not a powerful fleet when one thinks of what Athens had in days gone by, and we are no longer in a position to dispute the command of the sea, but it is sufficient for our needs at the moment. There are a few vessels which are used for diplomatic missions, but the main strength of the fleet is used to protect our commerce. There are still times when we have to send a squadron to seek out pirates, either directly, or as an escort for our merchant ships."

"If I am not mistaken, your ship is warping up to the wharf now."

"So it is. If you will excuse me, Sire, I will go and speak to the captain and load the treasure onto the ship."

"Of course. When all is in hand, Hippoclus, I would be pleased if you would join us for dinner. The harbor master, Philoneicus, has promised us a good meal with his best wine this evening, here in the office."

"I would like that very much, Sire. I should be free in two hours time, if that is satisfactory."

Hippoclus left to attend to his duties, and Pyrrhus returned to his wine and his book. The coming days were doubtless going to be difficult, and he was determined to prolong this short period of respite. Sometime later, when Pyrrhus finished reading his play, and was looking around for something else to read, Menestheus entered the office along with Philoneicus. "I hope you have had a bit of rest, Sire," said Menestheus.

"I have had a very pleasant read, Menestheus," replied Pyrrhus. "How are our preparations going?"

"Our ships are ready to sail at any time, Sire. I have spoken to Hippoclus, and they have safely loaded Demetrius's treasure and posted a suitable guard. After they finish loading fresh water onto the Athenian trireme, that will be ready for sea as well."

"Excellent," said Pyrrhus. "I have invited Hippoclus to join us for dinner. Philoneicus, perhaps you could send a man to tell him when he should join us?"

"Yes, Sire. Dinner should be ready in a half an hour or so. I will walk over and speak to him now."

A short time later Hippoclus joined them, and it was the signal for Philoneicus to begin his duties as a host. "I hope you will find the dinner to your liking, Sire. The local lamb is very good this year, and my wife has not failed me yet as a cook. I had been waiting for a special occasion to bring out this wine from Thasos, and tonight seems as good a time as I could ask for." Philoneicus poured the wine and said a short prayer to Athena for the safety of his family and their guests. The other men all added their own prayers privately, and then each of them poured a small amount of wine on the floor in a libation to the gods. With the brief formality out of the way, the men all drank to each other's health, and assured Philoneicus that they had rarely drunk better wine. Pyrrhus asked Theophrastus to tell them all about the sailing orders for the morning and where he hoped they would be able to intercept Demetrius at sea. There were no other decisions to be made tonight, and Pyrrhus then led the conversation to a discussion of the wealth of Athenian literature, and his pleasure in re-reading *The Persians* that afternoon.

CHAPTER IX

At first light the next morning, the three graceful warships left the Piraeus under oars. Pyrrhus asked Hippoclus to give his orders to the captain of the Athenian ship and then to travel with him on his vessel. Pyrrhus stood on the bridge of his flagship, with the captain, the pilot, Menestheus, and Hippoclus. They all watched the two beautiful ships following them negotiate the harbor mouth and then set their sails, heading first for Cynthos and then Delos, where they hoped to intercept Demetrius. Once they were settled on their course, Pyrrhus asked Hippoclus to join him in the captain's cabin.

"Please sit down, Hippoclus," said Pyrrhus. "I think it is fair that I should acquaint you with some details that I chose not to speak about yesterday. It is true that Demetrius is on his way to Athens with a large force, consisting of 5,000 infantry and 4,000 cavalry. What I omitted to tell you is that this force is all that remains of the army of Antigonus and Demetrius. Antigonus was defeated and killed at Ipsus three weeks ago. Demetrius is returning to Greece to try and rebuild his fortunes. Sadly, those fortunes are less promising than he currently believes. I am sorry to delay this confidence until now, but I am sure that you will understand that there was a need to temporarily retain an illusion of strength."

"I can well understand your caution, Sire," said Hippoclus. "What will Demetrius do?"

"I do not know. I expect that he will first go to Megara. He will see his wife, my sister, and try and consolidate his position in Megara and Corinth. After that, we can only wait and see. Come. Let us rejoin the others and take advantage of this pleasant cruise while it lasts."

The squadron sailed comfortably to Cynthos on that first day, and they spent the night anchored in the lee of the island. The following morning saw them set off for Delos. The wind failed them that day, and the journey was made under oars. Late in the afternoon, they approached Delos and anchored close to the island in a position where they could observe the sea lane that Demetrius's fleet would almost certainly use. One of a group of young lads with good eyes was kept constantly at the masthead, and after two days of watching and waiting, the cry came down that the fleet was in sight.

Pyrrhus gave orders for his ships to weigh anchor and to make their way to join the fleet. The three ships took up a position directly where the fleet was heading, intentionally blocking its path. Demetrius's captain signaled a halt and waited while Pyrrhus and his companions approached in a small boat. As Pyrrhus stepped onto the deck, Demetrius approached him with a smile on his face and shook his hand, "I must say that you have been very enterprising, Pyrrhus. I send you to Greece in two ships and you return with three!"

"It is good to see you, Demetrius," said Pyrrhus. "You remember Menestheus, of course, and I would like to introduce Hippoclus, who is one of the councilors from the Areopagus in Athens."

"It is a pleasure to meet you, Hippoclus," said Demetrius. "Please come and join me in the captain's cabin." Demetrius led the way to the cabin, invited the others to sit, and asked the captain's servant to bring wine, bread, and olives. "The sun is almost over the yardarm, gentlemen, so I think wine is in order to quench our thirst."

Once the servant brought the refreshments and left the room, Pyrrhus took a sip of his wine and said to Demetrius. "I am afraid I am the bearer of bad news, Sire. The political climate has changed in Athens. Hippoclus did what he could to dissuade the other councilors, as did your friend Cineas, but the fact remains that your garrison has been expelled from Athens, as have the garrisons of Thebes and Argos. Deidameia has been escorted to Megara, and I asked Cineas to join her there and to await word from us."

Demetrius said nothing while Pyrrhus delivered his bad news. Pyrrhus had seen him bear bad news before and been struck by the calmness of his manner in times of adversity. On this occasion, however, Demetrius was transported with rage and shouted at Hippoclus, "Is this what is called loyalty in Athens? Is this what is called gratitude? Do you not remember that it was me and my soldiers who fought Cassander and forced him to break off the siege of Athens three years ago? I drove him out of Greece as far as Thermopylae and brought peace and security to Athens and Thebes. Do you not remember the gift of honorable spoils that I gave to Athens after I defeated Ptolemy five years ago? Twelve hundred suits of armor I gave to the Athenians, thinking that they were honorable men who would understand the compliment I paid them. And now, you repay my services to your city by casting aside your allegiance as soon as you possibly can! You contemptible creatures!"

All of the men were struck by the ferocity of Demetrius's speech and, except for Pyrrhus, were afraid to speak. Pyrrhus felt that something had to be said, however, and he continued, "I must tell you, Sire, that your friends in Athens did what they could to dissuade the council from this course, including Hippoclus. There are other things that you should be aware of. Hippoclus has done the honorable thing and journeyed here to deliver this unpleasant news in person. He has also brought the treasure that your father left in Athens, and your ships that were left at the Piraeus have been taken safely to Megara."

"I understand that you are acting honorably, Hippoclus," said Demetrius, "but I feel that I am being treated shamefully by your city. I want to discuss these matters with Pyrrhus. I would like you other gentlemen to spend half an hour on the bridge, and then I will call you back to join us in the cabin." The others did as they were asked and left Demetrius with Pyrrhus in the cabin. "So, my friend, it seems there is always worse news to come. You have known of these matters for some time. Tell me what you think we should do now."

"The first step seems clear enough," said Pyrrhus. "I would suggest that we sail to Megara, and try and fill our friends in Megara and Corinth with confidence. You will be secure there for the time being at least, and you will be able to see Deidameia and get some rest. After that, I do not know."

"I am sure you are right. It would seem the only sensible thing to do. The pressing problem is how to acquire enough men and money for us to survive and have a country. That is a problem to solve once we get to Megara. For now, I propose to acquaint you with the state of the fleet, and then we will set a course for Megara."

Demetrius and Pyrrhus spent some time discussing their current state and the most immediate problems and then called the others in to join them.

"Gentlemen, please take a seat," said Demetrius, as the other men joined them. "I must repeat to you, Hippoclus, that I am extremely disappointed and saddened by the actions of the Athenians. I have always admired the Athenians for the great role that has been theirs in years past, both in peace and war, but I believe that their current position is both dishonorable and cowardly. Having said that, I acknowledge that you personally have acted both courageously and honorably. Therefore, I wish you to return to your people and to tell them that although I am extremely disappointed in their conduct, I intend to take no hostile action against them. I hope and believe that they will once more realize that my cause is the cause of a free and independent Greece and that we will again consider each other to be loyal friends. Having said that, I suggest you return to your vessel, and after the transfer of my father's treasure has taken place you return to Athens."

After such an outburst of undisguised anger, Hippoclus was more than happy to return to his own ship and attend to the transfer of the treasure. Before leaving Demetrius's flagship, Hippoclus sought out Pyrrhus and thanked him for softening Demetrius's anger, and for giving him the chance to return to Athens alive. It was not a happenstance that Hippoclus considered likely when they were in the captain's cabin.

Having seen Hippoclus off the ship, Pyrrhus left the preparations for the loading in the care of Menestheus and returned to the cabin. Demetrius was sitting in a chair, staring at his feet. "There you are, my friend. I was contemplating the callus on my left big toe and wondering how many of my loyal friends I can count on now."

"There is no need to be despondent, Demetrius," said Pyrrhus. "We have had to listen to bad news, it is true, but our situation is not entirely bleak. We have a strong position at the Isthmus of Corinth and the leisure to make our decisions after some deliberation."

"You always were a tonic at difficult times, Pyrrhus," said Demetrius. "If you would be so good, I would be grateful if you would supervise the transfer of Hippoclus's cargo, and then instruct the pilot to set a course for Megara. Once that is done, you could join me here again."

Pyrrhus left Demetrius to contemplate his problems and returned to the deck. He walked over to the bridge, where Menestheus and the captain were discussing the transfer of the cargo. One alternative was for the two ships to sail over to Delos and transfer the treasure while at anchor. The sea was flat and calm today, however, and the captain felt it would be a straight-forward exercise for the two ships to lie close to each other, and for the treasure to be moved from one to the other using a system of ropes and pulleys. This arrangement would certainly be quicker, and so would appeal to the military minds of Pyrrhus and Demetrius, where hurry and impatience were fundamental principles. Having decided on this course of action, the captain signaled Hippoclus's ship to approach and to lie alongside his own. There were many willing hands on both ships, and the transfer was completed quickly. Pyrrhus waved to Hippoclus and watched the Athenian ship creep away from the side of the flagship and then set off under oars for Athens. Once the other ship was under way, Pyrrhus turned to the captain and said to him, "Marsyas, once the treasure is carefully stowed, I would like you to set a course for Megara. Please signal the rest of the fleet to be ready to follow us shortly."

An hour later, the flagship sent up a flag to inform the rest of the fleet to get under way, and the oarsmen began their work. Looking behind him, Pyrrhus again admired the beauty of the other galleys. It was even more striking today, as it was the first time that he had seen such a large fleet at sea. The weather was kind to the rowers, and, after an hour or so, a favorable wind sprang up, and the ships were able to make their way under sails alone. Pyrrhus returned to the cabin and found that Demetrius was still contemplating his feet and had made a determined assault on the large flask of wine left on the table. "Come and join me in a glass of wine, Pyrrhus," said Demetrius. "It would be a shame to let it go to waste. The treasure came on board safely, I trust?"

"Yes, Sire," replied Pyrrhus. "It has been placed in a locked storeroom, and I have arranged a watch of reliable men to stand guard."

"Excellent. As I have taken such riches on board, I propose to give both you and Menestheus one hundred Attic drachmas each, and I will then try and win it off you at dice."

Pyrrhus called Menestheus into the cabin and the three men whiled away the afternoon playing dice. Demetrius did in fact win his 200 drachmas back, then returned it so that he could offer a rematch tomorrow.

CHAPTER X .

Two days later, the leading ships of the fleet entered the harbor at Megara. Demetrius decided to disembark the army and to set up an encampment on the plain outside the city. This naturally involved a furious level of activity. Shortly after their arrival, Pyrrhus and Demetrius went into the city, with Menestheus as their guide, and found the house of Sotion, who was acting as Deidameia's guardian in Megara. Pyrrhus's visit was brief, however, as he had been entrusted with the encampment of the army, and he had much work to do. He did, however, accept Sotion's invitation to dinner that evening. Demetrius stayed at the house, delighted to be able to enjoy the company of his lovely young wife after their long separation. As he and Menestheus returned to the port, Pyrrhus said to his friend, "I was delighted to be given this responsibility, Menestheus. In my opinion, the art of encamping an army has never been given enough attention by anyone apart from Alexander. It is all very well to set out an encampment in an orderly fashion, but a good camp should be fortified so that it is as defensible as a city."

As he looked at Pyrrhus's face, Menestheus could not help but take on some of his king's enthusiasm, and he listened keenly to his description of his proposed fortifications. Pyrrhus kept talking as they walked, and they were just about to reenter the harbor precinct when Pyrrhus was making his final point. "The last crucial point, Menestheus, is that the materials for the fortification should not be too bulky, so that when the army moves from one encampment to another, the materials can be transported with the army's baggage. What I have envisaged is that I would start with digging a channel or moat around the camp. The earth moved would be piled up on the inward side of the moat and would form the basis of the protective barrier. The upper part of the barrier would be a wooden palisade, held together with bolts and ropes, rather than nails, so that it would be a straightforward matter to disassemble it when the time came. Naturally, the preparation of the materials will take us some time, but I believe that when we are finished we will have developed a system of protection for a camp that can realistically be erected in two hours, using half the army for the manpower required. Once we have built the walls for this camp, it will be a straight-forward exercise to catalog the materials and use that as a basis to work out the requirements for an encampment for an army of any size."

"You have clearly given this matter a great deal of thought, Sire," said Menestheus.

"That is true, my friend," replied Pyrrhus, laughing. "I have wanted to do this for years. It has been said that, compared to war, all other aspects of human endeavor pale into insignificance. It may be something of an exaggeration, but I believe it is true in principle. Can you imagine any other situation where one could instantly have 9,000 men, such as the soldiers in our army, together with hundreds of ships and seamen, all ready to undertake our orders at a moment's notice? And ours is only a small army. Consider the resources at the command of Antigonus before his death, or Seleucus now. A great deal may be achieved with such a wealth of manpower."

As they approached the docks, Pyrrhus saw a group of Demetrius's officers talking with the captains of the three ships that were tied up to the wharf. There was Antimachus, the admiral of the fleet, and the two army commanders, Archesilaus and Pantauchus. Archesilaus smiled as he saw Pyrrhus approaching, "Good afternoon, Sire. It is good to see you."

"Good afternoon to you all, gentlemen," replied Pyrrhus. "I see that you have the disembarkation well in hand."

"Yes, Sire. We were just discussing the details. Pantauchus will take a company of men and lay out the arrangement of the camp shortly. We have sent word to the city to invite them to set up a market for the troops at our expense, and Archesilaus will take his men and arrange for the stables for the horses. Demetrius's newly acquired funds have proved a godsend. We will be able to give each of our men thirty drachmas. That would be the equivalent of a month's pay, and should keep them happy for a while. It also enables us to keep the goodwill of the city populace, as they should make quite a bit of money out of us over the next few weeks."

"Excellent," said Pyrrhus. "Pantauchus, I would like to accompany you when you survey the campsite. I propose to formally fortify the camp, and I will start work on preparing the materials as soon as you have laid out the site."

Pantauchus appeared to be secretly amused that this youth would go to all this effort on a safe encampment.

"You find something humorous, Pantauchus?" said Pyrrhus.

"Merely that it seems a lot of effort to go to, Sire, when we are not in any danger."

"It is as easy to cut our throats in our sleep in Greece as it is in Phrygia, Pantauchus," said Pyrrhus. "If I were Cassander, I would send an elite force to attack us at night, while we believe ourselves to be safe in our beds. It will not take him long to find out that we are at Megara, with only a small army at our command."

Pantauchus did not reply to this rebuke, but he had clearly taken offence. Experienced generals do not like to be told how to manage their affairs. His position was all the more difficult, as he knew that Pyrrhus was right. Although Pyrrhus could not know it at this time, this was to be the beginning of bad blood between them that was to last the remainder of their lives. Leaving these thoughts aside, Pyrrhus said to Pantauchus, "After we have surveyed our campsite, I would like you to detail 300 men to assist me, men with some experience in carpentry. I would also like you to send some shipwrights tools from the ships. I will need as many axes and saws as you can provide, as well as a variety of smaller tools and rope."

"Very well, Sire," said Pantauchus, for whom this conversation was becoming less pleasant as it went on. "Perhaps you would like to accompany me now; our surveyors are ready and waiting for us. I will send messengers to the largest ships to find your tools."

Pyrrhus nodded to Pantauchus, and he and Menestheus walked off toward the plain where the camp would be sited. Pantauchus signaled for his surveyors to join them, and they walked in silence onto the plain. The surveyors of the army were well experienced in the task of setting up a camp, having done it many times before. The basic arrangement was constant, and each encampment was set up to enclose an area that was appropriate for the size of the army at a particular time. It should be large enough that the troops should not be crowded together too closely, and to leave a clear perimeter so that the troops could form a defensive position in case of attack. On the other hand, the area of the camp should not be so large that the preparations would take too long to set up with the manpower available.

Once the surveyors made their calculations regarding the size of the camp, they set to work to set up the markers that would form the skeleton of the camp. They used stakes that were color coded to indicate their purpose. Black stakes indicated the perimeter of the square encampment, blue stakes the placement of tents for the soldiers, and yellow stakes showed the position of the tents for the king and the army commanders. Red stakes were used for the cavalrymen and the stables for the horses. The arrangement was essentially the same as had been used at Ipsus, with soldiers' tents on three sides of the square, the command area in the center of a large interior clearing, and the cavalry occupying the remaining side of the square. The army's baggage would normally be brought into the central area and left on wagons until needed. In this particular case, however, the baggage that was not likely to be immediately needed would be left on the ships until Demetrius made a decision regarding his next step.

While the surveyors were at work, the disembarkation of the army had been proceeding steadily and a messenger came from the port to speak to Pantauchus.

Pantauchus heard what the man had to say and then spoke to Pyrrhus. "Enough men have disembarked for us to begin setting up the camp, Sire. I can let you have one hundred men now and I can detail the other 200 that you asked for once some other ships have unloaded. The men have been given a meal before leaving the ships, and some of the tools have been collected. I will be able to get more tools as the disembarkation continues."

"Excellent," said Pyrrhus. "When the men are ready, we will get to work collecting timber. Menestheus, it is time for you and I to change into some working clothes and get our hands dirty."

An hour later, Pyrrhus had his hundred men ready to make a start. They left their weapons, armor, and kit in a safe spot and were dressed in their tunics only. Carrying their carpentry tools, they followed Pyrrhus and Menestheus to the nearby pine forest. After the confinement of the ships, the men found the prospect of peaceful activity on land a pleasant one. As Pyrrhus was obviously going to share in the work himself, there were few men who felt they could grumble about their duties. A group of fifty men made a start, cutting down trees and removing the branches, while another group set themselves up to trim and cut the timber to the required shape, and others were deputed to carry the timber.

As the afternoon went on, Pyrrhus made sure the men were able to have periods of rest and rotated their duties. It was going to take a considerable time to make these preparations, and he did not want to tax their goodwill too early. They had made considerable progress when Pyrrhus called a halt to the work at the end of the afternoon. He and the men walked to a nearby stream to wash and then returned to the campsite, which was now complete. The men left their tools in a pile in the center of the camp, collected their kit, and found their tents.

The disembarkation of the army would continue until night fell, and the remainder of the army would come ashore tomorrow. For the moment, the focus would be the preparation of the men's dinner, and the camp followers had already lit the cooking fires. Pyrrhus said good night to his men and sought out Pantauchus and Archesilaus.

"Everything has gone smoothly today, gentlemen," said Pyrrhus, "you have done well to get the camp set up so quickly."

"Thank you, Sire," said Archesilaus. "We should have all the men and horses ashore tomorrow."

"I will continue the collection of timber tomorrow, Pantauchus," said Pyrrhus. "Once the materials are all prepared, I will use half the army to build the fortifications, and then we will be ready to deal with any surprises. But now, I will say good night and join my sister for dinner."

Pyrrhus and Menestheus collected their things and walked slowly back to the city. As they walked, Pyrrhus said to his companion, "I would not like to admit this to the men, Menestheus, but every muscle in my body aches, and I am desperate for a hot bath."

"I feel the same way, Sire," replied Menestheus. "They did not teach us carpentry at the Academy, but I did quite enjoy the exercise, at least to start with."

As it was growing dark, they arrived at Sotion's house, and, after their knock, Deidameia opened the door herself. "I thought it must be you, Pyrrhus, but whatever have you two been doing with yourselves this afternoon?" Pyrrhus kissed his sister and replied, "An honest day's work for a change, my dear. Could you possibly arrange a hot bath for the two of us?"

"I am sure we can manage something," said Deidameia, laughing. "Come and have a glass of wine while your baths are being prepared. Demetrius has been waiting for you inside."

Deidameia took them inside to where Demetrius was chatting with Sotion and Cineas. He also seemed amused at the bedraggled appearance of his two friends. "Welcome, Pyrrhus. You too, Menestheus. Sotion has just poured us a cup of his best wine, and I am sure that I can persuade you to join us."

Sotion walked over with two cups of wine. "Please sit down, gentlemen. You must be exhausted after your day's activities. Is everything proceeding well?"

"Thank you, Sotion," Pyrrhus said as he accepted his cup. "We have made a good start today, and it will be much easier when all the men are ashore and I can have some more helpers."

Deidameia sat next to Pyrrhus and took his hand in hers. "Demetrius has told me of what happened at Ipsus. I am so glad that you three are safe after that terrible battle." She smiled at Pyrrhus, and she seemed even more beautiful than he remembered. Little wonder that Demetrius fell in love with her in Argos. Deidameia looked up at the maidservant who came to tell her that the baths were ready for the gentlemen. "Pyrrhus, you and Menestheus can go and have your baths now. Dinner will be ready when you rejoin us."

The maidservant took Pyrrhus and Menestheus through to the bathroom, where two steaming tubs were ready for them. Both men groaned in delight as they settled into the deliciously hot water. "This almost makes the day's activities worthwhile, Menestheus," Pyrrhus said as he lay back in the tub. As they were soaking, the maid quietly took their dirty clothes and left clean towels and fresh tunics for them.

Refreshed by their bath, and now looking reasonably respectable in clean tunics, Pyrrhus and Menestheus rejoined the others, and they made their way to the dining room. Sotion settled his guests on their couches, and his servant poured wine for all of them. After the meal was brought in, Sotion dismissed the servants, telling them that they could retire to their quarters for the evening. Once the servants left, Demetrius said to Pyrrhus, "I spoke with Sotion and Cineas about our situation in Greece this afternoon, Pyrrhus. They tell me that there is no problem with wavering loyalty here in Megara, nor in Corinth. It does appear, though, from what Cineas tells me, that there is little chance of our regaining the allegiance of the Athenians. What I propose to do is to spend some time with the city leaders here, and then travel to Corinth. I will do what I can to encourage our friends in these two cities and paint as optimistic a picture as I can. After that, the question remains as to what we can do to try and improve our fortunes."

Pyrrhus nodded in agreement. The measures that Demetrius proposed so far were as expected. He waited patiently for Demetrius to elaborate on the means of restoring their fortunes.

"We are in a situation where being too cautious could be the end of us," continued Demetrius. "If we remain here quietly for too long, Cassander will eventually find the means to attack us. As Lysimachus has played a large part in our defeat, I propose to make him pay the cost of his actions. I will recruit as many men as I can, both here and in Corinth, and I will then sail to Thrace, plunder his territory, and try and entice his men to change their allegiance to us."

"Do you know how strong Lysimachus's forces are in Thrace, Demetrius?" asked Pyrrhus. "He would have left part of his army at home, but I am sure that the bulk of his forces are still in Anatolia."

"Sotion and I talked about this at some length," replied Demetrius. "We both felt that he could not have left more than 10,000 men at home. These men would also not all be assembled in the same place. They would be dispersed to cover several key cities. That would be in our favor, as we could have all our forces together, which would give us superiority of numbers at a given place with a force of at least 5,000 men."

"It seems to be a plan that could work," said Pyrrhus. "I am at a loss to suggest any other course that would achieve your aims. The main risk would be that his forces could anticipate us and join together into one large body."

"Just so," replied Demetrius. "Our preparations will need to be done quickly before word can reach Lysimachus. One thing I am sure of is that the main thing on his mind now is trying to get the best result for himself in his bargaining with Seleucus. Both of them will greedily try to get the larger share for himself from the territories my father ruled. With our rapid escape fresh in their minds, I do not think that they will be expecting any aggressive act on our part."

Looking at Pyrrhus, Demetrius continued, "That brings me to the next point that I wanted to make. You proved yourself a good and courageous commander at Ipsus, Pyrrhus, but I do not want you to accompany me on this expedition. I need someone here in Greece who can command the respect and obedience of the troops and also try and stop any further defections from our cause. My expedition to Thrace will achieve nothing if my absence leads to the remaining cities abandoning their loyalty to us."

"I must say I am disappointed that I cannot go with you, Demetrius, but I understand that there are important tasks here. I will do as you wish."

"Excellent," said Demetrius. "Let us regard the matter as settled, then. I will make a visit to the ruling council tomorrow, and then I will start the process of raising new troops. I hope to find enough men that I can leave you a decent force here after I take the men I need."

"Lastly," continued Demetrius, turning to Cineas, "I must thank you, my friend, for all you have done for me in Athens and here at Megara. I am sure that the honorable treatment of my wife and the peaceful withdrawal of my forces from Athens are in no small measure a result of your actions. I would now ask you to return to Athens. With both you and Pyrrhus in Greece, I know my affairs will be in the safest hands."

CHAPTER XI

The next morning saw Pyrrhus and Menestheus rise early so they could resume their task of preparing the materials for the fortification of the camp. They breakfasted with Cineas at a time when only the most energetic of the servants had risen. Cineas was anxious to return to Athens as soon as possible, both to keep an eye on that rogue, Stratocles, and also to hear any news of events from northern Greece. Pyrrhus promised to visit Athens as soon as practicable, and Cineas would send word of any important events.

As Pyrrhus and Menestheus walked to the camp they were treated with the sight of a magnificent dawn, which lifted their spirits. It would be hot today, and the morning would be the most productive time of the day. As they approached the camp, Pyrrhus was glad to see that it was busy with the activity of the men preparing for the day. Pantauchus approached them as they came near the camp. He was clearly determined to appear more helpful today. "Good morning, Sire. I thought you would be early this morning. The men are just finishing their breakfast, and I have let them know that you intend to keep them busy today."

"Thank you, Pantauchus," said Pyrrhus. "I hope that we can deal with most of the heavy work this morning. Since the men are all so eager, I would like to get the surveyors to mark out the position of the perimeter of the fortification, and half of the men can get to work digging the trench. Once that is done, we can start the framework of the wooden barrier."

The surveyors joined the commanders as soon as they finished their breakfast, and Pyrrhus walked around the camp with them. In a short time, the black markers were repositioned to Pyrrhus's satisfaction, creating a square with a central gate on each of the four sides, and he then asked them to oversee the digging of the trench. The trench was to be three feet deep and three feet wide. His detail of men would continue to supply the timber, which would form the vertical posts of the wall. These would be delivered soon enough that they could be incorporated into the earthen mound created with the soil that would be provided by the excavation of the trench. Pantauchus detailed the other 200 men that Pyrrhus asked for yesterday, and they were all equipped with the necessary carpentry tools. Pyrrhus spoke to the men briefly, instructing them that the fashioning of the posts would be their first task this morning. He promised that if he dropped to the ground with fatigue, the other men would be given a short rest as well. This brought a laugh from the men, and they cheerfully followed him to the forest to begin their day's work. As they walked, Pyrrhus said to Menestheus, "This is another part of the experiment, Menestheus. For the fortification of the camp to be realistic in the field, the work should take no longer than three hours. We will obviously have to take into account the extra time it takes to fashion the timber materials, but at the end of the work on this camp, we should have an idea of how long it would take if the timber was already prepared and transported with the army. Also, for the purposes of our experiment, I will not have more than half the soldiers at work, as in the field we would have to leave a considerable number of men standing at arms to deal with any unexpected attack."

Menestheus nodded while Pyrrhus outlined his plans, and it was clear to him that the young king worked out his mental picture of the ideal encampment some time ago and was clearly relishing the opportunity of putting it into practice. As they reached the forest, Menestheus prepared to make a start on cutting down his first pine tree of the day with something of an inward groan as he thought of his aching body last night.

The men worked well that morning, and Pyrrhus called a halt to the work at midday. The day became hot, and it was time for the men to rest and have a meal. After a refreshing wash in the stream, Pyrrhus and his men walked over to the camp to inspect the progress. The trench had been dug, and most of the timber uprights were in place. Food and water were brought out and the men who were working on the campsite gratefully put down their tools and began their meal. Pyrrhus made sure all his men had been provided with food and drink and then walked over to join Pantauchus and the surveyors. "You arrived at just the right moment, Sire," said Pantauchus. "I was just about to send a messenger to tell you that our meal was ready."

"Thank you, Pantauchus," said Pyrrhus. "The men have done an outstanding job this morning. Once we have sat down, I will ask you to tell me how smoothly or otherwise the work went." Pyrrhus passed a plate of bread and cheese to Menestheus, and then took one for himself. The two men then sat down with Pantauchus and the surveyors. Pantauchus put his plate on the ground beside him and turned to Pyrrhus. "There were no particular problems here this morning, Sire, but it took the men two and a half hours to dig the trench and incorporate the timber posts in the new mound."

"And that was with half of the army working?" said Pyrrhus.
"Yes, Sire."

"In that case, we will have to modify the design, as the digging should take less than an hour and a half. For the next time, I will reduce the depth of the trench to two feet. After we have had lunch, the men who have been working this morning can rest this afternoon and the other half of the army can work on fashioning the timber for the walls." Pyrrhus turned to the surveyors, and asked them what would be the best way to build the remainder of the timber wall. Having decided on the best method, involving steps on the timber uprights for the crossbeams to rest on and fastening with rope, Pyrrhus asked Pantauchus to send an officer to the shipyard to purchase as much rope as he could, as the fleet could not be expected to provide as much as was needed.

Having made this last decision, Pyrrhus stood up and stretched his aching limbs. "Come, my friend," he said to Menestheus, "the sooner we get back to work, the sooner it will be over and done with." The men who had been working during the morning exchanged light-hearted banter with those who were about to start. Pyrrhus explained to the men that they could concentrate on felling trees and trimming off branches, as there would be enough men at the camp to cut the trees into planks as well as to fit the planking onto the uprights. With no further digging required, the large number of men available made the work proceed very quickly, and by the time work ceased that afternoon the walls were half completed. It was with a feeling of relief that Pyrrhus and Menestheus made their way back to the city as it was beginning to grow dark. It was likely that the walls could be finished tomorrow, and Pyrrhus could again direct his attention to the broader issues facing them.

Deidameia again opened the door for them when they arrived at Sotion's house. "Come in my dears," she said. "I have your baths ready for you."

Pyrrhus smiled at her and said, "You are indeed an angel, sister. I have been dreaming of a bath for the last hour."

Pyrrhus went in to greet Sotion and Demetrius and then joined Menestheus in the bathroom. "This the best time of the day, my friend," Pyrrhus said to Menestheus as he gratefully lowered himself into the tub. The maid brought in fresh tunics for them and a large flask of water, as her mistress was sure they must be parched after working all day in the heat. It was at the sight of the drinking water that they realized how thirsty they were, and between them they quickly drank all the water in the flask.

Once again looking presentable, Pyrrhus and Menestheus joined the others. Sotion, always the gracious host, stood up when they entered, bade them sit and make themselves comfortable, and handed each a cup of wine. "Thank you, Sotion," Pyrrhus said, gratefully accepting his wine. Demetrius took a sip of his own wine and said to Pyrrhus, "I visited the camp myself this afternoon, Pyrrhus, and I must say I am extremely impressed with the work that you have done there."

"Thank you, Demetrius," replied Pyrrhus. "The men have all worked very hard, and I hope the work will be mostly finished tomorrow."

"That is good," said Demetrius. "I have sent a messenger to the council at Corinth to tell them that I propose to visit them the day after tomorrow, and I would like you and Menestheus to come with me. It is important that you meet them since you will be my representative here soon."

"I understand," said Pyrrhus. "Have you spoken to the council here yet?"

"I saw them this morning. They seemed to accept the unpleasant news of our defeat at Ipsus without coming to the conclusion that our situation was desperate. I told them you will be looking after our affairs for a while and that you would call on them when time permits. I also spoke to some mercenary commanders who live here when they are not employed, and they will start recruiting men to join us."

"That is excellent," said Pyrrhus. "It seems it will not take too long for you to make your preparations. I imagine that we will be able to contact other military men in Corinth as well."

"Just so," replied Demetrius. "Corinth has provided many good fighting men, and I would be surprised if we are disappointed there."

Now that Demetrius and Pyrrhus had a chance to acquaint each other with their respective progress during the day, Sotion said to them, "I have arranged something which I hope you will all enjoy. Here in Megara, we have a number of poets who are widely admired, and I have invited one of them, a man named

Antalcidas, to come and join us tonight. He will read some of his poetry to us while we have dinner, and after dinner he will read us some sections of the Iliad."

"A marvelous idea, Sotion," said Demetrius. "We have all been preoccupied with military affairs for so long, some pleasant recreation will be most welcome." Demetrius's enthusiastic reaction was shared by them all, and as the evening progressed they were all sincerely delighted with their entertainment. Antalcidas possessed that most wonderful combination of skill in writing poetry and an excellent speaking voice. His own poetry was graceful and lyrical and told of the beauty of nature and the noble side of man. It was after dinner, however, when he captivated his audience. He recited several passages of the Iliad that were familiar to them all, and his skill as an orator made the story of the great Trojan War even more moving. As they listened to his reading, the small group was aware that they, too, were players in a momentous time in history and were inspired to emulate the great deeds of Achilles and Hector.

Chapter XII

It was with extreme reluctance that Pyrrhus and Menestheus rose early and made their way to the camp. It seemed to them that there was not a single muscle in their bodies that did not cause pain while they walked. They were indeed a curious sight, moving their arms and twisting their upper bodies as they walked to try and loosen up these stiff muscles. As they entered the camp, they acknowledged the greetings of the men who were still surprised that a king should share in this heavy manual labor.

Pantauchus walked out to greet them and told Pyrrhus that the men were all ready to begin the day's work. "That is very good, Pantauchus," said Pyrrhus. "I hope that we will have the fortifications finished today. What I propose to do is to spend a short time working with the men felling the trees and then to sit down with the surveyors and catalog the materials that we have used." They had already felled almost all the trees required to provide the wood needed for the walls, so that the main work today would be the cutting of planks and the final erection of the timber walls. The felling of trees was finished by mid-morning, and, after their usual refreshing wash in the stream, Pyrrhus and Menestheus walked around the perimeter of the wall. The result was even better than Pyrrhus had hoped. The engineers had done an excellent job of embedding the uprights and attaching the transverse planks so that the part of the wall that was completed was extremely rigid.

Pyrrhus spent the afternoon with the surveyors, preparing the catalog of the materials. Once this was finally completed, he felt that he had achieved his two aims. The men had finished building the walls, including the gates on each side, so that his camp was now protected against any attack. Secondly, and possibly more importantly, he defined the method whereby a similar fortification could be prepared for a camp for an army of any realistic size, along with the number of wagons and other materials that would be required to be transported with the baggage train of an army.

When he finished with the surveyors, he sought out Pantauchus and Archesilaus. He found them in the command tent discussing the various items commandeered from the fleet and arranging for their replacement so the fleet would be properly equipped once again. "Good afternoon, gentlemen. I hope I do not interrupt you. I have finished my tasks, and I hoped we might be able to drink a cup of wine together."

"Of course, Sire," replied Archesilaus. "Please come in and sit down. Pantauchus has found an excellent wine merchant, and we were hoping you would join us."

"The men have done marvels over the last few days," said Pyrrhus, "but I must say that I am glad the work is finished. I have discovered sore muscles that I did not know I had."

Pantauchus poured wine for all of them, and, after they sat down, they naturally began to discuss the options that were open to Demetrius and themselves. Archesilaus used his time very effectively over the last couple of days. He sent men whose discretion he could rely on into Megara to speak to various merchants and stevedores. These men were to arrange purchase of various items that would be required to reequip the fleet. They were also instructed to try and glean any useful information regarding the current political situation in Greece. Archesilaus turned to Pyrrhus and said to him, "I have had some interesting information passed on to me by my men in the city, Sire. As you would expect, there is a constant movement of various traders and merchants between the various cities in Greece. It is now generally known that Antigonus was defeated in Phrygia and that our forces here represent the remnant of his fleet and army, with the exception of the garrisons in Tyre and Sidon. The good news is that, for some time, Cassander has been preoccupied with his own affairs. There have been rebellions in the outer areas of Macedonia that have tied up a large part of his army. For the time being, he does not have the resources to make an attempt to attack us."

Pyrrhus nodded. "That is good news indeed, Archesilaus. As you say, if our situation is generally known to the traders, then Cassander would also be familiar with our affairs by now. He is the one person who could undo us if he was able to bring an army against us from Macedonia now. Have you been able to speak to Demetrius about this?"

"Yes, Sire," replied Archesilaus. "I spoke to him this morning. It was a fine thing to see a broad smile on his face again. He told me that I should tell you as soon as I could, rather than waiting until you see each other tonight."

"That is good of him. Is there any news of Lysimachus?"

"There is good news there as well, Sire. It seems that he and Seleucus are still wrangling over the division of Antigonus's territories, and it will be some time before Lysimachus is able to return to Thrace. On the other hand, it appears that the largest part of the territory will be taken by Lysimachus, so if and when we do have to face him, he will be an even more formidable opponent."

"That is very true," said Pyrrhus. "However, it does leave us with something of a free hand for the moment, which is the best we could have hoped for." Pyrrhus stood up and said to his hosts, "Menestheus and I will make our way back to the city now, my friends. I must thank you for your help with the camp and the cup of excellent wine."

Pyrrhus and Menestheus walked through the camp to speak to as many of the men as they could and then made their way back to Sotion's house. As they walked, Pyrrhus said to Menestheus,

"We must make some sort of offering to the gods tonight, Menestheus. I have had the gravest concerns that we would have to face Cassander's army at any moment. What a stroke of good fortune it is that he appears to be unable to leave Macedonia."

"We could not have been more fortunate, Sire," replied Menestheus. "All the same, it is a fine thing that we have a defendable position in our newly fortified camp. You never know what is around the corner."

"Spoken like a true philosopher, my friend. Your time at the Academy was obviously well spent. There have been too many examples of disaster following overconfidence for us to be complacent." The two men spent the remaining time of their walk home thinking of these examples, and both were resolved to not allow themselves to fall into such a trap.

The routine of their welcome at Sotion's house, their baths, and the grateful cup of wine was followed as usual, and they sat gratefully on the cushions in the living room. Once again, Sotion fulfilled his duties as host and proposed a toast to the efforts of Pyrrhus and his men on the fortifications. "Thank you, Sotion. I am glad to have the work finished, although it appears that we may be very fortunate in not needing to defend ourselves in the immediate future."

Demetrius nodded and put down his cup of wine. He also signaled to the others in the room that he was about to say something serious as he took his right hand from its semi permanent resting place on Deidameia's leg. "I gather you have heard the news that Archesilaus had for us?"

"Yes, Sire. Menestheus and I spoke to him this afternoon."

"Good. Now, Pyrrhus, as my councilor, tell me what you think about our position, and what I should do."

Pyrrhus had been thinking of little else for the last two hours, and he was ready for the question. "In my opinion, Demetrius, your plan to enroll an army of mercenaries and to harass Lysimachus's territory remains our best option, but it must begin as soon as possible. With Cassander's hands tied for the time being, you will be able to be comfortable about leaving Megara if you can leave me with a reasonably strong force here. With 5,000 men, half cavalry and half infantry, I am sure that I will be able to hold our position here until Cassander can mount a campaign against us. It would appear that he would not be able to consider such an attack for some months at least. Lysimachus is unlikely to return to Thrace for some time, which will give you the opportunity to acquire both men and money in raiding his territory. That will also have the effect of making Cassander even less likely to leave Macedonia to attack me here in southern Greece, as he may feel that you present a direct threat to him from your position in Thrace."

"That is how I see it as well," replied Demetrius. "I believe that a force similar to what you suggest for yourself would be sufficient for me to campaign in Thrace. If I leave you here with 5,000 men, our current army would leave me with a force of 2,500 infantry and 1,500 cavalry—4,000 men in all. If I can recruit another 2,000 men, I believe my force will be adequate for our purposes."

"From what you have told me, Demetrius," said Sotion, "that would not be a difficult task."

"I think it is entirely possible," said Demetrius. "We have already recruited several hundred men here, and I am told that a considerable number of men arrive each day from nearby villages, and we are yet to see what we can manage in Corinth. And now, gentlemen, I propose to retire. Deidameia and I will part again soon, and my nights with her are precious. Pyrrhus, if you are agreeable, I would like to leave for Corinth at first light tomorrow. Good night to you all."

Deidameia embraced Pyrrhus, smiled her good night to the others in her charming way, then took her husband's hand. After they had retired, Sotion said to Pyrrhus, "I must say, Pyrrhus, that I did not believe until tonight that we would be able to indulge in some cautious optimism."

"That is so true, Sotion. I had pictured ourselves defending our camp within weeks against Cassander's army. We can sleep more peacefully tonight perhaps. Can I interest you gentlemen in a game of dice? I find that I have acquired a taste for it from Demetrius."

Sotion and Menestheus gratefully accepted the invitation as a pleasant diversion from their complicated lives, and they played for an hour or so before saying good night to each other. Pyrrhus had not only acquired a taste for dice from Demetrius, but also some of his luck. He was fifty Attic drachmas richer when they finished playing, but promised the others an opportunity to win the money back as soon as possible.

CHAPTER XIII

Pyrrhus and Menestheus were determined not to delay Demetrius the following morning. They were washed, shaved, and prepared for their journey to Corinth well before dawn, and were halfway through their breakfast when Demetrius joined them. The two men stood up and greeted Demetrius as he entered the room. "Good morning, gentlemen," said Demetrius. "I am glad to see that you understand punctuality so well. Have we been left anything edible for breakfast?"

"We have, Sire," replied Menestheus. "The cook was at work when we came down, and there is fresh bread, pastries, and freshly boiled eggs."

"Excellent," said Demetrius. "A day without a good breakfast is an ordeal. Please sit down and I will ask the cook to bring some more food in." Demetrius had barely finished his sentence when the cook brought in two more hot eggs and filled the bread basket again. On her second trip, she brought in a pitcher of fresh milk and a jug of wine and water. She was relieved when Demetrius told her that nothing further would be required, and she gratefully left the room. Servants who are not used to such august company always seem to be pleased to have their heads still on their shoulders after serving kings.

The three men, with an escort of twenty cavalrymen left Megara for Corinth as the first rays of sunlight lit up the eastern sky. They traveled as quickly as they could without overly tiring their horses. The road to Corinth was a good one in Greek terms and they were able to make good progress. Demetrius had received a reply to the message he had sent the council, and an audience was arranged for the afternoon. He also wanted to be able to spend some time in Corinth this afternoon speaking to several mercenary commanders whom he was acquainted with and to begin recruiting men for his expedition. They stopped at a wayside inn after riding for about three hours to rest their horses and to have a meal themselves. Demetrius was a man with a ravenous appetite, and he was always generous to those whom he considered his guests as well as to his soldiers. Replete once more, they resumed their journey, and were within sight of Corinth after another three hours of riding.

The last few miles leading to Corinth were taken mostly at the walk, as the road was busy with traffic to and from the city. Corinth had always been a rich city. Their political institutions favored the stability that encouraged commerce, and the city's merchants had long taken advantage of Corinth's unique position straddling the isthmus of the same name, which connected the Peloponnese and central Greece. As they approached, they were impressed by the stately grandeur of the city walls and the fine buildings, which they could see through the wide city gates. Corinth did not exhibit the trappings of extreme wealth so apparent at Ephesus, but, nevertheless, it created a fine impression on those who visited the city.

All Greek cities forbade or discouraged the use of horses within the city walls, with the exception of their use as beasts of burden or pulling wagons necessary for commerce, and, as at Athens, Demetrius and his party left their horses at a stable outside the city walls. They entered the city on foot. Corinth was well known to Demetrius, and he led them through the city toward the civic buildings where they would meet the council. Their rapid journey meant they were early for their appointment, and they naturally spent some time at a roadside stall that offered bread, cheese, and wine to passersby.

With his hunger again temporarily at bay, Demetrius was again able to concentrate on the political matters at hand, and the group approached the council building. The escort was instructed to wait outside while Demetrius, Pyrrhus, and Menestheus made their way up the stairs and through the wide doorway. They were led through to the council chamber where the councilors were already assembled. The meeting began with the familiar and genuine expressions of regret and continued with discussions of plans and assurances of loyalty. It was such a familiar scene to Pyrrhus that he felt he had little need to attend to the details and was able to concentrate on forming an idea of the strengths and capabilities of these men. Corinth was the strongest city in Greece to remain loyal to Demetrius, and the actions of these men would be crucial to his political survival. Pyrrhus was pleased to note an impression of calm honesty and authority in these councilors, especially in the city leader, Archias. Demetrius had reached a point in the discussions where Pyrrhus needed to be attentive to detail once more. He was explaining to the councilors that he would be absent from Greece for a short time and would be leaving Pyrrhus in command of his forces. Archias nodded. He clearly understood that Demetrius would need to take some actions to build up his strength and also had the sense not to press him for details that, if generally known, would compromise his aims. Grateful for the man's subtlety, Demetrius felt he should tell him about his intention to recruit soldiers in Corinth. It would be impossible to keep it from being common knowledge anyway.

Archias felt as if he had been taken into Demetrius's confidence sufficiently and turned to Pyrrhus. "I am told that you have done wonders in fortifying your camp at Megara, Sire. I hope they will not be required in earnest."

"So do I, Archias. It is a wonderful stroke of good fortune that Cassander is not able to contemplate any action against us for the time being. If you are agreeable, Archias, I would like to meet with you after Demetrius has left, and I will be able to keep you informed of events which are of interest to all of us."

"I will look forward to it, Sire. I know you gentlemen have had a long ride and must be eager to rest. If you have not already made your arrangements, perhaps I could help you find suitable accommodation. There is a very good inn a five-minute walk from here, which I am sure you would find comfortable. I would be pleased if you would consider yourselves as guests of our city. Is that satisfactory? Excellent. If you would come this way, I will walk there with you and make sure that all is in order."

Archias led the way out of the council chambers, and after collecting Demetrius's escort, the group walked to the inn. It was called The Shining Helmet, and a fine helmet of Corinthian design was mounted above the front door. The beauty of the design impressed all of the visitors as they waited outside while Archias made the arrangements for their accommodation. After a short time, Archias came out and said that all was in readiness if the party would enter and let the innkeeper show them to their rooms.

"All that remains is for me to thank you for your friendship and loyalty, Archias," said Demetrius.

Archias shook Demetrius's hand and replied, "You and your father have been good friends to Corinth, Sire. I hope you will find that Corinth is a good friend to you." He then left, and Demetrius said to Pyrrhus, "And now, my friend, while there is something left of the day, I will go and speak to my prospective mercenary commanders. Make yourselves comfortable in your rooms and I will meet you for dinner." Pyrrhus made his usual arrangements for posting a watch of two men at the front of the inn, and the customary threats of what would be the result of absenteeism and drunkenness. The men had no intention of spoiling what was to them a very pleasant holiday, with no heavy work to do and a fine meal at the end of the day, and were quite content to fit in with Pyrrhus's arrangements.

"I am sure Demetrius will keep us up late tonight, Sire," said Menestheus. "Perhaps a rest now would be in order."

"I am sure you are right, Menestheus," said Pyrrhus. "I am still recovering from our labors at the camp." Without any further ado, they made their way to their rooms and gratefully slept.

Some time after dark, Pyrrhus was woken by Menestheus. Aware that a king in these dangerous times should be instantly awake following any disturbance, Pyrrhus sat up with something of a start. He had not quite yet managed the instant alertness that was so desirable, but seemed to be gradually improving. There was no way to predict which sudden wakening would be the beginning of a crisis that demanded instant action. As always, he was a little angry with himself for his short, half-awake state and made another resolution to try harder.

"Demetrius has returned, Sire. He asked me to tell you that dinner will be ready for us after you have had your bath."

"Excellent," said Pyrrhus, "I am looking forward to hearing how his recruiting went."

A short time later, Pyrrhus and Menestheus joined Demetrius in the dining room. Demetrius was in excellent spirits, took his friends to a table in the corner of the room, and poured wine for them. "Corinth is a good place to buy wine, it seems. This wine from Chios is as good as I have had for a long time. The innkeeper tells me the meal will be ready in a few minutes."

"Thank you, Demetrius," said Pyrrhus, lifting his cup to his host and then drinking from it. "It is excellent, as you say. Have you had a successful afternoon?"

"Extremely so. I met with two of the mercenary commanders that I told you about, and they are both keen to join us. They told me that they can guarantee at least 500 men in two weeks time. We can probably expect to have the same number from Megara by then. I had hoped to engage 2,000 men, but a minimum of 1,000 would be a good start. I am very keen to leave for Thrace as soon as possible before Lysimachus gets wind of what we are up to. It may mean that I will leave you with a slightly reduced force, Pyrrhus, but we shall see. We may also be able to recruit some men from Argos, but we will have to wait and see about that."

Pyrrhus nodded. He was not concerned about the results of Demetrius's recruiting efforts. Peace did not sit well with many Greeks of this era. They had been the finest soldiers in the world for 300 years, and there were many men whose only trade was war. The prospect of well-paid employment as mercenaries was attractive to men whose temperament and prejudices could not allow them to tolerate peaceful menial lives as farmers. At a time when conditions were peaceful in Greece, there would not be a shortage of men to recruit.

"What I propose to do is to meet again with these two commanders tomorrow. They will have a better idea of how many men they will be able to assemble, and I will arrange for our ships to pick them up here at Corinth in two weeks time. We have enough funds to cover all our expenses for a number of months, and in that time I hope to be drawing on some of Lysimachus's funds."

Demetrius took Pyrrhus and Menestheus with him the next day when he called again on the two mercenaries. Demetrius introduced them, and they sat down to discuss their business. Pyrrhus liked what he saw of these two men. They had a natural authority, and they pointed out that they had to agree with the aims of an expedition before committing themselves and their men. The older of the two men, Phillidas, explained that although they were mercenaries, they were also loyal sons of Corinth and would not be prepared to act in a way that was contrary to their city's interests. Even Agesilaus, the great king of Sparta, he continued, had offered the services of his sword to those who would pay for it, but only for the benefit of Sparta. Phillidas had conferred with some of his file leaders, and he confirmed his undertaking to have at least 500 men ready to embark in Corinth in two weeks time. Demetrius for his part promised to provide the men with one month's pay in advance after they boarded his vessels.

After such a satisfactory conclusion to the interview, Demetrius and the others returned to their inn. Demetrius brought them into the dining room, and, after they had sat down, he called for wine, bread, and cheese for their midday meal. "I will have to let the city elders in on my plans in due course, Pyrrhus, but at a time when any spreading of the information would not affect us. What I suggest is that you and I return to Corinth the day before the mercenaries are ready to embark. I will tell Archias then that the fleet will be arriving the next day to pick the men up, and we will depart for Thrace as soon as they are aboard, weather permitting."

Pyrrhus nodded. Demetrius's plans seemed satisfactory. "That means we will need to complete the work of reequipping the fleet as quickly as possible. If you are agreeable, Sire, Menestheus and I will return to Megara this afternoon, and I will speak to Antimachus early tomorrow morning to try and hurry the men up as much as we can. At some stage, I should also visit Athens and speak to Cineas. Perhaps the best time for that would be just after you have left Corinth in two weeks time."

"That is an excellent idea, Pyrrhus. If Cineas can regularly remind the Athenians of improvements in our position, they may again choose to throw their lot in with us. There are some other people I wish to see here in Corinth, and I will return to Megara tomorrow."

Pyrrhus and Menestheus quickly ate their meal and made ready to return to Megara, and at Demetrius's suggestion they took ten men of their escort with them. The men were not surprised at the short notice of their departure, and before long they mounted their horses and rode at their best pace for Megara.

CHAPTER XIV

It was the middle of the night when Pyrrhus and his party knocked on Sotion's door. Sotion opened it himself with a sword in his hand, as late callers were not always welcome. "It is you, Pyrrhus! You look half done in. Please come in and sit down."

"I am rather tired, Sotion, it is true, but our trip to Corinth has been a productive one. I have much to tell you." Sotion took Pyrrhus and Menestheus into the living room, bade them sit, and called for wine and food. Deidameia came in, clearly afraid that something terrible had happened. "It is all right, sister," said Pyrrhus, walking over to her and taking her hands in his. "All is well. Demetrius will return tomorrow after he finishes his business. Menestheus and I have returned early to get to work making the fleet ready."

"Thank the gods, Pyrrhus. You gave me such a start; it was very uncharitable of you," she said, her humor quickly returning.

"I will make it up to you, my dear. Please accept my apologies for startling you."

"You cannot have your dinner looking like that, Pyrrhus," continued Deidameia.

"Finish your glass of wine, and you can both have a bath while the food is being prepared."

Pyrrhus had been wondering how he could persuade the servants to prepare a bath for them at this late hour, and Deidameia had kindly resolved that dilemma for him. He would enjoy his meal much more when he was no longer covered in dust and sweat.

As they rejoined the others, now comfortable in clean tunics, Sotion gave Pyrrhus and Menestheus a cup of wine each and said to them, "Now, Pyrrhus, perhaps you could tell us the news while you have your meal, and you can end our suspense."

Pyrrhus gave them an account of their trip to Corinth, the most critical element being the plan to put to sea for Thrace in two weeks time. "That clearly explains your haste," said Sotion. "I am able to give you some good news which may make things somewhat easier for you. Antimachus has been hard at work reequipping the fleet, so you have something of a head start there. Pantauchus and Archesilaus have been busy recruiting soldiers. There will probably be 500 mercenaries from Megara and its surrounding towns, and Archesilaus will return from Argos in a few days. He expected to find a strong contingent of men there, so that together with the men from Corinth, you may have close to the 2,000 men that you wanted."

"That is excellent news, Sotion," said Pyrrhus. "We should probably find a position for you as quartermaster general."

"I am getting too old for this sort of thing, my friend. If I was ten years younger, I would hold you to your offer."

"I will put you two to bed now, Pyrrhus," said Deidameia. "You can organize your meeting with Antimachus tomorrow morning."

Pyrrhus nodded. He was very tired after his long ride, and for once was quite happy to be managed as a child by his sister.

The next morning saw Pyrrhus rise early, quite recovered from his exertions and eager to start his day. As he and Menestheus ate their breakfast, they were joined by Antimachus.

"Sotion insisted I come to see you early, Sire. He said you had important news that you would want to give me personally."

"That is true, Antimachus. Please join us for breakfast, and I will let you know of the new developments."

"So we will put to sea in two weeks, Sire?"

"Yes. Will you be able to fully reequip the fleet in that time?"

"I believe so. The shipyard here has been very generous. They have made all of their shipwrights' stores available to us at cost, and they are so well equipped that we have only had to send to Corinth for a small proportion of our needs. The material from Corinth should arrive within a week."

"Excellent. And how are the finances holding up?"

"Well enough so far, Sire. Antigonus's funds from Athens will cover the refitting of the fleet and probably two months pay for the seamen and the soldiers. He also has a considerable part of the treasure from Ephesus still intact."

"If the gods are with us, then we will be able to use some of Lysimachus's funds before the two months are up. If you are agreeable, Antimachus, I would like to look over the fleet this morning. I do not know when I will have another opportunity to see such a magnificent sight."

"By all means, Sire," replied Antimachus. "I had planned to sea-test two of the triremes today which have just finished having some storm damage repaired. If you wish, you would be most welcome to accompany me."

"It would be the delight of my life, my friend. After I speak to Pantauchus, I will be at leisure, thanks to your hard work."

After they had all finished their breakfast, Pyrrhus said good-bye to Deidameia and Sotion, and he left with Menestheus to find Pantauchus at the camp. He promised to meet Antimachus at the dock at midday.

As they approached the camp, Pyrrhus felt a glow of satis-faction when he looked at the fortifications. The fine detail had been completed while he was away in Corinth. There were reg-ularly spaced elevated observation towers and standing plat-forms had been put in place along the whole length of the wall, so his men would have a protected but still elevated position to launch missiles at any attacking force. Such refinements would not necessarily be able to be put in place for a short encamp-ment but would be available if needed. As they walked through the open gate, many of the men greeted him personally; he had built up a great deal of goodwill when he shared in the toil setting up the camp.

Once they were inside the central command area of the camp, Pantauchus came out to greet them. On this occasion, he seemed genuinely pleased to see them. "Welcome back, Sire, I did not expect you back until tomorrow."

"Thank you, Pantauchus. If we could prevail upon you for a glass of wine, I have some news which I think will be of interest to you."

As they sat together in the general's tent, Pantauchus was clearly pleased that their expedition was now beginning to take shape. "I am a simple soldier, Sire, and I am happier when I have something concrete to work with. If we are able to set sail in two weeks time, I will be very pleased. I am ill at ease with staying too long in one place if it means leaving our enemies with the initiative."

"You and I are of the same mind, Pantauchus," said Pyrrhus. "Demetrius and I have both been thinking of Cassander over recent days, and it will be a good thing if we can keep him distracted. I must add that I am very impressed with the additional work you have done on our fortifications."

"Thank you, Sire. It was a simple task when we had your work completed. I was hoping you would approve of our additions."

"There will not be a great deal for me to do until Archesilaus returns from Argos, and we can look at training the men into a cohesive force. Antimachus has invited us to join him on a seatest of two of his warships, so, if you will excuse us, we will make our way down to the harbor."

"It was quite a change to have such a pleasant conversation with that crotchety old bastard," said Pyrrhus as he and Menestheus walked down to the harbor. Laughing at the thought, he continued, "I am not sure he will ever forgive me for insisting on fortifying the camp when he thought it was unnecessary."

"Perhaps you will eventually become friends, Sire," said Menestheus.

"We will see. I will try not to offend him again too soon. One thing that I am sure of though is that he and Antimachus can be

relied on to thoroughly fit out the fleet and take care of the provisions for both the fleet and the army. So you and I, my friend,
can relax and enjoy our boating excursion this afternoon." As
they walked down to the harbor, they both admired the fleet as
it rode at anchor. Pyrrhus could not quite explain his fascination
with ships and the sea, whereas Menestheus was able to describe
the beginnings of his love of ships during the time he spent at
the Academy at Athens. No one who took an interest in Athenian
history could ignore the great role their navy had played in the
defeat of Xerxes' invasion in ancient times. The two men had
now entered the dockyards, a little before the appointed time.
They saw Antimachus on the wharf, supervising the loading of
water and emergency provisions into the two triremes he was to
take to sea this afternoon. He turned and caught sight of Pyrrhus
and Menestheus and walked over to meet them. "You are a little
early, Sire, but we should be able to leave shortly. My men are
just loading some stores in case we are unable to return this evening because of bad weather." Antimachus reached out to touch
the nearest piece of wood that he could find, a mooring post on
the edge of the wharf.

"We will leave you in peace then for a while," said Pyrrhus, and
the two of them walked along the wharf to get out of the way.

About an hour later, Antimachus sent a man to invite Pyrrhus
and Menestheus to come aboard. He apologized for the delay,
but said he was too old a sea dog to leave any port unprepared.
"I understand fully, Antimachus," replied Pyrrhus. "If Odysseus
had had you to help him, I am sure that it would not have taken
him so long to get home to Ithaca."

The admiral seemed pleased with the allusion and nodded.
"If you will excuse me, Sire, I will get us on our way. You might
find the best view from the rear of the bridge." He was too polite
to say that the rear of the bridge was where passengers would be
least likely to get in the way.

Pyrrhus and Menestheus made their way to the rear of the
ship, to the elevated platform that formed the bridge of the trireme. They took their places to the side of the bridge, so they

would not hinder the movement of the helmsman. The helmsman worked the beam that controlled the two steering oars. A galley would normally use the oarsmen to execute very tight turns, and the helmsman would control the more subtle changes in direction. In some navies, slaves were used for oarsmen, but in Antigonus's navy, following the example of the Athenians, the oarsmen were free men and were engaged at the same rate of pay as the soldiers. This naturally led to a far more effective fighting ship. The men knew that the officers would spare them unnecessarily hard rowing if they could, and in turn the officers knew that the men would give of their best when the occasion merited it. There were also times when the men could enjoy the sensation of speed that these fine vessels were capable of, and they were sure that there would be a short sprint today to impress the visitors and to fully test the ship.

Antimachus and the captain of the ship made their way to the bridge. Antimachus made the introductions, and then invited the captain to begin to warp the ship away from the dock and to head out to sea. With seemingly little effort, the oarsmen gently rowed the ship backward, then, with one side of the ship's oarsmen rowing backward and the other side rowing forward, the ship slowly turned 180 degrees in a boat's length. Pointed out to sea, the flagship slowly pulled away from her companion while the other ship made the same evolutions in her turn.

When the two ships were headed out to sea, Pyrrhus and Menestheus clapped their hands in appreciation of the precision and subtlety of the ships' movements. This naturally pleased both the officers and the crew, as they were keen to impress their royal visitor as much as they could.

The two ships made their way slowly and gracefully out of the harbor, and, when both of them had cleared the end of the breakwater, the timekeeper began to beat a faster rhythm. "This is our standard oar rate, Sire, when we are making a journey and there is not enough wind to use the sail. There is a reasonable breeze today, so we will continue under oars for a time, and then have a spell using the sail. Later on, we will resume oars and have a short spell of battle speed and then ramming speed, which is the fastest speed that the boat can reach. Even with a crew as good as this one, we can sustain ramming speed only for a short period."

Pyrrhus nodded as he took in the nature of managing a galley. The energy and stamina of the crew were clearly a precious resource and had to be used wisely in battle, so the maximum speed could be attained at precisely the right moment.

Antimachus continued, as he warmed to his topic. "The critical moments for boat speed, Sire, are when we have an opportunity to ram an opposing vessel, and also when we try to shear off their oars and disable her. In this case, we approach at our best speed, and, just before we come up to our opponent, the oarsmen on the side nearest the enemy suddenly ship their oars and the ship is brought to almost scrape the hull of the other ship. If they have been taken unawares, the prow of our vessel shatters all of their oars, leaving them defenseless. Depending on the progress of the battle, we would either board and take possession of the other boat or go to look for another ship to fight."

"It must be difficult to remain the hunter and not the prey in the melee of battle, Antimachus," replied Pyrrhus.

"That is what Demetrius pays us for, Sire," said Antimachus with a grin. The old man clearly loved his work. He called to the captain to set the sail and to instruct the men to ship their oars. The oarsmen cheerfully took their rest and looked forward to giving a spirited performance in due course.

"We had to replace the mast on this ship, Sire," continued Antimachus. "With the other boat, the mast held but the rigging was torn to pieces. It was the same storm you were caught in on your way from Ephesus." Pyrrhus nodded. It was quite a shock to realize how short a time ago it was that he and his companions huddled together in the lee of that small island. It seemed a lifetime ago. However he might describe his life, it was never boring.

Pyrrhus leaned on the rail of the bridge and looked back at the other trireme. She was also running under sail, and was spreading a fine bow wave. The two ships spent a considerable time under sail and executed several maneuvers to test the new mast and rigging. Antimachus turned to his captain and said, "Pherenicus, if the men have had enough rest, we might show our guests what the boat will do."

"They are champing at the bit, sir." The captain called down for the sail to be taken in and for the men to be ready at the oars. When all was secure, he nodded for the timekeeper to begin at standard speed. The other ship had also been waiting for the order and was under oars at almost the same time. After a short period to settle the men at their work, the captain called for the ship to go to battle speed. The increase in speed was sudden and impressive, but when the signal was given for ramming speed, it became truly invigorating. Pyrrhus was deeply impressed at what could be achieved by one of these vessels. He looked back at the second ship and wondered at the way that the ninety oars on each side of the ship could move as one. Strikingly beautiful.

Having covered twice the distance that his ship would be likely to run at ramming speed in battle conditions, Antimachus gave the signal for the men to rest. The oars were brought into the horizontal resting position and loud expressions of relief came from the lower deck, as well as some questions regarding Antimachus's legitimacy. The comments appeared to be good natured, however, and no offense was taken where none was intended.

"Well Sire, I think the boats have passed their seaworthiness test," said Antimachus.

"I am deeply impressed, my friend," said Pyrrhus. "Menestheus and I have enjoyed ourselves immensely. After we return to the port, I believe the drinks are on me."

"We will still have some time to enjoy ourselves, Sire. If you are agreeable, we will keep on sailing away from land for a while longer. I will try and time it so we run into the harbor at sunset. There is nothing quite like a sunset at sea."

His guests were more than willing to stay at sea for the remainder of the day, and for much of the time they admired the view of their own boat and their consort. Pherenicus, the flag captain, was able to spend some of his time explaining the intricacies of these sleek warships. To prepare even a single ship for sea was a formidable undertaking, with the many shipwrights' stores that were required for the maintenance of the vessel, as well as the water and provisions that were required to make the ship independent of the shore even for a short period—all this in a vessel that was not primarily designed for transport but for speed and fighting ability.

Pyrrhus also became aware of the subtleties of command in the navy. Pherenicus was the captain, and it was his prerogative to run the ship. Antimachus, as admiral of the fleet, was entitled to give the tactical commands, but these would always be given to the ship's captain, and the admiral could only interfere with the actual running of the ship in exceptional circumstances. Happily, Antimachus did not have to worry about finer points of etiquette in any vessel commanded by Pherenicus. They had sailed together many times over the years and had become friends. On the few occasions when Pherenicus took offense at Antimachus trying to run his ship, he was able to tell his admiral what he thought of it. These conversations were heated at times, but always ended in a bilateral acknowledgement of obstinacy and a smile.

After the frantic days of providing materials for Pyrrhus and his soldiers to use, the sailors were glad to be working on the fine instrument that was their navy, and, to them, it was a good thing to be at sea.

Pherenicus had been watching the sun drift lower in the sky, and he was now ready to turn his ships around and sail westward back to port. He was quietly confident of providing a magnificent nature show for his guests (and himself) entering the harbor while basking in a glorious sunset. The return trip would be all under oars, and even the mariners were entranced by the rhythmic beauty of these two triremes.

The afternoon progressed as smoothly as Antimachus had hoped. The clear and warm weather had remained with them throughout the day. As planned, the approach to the harbor at Megara was made during the sunset, and Pyrrhus and his colleagues were treated to a magnificent demonstration of colors from the west, partly reflected on a series of high-level clouds sitting above the horizon. The two warships were tied up at the main wharf just as the light was fading. Pyrrhus and Menestheus said their good-byes to Pherenicus, together with their genuine thanks for his hospitality, and alighted onto the wharf with Antimachus. Torches were lit along the full length of the wharf. It would be some time before the ships were made ready to be taken off to their harbor mooring.

"Antimachus, I must thank you for a magnificent afternoon," said Pyrrhus. "If you are agreeable, I will send some food and wine over to the ship this evening so the men can have an appetizing dinner. They worked hard to please us this afternoon."

"They would be very grateful, Sire. There are another two ships which are not yet ready for sea, which are having similar repairs done. If it is convenient, you would both be very welcome as my guests on their sea trials."

"I would not miss it for the world, my friend," said Pyrrhus. "Thank you again, and we will say good night."

CHAPTER XV

The afternoon Pyrrhus spent with Antimachus sea trialing the two triremes had such an invigorating effect on him that he could not spend the following days in idleness.

Although he had planned on spending time training the soldiers after they had been joined by their new recruits, he found he could not wait. The morning after their day at sea, he was awake at dawn and sent a servant to wake Menestheus while he washed and shaved. Menestheus made a heroic effort to not be late and joined Pyrrhus at the breakfast table only five minutes after Pyrrhus had sat down.

"Good morning, Menestheus," said Pyrrhus. "I am sorry to wake you so early, but I have decided to start training and exercising the troops today and would be very grateful for your assistance."

"Would that be related to the nature of prime numbers, Sire, or more practical military exercises?"

"Practical military exercises, my friend," replied Pyrrhus, amused. "I would like to see what you are able to pass on from what you learned in Athens."

"Little enough, Sire, in all probability. However, there is one piece of advice that Crates gave me, once he seemed to think I was mature enough to use it wisely. It is what he described as the art of confounding your opponent with superfluous detail when you are in trouble."

"The art of bullshit, Menestheus?"

"Exactly so, Sire."

"Well then, my friend, we are better equipped for our task than I had expected. Pleasantries aside, what I plan to work on is fitness and the ability to work together. All these men are experienced, and do not have to be told how to throw a spear or hold their shield. The issue is that they have come from a battle where they suffered a terrible defeat and have had no training time since then. The aim will be to get them to think as soldiers again and to regain their confidence. They will work with men who are now their comrades but are men they are not necessarily acquainted with. We need to work on their endurance and their ability to work together. A phalanx depends for its very survival on cohesion and cooperation. If these qualities are achieved, a phalanx is almost invincible; if it breaks up into small groups, it loses any chance of victory. We also need to make sure the hypaspists and cavalry are able to give the support that is required."

"I will do my best, Sire. I would not presume to teach veterans their combat skills, but I believe that I have a good grasp of tactics and deployment of an army. I spent some time working on just these matters when I was in Athens, and I will try to be useful."

Pyrrhus discussed his plans for some time and asked Menestheus to take notes. He wanted to be able to present a workable timetable to the army commanders. Each day would begin with a run, initially a short distance, say one mile, and in tunics only, then would come gymnastic and wrestling exercises, and after a break for the midday meal and a rest, he would work on weapons skills and phalangeal tactics and maneuvers. He would end the day speaking to the men after they had had a chance to wash and change their clothes. This session would be based on the generalship of Alexander. No man before or after him, with the single exception of his father Philip, had such an understanding of the tactics of a Greek army, or was able to make it invincible. The evolutions of the troops that were required to gain victory in all situations would be his subject for these evening discussions. These evolutions were not necessarily complex but also were not intuitively obvious.

"Now, Menestheus, we must go and tell Pantauchus about our plans. This may prove to be a greater affront to him than the fortification of the camp."

As they approached the perimeter, Pyrrhus was again pleased to see the amount of activity about the camp. Most of the soldiers had not yet become sufficiently relaxed to become lazy, and Pyrrhus was keen to make sure they had no opportunity to become complacent.

Over the last few days, since the work on the fortifications had finished, some of the men helped with the domestic duties of the camp and the care of the horses, some worked on their own fitness and weapons exercises, while others played dice and began drinking wine at the earliest possible moment.

Pyrrhus caught sight of Pantauchus just after he entered the western gate of the compound and walked over to speak to him. Pantauchus felt immediately at some disadvantage, as he was clothed only in his towel. He had just had his morning bath and was making his way back to his tent. Pyrrhus and Menestheus, in contrast, were fully dressed in their armor and were carrying their shields and spears.

"Good morning, Sire," said Pantauchus.

"Good morning, Pantauchus," replied Pyrrhus. "I have come to start exercising the men, and I would like to discuss my plans with you."

"Of course, Sire," replied Pantauchus. "If you will join me in my tent, I will be happy to hear your ideas." Pantauchus had become accustomed to being finessed by the young king and had some pangs of guilt that he had not started formal training before now. This naturally led to an increased feeling of hostility toward Pyrrhus rather than a reduction in his own self-esteem.

Once inside the tent, Pantauchus dressed in a simple tunic and invited the other two men to join him in his breakfast. They ate enough to be polite, and then Menestheus passed a piece of papyrus to Pantauchus, which showed the outline of the day.

"As you will see, Pantauchus," said Pyrrhus, "I have made a basic plan for a day's activities, and after the men have become settled and their fitness has improved, I will increase the intensity of their training. I would imagine that two weeks from now, the morning run will be five miles rather than one. I have considered my own fitness in this as a guide, and I am sure that my body would complain if the very first day started with a five-mile run."

"It seems a very reasonable starting point, Sire," said Pantauchus. "How would you like me and the other officers to help?"

"I would like you and the other senior officers to join me as expert instructors, my friend. We will need to have enough instructors that we can break up the army into smaller groups that are manageable. What I would envisage is that we would work with each of the smaller groups initially and try and work on their motivation as well as their skills. We would then leave them to sort out a training schedule of their own when they do not have formal sessions with an officer. If you could oversee part of the army, Menestheus and I will take other groups, and Diomedes and the other younger officers could take a group each. The junior officers will have to take part in the training exercises themselves, and I would ask the senior officers, such as yourself, to take on an advisory capacity."

"It is good of you to excuse me the exercises, Sire, but I think I can keep up with this lot, and I will be let it be known that I will look with disfavor on a young soldier who cannot beat his middle-aged general in a morning run."

"Excellent," replied Pyrrhus. "I am very grateful for your support, Pantauchus."

"We are both working towards the same end, Sire, and old soldiers are happiest when they are working with the men in their armies."

"If you would like to call the other officers into your tent, Pantauchus, I will explain our plans to them."

The first day of training ended in exhaustion for all concerned, partly because of the unaccustomed exercise, but also because of the fierce competition that developed. Pyrrhus and the other officers who took part in the training exercises were determined not to lag behind any of the soldiers, and the rank and file were equally determined not to disgrace themselves. For Pyrrhus, the last session of the day made up for all his tiredness. He was able to talk about the subject that was dear to him above all things, the generalship of Alexander. He spoke for an hour on this first day, and felt that was probably all he could ask of the attention span of his audience.

Pyrrhus felt he had an almost perfect day. He rose to go, turned to the men, and said to them, with a smile, "You have all done very well today, soldiers. I think we may be able to make an army out of you after all." This brought a roar of cheering from the men, and one veteran at the front of the crowd called out to him, "I would get some rest tonight, Sire. I am determined to beat you home on our run tomorrow!" Pyrrhus waved at this man, whom he recognized as a file leader from what had been the right wing of Antigonus's phalanx, and he and Menestheus made their way back to the city.

After he had knocked on Sotion's door, Pyrrhus was surprised to see Demetrius's smiling face as the door was opened. "Welcome, Pyrrhus. I have just got in myself, and Deidameia has been telling me about your exercises with the men. Come in, come in."

Pyrrhus was given an equally warm welcome by his sister, who was obviously delighted to have her husband home. Menestheus was also not left out and received a charming kiss from the young queen. Deidameia then shepherded the two newcomers to their baths.

When they had all settled down to their evening meal, Pyrrhus could not wait any longer and inquired about Demetrius's recruiting. Demetrius turned to him with such a smile on his face that things could not have gone too badly. "Better than I had hoped, Pyrrhus. I have engaged 1,000 men from Corinth, and I understand that 500 men have been recruited here. Also, I have had word from Archesilaus, to the effect that he will have at least 750 men from Argos. So, my friend, once we have gathered in all our recruits, I will be able to have an expeditionary force of over 6,000 men, while still leaving you with 5,000 men here in Greece."

"That is good news indeed, Demetrius," said Pyrrhus. "Are you still able to leave on the day we spoke about in Corinth?"

"Almost certainly," replied Demetrius. "The mercenary commanders are used to managing large bodies of men, and they are all very motivated, as this is an employment opportunity that is not offered very often. I will have to speak to Pantauchus and Antimachus regarding the provisioning for the army and the fleet. That is the only thing that could delay us, apart from unsuitable weather for sailing."

"I think you will find that the provisioning is well in hand," said Pyrrhus, "Antimachus and the others are working very hard to make everything ready in time."

The servants came in to clear the tables of the remains of the meal, and after they were dismissed for the evening, Demetrius was able to elaborate further on his plans.

"Pyrrhus, I would like to discuss the deployment of the army with you. Our original force consists of 4,000 cavalry and 5,000 infantry. The infantry, as you probably know better than I, is made of 1,000 phalangites and 4,000 hypaspists. The mercenary force that I recruited is wholly made up of infantry, half of the soldiers being armed as phalangites and half as hypaspists.

"Of our original forces, I propose to take with me 2,000 cavalry, the 1,000 phalangites, and 1,000 of the hypaspists. This will leave you with a force of 5,000 men, all of whom you are familiar with, and I will have an expeditionary force of 6,000 men to try my luck with Lysimachus."

"That seems a very satisfactory allocation of forces, Sire," replied Pyrrhus. "As all of our men may end up having to fight a battle soon, I would like to keep up the training for as long as I can, and I will make sure that the men are allocated into the regiments where they will find themselves after the division of the army occurs."

Having reached these arithmetic conclusions satisfactorily, Demetrius and Deidameia excused themselves and said good night, leaving Pyrrhus and Menestheus with Sotion and the wine. Pyrrhus sat for a time digesting the plans for the army, and it was Sotion who broke in on his thoughts. "Pyrrhus, I think you should have some relaxation before retiring. Menestheus and I would like to offer you a rematch at dice. He assures me that the natural tendency of probability is towards equality of individual parts, so he and I may regain some of your winnings."

"It is only fair to give you a chance, Sotion, but I must say that I have high hopes of winning again. Demetrius has been a very good teacher at dice."

Pyrrhus's hopes were not unfounded, and he added another seventy-five Attic drachmas to his total before the evening was out.

Allocation of forces	Demetrius	Pyrrhus
Men from original army:		
Cavalry	2,000	2,000
Phalangites	1,000	
Hypaspists	1,000	3,000
Mercenary Reinforcements:		
Phalangites	1,125	
Hypaspists	1,125	
	--------	--------
	6,250	5,000

CHAPTER XVI

Three weeks later, Pyrrhus traveled to Athens to see Cineas, Demetrius's fleet having sailed from Corinth several days before. There had been a tremendous amount of activity in the days after Demetrius's return to Megara. The final preparations of the fleet had taken up much time, as had the organization and training of the army. The mercenary reinforcements had presented themselves punctually as promised, however, and Demetrius was delayed at Corinth by bad weather for only two days. This short delay was not entirely bad news for Demetrius, as it gave him extra time to spend with his lovely wife. Deidameia then made her second journey to Megara with a royal escort.

On this visit to Athens, Cineas invited Pyrrhus and Menestheus to be his guests in his home, and they duly presented themselves at Cineas's front door at midday. Cineas answered their knock on the door himself. "Welcome, Sire, and you, Menestheus. Come in and have a glass of wine while lunch is being prepared."

Comfortably seated on cushions in the dining room, the two visitors gratefully accepted the cups of wine that were offered. "Thank you, Cineas," said Pyrrhus. "It is quite a relief to be able to relax after the activity of the last few weeks."

"I am sure you have been extremely busy, Sire," replied Cineas. "From what I have been able to gather from the local rumors, Demetrius has left with quite a formidable force."

"I hope it will prove to be strong enough, Cineas. One thing I am sure of though is that Demetrius has acted with sufficient celerity to take Lysimachus by surprise."

"Let us hope so, Sire," replied Cineas. "With regard to the position here in Athens, I am afraid that little has changed. There is still this rather unrealistic expectation that Athens will be able to maintain her neutrality indefinitely. I should add, however, that within these limits, the other councilors are keen to engage your support and hope to see you while you are in Athens."

"I was hoping to meet with the council tomorrow, Cineas. Goodwill can be a precursor to active support. I will say, however, given the privacy of these walls, I have come to believe that, if it is possible, the Athenians would do well not to admit any of the kings into their city with their forces."

Cineas was almost as taken aback by this speech as he had been when he first met Pyrrhus and he was informed about Antigonus's defeat. Pyrrhus continued, "I am not wavering in my loyalty to Demetrius, my friend, but I find myself a little deflated when I consider the current political situation. I still believe that Demetrius retains some of his father's views about a free Greece. Since Antigonus's death, however, the means of aspiring to an empire founded on Alexander's great ideals have all but left us, and what we are left with, is, in the most cynical view, the squabbles of a number of petty dynasts."

Cineas remained silent, digesting this most remarkable commentary. Having taken such a stand, Pyrrhus seemed to feel the need to explain himself completely. "It is not a conclusion that I am pleased to accept. My disappointment must lie in my grief for the loss of the few great men who could have truly made a contribution to civilization that would have been remembered for all eternity."

Cineas felt as if his heart would break if he allowed himself to dwell on this topic for too long and suspected that the other men felt the same. "Sire, I appreciate your candor and your trust in telling me these things. I have had similar feelings when I allow myself to dwell on the many tragedies that have befallen the great cities in Greece over the centuries—Athens herself, Sparta, Thebes, Argos, and holy Mycenae, and all the others. As something of a remedy, I would like you to accompany me in a visit to the Academy this afternoon. I am sure that Menestheus would like to see his old school again, and I think that a glimpse of the continuing greatness of our philosophical schools may help atone for some of the political and military misfortunes that prey on your mind."

Pyrrhus and Menestheus were delighted at this suggestion, and all were relieved to turn the conversation toward the achievements of the members of the Academy. Not only did it attract some of the finest students in Greece, but other philosophers came to Athens to work in cooperation with Plato's school. Also, there was some amusement to be had in the long-standing bad blood between the schools founded by Plato and Isocrates.

Crates, Menestheus's old friend and teacher was still the Academarch, and it naturally fell to Menestheus to visit him and ask if he would receive Pyrrhus and Cineas this afternoon.

Menestheus left Cineas's house shortly after the men had finished their lunch and made his way to the familiar buildings of the Academy. He was inwardly delighted at the welcome he received from Crates and was able to take back with him an invitation for the three of them to attend Crates's evening lecture and to stay for dinner.

After indulging in the luxury of an afternoon nap, Cineas and his two guests left the house soon after the sun had begun to set. As they entered the Academy, they saw servants lighting the lamps in the small amphitheater used for lectures in fine weather. Crates came out to meet the visitors and said to Menestheus, "I am sorry we had so little time to talk earlier, Menestheus, but I hope we can remedy that this evening."

"Thank you, sir," replied Menestheus. "I believe you know Cineas, and I would like to present King Pyrrhus of Epirus."

"Cineas, it is good to see you again, and it is a pleasure to meet you, Sire."

"Thank you, Crates. I have heard much of the achievements of the Academy, and it is good of you to receive us at such short notice."

"Gentlemen, the lecture is due to start in a few minutes, and all of my students have been punctual for a change. If you would like to take your places in the amphitheater, I can begin the lecture. We will have plenty of time for our own conversation over dinner."

Crates walked over to the podium while his guests took their seats. When all was quiet, he began. "I would like to welcome my students to this lecture this evening, and also to welcome my three distinguished guests. Menestheus, who was one of my most promising students until he had to embark on a career in the real world some time ago; Cineas, who is one of the most enlightened councilors in Athens, and King Pyrrhus of Epirus, who has been entrusted with the duties of ambassador for King Demetrius.

"With such distinguished guests, I have changed the topic for the lecture this evening, and I propose to discuss some of the ideas presented in Plato's dialogue, *The Republic*. As we have a small group this evening, I would welcome comments and discussion from our guests."

Crates continued, and began with an overview of Plato's great work, and led himself to the topic of the philosopher-king, indicating that were such a concept possibly realized, it must surely lead to the best of all forms of government. Having reached the desired conclusion, Crates then said, "We have with us as our guests men who are actively involved with politics at its highest level, and I now ask them to share their thoughts with us."

Cineas motioned toward Pyrrhus, indicating that he felt that the young king should be the one to make a comment. Pyrrhus nodded and stood up. Crates invited him to take his place on the podium with him and introduced him as he took his place. Pyrrhus took a deep breath and began. "Gentlemen, I must first thank you for the honor of being allowed to join you this evening to share in the wisdom of your teacher, and then for the privilege of being able to address you. The idea of a philosopher-king is,

I believe, one that will always please the intellect of contemplative men. Many difficulties present themselves, however, most of them discussed by Plato himself.

"We here tonight are in a unique position, as we are able to discuss the idea as a theoretical goal, but also lament the passing of a king who possessed many of the virtues demanded by Plato. To begin with, I would like to ask you to consider the two most difficult problems that, to me, stand in the way of humanity achieving such a wonderful goal.

"Firstly, there is the problem of finding such a man, and the ability to give him the opportunity to exercise his kingship. Secondly, there is the more difficult problem of succession. How does a city or nation replace their great philosopher-king?

"In the memory of men only a little older than myself, Greece had such a ruler. Alexander. He was a man with many of the virtues of our conceptual philosopher-king, a man greater than his own father. When on the verge of turning his military conquests into a benevolent and stable Greek empire, this great man was taken from the world. This man came to the kingship of Macedonia in the orderly process of the hereditary line of kings. A chance of fate, if you like, but quite separate from any conscious human choice, with the exception that his accession to the throne had to be confirmed by the Macedonian army.

"The legacy of a united Greek world under his rule was taken from us all by his untimely death at the age of thirty-two years. After his death, all the vanities and aspirations of ordinary men conspired to bring the world of Greek politics back to the turbulent state that has been the lot of Greeks since ancient times. Our world does not seem to have the ability to actively seek out and replace such men as Alexander, and I fear that such a dream will sadly remain just that. The best that we seem to be able to hope for is that niggardly Fate will offer we mortals such a man from time to time, so that if we fail to have a golden era with a series of philosopher-kings, we may hope to have occasional intervals of living in the shadow of such a man."

Contrary to their expectations, Crates and his students were clearly moved by what Pyrrhus had said and showed their appreciation with loud clapping, all rising to their feet. Crates drew the lecture to a close and invited his guests to follow him to his house, which was on the grounds of the Academy, where dinner would soon be ready.

Comfortably seated, with cups of wine in their hands, Crates and his guests were able to relax, all of them contemplating what Crates and Pyrrhus had said to them this evening. As the host, it seemed natural for Crates to begin the conversation. "I must confess to being rather moved by your thoughts, Pyrrhus. You have obviously given these matters a great deal of thought."

"That is true, Crates," replied Pyrrhus. "The death of Antigonus has preyed on my mind since Ipsus. He was the only one of the kings who believed that Alexander's empire could survive intact and who shared his vision of the society that could be created in such an empire. Even if he had been victorious in that battle, the idea of a philosopher-king may still have proved illusory. Antigonus was eighty-one years old when he was killed, and it is highly likely that he also would have run out of time before his goals could be achieved."

"So we are left with a world of ordinary men?" said Crates.

"I fear so, Crates," replied Pyrrhus. "Unless, of course, you and your colleagues are able to find a replacement."

This brought a smile to all their faces, and it was time to leave this insoluble problem behind them. "Considering the world of ordinary men then, Sire," said Crates, "where do you see a part in it for you and me?"

"I believe that your place is far more secure than mine, Crates," said Pyrrhus with a smile. "You and your colleagues have rightly become regarded as the greatest philosophical minds in Greece. Despite their faults, Demetrius and Cassander, along with Lysimachus and Seleucus, are not barbarians, and they esteem the teaching that goes on here and in other colleges. My place in life has not yet become clear to me, but it is certain that in one way or another it will depend on the results of the squabbling of the same petty dynasts that we spoke about earlier."

"Very well said, Sire. If you gentlemen are agreeable, I have asked one of my students to stay behind and join us after we have finished dinner. He has become quite an accomplished poet, and has agreed to give us a reading this evening of his own poetry, and also a selection from Aeschylus's plays." The guests were delighted at the suggestion, and Pyrrhus once again realized that Menestheus was a man to whom proper preparation was a life's work. He had clearly remembered his king's admiration of Aeschylus and arranged this reading with Crates.

At the end of the evening, Pyrrhus promised to come to the Academy again and thanked his host for his hospitality and the opportunity to address the students. As the three men walked home to Cineas's house, all felt uplifted by the noble poetry they had listened to during the evening. Despite the fact that the readings were mainly from tragedies, the noble purpose that drove them was inspiring.

CHAPTER XVII

The months that followed had a recurring sameness that Pyrrhus found frustrating. He liked and admired the governing men in Megara, and they remained firm in their loyalty to Demetrius. He regularly visited Cineas in Athens, and the two of them had become good friends. At each meeting, Pyrrhus's confidence in Cineas's political judgment and common sense increased, and it became customary for Pyrrhus to consult Cineas on every occasion where political acumen was required. Cineas's fellow councilors were fine men, on the whole, but Athens steadfastly declined to support Demetrius's cause with anything more than expressions of goodwill. Corinth remained loyal, and Pyrrhus was able to recruit another regiment of men whom he was able to send to Demetrius as reinforcements.

Pyrrhus's disappointment largely resulted from his inability to persuade any other major cities in the Peloponnese or central Greece to change their allegiance so they would materially contribute to Demetrius's cause, rather than merely offer protestations of friendship.

He was conscious of some success, however. After such a disaster as had befallen Antigonus at Ipsus, it was entirely possible that Demetrius could have lost all support in Greece. Demetrius, and Pyrrhus after him, were able to convince the cities that remained loyal that Demetrius was still a force to be reckoned with and whose friendship was valuable. Accordingly, there remained a reduced, but still formidable, alliance of loyal cities, especially when Tyre and Sidon were taken into account.

Also, Demetrius's campaigning in Thrace had been remarkably successful. This had the double effect of increasing his resources at the expense of Lysimachus and keeping Cassander's attention so fixed on his eastern borders that he had neither the resources nor the inclination to try another throw at Greece south of Thermopylae.

Demetrius began his campaign in Thrace in a masterly fashion. In the early weeks and months, he had clearly signaled his intentions. His force was large enough to exert a superiority of force at specific points, and the towns and cities that had received him in friendship he had treated with leniency and respect, while the first two cities that he had invested and taken after a short siege were treated with unrelenting harshness. Lysimachus was still in Anatolia, and was unable to quickly send any relief. The result was that many towns and cities welcomed Demetrius, and he was able to not only enlarge his financial resources but he also recruited many men from Lysimachus's garrisons. Six months after he had first set foot in Thrace, Demetrius was in a very satisfactory position with a large and well-trained army, and had a strong financial base. He had also been able to expand his fleet. Eventually, as was expected, Lysimachus returned to Thrace with his powerful army, and Demetrius withdrew from these territories. Lysimachus was not in a completely comfortable position, however, as his regal equals had not lifted a finger to help him in his difficulties. Even those who had been his allies recognized his power and were not inclined to help him, as no doubt they would have to fight him at some stage themselves.

Demetrius's standing had improved sufficiently to be acknowledged in far-off Egypt, and he was offered a treaty of peace and alliance by Ptolemy. As was usual in such affairs, Demetrius as the junior partner in this alliance was required to provide hostages to guarantee his fidelity. The only man who was able to qualify as an "eminent person" in this situation was Pyrrhus. So, in what was to prove to be the single most important moment in his life, Pyrrhus sailed to Egypt, initially as a mere pawn in the games of the great and powerful, but this moment was also the beginning of his own career in influencing the destiny of the Greek world.

Such events as the exchange of hostages are often extremely useful opportunities to deal with other troublesome people who have abilities sufficient to disturb the repose of those in positions of absolute power. Cineas was such a one, and after conferring with his exalted colleagues, Ptolemy required that he should accompany Pyrrhus in his comfortable exile. This was done at the request of the Macedonian ambassador, who related the wishes of his king, Cassander. This king had not let go of his designs on southern Greece, and he was keen to dispose of an Athenian politician who had a disturbing potential to rival his great mentor, Demosthenes.

Naturally, Pyrrhus and Cineas were permitted to bring either servants or attendants with them. Pyrrhus found it surprisingly easy to convince Menestheus of the attractions of Egypt to a natural philosopher, and Cineas chose to take with him a loyal and conveniently mute and illiterate servant who had been with his family for some time. This unfortunate man had lost his tongue in the aftermath of a Thessalian border dispute and was totally unable to communicate any secrets overheard in the course of his duties.

The arrangements made, Pyrrhus, Menestheus, and Cineas were once again treated to a voyage in their beloved triremes, and, as they approached their destination in Egypt, they gazed in wonder at the grandeur of that part of Alexandria that overlooked the harbor.

The harbor itself was dominated by the island of Pharos, where the second Ptolemy would build the great lighthouse of the same name.

As a mark of respect, Ptolemy and his wife Berenice, together with the royal court, were assembled at the dock when Pyrrhus's squadron entered the harbor at Alexandria.

Unlike pharaohs of native Egyptian dynasties, Ptolemy was not as immobile as a statue when in view of his people, and he chatted easily to his lovely wife as the ships approached the Grand Wharf, reserved for the use of royal vessels, under oars. What he did show was the cautious eye of the experienced general who does not yet have sufficient data available to him to form a clear picture of events. This young Epirote was thought to be capable and courageous, but was he able to be trusted? Time would tell.

After the flagship carrying the hostages had docked, an honor guard formed up along the walkway from the wharf to the royal platform. These men were dressed in the customary light clothing that had been traditional in the Egyptian army for centuries. They wore cloth headgear, a light linen vest and a short kilt. Their lack of convincing body protection was made up for by large oblong shields, and each man carried a spear and a short sword. As these men were an elite force and part of the Royal Bodyguard the headgear and the kilts were richly embroidered, and many of the officers wore gold jewelry such as necklaces or armbands.

As Pyrrhus stepped down from the ship to the wharf and began approaching the pharaoh, he turned to Menestheus and said, "We seem to be off to a good start, my friend. I never received a welcome such as this in Greece. It looks as if we will not be put in chains after all." Menestheus smiled and nodded, but was too caught up in his surroundings to think of anything to say, as the magnificent architecture of Alexandria took all of his attention. When he did recover some of his composure, he said to Pyrrhus, in an expression most resembling awe, "Sire, I may be mistaken, but I think that large building over to the left is the library." Pyrrhus looked at the building but was lost for words when he considered the enormous task that Ptolemy had undertaken in creating the great repository of the known world's wisdom.

When the three men and Melon, the unfortunate mute, had reached the foot of the dais, they bowed, and Ptolemy approached them. "Welcome, gentlemen. I hope you have had a good journey. My queen, Berenice, and I are pleased to see you. Come with us, and we will discuss our matters in the palace."

"Thank you, Sire," said Pyrrhus, "May I first present my colleague, Cineas, and my lieutenant, Menestheus?"

"Cineas, I have often heard your name in relation to Athenian politics, and it is always a pleasure to meet a man of principle. Menestheus, I hope we will have a chance to discuss your experiences at the Academy in due course."

Ptolemy was obviously well informed, as one would expect from a man who had chosen to advance his interests, and those of Egypt, by diplomacy rather than by force. In years gone by, he had joined in the military contests of the Diadochoi. Having been worsted in these struggles, he had subsequently found diplomacy to be both more effective and far more economical.

Pyrrhus and his friends followed Ptolemy and the train of courtiers down the avenue leading away from the docks and, with the court, continued walking after the pharaoh and his queen had stepped into their litters. It was perhaps one mile to the palace, and the newcomers gazed in wonder at the architecture of Alexandria. There was also the continual presence of statues honoring previous pharaohs, and the strange images of the many gods of Egypt. Many of these statues were of a style strange to a Greek eye. Most of the figures had the body of a man, but the heads were often in the form of animals such as birds and dogs. It was clear that the culture of Egypt was an extremely advanced one, but was strange and foreign to a Greek.

After their short journey, the cortege reached the royal palace. Ptolemy and Berenice stepped out of their litters and walked up the steps to the entrance of the reception room. The remainder of the court were dismissed by a wave of Ptolemy's hand, and he motioned toward Pyrrhus that he should approach him. "I am sure that you and your friends must be tired after your journey, Pyrrhus. I shall be busy with state matters until sunset. After that I would like you and your friends to join me for dinner. My servants will show you to your quarters, and you will have a chance to rest and bathe." Ptolemy smiled a farewell to the newcomers and left his chamberlain to show his guests to their new home.

The rooms that had been prepared for Pyrrhus and his friends were in the east wing of the palace and were grouped together. There was also a large living room at their disposal. This room was furnished with comfortable chairs and couches and a large bookshelf containing copies of many Greek works and also volumes of Egyptian history that had been translated into Greek. Large windows let in the afternoon light while awnings shielded the room from the direct and harsh glare of the sun. They also afforded a view toward the library and the harbor. The bedrooms were large and comfortably furnished, and each of them had an adjoining bathroom and dressing room. The dressing rooms were prepared with a full wardrobe for each of the men, including tunics, coats and cloaks for the cooler nights, hats and shoes. There was also a dress uniform for all of the men except Melon. Pyrrhus and Cineas had been provided with the uniform of a colonel in the Royal Household Guard, and Menestheus that of a captain. Waiting for them in the living room were four Egyptian servants who spoke fluent Greek, and, as they arrived, the chamberlain said to Pyrrhus, "These servants will settle you into your quarters, Sire. In each of the rooms you will find bowls of fruit, and pitchers of water and wine, which will be refreshed each day. I hope you will find your quarters satisfactory. If there is anything else you require, please let me know. I will call for you at sunset and take you to Pharaoh's private quarters for dinner. My name is Leontidas."

"Thank you, Leontidas," replied Pyrrhus, "the graciousness of our welcome is much appreciated." Leontidas bowed and withdrew, and Pyrrhus said to his friends, "I am sure that you gentlemen are as desperate for a bath as I am myself. I will see you when they call for us for dinner."

Pyrrhus followed the servant who had been allocated to him into his room and allowed him to remove his armor and tunic. "If you will follow me, Sire," said the servant as he helped Pyrrhus into his dressing gown, "your bath is ready."

"Thank you," said Pyrrhus. "What is your name, my friend?"

"I am called Hotep, Sire."

"You are Egyptian, are you not? But you speak excellent Greek."

"Yes, Sire. After Pharaoh was called to the throne, he educated many young boys and girls in the Greek language so we would be able to serve such dignitaries as yourself."

As Pyrrhus settled himself into his deliciously hot, and huge, bath, he began to understand how many Greeks had been seduced by the luxuries of Egypt and the East, and made himself promise not to embrace hedonism as a guiding principle. He would have to remind himself of how the Spartan king, Agesilaus, retained his simplicity of life when he was exposed to the luxuries of Egypt. For now, he was content to enjoy his bath, and he would work on discipline tomorrow.

Rested, clean, and dressed in fine new tunics, Pyrrhus and his friends sat and read in the living room until Leontidas called for them at sunset. "It is time to take you to Pharaoh, Sire," said Leontidas. "He has finished his business for the day, and his wish is that you and your colleagues join him and the queen for a private supper."

"That is good of him, Leontidas. Please lead on."

The walk to Ptolemy's private chambers took them to the other side of the palace. They walked past the reception room where they had first entered the palace, and Leontidas pointed out to them the banqueting halls and conference rooms where Ptolemy showed the face of Pharaoh to the world. They then entered the west wing of the palace, which held the private chambers of Ptolemy and his wives, as well as smaller dining and living areas used for smaller or more informal functions.

It was into one of these dining rooms where Leontidas led the newcomers and invited them to sit on the dining couches until Ptolemy joined them, with the exception of Melon, who was escorted to a different room to dine with other servants. Pyrrhus was pleased to find that this private chamber was furnished and decorated in a Greek style. There were a number of paintings on the walls, one of which depicted the flight of Darius at Gaugamela, another of the Acropolis and Parthenon in Athens.

There were also a number of beautiful busts of famous Greek and Macedonian figures, including Alexander and his father Philip, and others of Socrates, Pericles, Plato, and Aristotle. There was also a bust of Ptolemy's own father, Lagus.

A few moments later, Ptolemy and Berenice joined them. The guests all rose from their seats and bowed. Ptolemy smiled and said to them, "Your politeness is much appreciated, gentlemen, but in my private chambers I am satisfied with the courtesy due to a Macedonian king. It is something of a relief at times to be treated as a man, rather than the Living Incarnation of Ra. Please resume your seats, and we can begin our dinner." Leontidas signaled to the servants to begin serving the meal and instructed them to leave after the food and the wine had been laid out.

"Please help yourselves, gentlemen," said Ptolemy and turning to Berenice, "allow me to serve your meal, my dear." After passing a plate of food and a cup of wine to his wife, he received a kiss on his cheek for his trouble and then served himself. He then continued, "Pyrrhus, I have been following your career with some interest, although it takes some time for news from Greece to reach us here in Egypt. It seems you have become something of a commander during your time with Antigonus and Demetrius."

"Thank you, Sire. Demetrius was good enough to let me have a taste of command at Ipsus and later in Greece."

It was Berenice who asked Pyrrhus to tell them of the events at Ipsus and their escape to Greece, and she took a clear interest in the account. "So the elephants that Seleucus used to prevent the return of your cavalry were the critical factor at Ipsus, Pyrrhus?"

"Yes, my lady. Once that occurred, our right wing was so vulnerable that they surrendered in a panic and left the rest of us with no choice but to flee once we realized we could do nothing to save Antigonus."

"A terrible day, Pyrrhus," said the queen, "but you have retrieved your fortunes to some degree in Greece?"

"That is so, my lady. The loss of Athenian support was a cruel blow to Demetrius, but he has been successful in other ways. He had a successful campaign in Thrace until Lysimachus returned, and I think he planned to visit Tyre and Sidon after withdrawing from Thrace."

"I wonder how long it will be before these struggles stop?" said Berenice to Ptolemy.

"I do not know, my dear," replied Ptolemy. "It may be a case of fighting until there is only one man left standing." After a pause, Ptolemy turned to Menestheus, "Tell me of your visit to the Academy, Menestheus. Is it still the leader of the colleges in Athens?"

The conversation turned to peaceful matters for the rest of the evening, until Ptolemy brought it to a close. "It is time for me to retire, gentlemen. Leontidas will escort you back to your quarters. It may take you a few days to get to know your way around the palace. I will be occupied with state matters for most of the day tomorrow, but I would like you to accompany me in a ride later in the afternoon once the heat of the day has lessened.

"The only other matter I would raise is how you view your position here in Egypt. It is true that you are hostages who guarantee a treaty, but you are also my guests. Remember that great men have been in a similar situation. Philip of Macedon spent some time as a hostage in Thebes as a young man, and it is said that he learnt his trade as a soldier from Epaminondas. Good night."

Once back in their living room, Pyrrhus thanked Leontidas for his attentions and was about to say good night when Leontidas said to him, "There is one other small matter I would like to discuss with you, Sire, if you will permit me. As Pharaoh said tonight, he regards you and your friends as his guests, and it is his wish that you should have freedom of the palace and Alexandria. He has instructed me to give each of you a purse of gold pieces so that you will be able to retain some independence while you are with us. It will be my duty to replenish your funds when required."

"That is most gracious of Pharaoh, Leontidas. Please convey my warmest thanks."

Leontidas bowed and said good night. After he had withdrawn, Pyrrhus dismissed Melon and invited the other two men to join him in a glass of wine before retiring. They would be able to speak in privacy here, as the palace servants would wait in the bedrooms until their new masters were ready to be settled for the night.

"If it is our fate to be hostages, Sire," said Menestheus, "I feel we could do much worse than to be here in Egypt."

"That is true, Menestheus," said Pyrrhus. "The situation of hostages in the Greek world is a very strange one. As Ptolemy said, Philip himself was a hostage, and there are many similar examples. It is almost as if a hostage becomes a protégé of his ruler and jailor, so that he may become an ambassador for that ruler when he returns to his own country."

"I think you have described our situation very well, Sire," said Cineas, who had been very quiet during the evening. "There is also little doubt that Ptolemy is the most culturally enlightened of the remainder of Alexander's generals, and the most skilled in diplomacy. It is true that he has the unique advantage of being geographically removed from his rivals, but nonetheless, he has achieved great things here in Egypt."

"Am I right in thinking that he has three wives, Cineas?" said Pyrrhus.

"Yes, I believe so, Sire."

"Then there is no doubt that Berenice holds the greatest part of his affection."

"It would certainly seem so, Sire."

"Then we could do worse than to engage her support."

Leaving the others to contemplate his designs, Pyrrhus asked Menestheus to join him in weapons exercises after breakfast the next day and retired to his room.

The morning of the next day, Pyrrhus was woken at dawn by Hotep. As an apology for what would seem a very early hour to rise, he explained the daily routine in Egypt. "You will find that life here is somewhat different to that in Greece, Sire. The heat of the middle of the day is so intense that we begin our day early, rest during the hottest part of the day, and then resume our duties in the latter part of the afternoon and evening."

"I am sure that it is a sensible arrangement, Hotep, and one that I will soon accept as normal."

"I have prepared your bath, Sire, and your breakfast will be ready as soon as you are dressed. Menestheus's servant has told me that you have arranged a weapons practice with his master, and that he will be waiting for you in one hour. An exercise room has been made available to you in this wing of the palace."

Breakfast completed, under Hotep's guidance, Pyrrhus made his way to the exercise room, which was only a short walk from their quarters. As he entered, he saw that Menestheus was waiting for him, keenly admiring the items that decorated the walls. "Good morning, Menestheus," he called out from the entrance.

"Good morning, Sire. I hope you had a good night's rest in our new home."

"I slept like a baby, my friend," replied Pyrrhus. As he looked about him, his interest in the room grew quickly. There were a number of paintings on the walls, most of them having a military subject, but the variety was intriguing. There were several paintings showing men of the Egyptian army at important times in Egyptian military history. The largest of these, and the one which held the place of honor in the center of the main picture wall, depicted Pharaoh Thutmose the Third leading his army against the king of Kadesh at the Battle of Megiddo, the battle that was also known as Armageddon. Others showed battle scenes of Alexander's army, and one painting had as its subject the mistaken obeisance of Darius's family at the feet of Hephaestion instead of Alexander.

Also around the room were a number of armor stands, upon which were mounted complete suits of armor of varying design, including that of a Greek hoplite and a Macedonian phalangite. There were also a number of panoplies that were more in the nature of trophies, such as those from the various nationalities of the Persian Empire.

There were other stands that were of a more utilitarian nature and held a variety of practice weapons, together with protective clothing and helmets for practice use. After admiring their surroundings for some time, Pyrrhus and Menestheus began with gymnastic exercises and then spent some time on weapons drills with sword and shield. By mid-morning, both of them were ready to rest and sat down on a bench. "I have missed our exercise sessions over the last few days," said Pyrrhus. "Without them, one feels a certain lethargy creeping up."

"I am the same, Sire," replied Menestheus. "It became such a routine in Athens that, ever since, I have regarded some exercise as an essential part of any day."

"We still have some time before our Egyptian midday rest, Menestheus. I was hoping that you and I might collect Cineas and wander around Alexandria for a couple of hours."

"I am sure we could persuade him, Sire. He sent his servant to see me earlier and said he would read in our quarters until we had finished our exercises."

"Excellent. Let us wash quickly and collect him."

A little while later, with Hotep as their guide, the three of them left the palace to walk through Alexandria. The city had been founded by Alexander only thirty years before, but it had become the greatest city in Egypt. Enormous funds had been provided for its architecture and infrastructure, and it was both a cultural and commercial center of the first degree. The three visitors were keen to spend some time admiring the architecture of the central part of the city, but also wanted to leave some time to look through the library.

Late in the morning, as they approached the entrance to the library, they were struck by the grace and majesty of the building. The architect had not aimed for a technical masterpiece, but for an imposing and stately building appropriate for its purpose.

"Hotep, perhaps you could duck into the library and see whether they could receive us," said Pyrrhus. "It is a rare man who is comfortable when taken by surprise by complete strangers."

Hotep did as he was bidden, and a short time later returned, "The head librarian sends his greetings, Sire, and he would be pleased if you would join him in the library."

The four men entered the library, with Hotep leading the way. As they entered the reception chamber, an old man with a wise and learned face approached them and bowed.

"Greetings, Sire," said the old man. "My name is Menophis, and I am the chief librarian."

"It is a pleasure to meet you, Menophis," said Pyrrhus. "I would like to present my two friends and colleagues, Menestheus and Cineas. I was hoping that you would allow us to spend some time in the library. We have all heard a great deal about it."

Menophis bowed to Pyrrhus's friends and said, "It would be a pleasure for me to show the library to you, Sire. Queen Berenice told me you would be visiting us soon. As I am sure you are aware, Pharaoh began work on the library soon after he became governor of Egypt, following the death of Alexander. Once the work began, it became something of a passion with him, and he has continued to work with us even now when he has the great burden of kingship on his shoulders."

The three men spent three enthralling hours walking through the library. Menophis was an eloquent and enthusiastic guide and explained all aspects of the design and execution of the building of the library. He then spent a considerable time showing his guests the literary treasures that were housed in the great building and explained Ptolemy's plans to include literature from Italy and Mesopotamia. He then took them to the basement of the building where there were many offices for scribes who worked on creating additional copies of many of the works, and also the technicians' workshops where new scrolls were bound and older ones repaired.

When the men walked out of the library into the open air, they were struck by the intensity of the heat of the day. Pyrrhus turned to his friends and said, "I can see why the Egyptians avoid this time of the day. If you gentlemen are agreeable, I suggest that we return to the palace for our late midday rest until we meet Ptolemy." The others were in complete agreement. Menestheus said to Pyrrhus, "The coolness of the library did allow us to forget where we were for a while, Sire. I used to think that Greece was hot in summertime!"

"I am sure we will become acclimatized eventually, Menestheus," said Pyrrhus, "but I must say I did not know any place in the world could be so hot."

Pyrrhus and the others rested for a while in the cool of the palace, and punctually made their way to meet Ptolemy as arranged. With Leontidas as their guide once more they arrived at Ptolemy's private chambers at the time agreed.

"Welcome, gentlemen," said Ptolemy as they entered his office. "I have been able to finish my work for the day, and I would like you to join me in a ride in the country."

The four men made their way to Pharaoh's stables where their horses had been prepared, and waiting for them were a hundred men of the Household Cavalry who would be their escort. Without any further explanation, Ptolemy led the men out of Alexandria into the countryside, and, after two hours of riding, he stopped at the bank of one of the many streams that formed the delta of the Nile. Despite the fact that this river was only one part of the Nile, it was still a majestic sight and made any river in Greece seen like an unimportant creek.

"This is what I wanted to show you, gentlemen," said Ptolemy, looking over at the river in front of them. "It would have had a more dramatic effect if we had ridden further and had seen the Nile upstream of the delta, but I think you will understand my meaning.

"Egypt is essentially a desert country, but this river is its natural treasure. Every year the Nile floods its banks, and the silt that has been carried for hundreds of miles is deposited in its flood plain. As a result, my desert country has some of the most fertile pastures and fields in the world, and Egyptian farmers not only feed my people, but we export a vast amount of grain to our neighbors and to Europe. This river, gentlemen, is the true wealth of Egypt."

There was little more to be said, and the men contemplated the great river in silence. After a decent interval, Ptolemy said to the others, "I hope that I have been able to allow you to begin to understand my country, gentlemen. We should begin our journey home before we lose all daylight. I have arranged a late dinner for us when we get back to the palace."

Pharaoh's party rode at a good pace back to Alexandria, stopping once to rest the horses and to quench their thirst at a wayside inn. The innkeeper was suitably terrified at having Ptolemy as his unexpected guest and equally relieved to see Pharaoh and his company leave. His fears were somewhat made up for by the handful of gold pieces he had been given by Leontidas, and he would take delight in telling the story to his brother-in-law when they met in the marketplace tomorrow.

It was well dark by the time they arrived back in Alexandria, and the view of the city and the harbor at night alone would have made the journey worthwhile. After leaving the horses at the stables in the palace, Ptolemy dismissed his escort and arranged for his guests to come to his private dining room after they had washed and changed their tunics.

As Pyrrhus and his two friends entered the west wing of the palace, they were greeted by Leontidas. "Welcome, Sire. Please come with me. Pharaoh and Queen Berenice are waiting for you."

"I admire your efficiency, Leontidas," said Pyrrhus. "You have a remarkable ability to always be where you are needed. Pharaoh is a fortunate man to have you in his service."

Despite being a somewhat reserved individual, Leontidas smiled at this genuine compliment and replied, "I am glad you think so, Sire, but I consider myself the fortunate one to serve such a great man." Pyrrhus nodded, thinking that if he were not able to claim his birthright in Epirus, then he too may hope to stay in Egypt and remain with Ptolemy.

Leontidas led the men into the dining room where they had dined the previous evening and found Ptolemy and Berenice waiting for them. As they entered, Ptolemy smiled up at them and invited them to take their places. "There you are, gentlemen. I have been telling the queen of our outing today, Pyrrhus. I hope you enjoyed our ride."

"Very much, Sire. I have to confess that I did not understand until today how great the influence of the Nile is on every facet of Egyptian life."

"That is very well put, Pyrrhus. It is truly the soul of Egypt."

"I hope you and your friends are not too tired to enjoy your meal tonight, Pyrrhus," said Berenice.

"I am sure that we will manage, my lady," said Pyrrhus with a smile, "though my legs are telling me that they have done enough work today!"

The meal was set out by the servants and began once they had been dismissed. Ptolemy turned to Cineas and said to him, "Cineas, there is one aspect of your career in Athens that intrigues me. As I understand it, you are originally from Thessaly and went to Athens as a young man to study with Demosthenes?"

"That is correct, Sire. I spent a number of years as a pupil and assistant of Demosthenes and later chose to enter politics in Athens."

"That is what I find intriguing because I had always understood that to enter Athenian politics one had to be a landowner and that resident aliens were not permitted to own property in Athens."

"That is quite true, Sire. When I was getting to the end of my studies with Demosthenes, he regarded it as a personal challenge to help me gain citizen status in Athens so that I could follow him into politics. We had become close friends over the years, and it was my good fortune that in many ways he looked on me as his son. There was also the challenge of overcoming the Athenian laws, which he saw as an intellectual goal in itself.

"The means that Demosthenes found to help me centered around a small orchard at the far end of his own estate. He was able to fabricate a distant blood relationship between the two of us, too obscure to be disproved. According to this fallacy, I was his distant cousin on my mother's side. This enabled him to leave me this small piece of land, and I technically became a modest landowner, and that entitled me to begin a career in public affairs in Athens."

Ptolemy was clearly amused by this story and said to Cineas, "One could not ask for a better example of the superiority of genius over force. As he had done many times before, Demosthenes achieved a result that could never have been arrived at by threats of violence. Even Philip regarded him as a more powerful adversary than the Athenian army."

It was the queen's turn to save the conversation, realizing that all of the men in the room had experienced failure in military conflicts. "Tell me about your visit to the library, Pyrrhus. I hope Menophis was a good host."

"He was that, my lady. We spent several hours in the library, and it would be difficult to express our admiration for both the library and the aims that led to its creation. I understand that you are hoping to obtain literature from Italy."

"That is so, Pyrrhus," replied the queen. "I have seen some of the works of the Etruscans and the Romans, and they were quite wonderful, even after suffering translation into Greek."

"I have heard some of the men talk of the Romans, my lady. It seems they are becoming quite a force in Italy."

Berenice had only had a cultural exposure to the Romans and looked to Ptolemy to respond to Pyrrhus. "They certainly are, Pyrrhus. I try to get news of them, when I can, from traders and mercenaries who have been to Italy. Alexander himself was convinced that he would have to deal with them in the end. They would have been of great interest to him if he had lived to return to Greece and look at his western borders. If their power keeps growing, Italy and Greece cannot help but to come into conflict. There has already been fighting between the Romans and the Greek cities in southern Italy."

Pyrrhus sat back and digested these comments of Ptolemy's, and the wry smile that appeared on his face had a rather disconcerting effect on Cineas, although he could not explain why it should do so.

Chapter XVIII

Ptolemy was occupied with state matters over most of the next week, which left Pyrrhus and his companions free to explore Alexandria. They quickly became familiar with the city and its layout and soon regarded the Egyptian daily routine as normal.

Pyrrhus also visited the queen each day, late in the afternoon. He would tell her about the things he had seen in the city, and Berenice was always happy to talk about Ptolemy's achievements in Egypt. On one such afternoon, after Berenice told Pyrrhus about Alexander's original plans for the city, Pyrrhus said to her, "I am conscious of one important thing still undone, my lady. I understand that Alexander's tomb is here in Alexandria. Is it possible to visit the tomb and pay my respects?"

"Of course, Pyrrhus. The tomb is housed in a temple on the palace grounds. It is not open to the public, but I would be happy to show it to you. Alexander was worshipped as a god here in Egypt even before his death, and Ptolemy formalized his deification after he died. There are so many gods that are worshipped here in Egypt, one more did not pose any difficulties. If you wish, we could visit the tomb tomorrow morning.

Do you know that Ptolemy has written a biography of Alexander? I believe it is regarded by historians as the best of a number of such biographies written."

"Tomorrow morning would be very good, my lady. I will take my leave now, if you will excuse me. If it is convenient, I will call for you mid-morning tomorrow."

After leaving the queen, Pyrrhus returned to his quarters. Cineas and Menestheus had not yet returned from visiting the gymnasium, but Hotep was patiently waiting for his new master in the living room. "Hotep, my friend," said Pyrrhus, "I am glad to find you. I hope you will be able to do a service for me."

"I will do all that I am able to, Sire," replied Hotep.

"The queen has just told me of a biography of Alexander that Pharaoh has written. Could you obtain a copy for me? I would very much like to read it."

"I am sure I could do that, Sire. Pharaoh finished the work some time ago, and Leontidas has kept a number of scribes busy making copies of it. I will speak to him this evening, if you wish."

"That would be excellent, Hotep. I would like you to prepare my bath now, and then perhaps you could seek out Leontidas."

Pyrrhus lay in his bath feeling a warm glow of optimism flow through him. Since their arrival in Egypt, he had been conscious of a certain reserve shown toward him by Ptolemy. The great man had been kind and hospitable toward him, but Pyrrhus was conscious of his need to earn Ptolemy's respect. Pyrrhus had long been a great admirer of Alexander, and it was possible that this admiration could be the basis of a bond between the two of them. Even if it did not, Pyrrhus was eager to read the work, as he had not yet found a completely reliable document covering Alexander's great achievements.

Pyrrhus had just finished dressing when Cineas and Menestheus returned to their quarters, and Pyrrhus walked out to greet them. "Gentlemen, I hope you enjoyed your exercise. We will have our dinner here tonight. Would it suit you to have it served in one hour's time? I am famished, and there is some news I would like to share with you."

Some time later, Hotep called them to dinner. After seating the three masters and serving the food and wine, Hotep then approached Pyrrhus, "Sire, I hope you enjoy your meal. Leontidas asked me to give you these scrolls with his compliments. I will excuse myself now, until you have finished your dinner."

Pyrrhus gratefully accepted the parcel of some forty or fifty scrolls, "Thank you, my friend. I will not forget your kindness."

"Now gentlemen," said Pyrrhus, "it is time to tell you of some good things that have happened to us." Pyrrhus went on to tell the two men of his plans to visit Alexander's tomb and the biography of Alexander that he had just been given.

"I must apologize for not insisting that we all visit the tomb together, my friends. You will both have an opportunity soon, I am sure, but the queen has shown such goodwill towards us, I did not feel that I could force her generosity."

"That is entirely proper, Sire," said Cineas. The appearance of palace politics was quite a tonic to a professional politician, and Cineas was pleased to give it his undivided attention. He felt somewhat ill at ease with their existence in Egypt so far. He, like Pyrrhus, was aware that their small group had yet to find a purpose here in Egypt and a prolonged holiday was unnatural to him. "I agree that this may provide a bond between you and Ptolemy, and such a bond is essential if we are to achieve anything here in Egypt."

The following day, Pyrrhus called for the queen, and they made their way to the small temple that housed Alexander's tomb. The building itself was of an exquisite design. Ptolemy did not intend it to be monolithic or grandiose in the tradition of Mausolus, choosing instead a beautiful and subtle design, constructed of the finest materials both from Egypt and abroad. In some ways, the temple resembled a miniature version of the Parthenon. Above the polished marble columns, which were in the Ionic style, were beautifully sculpted friezes, where the metopes showed a variety of scenes that had some connection with the events in Alexander's life. Some showed battle scenes between Alexander's army and the Persians, while others showed glimpses of life in various countries that had become part of Alexander's empire. One metope showed architects studying drawings of proposed buildings in Alexandria, another presented a scene of a harvest in Persia, another the meeting of representatives of the various Greek cities proclaiming Alexander captain-general of all Greece. Inside the temple was a central chamber that housed the tomb itself. This chamber had its own four walls, in each of which was a wide doorway leading inside. Part of the temple outside the tomb was beautifully decorated with paintings of Alexander and his generals, and his father Philip. These paintings took up perhaps one third of the available area, and the remaining space was dedicated to inscriptions, both in Egyptian and Greek, listing the countries and cities that had been part of Alexander's empire and the names of the men who helped him create it.

The place of honor was given to the list of Greek cities that had supported Alexander and confirmed his role as captain-general of Greece. Following this were the names of Alexander's generals, as well as the other great men who had followed Alexander to Asia. These were the men whose names will be forgotten because their trade was science rather than war. They were the historians, the geographers, and cartographers, the engineers and the keeper of the royal diary. These were the men who showed the world that Alexander's conquests were different from those that had gone before. Other kings and other armies had conquered Asia—the Assyrians, the Babylonians, the Persians. These armies were for conquest and domination only. Alexander's conquests strove to create a brotherhood of men, not just a world that would provide tribute and satisfy a king's lust for power. It was in this chamber that the reader of these inscriptions could appreciate the true tragedy of Alexander's early death.

Pyrrhus and the queen had chatted easily as they walked through the palace grounds on the way to the temple. As they approached it, Pyrrhus was increasingly struck by the elegant majesty of the building, and he found it increasingly difficult to say anything at all. Berenice, who had had a similar feeling when she visited the completed temple for the first time, was content to leave Pyrrhus to contemplate the temple in silence.

As the two of them entered the temple, and Pyrrhus looked at the paintings and read the inscriptions, he had to acknowledge his own surprise. Since his visit to the temple of Artemis in Ephesus, he was convinced that no other building could affect him more profoundly. He now admitted he had been wrong, and he found himself deeply affected by the overwhelming humanity in Alexander's temple. After he had gazed at the paintings and read all the inscriptions at least twice, he turned and smiled at the queen. "Thank you for your patience, my lady. May we enter the tomb now?"

"Yes, Pyrrhus," replied the queen, "but I must tell you that it is no easier within than without."

Berenice took Pyrrhus's hand in her own and led him into the inner chamber, the tomb itself. At each corner of the tomb were large torches that were kept constantly lit and provided good illumination of the chamber once their eyes had adjusted from sunlight to interior lighting. In the center of the chamber, on a large dais, was a simply carved casket of dark, almost black, cedar wood, whose fragrance still filled the room. Its polish reflected the light from the torches as if it was a large diamond. The decoration of the tomb was simple. Apart from the casket, the only furnishing was an armor stand on which hung Alexander's favorite armor and helmet. This was placed in one corner of the room. There were paintings on only two of the walls. The first, on the wall to Pyrrhus's left, was a depiction of Philip holding his infant son, with his wife Olympias at his side. On the wall opposite, the second painting showed the spirit of Alexander rising above his funeral pyre, extending his hand to grasp that of his father Zeus, who was sitting on a cloud, reaching out to welcome his beloved son to heaven.

It was with some difficulty that Pyrrhus avoided dropping to his knees, quite overcome by this tomb. Berenice was aware of this and grasped Pyrrhus's hand more tightly.

"I understand your feelings, Pyrrhus," said the queen. "I have never been affected by anything as much as this tomb, with the sole exception of the birth of my children. Ptolemy insisted that

I wait until the temple had been completed before he brought me here. When I visited it for the first time, I wept for its sublimity. Come, my dear, we will walk back to the palace and have a glass of wine together, and then you must rest in your own quarters."

CHAPTER XIX

Pyrrhus spent several hours with Berenice after they returned to the palace from Alexander's tomb. She explained to him the view Alexander had of his own life, as it had been explained to her by Ptolemy. He believed himself to be the son of God, and it was this faith in his birthright and his destiny that enabled him to achieve superhuman feats in his short life. This also explained his conviction that he could achieve what no man had yet achieved, a world that could be united under a benevolent ruler, where peace rather than war could be the driving force.

Although he had always believed in his own power and destiny, it was here in Egypt that this belief was brought to its fruition. After making himself master of Egypt, he was taken to the oracle of Zeus-Ammon at Siwa. Whether it was the linguistic mistake, in unfamiliar Greek, of the priest who met him with the greeting of "Son of Zeus" instead of, "My son," or the ritual formula of the priests to a new pharaoh, on whom is bestowed, "The immortality of Ra, and the royalty of Horus, victory over all his enemies, and the dominion of the world," Alexander came away from that meeting with an unshakeable confidence in his own divine heritage.

The knowledge of Alexander's belief in his own destiny made Pyrrhus's experience at his tomb even more moving, as it provided the true understanding of the two paintings in his tomb, where both his human and divine parentage were acknowledged at the beginning and end of his life.

Pyrrhus left the queen to return to his own chambers. He rested and slept for the remainder of that day and night and then immersed himself in Ptolemy's biography of Alexander. After he had spent three days reading and rereading Ptolemy's work, taking his meals alone and politely declining Cineas's and Menestheus's invitations to take exercise or to stroll in the city, his friends had become sufficiently concerned to ask the queen for her advice. Berenice listened to their concerns, which added to her own fears that the young man could be overwhelmed by his admiration of, and grief for the loss of, the great Macedonian. With an insight that could have been surprising only to those who did not know her well, she confided her concerns to her husband. As a result, on the fourth day after his visit to the tomb, Ptolemy himself called on Pyrrhus in his rooms. He arrived unannounced at midday, and calmly informed Cineas and Menestheus that he had arranged for lunch to be served for Pyrrhus and himself, and that he would be grateful if the other gentlemen would spend the next few hours visiting the library.

Ptolemy waited for Hotep to escort Cineas and Menestheus out of the palace, and then directed Leontidas to serve a meal in the living room of the guest quarters. When this was done, he dismissed his chamberlain and knocked on Pyrrhus's door. "Pyrrhus, this is Ptolemy. I have come to invite you to dine with me." Pyrrhus opened the door in some embarrassment. "Forgive me, Sire. I have been neglecting my manners."

"Come and sit down with me, Pyrrhus. Lunch has been prepared for us, and I would speak with you." The two men sat on couches in the living room, and Ptolemy poured wine for the two of them. "Your friends are concerned about you, Pyrrhus, as is the queen." Ptolemy's face became very sad, and he continued, "I understand your grief, my son. I understand it because I have felt it myself. When Alexander died in Babylon, I felt that the light had gone out of the world, and that the world had lost its greatest hope of redemption. Perhaps the saddest part of it was the knowledge that Alexander himself knew that his great dream would die with him. When he was asked, "To whom do you leave your empire," he smiled wryly and said, "To the strongest." He knew himself there was no doubt that his generals would fight over his empire, as there was no clear succession that would follow his death. The only blood relatives who could succeed him were his infant son by Roxanne, who could never have universal support because she was a Bactrian princess, rather than a Macedonian, and his half brother, Philip Arridhaeus, who was a halfwit. Balanced against that, several of the generals were in too powerful a position to relinquish it to a rival, myself included. The world had been torn from its state of grace and returned to what it had been previously, a world of men, not of gods.

"What we must not lose sight of is that, although we do not live in a world of gods, we live in a world that will forever bear the mark of Alexander. We must be grateful for that and deal with our grief for him as we would for the loss of our own fathers. Life must go on, and we must all play our part in it."

Pyrrhus sat there for some time and then nodded his head in understanding. After another interval, he looked up at Ptolemy and asked, "Sire, is it wrong that I grieve for Alexander more so than for my own father?"

"No, Pyrrhus. It is not," replied Ptolemy. "It has been the way for all of us who knew him." Pyrrhus nodded once more and then buried his face in his hands.

CHAPTER XX

Pyrrhus's spirits gradually improved after his meeting with Pharaoh. Ptolemy visited him each day for the next few days and was pleased to find that Pyrrhus had put aside his grief and was eager to discuss various details of Alexander's campaigns that he had read about in the biography.

He had resumed his exercise sessions with Menestheus, much to his friends' relief. When the queen felt that Pyrrhus was sufficiently recovered, she invited the three men to dine again with herself and her husband.

As they walked through the now familiar palace to Pharaoh's private chambers, Cineas said to Pyrrhus, "I am very relieved to see you in your usual good spirits once again, Sire."

"As am I, my friend. For a while I wondered where the abyss might lead, but once I realized how great Ptolemy's loss was compared to my own, I knew that I must follow his example and put my own troubles behind me."

When the three men entered the customary dining room, they found Ptolemy and Berenice already there, standing at the window. Turning around, Berenice smiled and said, "Come in Pyrrhus, it is good to see you." The queen walked over to Pyrrhus, took his hands in her own and kissed him on the cheek. "We were all rather worried about you." Turning to the others, she continued, "Welcome, Menestheus, and you, Cineas. Please come and sit down."

Ptolemy then came over from the window and smiled at his visitors. "It is good to see you, gentlemen. Berenice and I were just admiring the sunset. Please sit down."

After the meal had been laid out and the servants had retired, Ptolemy served his wife's meal, as was his usual custom, and invited the guests to help themselves. He then turned to Pyrrhus and said, "I imagine that you three have seen most of Alexandria by now. I would like to suggest a trip to the countryside that we should make together, and then I will put you gentlemen to work."

Pyrrhus's eyes lit up at this suggestion, as he was not pleased with the idea of being a perpetual houseguest. "I will do my best at whatever task you set me, Sire," he replied.

"The trip we should make together is to the oracle of Zeus-Ammon at Siwa. You should see for yourselves the place that was seminal to Alexander's view of himself and the world. The journey will take us a week or more each way, and it will also give you a better feel for the geography of Egypt. After we return to Alexandria, I would like your help in training some of my troops. You have seen the Egyptian troops that form the Royal Bodyguard who fulfill the duties of protection of the palace, and who can be used in times of need in the city itself. The troops you have not yet seen are those whom I can actually rely on in a military context. Some of these men are Greeks, some are Egyptian, but they are all armed and trained in the same way as Macedonian phalangites, hypaspists, and cavalry. They have a permanent camp outside the city. These are the men I want you and Menestheus to help train. Unlike many of my officers, you have the battle experience, which is crucial in training such men."

Pyrrhus and Menestheus were both delighted at this suggestion, and Ptolemy was pleased at their enthusiasm. It would give his guests some purpose while in Egypt and would be valuable training for his troops. Turning to Cineas, Ptolemy continued,

"After we return from Siwa, Cineas, I would ask you to call on me each day at mid-morning. After a period of relative quiet, political affairs are beginning to become complicated once more, and I would be grateful for your insight into Greek politics."

Cineas was as pleased as his companions to be given a role in Pharoah's affairs and replied, "I will do all I can to be of service, Sire."

"Excellent," said Pharaoh. "Now, gentlemen, I propose to leave for Siwa at dawn, the day after tomorrow. Leontidas will make sure you have everything you need for the journey. Now that we have covered our business so satisfactorily, I think that we could all do with some relaxation. Leontidas has arranged for a visiting bard from Greece to recite some poetry for us this evening. I asked him to choose passages from Aeschylus and from the *Odyssey*. With our journey ahead of us, it seemed a suitable inspiration."

CHAPTER XXI

As planned, Ptolemy, with his three guests and his usual guard of one hundred men from his Household Cavalry, left Alexandria at dawn on the second day. They would follow the usual Egyptian custom in beginning the journey at first light, rest during the hottest part of the day, and then continue in the cooler part of the afternoon and early evening, before making camp for the night.

For Pyrrhus, this trip was one of exquisite delight. The last time he had journeyed far through unfamiliar country was after the battle of Ipsus, when he and his comrades rushed to escape Seleucus's pursuit on their way to Ephesus. On this occasion, he could wonder at the great parched country that made up that part of Egypt that was removed from the holy Nile and breathe in the sense of adventure of traveling in a foreign country in the company of one of the greatest rulers of his day. He was also aware of the destination that awaited them. The oracle of Zeus-Ammon at Siwa was the most ancient and respected shrine in Egypt, held in admiration as great as that of Delphi and Dodona in Greece. It was not beyond the realms of possibility that the priests would consider his own future and give some sign regarding his own destiny, at this time when his own expectations and hopes were so ill defined.

For the time being, his attention was taken up by the curious geography of Egypt. That a country so much composed of desert could be such a rich source of grain amazed him. As Ptolemy had explained to him previously, the Nile truly was the jewel of Egypt. The extent and fertility of the flood plain of the great river was greater than he could have possibly imagined.

There were a number of charming breaks in the desert through which they traveled. Their journey was planned so they could make their camp each night at an oasis. Ptolemy and his guests dined each night under the stars and a canopy of palm trees. A large advance party had gone ahead of the main group so that the camp could always be set up by the time Pharaoh's party was ready to stop for the night. Pharaoh would find a fully set up camp at the end of each day's traveling, complete with well-furnished tents and a large field kitchen.

This advance party consisted of fifty pack camels and their drivers, to carry equipment and stores, and a further fifty men, who set up the tents, cooked the meals, and acted as servants to Pharaoh and his guests. During the first night's stop, one half of the party left the camp shortly after midnight, carrying with them the second set of tents, stores, and mobile kitchen, to arrive at the next campsite in good time to make camp before Pharaoh's arrival. The remaining half packed up camp after Pharaoh departed and followed behind. In this way, one half of the support group was always ahead of the king.

Oases were not sufficiently numerous for them to take their midday break at one, and the group rested each day under the cover of awnings until the intensity of the sunlight lessened. Ptolemy was obviously a seasoned traveler in Egypt and seemed less affected by the heat than his guests and most of his soldiers.

This journey was to be a long one, probably taking eight to ten days. Each evening, Ptolemy would discuss their progress with Pyrrhus. He took into account the distance the party had been able to travel that day and with what degree of ease or difficulty, and the two of them would decide on the distance that would be traveled on the following day and where the camp was to be made for the following night.

The time that Pyrrhus spent with Ptolemy on this journey was something of a golden time when he reflected on it later in his life. Ptolemy was essentially on holiday from his usual pressures of affairs of state, and the two men were able to spend several hours together each evening. This allowed them the luxury of getting to know each other as men, not just from their respective positions as pharaoh of Egypt and a displaced king of Epirus who was in Egypt as a hostage. They naturally spoke of Ptolemy's time with Alexander and aspects of his campaigns described in his biography, but as the days went on they spoke increasingly of their own lives and aspirations. Ptolemy also encouraged Menestheus and Cineas to join in the after-dinner conversations, and, in time, they too would tell of their experiences once the great king had clearly signaled his friendship. Cineas held the attention of his audience when he spoke of his years with Demosthenes. That complex man was often seen by the Macedonians as one who held onto his city's heritage to an excessive degree. When the Athenian perspective was put forward in a clear light, both Ptolemy and Pyrrhus (whose ideas were strongly influenced by the powerful neighbor that Epirus had in Macedonia) found their admiration of Demosthenes surprisingly strong. In his turn, Ptolemy was able to paint a far more flattering picture of Philip than southern Greeks were accustomed to. This great man was not only the finest warrior of his day, but also a champion of all that the culture and philosophy of Athens and the other great southern Greek cities had achieved. It always saddened Philip that Athens remained his implacable enemy. His own belief was that the cause of the Greek world would have benefited enormously if they had been able to become friends and allies.

Philip had described the eve of the battle of Chaeronaea as the saddest moment in his life. He had approached the plains of Boeotia at the head of his army, determined one way or another to achieve, for himself and Macedonia, the leadership of Greece in the war against the Persians. Despite the military confrontation, he hoped until the last minute that negotiations for peace would be successful. These negotiations failed, and the Thebans would not let him pass. On the eve of the battle, after receiving the Thebans' final ambassador, he reflected on what the following day would bring. He would fight the Thebans, whom he had come to admire during his time there as a political hostage. At this time, the city was led by Epaminondas, one of the greatest men in Greek history. It was he who won for Thebes the military leadership of Greece after he broke the power of the Spartans at the battle of Leuctra. It was well known that he befriended Philip and treated him as his son..

He would also fight the Athenians, the acknowledged cultural leaders of Greece whose courage and determination had saved Greece from conquest by the Persians in ancient times. He allowed himself a short period to weep that night and then accepted that the coming tragedy was inevitable, and all he could do was to play his part in the drama to the best of his ability. When the battle was won, and he had cremated the Athenian dead with full military honors, he was able to soften his sorrow with the lenient peace terms that he offered to the Athenians, signaling his desire for goodwill to be a part of the confederation of Greek states whom he intended to lead. He was left with a heavy heart though. The battle that he had tried so hard to avoid left many Greeks with the cry of "Philip the Barbarian" still in their mouths, and he sent his general, Antipater, to Athens as his envoy to present his peace terms. There was another sorrow that he had to bear in his remaining days. As the result of a decision that he made in the immediate aftermath of Chaeronaea, in the full flush of victory and under the influence of wine, he had vented his anger toward those who had forced this battle on him, the battle that should never have been fought. This anger led him to his harsh treatment of Thebes. This sorrow was not immediately apparent to him, but in days to come he would know the despair of guilt.

Such was the picture of Philip that Ptolemy was able to portray to his fellow travelers. A complex and ambitious man, who was driven to fulfill his destiny and lead Greece against Persia, but also a man who deeply loved Greek culture. He was the man who truly Hellenized Macedonia, who desired the unconditional acknowledgement of his country as part of the Greek world, most of all by Demosthenes and the Athenians. His deepest sorrow was that this process would be attained by force.

As the journey progressed, the travelers came to know each other's minds and aspirations well. There were many times when they discussed events that held great sadness, but other moments held humor and wit, and were able to counterbalance the darker side of their lives.

As they came closer to Siwa, Pyrrhus's anticipation increased. On the ninth day after they had left Alexandria, they approached the oasis in the late afternoon. This was a particularly fine oasis, and it was in their view for over an hour as they approached it, situated as it was at the bottom of a deep valley. There was a ring of palm trees around it, and a group of several buildings in the center. Its size came as a complete surprise to Pyrrhus—large enough to build a small city on. Most of the space not taken up by buildings was filled with greenery, and, as they approached it, there was a delightful aroma of moisture and perfumed gardens, which was welcome after the barren dryness of the open desert. Outside the area of the temple and outbuildings and the cultivated gardens in the center of the oasis, orchards and pasture extended for at least a mile on each side, with many small dwellings scattered through the area, which housed farmers and shepherds and their families.

The advance party had arrived some hours beforehand, and Pyrrhus could see the group of tents that had been set up on one side of the temple complex.

Well before they were within hailing range, a large group of men had gathered at the entrance to the oasis to welcome Pharaoh. They were, presumably, the priests and attendants of the oracle, as well as the servants who attended to the needs of these learned men.

As Ptolemy, on his magnificent horse, entered the oasis, an elderly man stepped out from the group. Bowing deeply, the man said to him, "I bid you welcome, Pharaoh, you do us honor with your visit."

"Thank you, Ramses, it is good to see you again. I have brought some guests with me. I present King Pyrrhus of Epirus, his lieutenant, Menestheus, and his advisor, Cineas."

Ramses bowed deeply again and replied, "I welcome you and your colleagues, Sire. If you will come with me, we have prepared refreshments in the antechamber of the temple. You must all be tired after your long journey."

The men dismounted from their horses and handed the mounts to the many attendants, then followed Ramses into the temple. After the oppressive heat of the afternoon, the coolness inside the antechamber was as refreshing as cold spring water. The large room was generously furnished with couches and tables, and side tables groaned with the weight of the food and drink that had been provided for the party.

Ptolemy took off his hat and cloak and sat down on one of the couches. "It is a great relief to sit down on a comfortable chair, Ramses. Can you make sure that my men are provided for?"

"It has already been taken care of, Sire."

"Excellent. It has been too long, my old friend. Tell me of your activities and your health." As Ptolemy spoke, a flask of water and a goblet was placed by each of the visitors and they all drank deeply.

"My health is as good as an old man can expect, Sire. My bones creak more than they once did, but, God willing, they will serve me for some time yet. After you provided me with your fine tradesmen and the beautiful cedar wood, we have made some much needed repairs to the temple, and I am glad to say that it is once again fit to receive guests. Our young priests and students do well in their studies, although I must say that it is not always easy for them to forget the desires of the flesh. In our isolated position, though, they do well to accept the life of religious men. They also understand their privileges of living in such a beautiful house of God that Pharaoh has provided for them.

"I must not forget my manners, Sire. I trust the queen and your children are well?"

"They are all well, Ramses, thank you. The queen sends her regards to you."

Ramses bowed his head in acknowledgement, and Ptolemy continued, "Antigone has been traveling in Greece and is due to return from Argos next week. My son, Ptolemy, is currently in Babylon. It was time for him to undertake a visit of state as my representative, and in view of recent events I felt it would be appropriate for him to spend some time at the court of Seleucus. I expect him to return in two months time, hopefully much the wiser."

This was the first time that Pyrrhus had heard Ptolemy speak of his children in his presence, and he could not resist looking at Cineas with a wry smile. Cineas remained impassive with the exception of an almost undetectable raising of his eyebrows.

"I have brought my guests here to Siwa, Ramses, so that they can see for themselves the place where Alexander found so much inspiration. I am also sure that they would be grateful for any advice the oracle might offer them regarding their own place in the world."

"You have arrived at an opportune time of day, Sire. It is our custom to offer sacrifices to Amon in the early evening. If you wished, you and your guests could bathe and rest for a time and then you could join us in our evening prayer."

"Excellent. We will have an early dinner now as you have provided for us so well. I will let you return to your duties now, my friend. Perhaps you could instruct your servants to have our baths ready in an hour's time. We will then have plenty of time to join you in the temple."

Ramses rose and bowed to Pharaoh, then to Pyrrhus, and withdrew. Ptolemy stood up and said to the others, "Come my friends, we will have our meal now." Ptolemy dismissed the servants, and the four men helped themselves to the food and wine and resumed their places on the couches. "I imagine you gentlemen were surprised when I discussed my children in your presence for the first time." Ptolemy smiled at Pyrrhus and continued, "I am an old-fashioned Macedonian in many ways, Pyrrhus, and it takes me some time to take newcomers to heart. I am pleased to do so now, and I would be happy if you three would now consider yourselves part of my family, not only my guests."

Pyrrhus smiled at Ptolemy and said with considerable emotion, "Thank you, Father."

Menestheus felt no need to say anything, but smiled at Pharaoh and bowed. Cineas, who was rarely taken by surprise, found himself rather off balance but replied, "I thank you for your trust, Sire. It has been the wish of all of us to do what we can in your service."

Ptolemy raised his goblet and proposed it to Pyrrhus and then to Menestheus and Cineas in salutation. "Gentlemen, let us offer our own libation and prayer to Father Zeus." Ptolemy paused in thought, poured some of his wine on the floor, and then drank himself, each of the others doing the same in their turn.

Once again, the consummate diplomatist in Ptolemy saved the conversation. After reflecting for a short time after they had made their libations, he began to tell his guests about the history of the oracle of Zeus-Ammon. The recent history of the oracle, from the time of Alexander's visit was, naturally, well known to them, but he was able to tell them of its earlier history, from legendary times.

After their meal, Ptolemy and his friends were shown to their baths by the temple servants and provided with scented tunics prepared for dignitaries who were also supplicants of Zeus-Ammon. They spent a short time resting in the anteroom of the temple, and then Ramses came to fetch them. "We are about to start our evening prayer session, Sire," Ramses said to Ptolemy. "Our usual custom is for me to begin the prayer session, and then, when we have supplicants, I present them in turn to the high priestess of Zeus-Ammon, who then asks the god to respond to their requests."

"We will be pleased to follow your lead, my friend. Please lead on."

Ramses led Pharaoh and his company into the temple and seated them in the place of honor used by distinguished guests, and then made his way to the front of the altar. A goat, which

had been suitably sedated beforehand, was to be the sacrifice to
the God on this occasion. Ramses lit the candles held by his acolytes, and then his own, with a taper that he lit from the perpetual
fire maintained at the altar, and then filled the ceremonial goblet
with wine that was reserved for such sacrifices. He knelt down in
private prayer, then stood, and holding the goblet raised in front
of him, looked at the altar and said, "Father Zeus who is also
Ammon, I lead my company in prayer that you may continue to
guide us and give us your blessing. I also ask for your blessing
for our divine Pharaoh, who has given us his presence today. Let
him continue to guide Egypt in security and prosperity and pre-
serve our country as it has been for thousands of years, obeying
your divine will. I also ask your guidance for the great leaders
whom Pharaoh has brought to your temple to ask your will."

Ramses poured some of the wine on the floor, closed his
eyes once more in private prayer, and then drank from the goblet. Three attendants then joined him. One took the sacrificial
chalice and his candle and kept them out of harm's way while
the other two took hold of the goat. As one pulled the head of
the animal back, Ramses said another private prayer and then
slit the animal's throat.

"We offer this fine goat as a sacrifice, Lord, in thanks for
your continued blessing." The dead animal was taken away to
a rear chamber where the final details of the offering would be
performed. Ramses then retired to his position at the side of
the altar, and the temple choir sang a poignant Egyptian hymn.
While this lovely piece of music was being performed, a number
of temple servants cleaned the floor where the goat had met his
end. Ramses was an obsessively tidy man.

After the hymn, Ramses returned to the front of the altar and
said, "Father Zeus, who is also Ammon, I now call upon your high
priestess to come and deliver the signs of your will to our divine
Pharaoh and his guests who are also supplicants at your altar."

After Ramses had finished his prayer, he stood aside, and
from behind a curtain at the side of the altar a tall and striking woman appeared. Her face, though beautiful, was hard

and expressionless and bore the signs of years of penitence. Her eyes, however, were crystal clear and were softened by wisdom and compassion. She took her place at the altar, knelt in silent prayer, and then stood and turned to face Ptolemy.

"Divine Pharaoh, we welcome you to our shrine. If you will approach the altar and kneel, I will ask our god for his blessing for you. Also, I will ask him to disclose the future to you, if he chooses to reveal it."

Ptolemy then approached the altar and knelt in front of the priestess. She handed him the goblet of holy wine, from which he drank, and then returned it to the care of the acolyte. The priestess then knelt in front of Pharaoh and took his hands in her own and closed her eyes. "Divine Pharaoh, our god is pleased with you and will extend his protective hand over your labors, so that both you and Egypt will continue to prosper. Your children, who are far away, will return safely to our shores, and your line will prosper for generations to come." The priestess remained still for some time and then rose, keeping hold of Ptolemy's hands and bringing him to his feet also. Ptolemy bowed to the priestess and withdrew to his seat. The priestess then signaled to Menestheus to approach the altar. With the same introduction, she invited the god to pronounce his destiny.

"Menestheus, your fine mind and your compassion will always be gratefully acknowledged by your king, whom you will serve until the end."

Menestheus withdrew to his seat, and it was then Cineas's turn to be called to the altar. Cineas received a similar response from the priestess, something that a member of the Assembly in Athens might come up with when he really had very little to say, and then it was Pyrrhus's turn to approach the altar.

As Pyrrhus took his place at the altar, the priestess offered him the goblet of holy wine. He took a sip of the wine, and as he returned the goblet the priestess's face went grey. She offered Pyrrhus a fixed stare, and, after a pause that had put all of those in attendance in a state of anticipation, said to him, "King Pyrrhus, Zeus-Ammon has given me an insight into the future. You will claim your birthright in Epirus, and you will be known to the world to come as a great warrior. The god also sends you a warning of your doom.

"There will come a time when you will see a wolf fighting with a bull. This contest will be the sign of your death."

The priestess continued to stare at Pyrrhus, and, after attempting to stand up, fell to her knees, perspiration beading on her forehead. "Beware of the wolf fighting a bull," she repeated, and then she was picked up by her attendants and escorted back to her own quarters, shaking her head and weeping.

Pyrrhus remained kneeling, not knowing whether it would be appropriate to burst out laughing in such company. He managed to keep his mirth under control until Ramses approached him, took his hand and made him stand. "You seem to have a mixed blessing from God tonight, my son. I hope it will be a long time before you meet the wolf and the bull."

"Thank you, Ramses," replied Pyrrhus, manfully repressing a smile. Ptolemy then came up to him, winked at him, and said to Ramses, "Thank you for allowing us to share your prayer session, Ramses; we will retire now and leave you to finish your service."

Ptolemy then took his three guests out of the temple and said to them, "Gentlemen, I would like you to join me in my tent for a cup of wine."

"Well, Pyrrhus, you certainly made an impression on the priestess tonight," said Ptolemy. "After the platitudes that we others received, it was quite exciting."

"I have to admit, Sire, that I have regarded such palm reading as an amusement in the past, although this has been the most dramatic prediction I have ever heard."

"I am sure that it is just a bit of amusement, Sire," said Cineas, "but it does have an interesting source. There is a story that is told in Greece of such a contest, and it is well known in Argos where a statue was erected depicting a wolf defeating a bull in a fight to the death. It is said to have been dedicated by Danaus in legendary times. When Danaus had first landed in Greece near Pyramia and was on his way to Argos, he came upon a wolf fighting a bull. The rarity of such an event intrigued him, and he thought it must have represented a sign from the gods. As a stranger to the country, he identified himself with the wolf, also not a native inhabitant of Greece, and interpreted it as a struggle between himself and the native inhabitants. He watched the fight and was pleased to see that the wolf was victorious. He offered his prayers to Apollo Lyceius, the wolf god, and was encouraged in his own attempts to attack Argos. He was victorious and became king of the city. In gratitude for this sign from the gods, he had a statue made of the battle of the wild beasts that one can still see in Argos today." Cineas felt concerned for his king's safety, but as he was unable to alter an event that was in the hands of the gods, he felt obliged to soften the impact of the prediction, and said, "I would not like to vouch for it as a premonition, however."

"I am glad to hear that at least, Cineas," said Pyrrhus, clearly amused.

"Whatever we make of tonight's events, my friends," said Ptolemy, "this place is where Alexander was filled with divine light and was inspired to achieve what no man has yet achieved. It is of course a matter of debate whether the source came from God or whether it represented his own genius finding a course that could inspire it. One way or the other, it is important that you gentlemen should come here and see for yourselves a place which has had such an effect on the destiny of the world."

They spoke for a time about the nature of destiny and how many of the choices that one is faced with represent true free will, and what influence fate plays, independent of any decision making. Such a subject will intrigue men for all eternity, and this group, as all others before, left the question unanswered.

CHAPTER XXII

The return journey to Alexandria took twelve days, rather longer than the journey out, as the group rested for a full day at an oasis halfway home. It was partly due to the strong winds that they encountered, necessitating one full day spent sheltering from the storm, but also they were content to travel somewhat more slowly than on the journey out to Siwa. As with all journeys, the outward leg was full of anticipation and excitement, and the time traveling seemed to take an eternity, while on the return trip, the pressure of excitement was lessened and replaced by the pleasure of recollection of events and conversations that they had experienced.

Despite the foreboding nature of the priestess's prophecy, Pyrrhus was pleased to reflect on the encounter. There was little doubt that she had herself believed she had been given a message from God to pass onto him. There was much to be pleased about. Did she not tell him that he would regain his rightful place in Epirus and that the name he would leave behind would be remembered always as that of a great warrior by men of later generations?

As for the other? Well, all men must die at some stage, and it is not necessarily a tragic event for it to be signaled when the time comes. Some of the greatest heroes the world will ever know made that decision themselves. King Leonidas of Sparta, with the 300 men of his bodyguard, chose death and everlasting glory in their hopeless defense of the Pass of Thermopylae against the overwhelming might of Xerxes' army. The same choice was made by the Thespians, who refused to leave Leonidas and retreat with the main body of the Greek army, and so died with the Spartans. Such courage should always be acknowledged and recorded. The Thespians were led by Demophilus, the son of Diadromes.

There is a headstone at Thermopylae one can still see today, which bears the epitaph of Leonidas and his men, written in hexameter verse:

> Go tell the Spartans, Passerby,
> That we obeyed our orders,
> And dead, here we lie.

Was it a good bargain for a man to lose the second half of his life, a few paltry years, in return to gain the admiration of men for all time? Leonidas obviously thought so, as did his men. Pyrrhus also thought that such a bargain was favorable and as a result was not troubled by the prophecy. It brought a smile to his face when he considered that a short life filled with glory was chosen over a long and uneventful life by both Alexander and Achilles. He would accept the bargain that God seemed to be offering him, but he would also make sure that not a single day was wasted.

Pyrrhus discussed these matters with his friends and Ptolemy over cups of wine in the luxury of their camp. Ptolemy and Menestheus were perhaps the ones who could most easily identify with the heroic streak in Pyrrhus's nature. Cineas, however, could not help but be somewhat troubled by the enthusiast in Pyrrhus. No one could argue about the greatness of Alexander's contribution to the advancement of mankind. Achilles, on the other hand, was a difficult individual to either admire or condemn. Yes, he was the greatest of the Achaean warriors who sailed to Troy, but what did his pride and arrogance achieve when he fell out with Agamemnon? Their quarrel almost destroyed that great expedition, as well as filling Achilles' heart with guilt and remorse when his dearest friend, Patroclus, was killed by Hector, a man less strong than Achilles, but far more admirable. Even Achilles needed the help of Pallas Athene when he fought his final duel with Hector. If he had lived, and Troy had not been sacked by the Achaeans, Hector might now be regarded by posterity as the finest man to grace those dark ages, not only a great warrior, but a man endowed with the greatest gifts of humanity, alongside whom Achilles would be judged as a savage.

Although he could neither form a decision in his own mind, nor present his mind's dilemma to his dinner companions, Cineas could not help but be troubled by the contrasting sides of Pyrrhus's nature. Yes, he would be a great warrior and would claim a place in history, but would that place be that of Alexander or Hector, whose words were as wise as their arms were strong, or would he be a man to whom the struggle was everything, like Achilles?

The one thing that Cineas could be sure of was that his own destiny was inextricably linked to that of Pyrrhus. He would follow his king and do what he could to soften the ambition in that great heart, so that his epithet would not just be that of Odysseus, the "Sacker of Cities."

Their experience at Siwa formed a bond between these men that would last the remainder of their lives, and they were all conscious of it. As a result, they spoke to each other with the candor that exists between members of a family. This did not necessarily imply equality, as Ptolemy would remain their king, but the other men came to love and respect him as they would their own fathers, and he in turn regarded the other three as his sons. As a result, by the time they returned to Alexandria, none of the men was now in Egypt alone, and they all had a common desire to fulfill their individual destinies, which were now bonded together forever.

CHAPTER XXIII

After the party had returned to Alexandria, Ptolemy gave his guests two days to rest after their journey, and then, true to his word, put them to work. On the third day after their return, Pharaoh took Pyrrhus and the other two men to the permanent camp of his Macedonian army, which was stationed an hour's ride from the city. They arrived at the camp at mid-morning, and they found all the officers assembled at the gate, and an honor guard that was formed up inside the camp.

As Ptolemy approached, the general of the army stepped out in front of the other officers and bowed deeply. "Welcome, Pharaoh. It is always a pleasure to receive you."

"Thank you, Damocleides. I have brought King Pyrrhus and these other gentlemen to see you, to discuss how they may help you with the training of the troops."

"I will be grateful for their help, Sire. It can be difficult to maintain motivation and battle readiness without fresh ideas." Damocleides approached Pyrrhus as he was dismounting from his horse. "It is a pleasure to meet you, Sire. I have been told of your exploits at Ipsus and afterwards, and it is a fine thing to have the advice of a man of courage."

Pyrrhus was slightly surprised at this greeting from an experienced general but was inwardly delighted. Both men smiled
with pleasure when they shook hands. "I thank you for your
welcome, Damocleides. Pharaoh has told me how much he val-
ues having such a fine commander for his troops." Damocleides
smiled and nodded. Both men knew that they would work well
together and, possibly, become friends. "I would like to introduce my two associates, General. Menestheus, my lieutenant,
and Cineas, my political advisor."

"It is a pleasure to meet you both, gentlemen. If you would
like to come with me into the camp, you could review the troops,
and then join me for refreshments in my offices."

Damocleides led Pharaoh and his friends into the camp,
which was the size of a small city, complete with stone walls and
permanent buildings for both the command center, which contained both Damocleides's offices and his private quarters and
also the men's barracks. The command building also boasted an
exercise and training hall and large lecture rooms where Damocleides and the other senior officers attempted to impart some of
their wisdom and experience to the junior officers.

Damocleides took his guests into the middle of the central
marshaling and exercise area and presented his officers to Pharaoh
and his party. He invited the group to follow him in an inspection
of the guard of honor. This camp was home to 5,000 men, all
picked soldiers, who formed the backbone of Ptolemy's standing army. The men on parade today were the elite hypaspists of
the Royal Foot Guards. This battalion was made up of the finest
infantry that Ptolemy possessed and numbered 1,000 men. The
remainder of Ptolemy's Macedonian army consisted of another
battalion of 1,000 hypaspists, 2,000 phalangites, and 1,000 cavalry. Ptolemy had initially used the men who had been allocated
to him by the Council of Generals to form his "Macedonian army
of Egypt." Most of the men from his original army who were still
alive had completed their service. These men were given generous retirement benefits and were encouraged to remain in Egypt.
They were a rich source of training officers, and there were also

others who offered a contribution from their skills in civilian life. Some had expertise as engineers, others were craftsmen, such as potters and artisans. All these men would contribute to the Hellenistic culture that Ptolemy hoped would blend with that of the Egyptians to form a new and greater Egypt.

Ptolemy had gone to great lengths to form a new army on Macedonian lines and to change the nature of the force from one made up mainly of mercenaries to that of a national army, loyal to himself and Egypt. In achieving this goal he had the great example of Philip of Macedon, who had achieved such an end himself. Philip had increased the authority of the king of Macedonia, and with this greater power he had created a permanent standing national army, in the place of feudal levies with little military prowess. He created the army that was to be virtually invincible in the hands of himself and of his son, Alexander.

Philip's task was undoubtedly the more difficult, but, nevertheless, Ptolemy's achievement was most admirable.

When he recruited his second generation of soldiers, he made it clear that he was not engaging them as mercenaries for a limited period. He sought out the best men he could find through his recruiting officers in Greece, Macedonia, and the eastern Aegean. He offered these men generous pay and living conditions and recruited them on the basis of twenty years service in his army, followed by a period of five years where they formed a veteran reserve. On retirement from full-time service, the soldiers were granted a means of earning a decent living in a trade of their own choosing, remaining in the army as instructors, or in positions in the Egyptian civil service. As well as Greeks, Ptolemy had also enlisted the most promising of his Egyptian soldiers. About 1,000 men in this army were native Egyptians, and Ptolemy had been very pleased with how well they had adapted to Macedonian military theory and practice. Their presence in his army added significantly to the idea that it was a national army of Egypt.

These were the soldiers then, who stood to attention while the battalion was inspected by Pharaoh. Ptolemy was, of course, familiar with the officers and many of the men. Pyrrhus, for his part, was extremely impressed with these men on this first encounter. They were all fine looking soldiers, well armed and confident. He felt that if they had the best training available, they would be almost invincible. He smiled at this thought and hoped that he and Menestheus could make a worthwhile contribution to that training.

Damocleides and Ptolemy led the inspection group past rank after rank, until they had surveyed every soldier. Pyrrhus stopped and spoke to several of the men during the inspection. These conversations were, naturally, quite innocuous, but it was a very useful way of gaining a first impression of the morale that was present in this battalion. He was pleased that the responses from all the men he spoke to showed cheerful confidence as well as respect and trust toward their officers. Much might be done with these men.

Now that the formal inspection was over, Damocleides led his guests up to the balcony at the front of his offices. Pharaoh received and returned the salute of the army and then led the other men into the general's office. As Ptolemy entered the main office where refreshments had been laid out, a group of servants attended to him, and then the others. The servants relieved the dignitaries of their cloaks and armor and directed them to chairs around the central table. After accepting a glass of wine from a servant, Ptolemy said to Damocleides, "I am pleased with the men, Damocleides. They look fit and confident."

"Thank you, Sire," replied Damocleides. "They are coming along well, I think. They are probably as good as a man who has enjoyed peace for as long as I have can make them. I will be grateful for the advice of King Pyrrhus when we can meet together. There is nothing quite like the presence of a man who has recently been in battle to focus the minds of the young men on their military prowess."

"I was hoping that I could share some of my ideas with you, General. First, I would like to talk to them about our defeat at the battle of Ipsus. The tactics of Antigonus and Seleucus and Lysimachus were admirable and represented the principles of

Alexander. The result of the battle was not due to poor tactical thinking on the part of Antigonus but rather the unexpected
event that can leave one at a grave disadvantage. Because it was
such a good example of three outstanding commanders in the
field, I would like to use it as a teaching example, if Pharaoh and
his officers would not find the recollection painful."

"All battles, with their loss of lives and suffering, are painful
to recall, my son," said Ptolemy. "In that context, however, Ipsus
does not trouble me more than battles I have seen myself. I am
content for you to choose your own teaching methods, if you can
bear to talk about Ipsus yourself. You mentioned that you had a
number of ideas for us to consider. Please continue."

All of the men present had quietly nodded their heads while
contemplating Pyrrhus's description of Ipsus. Antigonus had
been one of the finest commanders of an army in the known
world. If he could experience such a disaster, who could not?

Pleased that his idea had landed on fertile ground, Pyrrhus
continued. "As well as such philosophical matters, I would also
like to work on shield, spear, and sword drill with them. From
what I saw at Ipsus, the armament of our adversaries has changed
over the last few years, and I would like your advice on any
changes you would recommend, in either tactics or equipment,
to best be able to meet the enemy."

"I would be pleased to discuss these matters with you, Sire, at
your earliest convenience. I do not know how long you will remain
with us in Egypt, but I hope to make the most of your knowledge
while I can. Perhaps you could remain here this evening as my
guest, after Pharaoh leaves. We could dine together and discuss our
matters. I have a guest suite which is available to you and Menestheus, and I could escort you back to Alexandria tomorrow."

"That would be excellent, my friend, if Pharaoh is agreeable." Pyrrhus looked over at Ptolemy. "I was hoping that you
and Damocleides would work together well, Pyrrhus. Do remain
here as long as you wish. I am sure that our host will find duties for Menestheus as well, so he should remain here with you.
I would ask Cineas to return to the city with me, as there are

a number of matters that need to be dealt with urgently, and I would like his advice on my response to several ambassadors."

Ptolemy stood up and walked over to Damocleides. "I will take my leave now, my friend, as there is much for all of us to do. Pyrrhus, stay as long as you wish, but I expect that a report on your progress will arrive on my desk each morning."

Pyrrhus smiled and nodded, and then bowed to Pharaoh. "I will be a good correspondent for the first time in my life, Sire."

"I will hold you to that, my son," replied Ptolemy, returning Pyrrhus's smile. Then looking toward Damocleides and Menestheus said, "Gentlemen, I will see you soon." He then collected Cineas and left the room to prepare to return to Alexandria.

Pleased to be left to discuss military matters to their hearts' content, Pyrrhus, Menestheus, and Damocleides grouped their chairs together, and Damocleides called for his servants so that they could bring more figs, bread, and wine. This would be at least a three-goblet conversation.

After Pyrrhus had described some of the changes he had observed at Ipsus, Damocleides said to him, "From what you say, Sire, it is clear that in Seleucus's and Lysimachus's armies they have lengthened their sarissas. This would clearly have given their phalanx an advantage. Do we lengthen ours to meet them?"

"I think we must, General," replied Pyrrhus. "I have to say, however, that this is not the most pressing issue. We must not forget that the armament of the phalanx is not everything. Yes, we must make sure that the equipment of our phalanx is a match for that of our enemies. More importantly, we must remember that Alexander trained his phalangites so that they could maneuver to meet the advance of an enemy from any direction. This is one of the areas where Antigonus failed to beat his opponents. Also, we must not lose sight of the fact that the definitive blow is delivered by the hypaspists and the cavalry on the enemy's rear or flank. If our enemies concentrate all their attention on their phalanges, and lessen their focus on hypaspists and cavalry, then these changes may work to our advantage." The other men were completely in agreement with Pyrrhus's ideas, and they continued their discussion until well after sunset.

It was indeed a three-goblet conversation that took place in Damocleides's offices on this day. Two of the goblets were consumed in practical, tactical details, and, by this stage, the three men understood each other and had thrashed out a framework whereby they would work with the men to improve their battle capabilities. The third goblet was consumed while they considered the broader issues facing them, related to both strategic and political matters. Old soldiers could smell when a war was looming, and all of them had picked up the scent over recent months.

CHAPTER XXIV

Pyrrhus and Menestheus spent four days at the army camp. They began each day breakfasting with Damocleides and finished the day dining with him. As Pyrrhus had initially thought, Damocleides was an extremely competent soldier, perceptive, and devoted to Ptolemy. He was also very receptive to any advice he could get to improve the effectiveness of his army. Such open-mindedness and lack of pretention made him a fine man to work with.

The first day was spent working out a program whereby time could be spent with all of the officers in turn. Once they were confident conceptually in the maneuvers that they would teach the men, Pyrrhus and Menestheus would work with them in the instruction of the troops. Pyrrhus made a mental note to try and engage the help of Spartan mercenaries who had been file leaders. The Spartans had been the masters of phalangeal maneuvers for centuries. Their skill in drilling men, when adapted to Macedonian weapons and tactics, would be invaluable.

The best use of Pyrrhus's time, as they agreed, would be for him and Menestheus to spend three days each week at the army camp. It would allow him a good deal of teaching time, and it would leave the officers and men the remainder of the week to work steadily on their skills without being overwhelmed by detail. With such a timetable, Pyrrhus hoped that in three months, the army would be sufficiently confident in their execution of phalanx movement that they could earn a place in the army of Alexander himself.

While Pyrrhus and Menestheus spent their three days at the army camp, Cineas spent much time with Ptolemy. As Pharaoh had said earlier, Hellenistic politics had become complicated once again. He had hoped that the battle of Ipsus would lead to a definitive treaty between himself and the other kings. The constant risk that Antigonus would mount a campaign against one of his rivals was now removed, and Ptolemy had hoped that he and the other kings would be able to agree that the current positions of all of them represented an acceptable balance of power.

There were two grave complications, however. Antigonus's power had not been extinguished at Ipsus and lived on in his son, Demetrius, who was once again a force to be reckoned with. At the moment, Demetrius was a powerful figure, with considerable resources at his command. He was an enthusiastic ally now, and such an alliance was extremely desirable. The difficulty lay in his unpredictability. If he harbored his father's ambitions to create a single empire once again, he may prove to be an enemy to be feared in the future.

The other complication was the bad blood that appeared to have developed between Lysimachus and Seleucus. It became apparent that the main reason why Lysimachus delayed his return to Thrace was the quarrel that had developed between himself and Seleucus. Lysimachus had demanded the lion's share of Antigonus's domains for himself, following the battle of Ipsus. Eventually, Seleucus had acquiesced to Lysimachus's demands, but the two of them remained both distrustful of, and hostile to each other. There seemed little doubt that they would eventually fight each other. While the kings were at each other's throats, they would be less able to keep at bay the perpetual threat from the barbarian nations that bordered all of their territories, such as the Gauls who threatened northern Greece.

It was this potential instability that Ptolemy discussed with Cineas when they met each morning in Pharaoh's office. There were also other topics they considered. It was during the second of their meetings that Ptolemy raised a dilemma of a more personal nature.

"Cineas," began Ptolemy, "there is another matter that I would like to discuss with you. Berenice took me rather by surprise last night. She is keen to introduce her daughter, Antigone, to Pyrrhus. She arrived home from Argos yesterday, and I will have to make a decision today as to whether or not I give my approval for this introduction to take place."

"Such things trouble all parents, Sire. From what I understand, your stepdaughter is a beautiful and talented young lady. All I can say is that if Pyrrhus was to form an attachment with Antigone, it could only be one of love and devotion. He looks to you as a son does to a father, and that alone would compel him to treat Antigone as a goddess. His own part on the world's stage is yet to be determined, but if he can avoid a premature death, there seems little doubt that he will achieve greatness."

"One cannot ask for more, my friend," replied Ptolemy. "My own view is much the same as yours. I really cannot object to an introduction to a man who has much to offer Antigone."

Ptolemy was relieved that he had been able to share his troubles with Cineas. Being able to discuss such personal matters with a trusted confidant is a rare luxury for a king, who normally has to deal with the loneliness that comes with monarchy. Ptolemy would give his approval for the introduction to take place.

CHAPTER XXV

Now that Pyrrhus and Ptolemy had both had time to settle back into their lives in Alexandria, Berenice felt it was time to again tell her husband that she wanted to introduce Pyrrhus to her daughter, Antigone. Although Ptolemy loved her as if she were his own child, she was Berenice's daughter from her first marriage. As such, Berenice felt she should be the one who would have the right of suggesting a likely match for the young princess.

Ptolemy had already decided that he could not, in all conscience, object to this, despite the fact that he had his own ideas on an ideal husband for Antigone. For any king, the betrothal of his children was an extremely important part of diplomacy. Still, it was not totally impossible that Pyrrhus could once again be king of Epirus and become a very valuable ally. So, it was with almost no reluctance that Ptolemy gave his approval for the introduction to take place. As was her nature, Berenice spoke to the two young people at leisure and gave both of them time to think about whether they could picture such an attachment. Of course, they spoke to friends and mutual acquaintances to find out what they could about the other. Antigone naturally spoke to

her parents, and Pyrrhus was flattered when both Ptolemy and
Berenice took time to speak to him about Antigone.

What Pyrrhus was able to learn about the young princess
seemed a mixture of truth and idealistic image making. He was
told, predictably, that Antigone was as beautiful as her mother
and also that she was an intelligent girl who took an interest
in politics and the history of both Egypt and the Greek world.
There also appeared to be no doubt that she would insist on
having the final word in the choice of a husband, no matter
how desirable any such match would be from a political point
of view. The easiest piece of information to take at face value
was that the two of them were the same age, their birthdays
only a matter of weeks apart.

In due course, the meeting was arranged. Both Antigone
and Pyrrhus would call on the queen in her chambers late in the
morning on the chosen day. Antigone arrived early, so that she
and her mother could talk between themselves before Pyrrhus
arrived. As they sat in comfortable chairs, Berenice said to her
daughter, "Ptolemy has been surprisingly quick to approve this
meeting, my dear. This is partly because of his love for you,
partly because of his love for me, as he grants me the privilege
of suggesting a match for my own daughter. Also, he admires
Pyrrhus and is very fond of him. It is not unlikely that he would
have eventually made the same suggestion himself. As far as
Pyrrhus's own prospects are concerned, I would have to say that
they are good, if uncertain."

Antigone showed a natural distrust of arranged marriages,
despite her unshakeable belief in her mother's best intentions.
She would wait and see how this young king of Epirus could
present himself before making any binding comment.

Pyrrhus was shown into the anteroom of Berenice's chambers by Leontidas at the appointed time and waited somewhat
nervously for the two ladies to join him. He had by now heard
much of the young princess, and, while feeling himself com-
plimented by Berenice's suggestion that the two young people
should meet, he had also seen too many arranged matches to

feel optimistic. He was excited despite his reservations and had taken particular care to look his best. He had bathed and shaved as late as possible before leaving for his appointment, taken particular care with his hair, and chose to wear the best of the few tunics he still had with him from his wardrobe in Epirus. He wanted to remind Antigone that his world was not just made up of his life in Egypt, and that something did remain of his previous existence as king of Epirus.

After he had waited for a few moments, Leontidas informed him that Queen Berenice and Princess Antigone would join him shortly. After he had taken a few more anxious turns around the room, the chamberlain announced the two women. Berenice entered first, looking as beautiful as ever, and he smiled and bowed to her, then took her hand in his after she had offered it.

"Pyrrhus, I would like to present you to my daughter, Antigone."

The young princess, who had followed her mother into the anteroom, now stood beside her mother and looked Pyrrhus in the eye. "I am pleased to meet you, Pyrrhus. My mother has told me much about you."

Antigone offered Pyrrhus her hand, which he took in his own, and with a bow of his head replied to her, "The pleasure is mine, my lady." Pyrrhus's initial response had been one of customary court politeness, but on raising his head from his bow, he looked into the eyes of the most elegant and graceful woman he had ever met. All of his previous caution and reserve seemed to disappear at that moment. As Antigone's eyes returned his gaze, he saw that she had the same reservations about their meeting. At this moment, however, these reservations receded for both of them.

The young princess who stood before him was different than the girl he had pictured in his mind's eye. When told about her beauty, he had distrusted the term, which is so commonly misused. The face that now smiled at him was indeed beautiful, however, but different to the beauty one normally expected in a young courtesan. Antigone's beauty was less perfect, but infinitely more serene. Her face was young and gentle, and her smile something he wished to capture in his mind's eye so he could dream about it at night. Her long black hair, beautifully set and decorated with pearls and other jewels, was showing signs of premature grayness. She stood tall, as straight and fine as a young sapling. Her white linen gown swept down from her tanned and square shoulders, following the contours of her slim and muscular figure until the final folds rested on her ankles. Her arms, bare from the shoulder, were tanned and firm from regular exercise and adorned with gold bands and bracelets. Her hands, beautifully manicured, were as elegant as the arms that moved them, but also showed some roughening of the skin, showing that the stepdaughter of Pharaoh was prepared to look after her own linen and tend her herb garden.

Pyrrhus knew from the first moments that he would love her, and the warmth in his eyes was clearly noticed by Antigone.

Antigone smiled at Pyrrhus again and invited him to walk in the palace gardens with her. Pyrrhus gladly accepted the invitation and offered his arm, which Antigone took. Even this slight touch was intoxicating. Walking through the queen's apartments and through the wide doors out to the garden, with this beautiful lady on his arm, close enough to her to smell the subtle but exquisite perfume she always wore, left Pyrrhus in a mental turmoil. He was already aware of the stirrings of both love and desire that he had only experienced briefly in his young life, and that a long time ago, in Epirus, when his life had been peaceful and ordered. On that previous occasion, he had felt desire but little love, the object of which was the particularly pretty daughter of an Epirote nobleman who brought his daughter to a reception at the royal palace. On that occasion, he had been the great man, the king, and his confidence had known no bounds. Now, however, he was confronted with a combination of beauty and grace he had not imagined possible and feared more than anything that he would appear to be an uncouth boor to the lovely young princess whose hand rested on his arm.

"My mother tells me that you and Pharaoh had an eventful journey to Siwa, Pyrrhus."

"That is true, my lady. The journey itself would have made the trip worthwhile, but the visit to the oracle was quite illuminating."

"From what my mother told me, 'illuminating' would be something of an understatement."

Pyrrhus laughed at this rather accurate statement. "That is true, I must admit. The priestess appeared to believe she was giving me a message from God. The difficult part is how much of it I should believe myself. I would be quite happy if it did turn out to be a true prediction, as there was much more good news than bad. Have you ever had such an experience yourself?"

"Not really," said Antigone. "I have been to the oracle twice and on both occasions the priestess gave me the sort of sugary sweet platitudes she usually gives my father. I say my father because that is how I think of Ptolemy. I was very young when he and my mother were married, and he has always treated me as if I was his own daughter. Also, my real father always lived in Macedonia, and he died before Mother and I came to Egypt."

The two young people spent hours walking in the gardens, chatting easily, both of them taking pleasure in their new acquaintance. They sat in a shady grove close to the palace, which was well furnished with stone benches and chairs and decorated with several beautiful statues and a large fountain. Sitting next to Pyrrhus, Antigone leaned over and kissed him. "That has broken the ice, Pyrrhus. You must call me Antigone, now, rather than 'my lady.'"

"As you wish, Antigone," replied Pyrrhus. He then returned her kiss and said, "Now the ice is properly broken for both of us."

Antigone stood up and took Pyrrhus's hand. With that exquisite smile on her face again, she said to him, "Would you like to walk over to the stables and have a look at my horses?"

"Very much," said Pyrrhus. Hand in hand, they walked to the stables. The horses Antigone took so much pride in were magnificent animals, but Pyrrhus was only able to give them a very small amount of his attention. He had eyes only for Antigone at this moment. Antigone clearly spent quite a lot of time in the stables looking after the horses and invariably riding at least one of them every day. There were six of them altogether, and she maintained her own private stables on the edge of the palace gardens, separate from those where Ptolemy and Berenice kept their mounts. Being her own private domain, there were charmingly feminine features to the stables. Pictures of pastoral scenes adorned the walls, and she insisted the stable boys kept everything very neat and tidy. All of the horses had beautifully embroidered rugs, some of which she had made herself.

After a complete tour, Antigone said to Pyrrhus, "We should probably make our way back to Mother's suite soon, my dear. She will probably be wondering what has happened to us."

Pyrrhus nodded and replied, "I am sure you are right, Antigone. But I must say that I am sorry our afternoon together has come to an end." They looked at each other for a moment, comfortable in their privacy, as the stable hands were all at the far end of the area, preparing the dressage ménage for the princess's morning ride tomorrow. Again, Pyrrhus was struck by the grace that was so much a feature of Antigone's nature. Unsure of himself, but convinced that he would regret the attempt if he did not try, he placed his hands on her waist and kissed her. To his enormous relief, she returned his embrace and they remained in each other's arms for what seemed an eternity. Antigone eventually lifted her head from his chest, looked into his eyes and placed her hand on his cheek. "We really must visit the stables again, Pyrrhus." Pyrrhus pressed his cheek against her hand and nodded once more.

Hand in hand, Pyrrhus and Antigone walked slowly back through the garden to the palace. Just before leaving the gardens and entering the palace, they embraced once more, and then made their way back to Berenice's chambers. After walking through the open doors that led from the gardens, they went through into Berenice's living room, where they found the queen sitting on a couch sewing one corner of a large tapestry. As they entered, Berenice looked up and smiled at them. "Come in, my dears. I am glad you are back. If I spend any more time sewing today, I am sure I will be cross eyed. You must both be thirsty after your walk. Please sit down, and I will arrange some refreshments."

Berenice called her maid to arrange cool drinks and something to eat. Pyrrhus and Antigone had sat down on adjacent couches opposite where the queen had been sitting. This would allow them to hold hands briefly while Berenice was out of the room.

A short time later, the refreshments were brought in, and the servants dismissed. Berenice, as the hostess, naturally got the conversation going. "I hope Antigone was able to show you some of the interesting flowers that are blooming at the moment, Pyrrhus."

"She did indeed, my lady. I did not realize that so many beautiful flowers were native to Egypt."

"Some of them are native to Egypt, Pyrrhus, but I have collected many plants from Greece and Persia over the years, and I am glad to say that some of them have done very well here. They need quite a lot of extra watering, of course, but they are a pleasant reminder of home. I love Egypt and my life here, but I try and keep some ties with my previous life in Greece."

They spoke of Greece and mutual acquaintances for some time, until Pyrrhus felt he should excuse himself, however reluctantly. Antigone walked him out of the queen's chambers. "I hope we will see each other again soon, Pyrrhus. If I can persuade Mother, could you have dinner with us tomorrow?"

"Nothing could keep me away, my dear," replied Pyrrhus. As they were now outside the queen's private domain, in the 'public' area of the palace, Pyrrhus kissed Antigone's hand as his farewell, and took her smile away with him in his mind's eye.

CHAPTER XXVI

The next evening, Pyrrhus dined with Antigone and her parents. He had been true to his word, and had sent a courier to Ptolemy an hour after sunrise with the details of the previous day's activities, having returned to the army camp after he had left Antigone.

The more sensitive issues he left to discuss with Pharaoh in person. Ptolemy appreciated the dilemma that faced the young man when he was to dine with the royal family. He had much to tell Ptolemy but was also eager to spend time with Antigone. Ptolemy therefore arranged for Pyrrhus to join him in his chambers two hours before they were to dine together so the young man could then spend time with Antigone after the meal. This arrangement allowed Pyrrhus just enough time to bathe and change his clothing between arriving back in the city and meeting with the king.

Settled on a comfortable couch at Pharaoh's invitation, Pyrrhus's enthusiasm could not fail to impress the king. "They are a fine body of men, Sire. With the right training, they could work wonders."

"I am glad to hear you say that, Pyrrhus," said Ptolemy. "I hope that my fears do not eventuate, but the fact remains that the politics of the Mediterranean are in turmoil, and who knows when I may need to use them to counter some military move against Egypt. I had hoped that after Ipsus, the kings could agree on a mutually beneficial peace, but there is as much brinkmanship now as there has ever been. The only comforts are that Egypt is a difficult country to invade, as Perdiccas and Antigonus found out, to their cost, and that the war that will eventually take place is likely to be either between Seleucus and Lysimachus, or the two of them against Demetrius.

"Cassander may take a side if he sees a clear advantage. I would expect to be able to avoid being involved, but the cost to Europe could be disastrous if their borders are so neglected that the barbarians decide to invade Greece or Italy. I can only hope that Cassander keeps his wits about him and pays attention to his northern borders. The Gauls always have their eyes on the riches of northern Greece."

"He may not be particularly likeable, Sire," said Pyrrhus, "but he is no fool. I am sure he has the same concerns as yourself."

"I hope so, Pyrrhus, I hope so. Anyway, we have done all we can, and we shall just have to wait and watch. However, I would like you to begin work preparing the materials needed to fortify an army camp in the field. Much of the timber required will have to be imported, so please provide me with an inventory of your needs. The minimum size of the army would be 5,000 men. Menestheus told me of your fortification of the camp outside Megara, and I was very impressed. In any conflict, my army is likely to be outnumbered, so I must do all I can to protect my soldiers.

"Now, my friend, tell me about your meeting with Antigone."

"She is a very lovely woman, Sire, and I thank you for allowing us to be introduced. It is my hope that I can win her heart. Any man who could do that would consider himself blessed."

Pyrrhus and Ptolemy spent their full two hours deep in conversation. Pyrrhus spoke candidly of his admiration for Antigone, and it was clear to Ptolemy that it was no fanciful infatuation. The young man was clearly deeply in love with his stepdaughter.

They spoke again of military matters, and Ptolemy was pleased to acknowledge the genuine regard that Pyrrhus had for Damocleides. It can be difficult for a king to accurately judge the capabilities of a military commander who has held his post through many years of peace. There was no doubt that Pyrrhus was completely candid with Ptolemy, nor was there any doubt that he regarded Damocleides as a fine soldier. Together with his confidence in Pyrrhus, Ptolemy could assuage his political concerns with the knowledge that the men who served him were as good as he could wish for.

They had just finished discussing the process of cataloguing the materials needed for the fortified camp, when Leontidas entered Pharaoh's office. After a deep bow, Leontidas said, "Sire, I am sorry to interrupt you, but the queen wishes you to know that dinner will be served shortly." This seemed the best way to put it, so that Ptolemy could not blame him for disturbing important work.

Ptolemy looked up at Leontidas and replied, "Thank you, Leontidas. King Pyrrhus and I have just finished our work. Please tell the queen that we will join her shortly."

After Leontidas had left, Ptolemy sat in a comfortable chair and invited Pyrrhus to do the same. "I think that we have covered most of the important matters, Pyrrhus. I will be happy for you to use your own judgment in any additional material that you feel we require. I would be grateful, however, if you would include any additional requisitioning in your daily reports. I feel much more comfortable when I understand all that goes on with my troops, it gives me a feel of their battle readiness. And now, my friend, we can enjoy a relaxing dinner. Let us join the ladies."

Ptolemy and Pyrrhus made their way to the dining room to find Berenice and Antigone waiting for them.

CHAPTER XXVII

When Pyrrhus and Menestheus first commenced their duties at the army camp in earnest, they worked at a furious pace for several weeks. They came to understand, however, that they could not train a whole army in a matter of days, and eventually established a routine and a pace of work that they could be comfortable with that avoided a state of perpetual exhaustion. They were able to be satisfied with the progress they made in the three days that they spent at the camp each week and delighted in the remaining four days spent in Alexandria.

Pyrrhus spent as much time as possible with Antigone. His love for her was returned in kind, and they also developed a friendship based on respect and trust. Pyrrhus's natural ingenuity allowed him to hold Antigone in his arms at least once every day he spent in Alexandria.

He also spent much time with Ptolemy. A large part of this time was spent dealing with practical, tactical matters, such as the progress that was being made on the preparations for the mobile fortified camp for the army. Ptolemy was determined, however, not to neglect Pyrrhus's education and spent as much time as he could teaching the young man about the broader issues of political and strategic thinking that must be considered by a king. To be able to lead an army in battle was all very well, but a victory must serve a political end for it to achieve anything. This was the true art of war. That most warlike of nations, the Spartans, paid their greatest honors to the commander of an army who could achieve the ends of a campaign without bloodshed. They were too wise to believe that the greatest glory should go to the Spartan king who fought and won the bloodiest battles.

There was another goal that Ptolemy had set himself. He recognized that Pyrrhus was as good a student and protégé that a king could ask for. Was Ptolemy less of a man than Epaminondas? Could he not present to the world a man as great as the Philip who returned to Macedonia after his time in Thebes? Ptolemy had witnessed the deeds of Alexander and played his part in the turbulent world that existed after his death. There was still much to be done, and Pyrrhus, possibly, would be one of the men who would shape the world of the next generation. It brought a smile to Ptolemy's face when he reflected that the age of military and political high adventure was not yet over.

Weeks became months. The news of Pyrrhus's engagement to Antigone was expected by the day. The army being trained by Pyrrhus was reaching a fine state of discipline and expertise, and he had completed most of the preparations for the fortification of an army camp.

It was now Ptolemy's opportunity to surprise Pyrrhus. Ptolemy had sworn all of his officers and servants to silence regarding this topic, as he wished to be the one to present Pyrrhus with the announcement of a completely improbable event. This event was the annual Grecian Games that Ptolemy held for his army. The games were modeled on the Olympic and Isthmian games, to name but two, which had been held in Greece for many hundreds of years. Unlike the Greek games that inspired him, these games were solely athletic contests, there being no contests for poetry or drama. Ptolemy had had reservations about the degree that he could expect his soldiers to contribute to and appreciate Greek literature, and had no desire to see his pet project fail because of excessively grandiose expectations.

It was still Pyrrhus's habit to spend several hours with Ptolemy on the day that he returned to Alexandria after his three-day spell at the army camp. It was on such a day that Ptolemy invited Pyrrhus to sit down and join him in a cup of wine after he had finished presenting his report of military matters at the army camp.

After they had settled themselves comfortably on couches in Ptolemy's office, Ptolemy said to Pyrrhus, "I am very pleased with the progress you have made, my son, both with the training of the troops, and also the preparations for the fortified camp for the army."

"Thank you, Sire," replied Pyrrhus.

"I imagine your duties keep you very fit?"

"If I cannot keep fit now, Sire, there is no hope for me. I have to try to be faster and stronger than the men, or I lose some of my authority."

"That is good, as I have a suggestion to make to you. Each year, I hold athletic games for the men in my army. As at Olympia, we hold a complete contest, and the events are open to all my soldiers and officers, and on this occasion all competitors are equal. I would like to invite you to take part. The only event I do not include in these games is the chariot race. I wanted to create an athletic contest that reflected on the skill of the individual athlete, rather than events which were determined by wealth.

"I will send you a program of the events, and you could enter any event you feel comfortable with."

It took Pyrrhus a short time to overcome his surprise, but his smile of delight appeared almost immediately. "I would be pleased to take part, Sire. I have to confess that it did not occur to me that such games would be held here in Egypt. It will be a charming reminder of home."

"That is how I feel about them, Pyrrhus. Just as Berenice keeps her flowers to remind her of home, these games are my reminder of my life in Macedonia. The games will begin in two weeks and will be held over four or five days, depending on the number of competitors. Leontidas will bring you a program, and you could let him know your choice of events in two or three days."

After the meeting, Pyrrhus made his way to the gardens outside Antigone's stables. It was here the two of them met after Pyrrhus's conference with Ptolemy. He found Antigone waiting for him. After their initial embrace, Pyrrhus said, "You might have warned me about these games. I have only two weeks to train for them."

Antigone began to laugh, and, despite his intentions, Pyrrhus also saw the amusing side. Antigone took his hand and replied, "Pyrrhus, I could not tell you. My father insisted on being the one to tell you, and, after all, the games are only a modified version of what you do every day, either with Menestheus or the soldiers at the army camp."

"That is true, I must admit, but there is such a thing as mental preparation." Pyrrhus could not keep up his pretence of irritation any longer. The sight of Antigone laughing brought him more happiness than anything else, and his own smile matched hers. "You realize, of course, that I will get you back with a surprise of my own, when you least expect it?"

"I would be disappointed if you didn't," replied Antigone, "and to partly make up for this one, I will help you choose the events that you will enter, and act as your coach." Antigone kissed Pyrrhus on the cheek, smiled mischievously, and then said to him, "Off you go to make your plans with Menestheus. When we meet tomorrow, I will let you know which events I want you to enter for."

CHAPTER XXVIII

When Pyrrhus returned to his quarters, he found Cineas and Menestheus waiting for him, apparently reading in the living room. On this occasion, however, their concentration was such that they could have absorbed just as much if their scrolls were upside down. They knew they would have to explain their silence about the forthcoming games, about which Pyrrhus seemed to be the only person in ignorance.

"I hope you gentlemen are enjoying your afternoon read," said Pyrrhus. "I have just received a very tempting invitation from Ptolemy to take part in the army games, which are to take place shortly. Perhaps you have heard of them?"

Menestheus stood up and placed his scroll on the table beside him. "Good afternoon, Sire. I must admit that I was told about the games some weeks ago. All I can say in my own defense is that Pharaoh himself swore me to silence. He insisted that he be the one to tell you about them." Having confessed to keeping his king in the dark about an important subject, he stood and awaited his fate. Pyrrhus intended to let Menestheus sweat for a few moments, and so he casually walked to his usual chair and sat down, keeping a grim expression on his face. After a suitable interval, Pyrrhus replied, "I would like to point out to you, Menestheus, and to you Cineas, that the two of you are my royal council and my eyes and ears in the world around us. In the future, I expect that neither of you will keep secrets from me." Pyrrhus let his words have their effect for a few moments, then put aside his demeanor and said to them with a smile, "Having said that, my friends, you have done the right thing. Ptolemy is the only man in the world whose instructions may take precedence over my own. Now, tell me, Menestheus, do you have a list of all the contests that will be held in the games?"

"Yes, Sire," replied Menestheus, relieved to have survived this conversation. "I have the list right here."

Cineas felt that he too must atone for his silence and added, "I have prepared a list of previous winners of the various contests, Sire. Some of the sports are dominated by people of exceptional ability, but there are several contests where you would have a very good chance of taking the laurel wreath."

"I am glad that you have been doing your homework, Cineas. Please continue."

"I have excluded the discus throw, Sire, because the current champion is something of a freak. He has always been able to out throw his nearest competitors by at least three cubits and appears to still be in fine form." Cineas began to warm to his topic and continued. "I have excluded boxing, of course, as it is ridiculously brutal. Also, the current army champion is a man before whom Heracles himself might experience fear. The three most important events that remain are, wrestling, running, and the javelin throw. I believe you would be able to do very well in each of these three, particularly wrestling and javelin. Menestheus would be one of the men who could take the running race from you."

Pyrrhus nodded, giving this information the full attention it deserved. "I will be more than happy to give Menestheus the running race if I can take out the other two. You gentlemen will be happy to know that I have engaged a coach, whom I am sure will not tolerate half measures. Menestheus, if you can keep my coach under control, I will be happy to be your pace man in the running race."

"This coach would not happen to be a beautiful princess, would she, Sire?" replied Menestheus.

"I am afraid so, my friend, and I suspect she will be a hard taskmaster. Cineas, do you have the measurements for the winning javelin throws at previous games?

"Yes, Sire."

"Very well then. Let us discuss this over dinner, and we can start our training tomorrow."

Leontidas had been warned by Pharaoh to serve a particularly good meal in the guest quarters tonight, as a peace offering for the surprise that he presented to Pyrrhus. The gift was accepted in the spirit in which it was offered, and Pyrrhus was happy to make his plans for the games while his spirits were lifted by Pharaoh's best wine.

CHAPTER XXIX

At dawn the next morning, Pyrrhus and Menestheus went through their warm-up routine while Cineas paced out the athletic fields that they had selected in suitable flat ground in the open area of the palace gardens. On one side was the track for the running race of one stade, a distance of about 200 paces. The other side was marked out for the javelin throw.

After finishing his task, Cineas sat down and waited for the two athletes to finish their preparations. He had just settled himself when he saw Antigone approaching them, carrying three javelins. Despite the early hour, she was impeccably presented. Her hair was beautifully set, and her modest makeup perfect. Her concession to the informality of the moment was her choice to wear the light linen sporting dress she usually wore if she accompanied Ptolemy on a hunt.

"Good morning, Cineas," she said as she approached him. Cineas rose and bowed.

"Good morning, my lady. I was hoping you would be able to join us this morning."

"I would not miss it for the world. I have not yet had the opportunity to coach such a fine athlete. I am glad to see that he is punctual."

Antigone's approach had also been noted by Pyrrhus and Menestheus. As they continued their sit-ups, Pyrrhus said, "My coach has arrived, Menestheus. She has a very determined look on her face, and there does not seem any doubt about which javelins we are to use."

"So it would seem, Sire," replied Menestheus. "At least we can be sure that we will not be supplied with shoddy equipment."

Antigone continued her way onto the newly created athletic fields and approached her two protégés as they continued their sit-ups. "Good morning, Pyrrhus," she said with a smile, "and to you, Menestheus. I was sure I could interest you two in the javelin event, and I have brought the three best javelins from my father's collection."

"Good morning, my lady," they both said in unison. Pyrrhus stood up and took Antigone's hand. "Is it customary in Egypt for an athlete to kiss his coach?"

"I think we can bend the rules from time to time," replied Antigone, who then kissed Pyrrhus before giving him a hug that would inspire any man not yet dead. "And now, my dear, please tell me your ideas on the events that you two intend to enter for, and I will let you know if I agree."

"Come sit down and I will tell you." Pyrrhus took Antigone by the hand and led her over to the group of chairs that had been brought for them, invited Cineas to resume his seat, and motioned for Menestheus to join them. After Antigone had sat down, the three men also took their seats. "After considerable thought, Menestheus and I agreed that we would both enter for the running race, the javelin, and wrestling. We will act as training partners for each other, and we have also agreed that we will not bear any grudge against the other if he wins."

"That sounds very satisfactory, Pyrrhus. I had come to the same conclusion myself," replied the princess. "I am very glad that you have not considered entering for the boxing. It seems as if even the winners are always at death's door for a considerable time afterwards."

"As we are both in the prime of our lives, the idea of entering for boxing seemed a poor choice, my lady," said Menestheus.

"After our warm-up session is completed we thought we would have a few practice sprints, and then work on the javelin. We will only have each other to measure ourselves against with the running, but Cineas has been able to measure out the distance of the winning javelin throw from last year's games, so we will have something tangible to gauge our progress against."

"Excellent," replied Antigone. "Have you been able to make any plans for the wrestling?"

"Not as yet," said Pyrrhus. "I hope to engage some of our men as sparring partners in the wrestling. It is very desirable to be able to measure oneself against a variety of opponents, and we do not want to get to know each other's methods too well, in the interest of fair play."

"I will not press you as to your motives in that, Pyrrhus," said Antigone, "but as you both accept it as the desirable method, I will go along with it. And now, are you two gentlemen sufficiently warmed up to make a start?"

"I think so," said Pyrrhus, turning to Menestheus, who smiled and nodded. "Very well then, let us make a start. What do you think, Menestheus, two slow practice runs, and then a run at racing pace?"

Cineas made his way to the start of the race and brought the two runners up to the line. Antigone made her way to the end of the track to judge the interval between them at the end. When all was in readiness, Cineas said, "The customary method of starting the race, Sire, is a count to three. As starter, I will count one, then two, and on the third beat I will clap my hands. The clap of my hands is the signal to start running. That is clear to you both?"

"Yes, my friend, I think we can both grasp that."

"Excellent. If you would both approach the line and make yourselves ready. Good."

Cineas went through the starting ritual, and on the clap of his hands both Pyrrhus and Menestheus made a good start and ran gently to the end of the track. The second practice run was made, and as in the first run they reached the end of the track together, then walked slowly back to the start. As they made themselves ready on the starting marker for the full-pace run, Pyrrhus said to Menestheus, "I expect you to have no mercy on me, my friend. None of our other competitors will."

"Be assured that I will do my best, Sire," said Menestheus in reply. "This is my best event, and I would like to gain one laurel wreath if I can." Pyrrhus nodded, and the two of them waited for Cineas to start them. Menestheus was the taller of the two and was of a slimmer build. He hoped that this would give him some advantage in this event, as the strength in Pyrrhus's upper body would make him a fine competitor in the javelin and wrestling.

The two men waited eagerly for Cineas to start them, and, when he clapped his hands, both of them leaped away. The decision would not result from a poor start. They gave their all in this race, and at the half-way mark, there was nothing between them. As they continued, the strain of the exertion showed on both their faces. From then on, determination became the most obvious feature. Inch by inch, as they approached the finish line, Menestheus was able to run ahead of his opponent. With a desperate attempt to regain the lost ground, Pyrrhus put everything he had into the remaining few paces, but as they ran across the line, Menestheus had beaten him by a half pace. Both of them stopped slowly and then bent over, resting their hands on their knees and gasped for breath until their hunger for air had begun to recede. Pyrrhus was the first one to straighten up and rest his hands on his hips. "Well done, my friend. Those long legs of yours do seem to serve a purpose after all."

"Thank you, Sire. My opponents in Athens were much easier to beat than you have been."

Antigone was clearly pleased with the performance and smiled at the athletes as she approached them, and then gave each of them a cup of water. "Well done, gentlemen. If you keep this up, we may have a chance after all. After you have a bit of a rest, you can show me what you can do with a javelin."

Pyrrhus and Menestheus walked around the palace gardens for a while to recover from the exertions of their sprint and then returned to the area where the seats had been set out, to find Antigone and Cineas chatting away. They then went through another warm-up routine before starting their session with the javelin. When they were ready, Pyrrhus approached Antigone. "We are ready, at last. May I have a look at the javelins you brought?"

"Of course," said Antigone. "Father assured me that they were the best in his collection." Antigone picked up the javelins and handed one to Pyrrhus and one to Menestheus. As the two men felt the weight and balance of the javelins, they could not help but agree that they had never seen better. Pyrrhus looked at Menestheus and said to him, "If we cannot throw well with these, Menestheus, there is no hope for us. Shall we make a start?"

The two athletes walked up to the line that Cineas had drawn on the ground earlier, and then paced out their run-up. After they had placed their markers, they took turns in practice run-ups, and Pyrrhus invited Menestheus to try a few gentle practice throws. After four throws each, they were both ready to test themselves against the distance Cineas had measured out. Menestheus picked up his javelin and approached his marker, tested his grip and raised the javelin over his right shoulder. After some adjustments, he was happy with the balance and began his approach to the line. His time in Athens was clearly not misspent, and he threw with classic technique. Balanced on one foot on the line, Menestheus watched to see how close his throw would be to Cineas's marker. It was a good throw, but it fell two paces short of the mark.

Pyrrhus then approached his marker for his turn. He was aware of the expectant eyes focused on him and determined to put everything into this throw. Physical prowess was still a goal that army commanders and kings had to aspire to in their younger years, and this was the event in which he had his greatest chance of taking the winner's prize. Pyrrhus made his throw and then anxiously watched the javelin's flight. From where he stood, it was going to be a closely run thing, and he walked down the field to see if he had thrown past the mark. When he approached his still quivering javelin, stuck in the ground at the textbook angle of forty-five degrees, he could not suppress the beginnings of a smile. He had indeed thrown past Cineas's mark, showing the distance of last year's winning throw, but only by the breadth of two fingers. As he contemplated his win, Antigone came up to him and took his arm.

"Well done, my love," she said to him, "but as your coach, I will get you to work on a safer winning margin. The javelin is the best event for a gentleman to win." She kissed him on the cheek, pressed his arm closer to her, and said, "I am very proud of you."

Pyrrhus could have died happy at that moment, and then felt extremely gratified that if his luck held out he may have other moments as good as this in his life. As he basked in the mellowness of the moment, Cineas and Menestheus also joined him. Both of them were presenting him with beaming smiles of delight, Menestheus being the first one to say, "Well done, Sire." Menestheus then shook Pyrrhus's hand, producing a shoot of pain up his king's arm as a result of the strength of his enthusiastic grip.

"Thank you, gentlemen," replied Pyrrhus with a benevolent smile. "I must say that my coach has pointed out to me that I must work on achieving a more comfortable winning margin, but I think we can all be satisfied with our first day's work."

Pleased with themselves, the three men made their way back to their quarters for the customary rest during the heat of the middle of the day. Cineas had already arranged for some of the men under Pyrrhus's command who had some prowess in wrestling to join them in their exercise room late in the afternoon. There seemed little doubt that the work of the afternoon would prove to be more demanding than their activities of the morning.

CHAPTER XXX

The afternoon session of wrestling did indeed prove to be less pleasant than the more ethereal events of the morning, but both Pyrrhus and Menestheus felt happy with the progress of their first day of training. They felt that between them, they had good prospects in the running and javelin, and in their first session of wrestling, both made as many throws of their opponents as they had been thrown themselves and so far had not suffered any significant injury.

They followed the same training routine on each of the four days of the week that they spent in Alexandria and also managed to fit in some training time while they were at the army camp. On Antigone's insistence, the day before the games were to start was spent resting. When the first day of the games arrived they were in fine spirits and eager to compete. They were to be just spectators on this first day, however, as this day was dedicated to the discus throw. So many competitors had entered this event that no other sport would take place on this day. To make sure that they would not lose any of their competitive edge, Pyrrhus and Menestheus continued with their running and javelin exercises at first light and then returned to their quarters to wash and shave. Ptolemy and

Berenice had invited them to breakfast with them and Antigone each day of the games and then they would make their way to the athletic fields that had been set up outside the city.

As they approached the athletic fields on the first day of the games, the newcomers were delighted at the festival atmosphere that prevailed. A large crowd had gathered from the city, and the pavilion that was set aside for the men from the army, on the southern side of the track, was filled with competitors and their friends. As there was no need for the large circuit required for a chariot race, banked seats had been set up on all four sides of the arena, and almost all of the spectators had a good view of at least part of the arena. A large box in the middle of the northern side of the track had been set up for Pharaoh and his court, and this naturally dominated the spectators' accommodation.

As Pharaoh and his family and guests entered the royal box, a great cheer of delight welled up from the crowd. The people of Alexandria clearly loved and admired their king. Ptolemy and Berenice took their places at the front of the box and acknowledged the salutation from the crowd. When the din had lessened, Ptolemy and his lovely wife took their seats, Ptolemy signaled to his chamberlain, and Leontidas announced that the annual military games were to begin. Once the next burst of cheering had subsided, Leontidas announced the first group of competitors for the discus throw. The heats were arranged so that as the morning progressed, the ability of the competitors would steadily increase. This naturally heightened the anticipation of the crowd, and the last group to be announced before the midday break contained the names of the current army champion, Cleisthenes, and the three other men who had some chance of beating him.

As Cleisthenes walked out onto the field, carrying the discus that he always used, the crowd burst out into another cheer. This man had won the discus throw every year for the last four years. As such, it was his right to throw last. Cleisthenes acknowledged the crowd's applause, and took his place near the throwing mark. Following him came the three other competitors in this final, elite heat. They, too, earned a loud cheer, not so much for their considerable ability, but for their willingness to be directly in opposition to a seemingly unbeatable champion. As was the custom with the discus event, the distance of the previous year's winning throw was marked out on the field, and this was the first point of reference for the current contest. Each throw would be given a measurement relating to its distance from this mark, as well as a measurement from the throwing mark.

Each of the competitors would have three throws, Cleisthenes throwing last in each round. In the first two heats, all four competitors threw just short of the mark from last year, and the man who had thrown second in this group, Stasicrates, had thrown further than the champion by several inches. As the third and final round of this heat began, the crowd became silent in anticipation. The first man to throw was short of his competitors' previous throws by a hand's width. His contribution to the contest was only to increase the suspense. Stasicrates then approached the mark and made his throw, which was better again so that his distance was two fingers' width greater than last year's winning throw. Number three's throw was short of the mark, and so came Cleisthenes's last throw.

Up until now, his demeanor had been that of a man who was slightly bored with his surroundings, but in his approach to the mark for his final throw, his face showed grim determination, as if the preceding throws had been made in a practice arena, and this one the only throw made in front of the crowd and judges. After bending his body around like a young sapling, he began his throw and sent the discus flying as if launched from a catapult. Silence reigned until the discus began its downward travel to the ground, when an excited murmuring began from the crowd. As the discus came to earth, a huge cheer erupted, as Cleisthenes had bettered his previous winning throw by a full cubit. As if the issue had never been in doubt, Cleisthenes smiled benevolently to the crowd, waving his hand to acknowledge their applause, and then shook hands with his competitors before walking to the athletes' dressing rooms.

Pyrrhus, who was also on his feet applauding the champion, said to Menestheus, "It is just as well we did not enter for this event, my friend. I think that Cleisthenes could bring himself to better any throw that his competitors could make."

Ptolemy signaled to Leontidas to announce the adjournment of the competition until the finals began later in the afternoon. Ptolemy and his guests then walked out of their pavilion and then mounted the chariots that would take them back to the palace. A large number of awnings had been set up outside of the arena so that spectators could rest and take their midday meal in the shade, if they did not return to the city.

Once at the palace, the royal party dismounted and went inside, having arranged for the guests to return to the palace steps in three hours time to return to the games.

Pyrrhus took Menestheus's arm as they walked toward their quarters, "I will leave you and Cineas to your afternoon rest, my friend. I have arranged to meet Antigone in the gardens."

"I was sure you would do that, Sire," said Menestheus with a smile. "I will see you at the steps later on." Pyrrhus made his way to the area near the stables, where he found Antigone waiting for him. When she caught sight of him, her face beamed a radiant smile, and she walked over to him and settled into his arms. After a time, they walked over to the seats, Pyrrhus sitting on the bench and Antigone sitting on his knee with her arms around his neck. "My father takes a great deal of pleasure in these games, Pyrrhus, and at the end of them he is always rested and happy."

Pyrrhus nodded, and replied, "Is that so?"

"Yes, it is." Antigone stroked his cheek and continued, "In such a mood, he is likely to consider any request favorably." Once again, Pyrrhus nodded, and was quite unable to avoid smiling. "It might even be a good time for you to suggest that you would be willing to take his daughter off his hands." A flood of emotion welled up in Pyrrhus's breast. This would be without doubt the happiest moment in his life so far. He looked deeply into Antigone's eyes and placed his hand on her cheek. "My darling, I do not know what my life will hold. There were ominous as well as good things in the priestess's prophecy, but, whatever transpires, I will love you more than any other for the rest of my life. Is that an offer that you could accept?"

"Yes, my dear. It is the only offer I will ever want."

"It is settled then. I will speak to Ptolemy when the games are over." They spent the next little while walking in the gardens until Antigone said, "I must go and spend some time with Mother before we return to the games. Can we meet again this evening? I will tell Mother that I have invited you and your friends for dinner."

"That would be perfect," replied Pyrrhus. The lovers embraced again, and Antigone then left to join her mother, looking back and smiling at Pyrrhus before going through the garden door of her mother's chambers.

Chapter XXXI

The events of the remainder of the day unfolded as expected. Cleisthenes had thrown the discus as far as he had in his heat and had maintained his winning margin of one cubit. Despite the boredom that he appeared to show early in the contest, he was quite overcome when it came time for him to receive the winner's prizes for the fifth time from the hands of his pharaoh. Ptolemy had added an inscribed gold medallion to the usual winner's prize of the laurel wreath. Also, in each of the sports, the winner and the next two place getters would be presented with a purse of gold pieces. As a soldier himself, Ptolemy understood that it was rare for men in any army to think of themselves as well paid, and occasional glimpses of generosity were a very cost-effective investment in their loyalty.

Pyrrhus and his friends dined with the royal family. The evening was not allowed to go too late, however, as Antigone, in her role as coach, reminded Pyrrhus that he and Menestheus had to compete in the javelin throw the following day. Ptolemy and Berenice had their own thoughts as to the nature of Pyrrhus's apparent state of grace at the dinner table, but chose not to make any comment on it. No doubt they would find out in due course.

At breakfast the next morning, the two athletes presented themselves in their athletic tunics and were clearly relishing the prospects of the day's competition. They would need to be at the ground earlier than the spectators and so excused themselves early and made their way to the ground in the chariots provided, Cineas having been deputed to carry the javelins.

Although Ptolemy broke with Greek tradition in allowing women to be spectators at the games, and in requiring the athletes to wear a loincloth while competing (instead of being naked), it would be too much to ask of any conservative Greek to allow women into the athletes' dressing rooms. Antigone, therefore, had to delegate some of her duties as coach.

There were almost as many entries for the javelin as there had been for the discus, so the full day was allocated for this sport. The heats that Pyrrhus and Menestheus would compete in were toward the end of the morning session, but they were not in the very last groups in which the most proficient competitors were placed. As a result, they both won their heats comfortably and returned to the palace to rest until the afternoon competition began.

When the time came to return to the ground for the finals, Pyrrhus was aware of his increasing desire to win this contest. He remembered Antigone's comment that this was the best event for a gentleman to win, and if he ever wanted to be seen as such, now was the moment. When their time came, he and Menestheus walked out onto the field. As they approached the throwing area, they, like all of the other athletes, were intoxicated by the cheers and applause of the crowd. As they removed their tunics and stood there in their loincloths, Pyrrhus looked as much like a god as Odysseus when his appearance had been enhanced by Pallas Athene before he fought Irus in front of Penelope's suitors.

Although of only medium height, his broad shoulders and muscular physique would have enabled him to stand favorably next to the king of Ithaca.

When both the competitors and the crowd were ready, Leontidas gave the signal for the contest to begin. The winner of each heat from the morning would throw three times. By the time all of the competitors had thrown twice, Pyrrhus was running second, his throw being just behind that of a young captain of hypaspists. Menestheus appeared out of contention in sixth place. So far, Pyrrhus and the captain had been the only ones to throw past the mark of last year's winner. As the turn of the young captain came up for his third throw, he walked past Pyrrhus on his way to the mark and said to him, "Good luck, Sire." Pyrrhus smiled to the young man and replied, "Thank you, Pheidon. I know you will keep me honest."

Pheidon carefully positioned himself and balanced his javelin over his right shoulder. Happy with his preparation he began his run-up and threw. It was his best throw of the day, and he had thrown half a cubit past the mark. It was now Pyrrhus's turn. Exhilaration and fear of failure were the two emotions competing in his heart. As he positioned himself and adjusted the balance of his spear, he thought of Antigone and the delight they could both take in the victory if he were to win. Running toward the throwing mark, his determination grew with every step, and he threw the javelin with every ounce of his physical being. The few seconds that it took for the javelin to fall to ground seemed to last an eternity, but when it finally stuck in the earth, the cheering of the crowd was the first hint that he had indeed thrown past his rival. The signal from the line judge confirmed it—he had thrown further than Pheidon by the breadth of a hand. The camaraderie of athletes was then exemplified by Pheidon. As soon as Pyrrhus's winning throw was confirmed, Pheidon approached him and offered him his hand. "Well done, Sire. I am sure that no one will be able to take this from you now."

"Thank you, my friend. I am sure that you will take the laurel wreath next year."

So it proved. The remaining throws did not alter the first three places, but Menestheus was able to rise to fourth place. He would have to make the running race his share of immortality.

When the time came for the victor's presentation to be made, Pyrrhus made his way to Pharaoh's pavilion, along with Pheidon and the young phalangite who had taken third place. Ptolemy walked up to him and placed the laurel wreath on his head and the cord of the gold medallion around his neck, then said to him, "Well done, my son." Pyrrhus bent his head and replied, "Thank you, Father." Fortunately, Pyrrhus was not required to say anything more, as he would have been quite unable to do so. Ptolemy smiled at him, presented him with the remaining prize of the purse of gold pieces, and then moved along to reward the other two athletes. Ptolemy then moved to one side and waved his hand toward the three finalists, indicating that the crowd could now show their appreciation.

The immense applause that came from the men from the army touched Pyrrhus deeply. He placed his hands on his heart and bowed, and then took the hands of his fellow finalists in his own, and raised them above his head, provoking another roar of cheering.

When it was over, Pyrrhus asked for the attention of all the athletes in the dressing rooms. "Gentlemen, as we have all had a successful day, I would like all of you to be my guests at dinner tonight. I am sure that Leontidas can recommend an inn that could accommodate all of us. Let us meet at the steps of the palace in two hours' time, and we can make our way there."

Leontidas had a fortunately phlegmatic nature and dealt easily with all the additional duties that were placed in front of him. Without any demur, he undertook to have his favorite inn ready to receive the celebrants for the evening's celebrations and, having made the arrangements, to be at the palace steps at the appointed time to guide the group to the inn. He also made one additional call to his friend, the imperial treasurer, to pick up sufficient gold pieces to cover the expenses of the evening.

Pyrrhus was able to meet Antigone briefly before the celebrations of the evening were to begin. "I am sorry that our meeting will be so short, but I felt that I had to offer my hospitality tonight," he said as he held Antigone in his arms.

"You are quite right, my dear. On this occasion, you are my father's ambassador, and the goodwill you will create among the men is priceless. Tomorrow is the day for the boxing, and you can be mine all day."

It was extremely fortunate for Pyrrhus that he did not have to compete the next day. His duties as host required him to drink with his guests until the evening finally came to a close. Having had an excellent meal, the athletes were pleased to talk over their many cups for what seemed an eternity. It was not for them to pay less than a full compliment to Pharaoh's hospitality.

It was a rather haggard Pyrrhus who presented himself at breakfast the next morning, Cineas and Menestheus being in only slightly better form. This naturally caused considerable amusement to Ptolemy and Berenice, and Antigone wavered between amusement and irritation at the backward steps that Pyrrhus had taken in his training program. She could not keep up the pretence of displeasure for very long, however, and disappeared from the breakfast table for a short time to prepare a tonic that would ease the throbbing headaches of her three patients. By the time the group left the palace, the three miscreants were beginning to feel human once again, although they were extremely glad to gain the shade of the imperial pavilion. Even the mild morning glare of sunlight was seemingly intolerable.

The boxing attracted a smaller field than the events of the first two days, but by its nature took longer to run its course, so that the full day was allocated to it. Despite changes to the rules to try and reduce the severity of the injuries, such as softer gloves and earlier decisions as to the winner, it remained a brutal sport. Berenice and Antigone could not bring themselves to attend the finals in the afternoon. The incumbent champion, as expected, made short work of all his adversaries, but even he could barely stand when it came time for him to receive his prizes from Pharaoh.

As Pyrrhus embraced Antigone in the palace gardens after the day's activities were over, she held him tight and said to him, with tears in her eyes, "I am so glad you did not enter for the boxing, Pyrrhus. It was terrible to watch all those brave men suffer so much."

"It has always been the same, my dear. Homer himself gives a very sobering account of it. Perhaps it will not always be included in the games."

"I hope not. And how are you feeling?"

"Much better, thank you," replied Pyrrhus with a laugh. "Your tonic was a godsend. Cineas and Menestheus also send you their thanks."

"Will you be fit for the wrestling tomorrow? You still look a little pale."

"I will be as good as gold tomorrow, but I have my reservations about taking the laurel. Some of the men are much better than I expected."

CHAPTER XXXII

The wrestling proved to be a struggle for both Pyrrhus and Menestheus.

Menestheus met the eventual winner in one of the early heats, and so was eliminated early in the contest. Pyrrhus had better fortune and was able to progress to the final. As he stepped into the arena for this final bout, he could not but help to groan inwardly. His opponent was the most muscular man he had seen in his life. After both men had been struggling for some time to throw the other, with welt marks over all of their upper bodies, Pyrrhus thought to himself that he might as well try to throw one of the pyramids. The slight relaxation of his grip that accompanied his inward amusement was not lost on his opponent, and the next thing that Pyrrhus was aware of was lying on his back on the ground, staring up at the sky.

"It appears you have won the day, Eudemus," Pyrrhus said to the man looking down at him.

"So it would seem, Sire," replied his opponent, taking Pyrrhus's arm and helping him to his feet. Eudemus was an extremely popular man in the army, and the crowd was very vocal in its pleasure of seeing him win the event. Oddly enough, if an artistic competition had been included in the games, he would have been one of the men to submit pieces of poetry.

After the award ceremony, Pyrrhus made his way, once again, to the gardens to meet Antigone. As they sat on the bench, Pyrrhus said to her, "Every part of my body aches after today's competition. I might just enter for the javelin throw next time."

This brought a charming laugh from his lady, who replied, "I can see that you are desperate for your bath, Pyrrhus, so I will not keep you from it for long. Tomorrow will be an easier day. Mother would like the three of you to have dinner with us tomorrow. She seems to think that there is something that you want to tell them."

"She might be right," said Pyrrhus with a smile. "I will rehearse my lines while I am in the bath."

"Very good," said Antigone, kissing him on the cheek. "Off you go now for your bath, and I will see you at breakfast."

Pyrrhus made his way to the guest quarters, aware of the happiness that was welling up in his breast. He was also aware of some conflicting emotions. One of the products of his current intense happiness was a stirring of his ambition to make his mark in the world, and this ambition demanded that it not be neglected. There would be time for that, but for now he would have his bath and one of Hotep's massages.

As he lay in his bath, content for the moment to have no guilt about hedonism, he reflected on the curious interplay of emotions that he had become aware of this afternoon. He was about to be betrothed to a woman whom he loved beyond qualification, who would offer him more happiness than any man could reasonably hope to experience in a mortal life.

The darker side of his character refused to be ignored, however. This martial aspect had been stirred over recent months with the work he had undertaken at the army camp, and the physical competition over the last few days had brought it increasingly to conscious awareness. He knew that part of him could only be satisfied by power and conflict. Also, he would not be satisfied with the role of a king or general who merely directed the actions of his army. He had an element of bloodlust, which demanded that he be part of the brutal hand-to-hand combat where men faced the ultimate test of courage.

It was as if he believed himself to be Achilles reincarnate, and he had to ultimately meet his Hector, the man against whom he could measure himself. The man who would be the one to finally give him the right to stand among the other great captains of history as an equal.

These thoughts turned around in his mind for the length of his bath. He continued his musing as he lay on the massage table and blessed Hotep for relieving the pain in his muscles. As he stood up finally and allowed Hotep to wrap his towel around his shoulders, Pyrrhus found peace in his mind. The realization of his role in the world came to him calmly and certainly. He understood at that moment that the two aspects of his nature could, and would, be realized without difficulty. There was no doubt that he and Antigone would soon be wed, and that he would have her love, and she his, for the remainder of their lives. The newfound certainty that had descended on him during his bath left him without any doubt that destiny would reward him with greatness. As with all great matters, there was a period of agony that leads to a decision. Once that decision is reached, as it was just before Ipsus, one's mind can return to a calm state of certainty. The outcome, naturally, is in the hands of the gods. The calmness comes from the realization that one can do no more to achieve that end, combined with belief in the inevitability of that end being realized.

Pyrrhus's life would have two foci. The understanding that they were not mutually exclusive was the source of this sudden inner peace.

As he allowed Hotep to towel him dry, Pyrrhus said to him, "Hotep, my friend, I have just realized that I am the most fortunate of men. Such opportunities as are presented to me may not come in all centuries."

Hotep paused for a moment and then replied, "I have known that for some time, Sire."

Pyrrhus turned to face Hotep, and then said to him, "You will achieve your own greatness, my friend. You may be the one to comfort Pharaoh when Leontidas is taken from him."

"That is my hope, Sire. All of us in the palace understand the privilege that we have been given by God in serving such a man."

The two men had no need for further discussion. They understood each other completely. Hotep resumed drying his master and brought him his clothing.

Pyrrhus and his friends left the breakfast table early again the following morning, as two of them would be participating in the running race. As it was the premier event of the games, it was held on the last day and attracted the greatest crowd. Pyrrhus did his best to help Menestheus cope with his anxieties. The man was desperate to leave his mark on these games, and the running race was both his best and his last chance. Cineas was in almost as great a lather, as he had developed an almost fatherly attitude to his two athletes.

Pyrrhus and Menestheus were in the same heat for this race, this being the third to last. Last year's winner and runner-up were leading the groups in the last two heats. As they took their places at the line, Pyrrhus said to Menestheus, "I will be right behind you, my friend. I know you can win this race. You will also make Antigone very happy by winning."

Menestheus nodded his gratitude, and they both made themselves ready for the start. At the signal, they both made an excellent start, and they were side by side at the halfway mark. Pyrrhus was trying his utmost, but he was able to turn to his left and say, "Now, Menestheus, get going!"

In the last hundred paces, Menestheus found his stride and was able to beat Pyrrhus to the finish line by more than one full pace. When they had recovered their breath, Pyrrhus walked over to Menestheus and shook his hand. "Well done, my friend. I will be cheering for you from the stand in the finals."

"Thank you, Sire. I will be glad when it is all over."

Menestheus managed to occupy himself in the interval before the finals by having a bath and a massage and was able to present himself at the track in a reasonably calm state of mind.

As he lined up for the last run, he saw Pyrrhus and Antigone wave to him from the royal box. Having supporters in the crowd when competing in a foreign land always seems to help athletes, and Menestheus was no exception. Summoning up as much resolution as he could, he took his place on the starting line. The race begun, he urged himself to make himself run faster than ever before, and, at the halfway mark, he and last year's champion were exactly side by side. From then on, however, Menestheus was able to keep running at the same speed, while his opponent's pace began to slacken, and he was the first to cross the finish line, half a pace ahead of the next runner, last year's champion. As he walked around the end of the arena, hands on hips, bringing his breathing under control, Menestheus acknowledged the congratulations offered by his fellow sprinters, then turned to face the royal box where Pyrrhus and Antigone, as well as her parents, were applauding him. He bowed and then waved in acknowledgement, and then made his way with the other place getters to the royal box to receive his awards from Pharaoh. Menestheus, like Pyrrhus before him, was surprised and gratified at the applause and cheers from the army stand and did his best to acknowledge it. Ptolemy seemed the most pleased of all and with a radiant smile presented him with his prizes, then shook his hand and said to him, "Well done, my son." Ptolemy then rewarded the other two athletes and, with a wave of his hand, invited the other spectators to show their appreciation. This was the most rousing applause so far, as it was understood by all that it was in acknowledgement of all the athletes who had taken part in the games.

When the applause had finally died down, Leontidas announced to the crowd that the games had come to a close, and that Pharaoh had arranged for supper to be provided for all the spectators in the tents outside the arena after the final ceremony of giving thanks to Zeus-Ammon had been completed. The crowd then fell silent as a group of priests made their way to the center of the field and offered the sacrifice and closing prayers of the games.

Finally back in their quarters, Pyrrhus embraced Menestheus, as did Cineas, and they both offered their congratulations.

"I knew you could win the running race, Menestheus," said Pyrrhus, "but last year's winner did press you hard. Let us sit down and have a cup of wine in your honor. We are not due to meet Pharaoh for dinner for two hours, and I think we all could enjoy a bit of relaxation."

Hotep presented each of the men with their wine as they made themselves comfortable in their chairs. "My congratulations, sir," he said to Menestheus, then to Pyrrhus, "and to you, Sire. All of us in the palace have taken great pleasure watching you compete."

"Thank you, Hotep," replied Pyrrhus. "If you could prepare our baths now, we will get ourselves ready for dinner."

As they lounged in their chairs, Cineas said to Pyrrhus, "You and Menestheus have done very well in the games, Sire. You certainly had very enthusiastic support from the army."

"That support was a wonderful surprise, Cineas. It is not always the case that a body of soldiers shows any regard for its officers. It may prove to be more difficult to leave Egypt than I expected, when that day finally comes."

"In more ways than one, Sire," replied Cineas.

Pyrrhus leaned back in his chair and again pondered on the various dilemmas that he would have to face. To leave Egypt, he knew, was a necessary event if he was to make his own way in the world, but it would mean saying good-bye to Ptolemy, a man whom he would be honored to serve for the rest of his days.

"At least I will not have to deal with that decision for some time," said Pyrrhus.

It was now Cineas's turn to leave Pyrrhus unsettled by the knowing look on his face on this occasion. Pyrrhus could not help but think that Cineas was privilege to some private information, but there was not sufficient suspicion for him to press for details. That would be a discussion for another day.

"And now, gentlemen, our baths should be ready, and we can then look forward to an excellent dinner. Shall we meet again here in an hour's time?"

At the appointed hour, Pyrrhus and his friends presented themselves to the royal family in the familiar dining room.

Berenice walked over to be the first to welcome her guests. She took their hands in turn and kissed each of them on the cheek and offered her congratulations. Antigone repeated the process, and Ptolemy then offered his welcome and invited his guests to take their places. When they were all seated, Leontidas poured the wine, and Ptolemy said to them, "You have all done honor to the army and to me, gentlemen. I hope you have also been able to enjoy your participation in the games?"

"Very much, Sire," said Pyrrhus. "It has been a wonderful thing to find aspects of Greek life here in Egypt."

"Enough for us not to be too homesick, my son," replied Ptolemy. "I hope you found my javelins suitable. I have to say that I could not quite manage your prowess with them. Now, my friends, dinner is ready, and I am sure you will all have a good appetite."

The conversation continued about athletic contests for most of the meal. Ptolemy was able to tell his guests about the various games that Alexander had held for his army. Some of these games had been held in the most far-flung parts of his empire, in the semi-barbaric nations that were at the periphery of the once Persian empire. The great king himself often competed, and, like Pyrrhus, the javelin was his best event.

Once the dinner plates had been cleared, and fresh wine had been put on the table, along with the usual cheese and figs, Antigone offered Pyrrhus a knowing look together with a single raised eyebrow. Pyrrhus had been inwardly dreading this moment. How does one ask for the hand of the daughter of one of the most powerful kings in the world?

Pyrrhus was able to find some courage and consolation in two things. Firstly, there seemed no doubt that Antigone would accept his proposal, and secondly, Ptolemy himself was once an ordinary, although distinctly aristocratic, Macedonian, before his existence as the Living Incarnation of Ra.

Convinced that he could not put it off indefinitely, and that he seemed to be faced with the ideal moment, Pyrrhus said to Ptolemy, "There is a matter that I hoped to discuss with you, Sire, and with you, my lady," turning to Berenice. "You were both kind enough to allow me to be introduced to your daughter, and I hope now that you will allow me to ask Antigone for her hand in marriage. If fate allows me to offer her nothing else, I will give her my love for the rest of my life."

There was, naturally, a short pause in the conversation. Ptolemy smiled at Pyrrhus and then turned to Berenice, inviting her to make the first response. "Pyrrhus," said Berenice, smiling at him, "I have been expecting such a request for some time, as has Ptolemy. If Antigone wishes it, I am pleased to give you my approval, together with my own love and my wishes for your happiness together." Berenice looked to her daughter, and Antigone said to her mother, "It is what I wish for, Mother."

Pyrrhus then looked to Ptolemy, and said, "And you, Father?"

"You have my blessing, my son. It saddens me that you and Antigone will not always be here with us in Egypt, but one cannot have everything in one's life. We will all remain one family, wherever our various destinies take us." Ptolemy then looked at Menestheus and Cineas, indicating that they too were part of this family that could not be divided by distance.

Ptolemy and Berenice rose from their couches and embraced Antigone and then Pyrrhus. Menestheus and Cineas were embraced in their turn, and Ptolemy then said to Pyrrhus, "Go to Antigone first, my son, and then I would like you to join me on the balcony."

Pyrrhus walked over to Antigone. Pyrrhus held her in his arms for a time, feeling her love course through him. Keeping his arms around her, he looked into her eyes and said, "It is done, my dear. You appear to be stuck with me."

"I will learn to bear it, Pyrrhus," said Antigone, laughing. "Off you go now and speak with my father. He and my mother have been contemplating this moment for some time."

Pyrrhus joined Ptolemy on the balcony of the palace. The king had brought their goblets of wine with him, and, as he entered, Pyrrhus's goblet was returned to him by Ptolemy. "I know that you must leave us in due course, my son," said Ptolemy, "and I must say that the knowledge brings me no joy.

This realization is part of my dowry to you, however. I propose to return you to Epirus with an expeditionary force of my army, so you can reclaim your birthright as king. I would like you to give it some thought, and then we can speak about the details. I have discussed this with Cineas, and he may be able to help you crystallize your thoughts."

"Thank you, Father," replied Pyrrhus, reaching out for Ptolemy's hand and kissing it. Ptolemy took Pyrrhus's head in his hands and pressed it to his shoulder. "We have spoken enough for tonight, Pyrrhus. Go and join Antigone, and we will speak of this matter again."

So this was what was behind Cineas's knowing expression earlier, thought Pyrrhus. There was too much for Pyrrhus to absorb from this evening's dinner, and he decided to spend the remainder of it with Antigone and to deal with his destiny tomorrow.

Chapter XXXIII

The next morning, Pyrrhus and Menestheus made their way to the exercise room, as was their habit. Before they left, Pyrrhus asked Cineas to arrange lunch for them in the guest quarters and warned him that he would ask him to share his thoughts on how they should plan his return to Epirus to reclaim his throne.

When they were all comfortably seated on their couches, and the servants had retired after serving the meal, Pyrrhus poured wine for the three of them and then said, "I know that you have been giving this matter a great deal of thought for some time, Cineas. Please tell me what you think about this plan to return me to Epirus."

Cineas sipped from his wine cup and replied, "I have thought of little else since Pharaoh first spoke to me about it, Sire. Some of the difficulties that will face us will merely be ones of logistics and will relate to the amount of force that you will need to effect the coup. The most important factors are unknown to us at the moment. What is the current political situation in Epirus, and how much loyalty can Neoptolemus rely on in an attempt to resist your return? These factors will determine the nature of your return, as will the amount of goodwill that you can claim from the people and the nobility from your days as king."

Pyrrhus nodded, having had identical thoughts himself. Cineas continued, "Sire, I must counsel against a direct invasion of Epirus without first understanding the current political situation fully. If the current Neoptolemus is a popular ruler, both with the army and the populace, we could be faced with a very difficult civil war. I know that a man such as yourself would not want his country to be faced with such a destructive prospect, if it could be avoided.

"Ptolemy has offered his full support, but he also charged me with considering the various means at our disposal to return you to your country and your kingdom. He is particularly keen for the transition to be accomplished without bloodshed. It would be to our advantage to learn what we can before committing ourselves. Once we have a full understanding of the situation, it may be appropriate for you to send an ambassador to present your claim, for the consideration of the people and the senior magistrates, including Neoptolemus.

"It may also be prudent to send an ambassador to Macedonia, so that Cassander could accept political changes in Epirus without feeling that his own interests are threatened."

"You have followed my own thoughts very closely, my friend," said Pyrrhus. "Would you consider making a trip to Epirus as my ambassador? I know of no one else who would have the skills required."

"I would be pleased to do so, Sire. The first thing we would have to consider is whether my visit would be a covert one, where I would try and glean what information I could about the various loyalties in Epirus or whether I would openly be traveling as your representative with the declared support of Ptolemy."

"I have to say that I prefer an open approach," said Pyrrhus. "I am not prepared to spend the lives of my own people and Ptolemy's soldiers in a civil war if the people of Epirus do not desire my return. If that were the case, it would be better for me to remain here in Egypt."

"In that case, Sire, I would think that it would be best if I was accompanied by a force that aimed to convey dignity and demonstrate Ptolemy's support, rather than a military force that would be taken seriously. Part of Pharaoh's Royal Bodyguard accompanied by a small fleet, would be ideal."

"An excellent idea," replied Pyrrhus. "Would you go to Macedonia after leaving Epirus?"

"Yes, Sire. It would be a great advantage to have some idea of our intentions regarding Epirus before meeting with Cassander. Equally, we must not delay meeting with him any longer than absolutely necessary or he may feel compelled to act, and his interference is the last thing we need."

"The next thing to do is to speak to Ptolemy about our plans," said Pyrrhus. "I will see if he can spare us some time tomorrow."

"There is some pleasure to be taken in using our time well, Sire," said Cineas. "It will take some time for the preparations for your wedding to be made. If I was to leave for Epirus relatively soon, I could be back in Egypt with some news in time to attend your wedding."

"I know how much you enjoy international politics, my friend, and you are clearly champing at the bit. Let us ask Leontidas to arrange a meeting with Ptolemy for tomorrow, and then we can stroll around the library for a couple of hours to settle our spirits."

Late in the afternoon, Pyrrhus and Antigone were walking in the palace gardens, and Pyrrhus was explaining the decisions that had been reached earlier in the day, and the meeting that had been arranged where their ideas could be presented to Ptolemy.

"Cineas is a very astute politician, Pyrrhus, isn't he?" said Antigone.

"Very much so, my dear," replied Pyrrhus. "Politics truly seems to be his life blood."

"I know my father truly desires your return to the throne of Epirus, Pyrrhus, but he desperately wishes it to be accomplished without bloodshed. I am sure that he will approve of your plans. Is there a nice house for us to live in when we get to Epirus?"

"The royal palace is a rather humble place when compared to the palace in Alexandria, but I am sure that after it has a fresh coat of paint and we buy some new curtains, it will serve us comfortably."

"That is good. Are there some stables where I can keep my horses?"

"As many as you would like to bring with you. The Household Cavalry keep their horses at the palace, so the stables are always ready to look after a few new mounts."

"And a nice garden where I can plant my herbs and flowers?"

"Oh yes. And now I am going to keep you quiet for a while," said Pyrrhus, picking her up in his arms.

It was mid-morning the following day when Pyrrhus and his two advisors made their way to Ptolemy's office to discuss their plans. Cineas presented their ideas succinctly, and Pharaoh was clearly pleased with what he heard.

"You have given me a set of workable ideas, Cineas, and I heartily approve. I am glad that you have avoided the idea of kingship at all costs, Pyrrhus."

"I do not want to be acknowledged king at the point of a spear, Sire. If the people do not welcome me, I will not press my claim. In that event, with your permission, I will remain here in Egypt and serve you to the best of my abilities."

Ptolemy nodded, contemplating the alternatives that were presenting themselves. In his heart, he wished that Pyrrhus and Antigone could remain here in Egypt. He was equally aware, however, that Pyrrhus's destiny would take him home to Epirus and that he would be deprived of both his presence and that of Antigone. Ptolemy had made many farewells in his life, and this was one more, perhaps the hardest of them all. He had lived and fought with Alexander and the other great men of his times. These journeys took him all over the world, and Egypt was his final resting place. It pained him to realize that at a time when he wished he could finally live in peace with the people most dear to him in a country that he loved, his daughter and three men whom he loved as sons would finally depart. It was as likely as not that he would never see these loved ones again.

"If that is your destiny, Pyrrhus, I would be the happiest of men. We cannot change the course of fate, but wherever you are, I will be with you in spirit." Ptolemy reflected for a time and then said, "Cineas, you are the key to this enterprise. I will arrange for a battalion of my household guards and a handsome fleet to accompany you. Time is of the essence if you are to return in time for the wedding. I can have the main body ready to sail in three days, and I will dispatch a trireme to sail tomorrow to let both Neoptolemus and Cassander know to expect my ambassadors."

To Pyrrhus, he continued, "All I ask in return, my son, is that in your new life you continue to be a good correspondent. It will enable me to keep you and Antigone in my thoughts. That will give an aging man great comfort, and, whatever transpires, you will always have a home here in Egypt, and I will stand ready always to give you my support."

CHAPTER XXXIV

At dawn, three days later, Cineas's fleet set sail from Alexandria, passing Pharos as the first rays of sunshine lit up the horizon. It consisted of the twelve finest triremes in Ptolemy's fleet, together with beautifully presented troop carriers, taking with them a full battalion of his Household Guard. Perhaps the most telling fact that impressed Cineas with the gravity with which Pharaoh viewed this expedition was that Leontidas accompanied him as his advisor. Cineas did not know of another time when the court chamberlain had left the presence of his king.

It would be difficult to imagine any other diplomatic mission that presented a more dignified and graceful appearance, doing honor to both Egypt and the Epirotes and Macedonians who would receive them. In days gone past, the great Croesus of Lydia had complained that the Spartans had sent one ambassador in a single ship. After protesting, he received the reply, "Yes, Sire. One envoy to one king."

Cineas had acquired some of Pyrrhus's love of ships in their time together, and he and Leontidas stood on the bridge of the flagship as it led the way out into the Mediterranean. All the ships were currently under oars, and the two men watched in admiration as the many decks of oars propelled the fleet out to sea.

"Come, my friend," said Cineas, "we have much to discuss before we arrive in Epirus."

Leontidas nodded, and the two men made their way down to the captain's cabin, which had been made available to them for this voyage. After settling themselves comfortably at the desk in the day cabin, the ever vigilant palace servants, sent by Pharaoh to see to the needs of his ambassadors, brought in wine and delicacies for the dignitaries to refresh themselves.

After they helped themselves to the refreshments, Cineas leaned back in his chair, and he and Leontidas began to discuss the many possible courses that their trip to Epirus could take, including a battle at the ships.

Standing at the wharf, Pyrrhus stood with Antigone, waving good-bye to their friends. Beside them, Ptolemy and Berenice gestured their farewells, as did Menestheus.

After watching the ships until they were low on the horizon, Ptolemy excused himself from the ladies and asked Pyrrhus and Menestheus to accompany him back to his office. Pyrrhus took the opportunity to embrace Antigone while Pharaoh mounted his litter, confirmed their meeting later in the day, and then assumed a demeanor more suitable for a member of the royal court.

Once in Ptolemy's office, the king invited the two men to take their seats and then said to them, "Gentlemen, it will be several weeks before we have news from Cineas. I believe we should use this time to make our preparations. There is no way of telling whether we will be required to send a military expedition to Epirus, but we should be prepared for it if need be. Pyrrhus, I would like you and Damocleides to prepare your men on the assumption that we will need to embark an expeditionary force of 5,000 men in two month's time. The fleet commanders will be able to prepare the transports for the men and the provisions, but they will need to speak to you to confirm the number of horses that need to be transported, and also how much field artillery and siege equipment you will need to take with you. I will leave you to speak to Damocleides, and I would ask you to present your needs to me before speaking to the admirals. One week should suffice for you to clarify your thoughts. Let us speak of these things again one week from today.

"There will be another demand on your time, Pyrrhus, over the coming weeks," continued Pharaoh. "My son, Ptolemy, will be arriving home later this week. He has, as you know, been with Seleucus and his court. I sent word to him two months ago, telling him that it was time for him to return home." Ptolemy relaxed in his chair, and a wide smile appeared on his face. "Recent events have meant that his homecoming could not have come at a more opportune time. He is of an age with you two, and I expect that he will have you both out on hunting trips as often as he can. So, gentlemen, I do not think that either of you will have a dull moment for some time."

Later that day, Pyrrhus and Antigone walked around the palace gardens, arm in arm. Pyrrhus told Antigone of his inward groaning when he was told of her brother's impending return. "But I thought you liked hunting, Pyrrhus," replied Antigone. "My father thinks that you are rather good at it."

"Yes, I do enjoy it, very much. It is just that I have an army to organize and a king to keep happy, and, if I have a spare moment, I like to drop in on a certain young princess from time to time."

"We will find a way, my dear, even if it is when all of my family and the servants are asleep," said Antigone, laughing and squeezing Pyrrhus's arm. Antigone kept a tight grip on Pyrrhus's arm as they walked and at length said to him, "Pyrrhus, there is something I would like to share with you. Something that happened when you held me in your arms, after we had spoken of our life to come in Epirus."

"I remember that night well," replied Pyrrhus. "It was a night I shall treasure in my mind for the rest of my life."

"Something very special happened that night. I cannot give you a rational explanation for it, it is too soon, but I can tell you of a thing that I am as certain of as the sun rising to open the new day."

Pyrrhus smiled at his lady, and took her hand. "And what is this thing you speak of?"

Antigone returned the love that Pyrrhus had offered her with his hands and smiled into his eyes. "I am to give you a son, my dear. There is no greater gift that is in my power to give you. I am no longer a princess of Egypt; I am your wife. I will give you my love, my life, and your children. If this will make you content, then we will have happiness for the rest of our lives."

Pyrrhus looked into Antigone's eyes and pressed her hand. Filled with love for her, he leaned over and kissed her. "I am the most fortunate man in the world."

"Now that the die is cast with no retreat, you could have your fill of me. If that is to your liking?" The smile that Antigone now offered Pyrrhus was the most erotic gesture that he had ever witnessed. Laughing despite himself, he replied, "I am sure we can arrange something, even if your brother is a rabid hunter. Did I tell you about the new blankets that I ordered for your stables that were to be placed in the vacant stable boy's room?"

"No, I don't think you did."

"If you were free for the rest of the evening, I would be pleased to show them to you."

"Perhaps we could walk down and have a look at them. To make sure I approve, of course."

"Of course. If you would take my arm, we could stroll through the gardens and then you could tell me if they are suitable."

Antigone took Pyrrhus's arm and nestled her head into his shoulder. "It is a fine night for a walk."

Up until now, Pyrrhus had been under the mistaken impression that he lived a busy life. With the return to Egypt of young Ptolemy, he realized his mistake. The two of them, with Menestheus, had quickly become friends, and it was with some difficulty that he was able to limit the days spent hunting to two days per week. There were also the evenings spent at dinner with Ptolemy. Initially, they had consisted of the young men and their carousing, but Pyrrhus was quickly able to convince his new friend that a good night's entertainment could have more to offer than dancing girls and an endless supply of wine. It was only a matter of weeks before the evenings were of a sufficient tone that he could invite Antigone to join them, and, one evening, when Pyrrhus had a solemn promise from the prince that he would behave himself, Pharaoh and Queen Berenice themselves were their guests for dinner and a reading of poetry.

Pharaoh was more at ease that night than Pyrrhus had seen him since they returned from their journey to Siwa. He had missed his son terribly during his long absence from Alexandria, and had taken delight in his return. Also, he and Berenice enjoyed the preparations for the wedding. They were content to take pleasure in their remaining time with Pyrrhus and Antigone and to deal with their eventual parting when the time came. The old soldier in Ptolemy was coming to the fore as well, and he took a leading role in the plans for the possible expedition to Epirus, rather than leaving it all to Damocleides and Pyrrhus.

There is nothing quite like a military challenge combined with an unquestionable belief in the justice of the cause to cheer the heart of a soldier. The final factor in Ptolemy's good humor was, however, to the credit of the queen. She pointed out to her husband that if he found it so easy to send Cineas off to Epirus with an army and a fleet with only three days warning, how difficult could it be to arrange the same thing for himself and spend some time with his daughter and her family once or twice a year? The idea of a holiday had become quite foreign to a man who spends his waking hours being treated as The Living Incarnation of Ra. Once the idea had been clearly and unmistakably pointed out to him, he began to think that eventually he could enjoy being Pharaoh.

The dinner was an unqualified success. Ptolemy the Younger was entrusted with making sure that the dinner was up to imperial standards, Hotep had procured an ample quantity of Pharaoh's best wine, and Pyrrhus had secured the services of the finest Greek sophist in Alexandria to recite the poetry, which was naturally chosen from works of Aeschylus and Euripides. Antigone, surprisingly, arranged the dancing girls. She had no aversion to eroticism herself and had taken it upon herself to teach her brother that subtlety could achieve things that flaunting could only aspire to.

This evening was such a success that Pharaoh's happy good humor continued for many weeks. He did not neglect his work, of course, but he spent as much time as he could with his son and Pyrrhus and Antigone. His presence became usual on the hunting trips that the young men organized, and he was able to show them that an experienced and wise old soldier could achieve results at least as impressive as the young enthusiasts. He and the queen often dined with the young people as well. Ptolemy used some of these evenings to speak to Pyrrhus and his children about the politics of the world around them. He knew that the time that remained to him to spend with Pyrrhus was growing short, and he was always mindful that when Pyrrhus left Egypt, he would have come to the end of his days as a student of world affairs, and would begin his own career as a figure in world events. Ptolemy was determined that his protégé should be as well prepared as possible for the role he was to play. It also would not hurt his own son to hear some of the basic truths that a king has to accept. Antigone was also carefully nurtured, and her natural bent for politics encouraged. She, arguably, was the most important of his pupils. She could guide Pyrrhus and help him in his role as king, giving her insight and moderation as a balance to his own genius in managing men.

This group of the Egyptian royal court enjoyed this golden time in the lead up to the royal wedding. The final event that threatened to overflow the collective cup of happiness was the return of Cineas and his expedition. True to his promise, the fleet sailed into the harbor of Alexandria three days before the wedding. The lookouts on Pharos signaled the approach of the fleet several hours before it would enter the harbor, allowing the court to assemble at the royal wharf in good time to meet them. The first ship to dock was one of the troop carriers. The guardsmen quickly disembarked, and under the guidance of their officers, formed a guard of honor, leading up from the wharf to the royal platform. Once the troop carrier warped away from the wharf, Cineas's flagship made its way into position, and to the sound of a fanfare of trumpets, Cineas, with Leontidas and the flag captain, disembarked. The three men made their way past the guard of honor, approached the royal platform, and then knelt in obeisance to Pharaoh. Ptolemy, who had had his own misgivings about the news he was about to receive, consoled himself with the thought that Cineas would not make such a show of his return if the news he bore was inconsolably bad. Cheered by this thought, Pharaoh said to Cineas, "Welcome home, my friend. It is good to see you. We have much to discuss. Leontidas, I am grateful for your return. Please rise, gentlemen." Turning to the flag captain, Ptolemy continued, "And to you, Demaratus, I give my thanks for the safe return of my friends and my soldiers."

Demaratus bowed to Pharaoh and replied, "The gods smiled on us, Sire. If you will excuse me, I will attend to the remainder of the disembarkation."

Ptolemy took Cineas's arm and led him over to where Berenice and the rest of the court were waiting. The queen beamed a smile of welcome to Cineas and took his hands in her own.

"Welcome home, Cineas. It is such a relief that you have all returned safely."

"Thank you, my lady," replied Cineas with a smile. "I promised to be back for the wedding, and, with that in mind, I gave the crew no rest." Pyrrhus and Menestheus then wrung Cineas's and Leontidas's hands in welcome, then they were both embraced by Antigone. Pharaoh then introduced young Ptolemy to Cineas. Leontidas, who had no idea the prince's return was so imminent, was more overcome by delight than Pyrrhus had ever seen him. He had missed him as he would have missed his own son. Kneeling at his feet he took the prince's hands in his own and kissed them. "I have prayed for your safe return, my lord. Thank God you are back with us."

The prince brought Leontidas to his feet and replied to him, "It is truly home now that you are with us again, my friend. Let us return to the palace. Father has prepared a meal for us all."

Young Ptolemy had shown a glimpse of the true dignity of his bearing on this occasion that was not always obvious in the informal and good-natured way he went about his life. His physical demeanor was always impressive, and, like his father, he stood lean and tall with his jet-black hair brushed straight back. His face, young and handsome, showed the hawk-like lines so common in the Macedonian aristocracy. It was clear to Pyrrhus that his friend would make a great name for himself in the annals of history. What was not to be known for many years was that as Ptolemy II, pharaoh of Egypt, he would be remembered as the king who built the great lighthouse of Alexandria, known as the Pharos, taking the name of the island on which it was built. Such then were the men who had taken Pyrrhus into their family.

Comfortably satisfied by the fine food and wine that had been prepared for himself and his guests, Ptolemy leaned back on his dining couch and turned to Cineas with a smile. "Now, Cineas, I hope that you will put me out of my misery and tell me of the details of your expedition."

"It will be my pleasure, Sire. The result of this voyage is, I believe, one that we can all be happy with, but it is different to the various outcomes that I had pictured in my mind while we were on our way to Greece. It is the basis of what Pyrrhus would call, a 'three-goblet conversation.'"

"We have plenty of wine at our disposal, Cineas, and the rest of the day to drink it in."

"First, Sire, I should point out that there is a great deal of goodwill remaining in Epirus towards Pyrrhus, and most of the country would be delighted to see his return. Neoptolemus has made himself very unpopular with many of his people, and is, to a degree, aware of his political vulnerability."

"I am pleased to hear this, Cineas," replied Ptolemy. "I gather that there is more to come."

"Yes, Sire. Despite his problems with many of the people and the nobility, Neoptolemus can still count on considerable support from the army, to whom he has been very generous. The army commanders are fine men as a whole and acknowledge their greater loyalty to their country, as well as that owed to a troubled king. So, you see, Sire, that a simple answer does not present itself."

"That is clear to me, Cineas. I suspect that you are going to tell me that there is, however, a solution which you are to propose to me?"

"Yes, Sire. A demand made to Neoptolemus to abdicate in favor of Pyrrhus would be refused, and a military confrontation to follow it would lead to civil war. Neoptolemus himself has proposed a solution. As far as I know, it is a unique political path out of an impasse." Cineas sat back in his chair and continued, "Neoptolemus has proposed a joint kingship between himself and Pyrrhus, to begin when Pyrrhus presents himself in Epirus. They will have a joint command of the army, the agreement of one being required to ratify the orders of the other. Both of them would also have a double vote in the assembly and also the power of royal veto in the assembly."

Ptolemy sat in his chair and looked at Cineas. After chewing his finger for a time, Ptolemy said to Cineas, "I imagine that Neoptolemus has looked to the royal houses of Sparta as an inspiration for this escape out of his dilemma."

"That must be the case, Sire," replied Cineas.

"The great difficulty is in the undefined base of power, my friend. The Agiad and Eurypontid kings of Sparta do not have the judicial authority that is traditional in Epirus. They are the hereditary commanders of the army, but their authority, in political terms, is balanced by that of the Ephors, so that there is not an automatic polarization of the state."

"That is true, Sire," replied Cineas. "It is not a perfect solution, but it does reinstate Pyrrhus in Epirus, while avoiding a civil war."

"Let me think about this for a time. Tell me about your meeting with Cassander, and then I will ask Pyrrhus to give us his thoughts."

"Cassander is happy for Epirus to find its own path if he can be sure that it does not threaten his own dominions. The proposed arrangements in Epirus would, if anything, reduce that country's military strength for a time, with so much attention being given to solving domestic political dilemmas. He is also aware of your support for Pyrrhus and is afraid to provoke your hostility."

Ptolemy rose from his chair and walked around the dining room. After a time he turned again to his advisor and said, "Cineas, it seems that we do not have to factor in Cassander's reaction to our ideas for the time being. It is time to ask Pyrrhus what he thinks of these plans."

Pyrrhus had been anticipating the need to respond to these proposals, and the answer that he would give was almost beyond any decision making. Events would take hold of his destiny, as surely as they had when he had come to Egypt as a political hostage.

"It is an opportunity I must take advantage of, Sire. Cineas tells me that the country is eager for my return, and that the only way I can make that return without civil war is to share the throne with Neoptolemus. I must take this step, if I am ever to reclaim my birthright as king."

"I know you are right in this, my son, but it will take some time for me to be comfortable with the dangers. If Antigone agrees, I will accept your decision. It would now be inappropriate for a large force to accompany you, as it would be seen as a threat to the Epirote army, but you must have some men whose loyalty to you is beyond question. I recommend you take an Agema of 500 men, the personal bodyguard of a Macedonian king, drawn from the men you have commanded here in Egypt.

"It is the one thing I shall insist on for this venture to proceed. If the need arises, all the resources of Egypt may be called upon."

"Thank you, Father. I accept your advice, and if I have Antigone's support, then we are all agreed."

Antigone walked over to Ptolemy and took his arm. "I will make sure that the guest quarters are always ready for you, Father."

Ptolemy nodded and smiled at his stepdaughter. "That settles it then. Now that your mother has pointed out to me how easy it would be for me to visit Epirus, we will be sure to take up the invitation."

Berenice was sure that no one in the room would be able to sleep tonight without some sort of relaxation and asked Leontidas to bring in their visiting sophist.

"Read us some more of your wonderful poetry, Chryses. Perhaps a love story might be appropriate at this time of the evening."

"As you wish, my lady," replied the poet. Chryses then chose one of his own poems to read to the assembled dignitaries. He saved this poem for special occasions, as it was too painful for him to recite it more frequently. He wrote it at a time when his own heart was to be broken by the woman he was to think of forever as the true love of his life.

They had been in love for many years, but their lives had taken very different and separate courses. Half a lifetime later, when they had both been free of earlier entanglements for some time, they were to meet again unexpectedly. Their love of old had found its greatest opportunity to be fulfilled, and they both took delight in each other's company after their long separation. Chryses himself was torn between fear of the pain of unrequited love and a feeling of fulfillment of his soul, that the love that was meant to be would finally be allowed to blossom between them. It was at this time, when his soul was torn between hope and fear, that he wrote this letter of love and always believed that it was the best thing he had ever written. The hope that gave him the courage to write this epistle was to be dashed in time. This woman, who would always remain a goddess to him, finally could not bring herself to accept his love. The pain of his failure would be with him each day for the remainder of his life. This poem brought both pleasure and pain to him in these remaining years. To reflect on it brought the pleasure of the love and hope that inspired it, and also the despair of his love being rejected.

This then was the poem that Chryses narrated to the assembled dinner guests, and the combination of hope and despair that it imparted affected all of his audience. So powerful was it that the only way any of them could find peace this night was to rest in the arms of their loved ones, Ptolemy and Berenice as much as Pyrrhus and Antigone.

CHAPTER XXXV

During the next three days, political concerns were put aside, and all attention was paid to the royal wedding. Ptolemy and Berenice, with the support of Leontidas and Hotep and Pyrrhus's friends, made sure the young couple was not worn out by the wedding preparations and undertook as many of the tasks as they could themselves.

Some things required their presence, of course. One such event was the arrival of Ramses, the high priest of Zeus-Ammon, in Alexandria. Ramses arrived with his train of colleagues, acolytes and servants at midday on the day before the wedding.

Ptolemy and all his court were at the palace entrance to meet him. As the old man stepped out of his litter, Ptolemy himself was there to take his hand. "Welcome to Alexandria, my friend. It is too long since we last had your presence. Berenice is eager to see you."

Ramses bowed deeply to Pharaoh and replied, "Thank you, Sire, both for your gracious welcome and the litter you sent for me. I am getting too old to spend many days on a horse."

"Come, Ramses. My family is waiting to see you." Ptolemy took Ramses' arm and led him up the stairs to where the court was waiting. Berenice was the first to welcome him, followed by Antigone and young Ptolemy. Ramses took the two children by the hand and said to them, "It brings joy to an old man's heart to see the greatest jewels of Egypt here in Alexandria together."

Young Ptolemy squeezed Ramses' hand and then turned to his father. "Sir, I will make sure that Ramses' party are shown to their quarters, and I will ask Ramses' secretary to call on him in one hour's time."

"Yes, my son. Come to see me after you have them settled."

Ptolemy then presented Ramses to Pyrrhus. "I am honored to conduct your wedding service, Sire, and to share in the celebrations. You have my sincere best wishes for your happiness."

"Thank you, Ramses," replied Pyrrhus, "you remember my dear friends, Cineas and Menestheus?"

"Of course, Sire. Gentlemen, it is good to see you again and in such happy circumstances."

Ptolemy walked Ramses to his quarters in the palace and left him in the care of his own servants, then returned to his office, where he had asked Berenice to meet him, together with Pyrrhus and Antigone. "There will be an exercise that none of us will be spared, Pyrrhus, and I would not plan anything else for the rest of the day. Berenice will be able to vouch for this as well. Ramses has become even more obsessive in his quest for religious perfection, and the rehearsal for the wedding ceremony will be merciless. I understand that you had some sort of dinner with your friends last night, to bid farewell to your life as a single man?"

"That is true, Sire," replied Pyrrhus, whose head still throbbed. "Menestheus and your son would not take no for an answer. I insisted that we not hold our celebrations on the night before the wedding, so I sincerely hope that tomorrow will be a better day."

Antigone nestled up to Pyrrhus and took his arm. With an amused look on her face, she said to Ptolemy, "Father, I don't think we should press Pyrrhus too much about his activities last night. He seems a little delicate today."

"As you wish, my dear. Ramses will no doubt let us know when we are to present ourselves in the palace temple. Until then I suggest that we all get some rest; we have a very long day ahead of us." The party dispersed until Ramses summoned them to the temple, and then they all understood that Ptolemy's warning was no overstatement. It was an exhausted group who returned to Pharaoh's private dining room for a late supper.

As the tired group nursed their glasses of wine after their meal, Berenice said to Pyrrhus and Antigone, "There is some pleasant news to finish your day, my dears. When your wedding was decided on, Ptolemy sent a number of ambassadors to let the other royal houses know of the betrothal and to present to them the customary invitations to attend the wedding. It is very rare for such people to be able to attend, but they have all replied through their own ambassadors. Time was obviously short, and the last of the replies arrived today. Pyrrhus, I thought I would wait until now to tell you of these letters after they all arrived. The letter that arrived today was from your friend Demetrius. The gifts have been placed in the anteroom of the temple, but I thought that you and Antigone might like to read the letters tonight."

Pyrrhus's face beamed a smile of delight, despite his tiredness. He had not heard from Demetrius since his arrival in Egypt and had often wondered how his friend's life had prospered or otherwise. "I would be delighted to read them, my lady, if Antigone is not too tired." Opening gifts and letters has as much charm for princesses as commoners, and Antigone was sure she could stay up a little longer. "Pyrrhus, read the letters in whatever order you like, and then you could show them to me."

The list of letters was long and had been sent by all of the Hellenistic kings, as well as other rulers. Despite the long history of antagonism and conflict between them, Seleucus, Lysimachus, and Cassander sent gracious wishes for the happiness of the betrothed couple, and no doubt the gifts were equally as generous. A rather formal but charming letter had been sent on behalf of the people of Rome by the consuls, Lucius Cornelius Scipio and Gnaeus Fulvius. They offered their felicitations—and their apologies for not sending representatives to the wedding, but explained that a looming war with the Samnites precluded them from diverting their attention away from domestic affairs.

Lastly, Pyrrhus opened the letter from Demetrius, and on Ptolemy's invitation read it aloud, which Pyrrhus was pleased to do after scanning it for lewd comments.

King Demetrius to King Pyrrhus, Greetings.

My friend, I was delighted to receive news of your betrothal from King Ptolemy, and send my sincere best wishes to you and Antigone.

What an enterprising fellow you are, Pyrrhus, to be sure. I ask you to be my representative in Egypt, to guarantee a treaty of peace, and you end up marrying Pharaoh's daughter, no less! Your charm is truly international.

My own affairs proceed well, despite some disappointments. I believed that Seleucus and I had finally put our antagonism to rest recently when he requested the hand of my daughter, Stratonice. I agreed to the match because it seemed the best way to achieve peace between us, finally. All seemed to go well, and he was a gracious host at the wedding, until he pressed me to cede Tyre and Sidon to him as dowry, the sniveling wretch. As you can imagine, we parted on less than good terms, the only consolation being that he appears to be a kind husband to Stratonice.

I hope to return to Greece in due course, but that is in the hands of the gods.

I have sent you gifts which I hope will be to your liking. I can only guess as to Antigone's tastes, but my wife, your own dear sister, admired this dinner setting with the gold decoration. Please accept it with our heart-felt best wishes for your happiness together.

Your friend, Demetrius.

Below this was a short note from Deidameia:

My dear Pyrrhus and Antigone,

I am sorry that we are unable to join you at your wedding. We will be with you in our thoughts, however, and send our love and best wishes. I pray we will meet again.

Your loving sister, Deidameia.

Despite the dark implications, Pyrrhus and Ptolemy could not help but be amused by Demetrius's letter and the earthy description of his relations with Seleucus. Pyrrhus was glad that his friend's fortunes had improved and that Deidameia was in good spirits. If only the protestations of friendship from the other kings were as genuine. Still, at this moment, they could temporarily think that all was well with the world.

When Pyrrhus awoke the next morning, even before Hotep's appearance, he felt more alive than he had in months. His throbbing headache had disappeared with his night's sleep, and he felt brimming with energy, looking forward to Antigone finally being his wife. With his thoughts taken up entirely by his beautiful bride, he walked out of his room onto the balcony and received his first shock for the day. Expecting to watch the dawn and admire the architecture of Alexandria before the city woke up, he found the square outside the palace filled with many thousands of people who had come to see the wedding of the Princess Antigone. Some of them caught sight of him as he stood on the balcony and waved to him. This provoked a loud cheer from the crowd, and Pyrrhus thought to himself that this was an outstanding omen and returned their wave.

His only regret was that he was standing on the balcony naked. Still, one cannot have everything.

After a final wave to the crowd, Pyrrhus walked back into his chambers to find Hotep waiting for him. "I find that I have been underdressed for my first meeting of the day, my friend. I will have to concentrate a bit harder if I am to get through today."

"I am sure you will manage, Sire," replied Hotep with a smile. "I have prepared your breakfast, and your bath will be ready as soon as you have finished."

As Pyrrhus walked into the living room of the guest quarters, he felt as preened as a sacrificial victim. Hotep had gone to extraordinary lengths to make sure that he was dressed and groomed to the degree appropriate for the royal nuptials. He found Menestheus and Cineas waiting for him. They too were in a state of perfection.

"Good morning, Sire," said Menestheus. "I hope you were able to sleep last night."

"Good morning, gentlemen," replied Pyrrhus. "I slept like a baby, my friend, and I have just waved to the people of Alexandria, all of whom seem to be in the square outside. Next time, I will wear some clothes while I do it."

This caused considerable mirth, and Cineas replied, "If that is the most awkward moment you have today, Sire, then I would not be too upset."

"We have some time before the ceremony begins, Sire," said Menestheus. "Is there anything you would like to do for an hour or two? It might make the time drag less."

"The same thought occurred to me, Menestheus. I am completely open to suggestions."

Cineas had already given the matter considerable thought and came prepared. "I have been speaking to some of the officers at your camp, Sire, to get some idea of which men might be willing and able to go to Epirus with you. It seems many more men are keen to go than we will be able to take, so we are in the happy situation of choosing the best men in the army. I have a list of the names of some of the officers as well as the men, if you would like to have a look at it."

"Excellent." replied Pyrrhus. "I don't think that I could concentrate on anything more philosophical right now. May I see the list?"

Pyrrhus read through the list Cineas had given him and sat back in his chair. "Gentlemen, this is extremely gratifying. As you said, Cineas, we will be able to choose the finest men in the army and still have to turn men away. Will we be able to find enough officers, do you think?"

"I am sure of it, Sire. I have not had a chance to speak to all of them yet, but I think that many of the officers who do not have families will be keen to go. Happily, that would include some of the best officers you have."

The conversation continued, and by the time Ptolemy and Berenice called on them, they had made considerable progress in assigning men to individual units and decided on the officers they would approach, in the hope that they would join them.

At mid-morning, Pharaoh and his queen entered the guest quarters, accompanied only by Leontidas and young Ptolemy. "Good morning, gentlemen," said Pharaoh. "I hope that you are all ready for the day's events."

"Good morning, Sire," replied Pyrrhus, relieved that this period of waiting had come to an end. "We are as ready as we will ever be."

"That is as much as anyone can ask, Pyrrhus," said Berenice, kissing him on the cheek. "If it is any comfort, Antigone has had as much difficulty with these early hours of the day."

"We have time for a glass of wine before making our way to the temple, gentlemen," said Ptolemy. "It may help us get through Ramses' service, which promises to be considerable. Please sit down."

Hotep and Leontidas made themselves busy providing their masters with wine, themselves quite affected by the moment. As a man not without sensitivity, Ptolemy said to them, "Leontidas, I am sure that you and Hotep would enjoy a glass of wine. Please do so, and we can propose a toast to Pyrrhus together." Leontidas silently blessed his king and poured a glass of wine for himself and his colleague, waiting of course, for Ptolemy to drink. When all were provided for, Ptolemy stood up and smiled to his wife and his friends.

"My lady and gentlemen, today is a momentous day. We will see the marriage of two young people who are very dear to us all, and soon, we will have to bid them farewell. Let us take this moment to offer Pyrrhus and Antigone our congratulations, and to offer all these friends who will leave our shores our best wishes for their lives and happiness."

Pyrrhus raised his glass to Ptolemy, and said, "Thank you, Father."

Nothing more needed to be said, and, after raising their glasses in salutation, they all drank, savoring the moment.

"I see you have been making your plans, Pyrrhus," said Berenice, looking at the list he and the others had made.

"Yes, my lady," replied Pyrrhus, smiling. "It was the only thing we could concentrate on this morning. It did pass the time quite well."

"I understand, my dear," said Berenice. "Ptolemy, I think that Ramses must be ready for us, by now."

"Yes, of course. Shall we go?"

As the party made their way to the temple, Pyrrhus could do nothing to still his racing heart and blessed Cineas for keeping him occupied for the last couple of hours. His whole being was taken up by his thoughts of Antigone. As they walked down the passage leading to the temple, Ramses approached them and bowed to Pharaoh. "Good morning, Sire." Ramses then walked up to Pyrrhus and shook his hand. "It will be an elegant service, Sire, but long. Just think of the prize that awaits you."

"I can think of nothing else, Ramses," replied Pyrrhus, smiling at the priest. Ramses nodded and said to Ptolemy, "If you are ready, Sire, I will take Pyrrhus and his best man to the altar, and the other guests could join the congregation. When we are ready, you and Queen Berenice could bring Antigone to join us."

Ptolemy nodded to Ramses and led the rest of his family to the anteroom of the temple, while Cineas, Leontidas, and Hotep joined the congregation.

Ramses was left with Pyrrhus and Menestheus. He was beginning to enjoy his duties as high priest of Zeus-Ammon, and, with a look of sublime happiness on his face, he said to Pyrrhus, "If you are ready, Sire, we can make our way to the altar now."

"Please lead on, Ramses," replied Pyrrhus. The old man made his way into the temple, the younger men following respectfully. As they entered the temple, Pyrrhus felt a deep sense of occasion at the magnificence of the preparations. All of the resources of Egypt had been called upon to decorate the temple for today's ceremony. The skins of lions and leopards were scattered over the floor, and flowers from the most exotic plants were gathered together in huge vases. Incense from far-off India burned in lamps in the alcoves, and feathers of huge tropical birds were arranged to decorate statues of Egyptian gods and pharaohs.

At the end of the aisle stood a large statue, representing Zeus-Ammon, a figure of enormous strength, but also a god who had some of the human qualities seen in Greek mythology, to balance the severe preoccupation with death seen in Egyptian religion. These Greek qualities of the figure calmed Pyrrhus's spirit to a degree and allowed him to think of the true object of the ceremony, his union with Antigone. More at ease than at first, Pyrrhus and Menestheus followed Ramses to the altar in front of the statue of the god. Ramses asked them to stand in front of the dais, while he walked around to the other side, to face and welcome Pharaoh and his family to the ceremony.

Just as Ramses had taken his place at the dais, the choir began singing the traditional Egyptian wedding hymn, and Ptolemy and Berenice led Antigone into the temple, each holding one of her hands. She looked as exquisite as Aphrodite must have stepping out of the sea at Cyprus, her beauty taking Pyrrhus's breath away.

Antigone made her graceful way to the altar, never taking her eyes away from Pyrrhus. Reaching the dais, Ptolemy and Berenice placed her hands in Pyrrhus's hands and retired to take their places in the front row of seats. Ramses then called on the two lovers to kneel at the altar, each keeping hold of the other's hand, Menestheus standing to one side, the traditional way to guard the couple from unwanted intruders. The wedding service then began, and wove itself through what seemed an eternity of ritual. At each stage, Ramses quietly reminded the young people of their responses.

Eventually, the rites were drawing to a close, and Ramses asked Pyrrhus if he would accept Antigone as his wife and queen. Pyrrhus looked into Antigone's eyes and then turned to Ramses. In a voice that was calmer than he had expected, he replied, "Yes, my lord Ramses, I do." Ramses nodded to the young man and asked Antigone if she would accept Pyrrhus as her husband and king. She repeated, "Yes, my lord Ramses, I do."

Ramses then gave the couple the blessing of Zeus-Ammon and pronounced them, "Man and wife, king and queen, father and mother." He then took each of them by the hand and brought them to their feet. "Accept an old man's blessing, my children. As you prosper, so Egypt will prosper. Pyrrhus, if you wish, you may kiss your bride."

Pyrrhus took each of Antigone's hands in his own, looked deeply into her eyes, and kissed her. They were able to embrace briefly, and Pyrrhus whispered into Antigone's ear, "I am more desperate to hold you in my arms than I have ever been." Antigone let out a brief giggle and squeezed Pyrrhus's hand more tightly. "Soon, my love," she whispered, and then it was time for them to walk down the corridor of the temple, acknowledging the unspoken congratulations of their friends and family as they went.

Once outside the temple, the more informal events of the day would begin. The many guests, too numerous to be part of the temple service, waited in the reception room, eager to congratulate the newlyweds, and to pay their respects to Pharaoh. The various men and women that Pyrrhus and Antigone were presented to were those whom Pyrrhus could have learned the secrets of the world from, if this was an ordinary day. He met, among many others, the ambassadors from Carthage, Syracuse, Rhodes, Ethiopia, Athens, Argos, and Sparta. Today, he put aside his hunger for knowledge and politely acknowledged their greetings. His only thought was Antigone.

Fortunately, they at last came to the end of the introductions, and Berenice came to their rescue. "Come, my dears, you must rest for a while before the banquet starts."

The queen then took them out to the gardens and bade them sit down on a stone bench. "I will send a glass of wine out to you, and you will have a half an hour before we go into dinner."

"Thank you, Mother," replied Antigone. Berenice smiled at her daughter and rejoined her guests. Very soon, Hotep arrived with two goblets of wine. Remembering the queen's instructions, he presented the wine and departed straight away.

"Cheers," said Pyrrhus to his bride.

"And to you," replied Antigone. They touched their goblets together, and Antigone continued, "I don't think we made any terrible mistakes in the service, do you?"

"I don't think so. Ramses was a very patient instructor. Have you heard about my early morning audience with the people of Alexandria?"

"No, Pyrrhus, I haven't."

Pyrrhus recounted his experience of waving to thousands of people in the square while standing on the balcony stark naked. This was too much for Antigone, who collapsed in laughter. "Pyrrhus, I wish I had been there to see it."

"I could arrange a rerun tomorrow morning, if you would like it."

"That's all right. I will arrange my own personal audience for the morning."

It was now Cineas's turn to interrupt the conversation. "Sire, excuse the intrusion, but Pharaoh would like to present you and Antigone to the people on the balcony, before we go into the banquet.

"Of course, Cineas. We will come straight away."

"At least you have some clothes on this time, Pyrrhus," said Antigone. Pyrrhus's amusement lasted well onto the balcony, and he was smiling in delight as he and Antigone stood next to Ptolemy and Berenice and acknowledged the cheers of the crowd. When the crowd showed signs of early hoarseness, the royal party gave a final wave to the crowd and retired to join the banquet.

CHAPTER XXXVI

Four weeks later, Pyrrhus and Antigone waved their fare-wells from the bridge of their flagship as their fleet made its way out of the harbor of Alexandria. Although they had all been anticipating this moment for months, it was a tearful good-bye. The parting from family was painful for both Pyrrhus and An-tigone, but Pyrrhus was also deeply affected by his good-byes to Hotep and Leontidas. They had almost become a brother and father to him.

Once Alexandria had dipped below the horizon, however, the resilience of youth allowed them to put their sadness behind them and to appreciate the excitement of this journey of destiny that had just begun.

The wedding banquet had gone extremely well, and, despite the obligatory rounds of the guests made by the newlyweds, they had moments where they could whisper to each other in the perfect privacy afforded by the levels of background noise from the guests and musicians. They then spent their first two weeks of married life on the royal barge, gently cruising down the Nile, where they saw, from a distance, many of the towns and cities of lower Egypt. They stopped at only two places, however, Naucratis and Memphis. These stops were made to satisfy the needs of the Egyptian people, desperate to see the royal couple, and limited to two to retain some privacy on their honeymoon. Pyrrhus was suitably dumbstruck by the sight of the pyramids and the monumental architecture of Memphis.

Once they had returned to Alexandria, Pyrrhus was kept extremely busy with the preparations for the journey to Epirus, and Cineas left one week before them to make sure that Epirus was ready to receive them. He also wanted to make sure that Neoptolemus did not break his word.

Now, standing on the bridge of their flagship, Pyrrhus found his anticipation thrilling. It was four years since he had been deposed from his throne, and in a matter of weeks he would set foot again in his native Epirus, once again recognized as king. At that moment, he felt as if the whole world was his for the taking. Smiling at this thought, he was pleased to reflect on the remaining time that he and Antigone would have to themselves on this journey back to Greece, an extension of their honeymoon on the royal barge. Antigone's smile matched his own, and he took her hand and retired to their cabin.

Despite two days of storms, which required the fleet to ride at anchor, sheltered by the southern coast of Sicily, the journey to Epirus was indeed an idyllic voyage. The young lovers spent many hours together, and Pyrrhus met each afternoon with Menestheus and Brasidas, the captain of the flagship. Menestheus had been given the command of the 500 men who had volunteered to form Pyrrhus's Agema. On these occasions, Pyrrhus reviewed the progress of the fleet and spoke to Menestheus about the men under their command. As well as continuing their military exercises, they did what they could to relieve their seasickness in the early days of the voyage.

Pyrrhus arranged for spacious and well-ventilated areas to be set aside in each ship for a sickbay. Pyrrhus visited the men in his own ship each day, hoping that his encouragement would help their recovery.

With custom and excellent nursing care, most of the men overcame their sickness in a few days, except for a few unfortunates who vomited their way across the entire Mediterranean and seemed within hours of death when the lookout at the masthead of the flagship shouted to the deck that land was in sight. This land was the mountains of Epirus.

The sight of their destination, with its attendant adventures and dangers, did more than any physic to bring the invalids back from the brink of death. The inmates of the sickbay elbowed their way to the deck rail, claiming their sufferings gave them the right to the best view in the ship.

The discoverers of a new continent could not have beheld land with more expectation than these mariners, who had risked everything to join in this expedition. They had left a comfortable and honorable service under a great king to join Pyrrhus. They knew in their hearts that this expedition would bring danger, honor and success at best, and an early death at worst. They found their confidence and courage in Pyrrhus, who had made clear to them that he would fight with them in their front line, if it came to that. They were also inspired by the courage of Princess Antigone, who had entrusted herself to them.

Such then were the thoughts of the soldiers who gazed at the land from the decks of their ships. Antigone had changed into her finest clothes at the cry of, "Land ho," while Pyrrhus had put on his best armor, holding his well known helmet with its plumes and goat's horns in his left arm.

The ships made their way through the narrow entrance of the Gulf of Ambracia and continued their journey until they approached the fishing village where the kings of Epirus kept a country house. There the ships would dock and the passengers would step onto the soil of Epirus.

Kings and soldiers alike watched the land as they approached. What sort of reception would they receive? Would there be a battle on the beach? Would they be treated as honored guests? The anticipation was exquisite. Two hours after the first cry of approaching land, the ships were close enough to the land that the figures on the shore were distinguishable. After a long and close look, Pyrrhus said to Menestheus, "All is well, my friend.

Cineas is standing at the dock, and the soldiers are a guard of honor. They are not there to fight us."

"That is well, Sire. I will speak to the officers, and we will hoist the flags of greeting."

Cheerful anticipation now infected all on board the ships. It appeared that they would be peacefully welcomed to their new home. Soldiers are a resourceful group of men, and they were able to replace the excitement of a possible battle with that of a hoped for peaceful reception and the good things that would accompany it. There was no need for a great imagination on their part, and good food, wine, and pretty women sprang to their minds. They were not to be disappointed, as a truly extravagant welcome had been provided for the new king and his retinue.

Neoptolemus, by nature a fearful and irresolute man, had his spine braced by his advisors, and was persuaded to honor his agreement in its spirit as well as its letter, providing a grand welcome for his new associate. Cineas, who earned the admiration and support of the army, encouraged the generals to provide a grand guard of honor for Pyrrhus. Such a spirit of optimism was congenial to them, as a gesture of hope for the political stability of their country, for which many of them had already bled.

As the flagship docked at the main wharf, an elite company of guardsmen formed a guard of honor and put in place a splendid gangplank for the royal party to walk down and to set their feet on the soil of Epirus. Taking a deep breath, Pyrrhus looked into Menestheus's eyes and smiled. He took Antigone's arm, and they walked down the gangplank together. Pyrrhus paused before he stepped onto the shore, briefly contemplating the moment. Antigone squeezed his arm and whispered into his ear, "We have come home, my love." Pyrrhus smiled and took his lady onto the soil of Epirus. Concentrating with all his will to maintain a steady gait down the dock, he looked into Cineas's eyes. His friend had walked ahead of the official party to be the first to welcome his king to his homeland.

"Welcome home, Sire," said Cineas, bowing his head.

"Thank you, Cineas," said Pyrrhus. "I would have your hand rather than your bow, my friend. It is your wisdom that has enabled me to come back to Epirus."

Cineas grasped Pyrrhus's hand with the strength that the moment demanded, then bowed to Antigone. "I am pleased to welcome you to your new home, my lady." Antigone embraced Cineas and replied, "I knew you would have everything ready for us, Cineas. It is good to see you again."

Cineas then escorted Pyrrhus and Antigone toward the reception party, at the front of which was Neoptolemus and his army commander. As they walked, Cineas spoke into Pyrrhus's ear. "You are safe for the moment, Sire. The army is pleased with your return and the peaceful accommodation you have made with Neoptolemus. If he were to offer any violence now, he would forfeit his own life."

Neoptolemus's spine was still straight, and as Pyrrhus approached he stepped out in front of his advisors to greet him. "Welcome, dear cousin. I hope you will again be happy in Epirus."

Pyrrhus shook the hand that was offered him. "Neoptolemus, I would like to introduce my wife, Antigone." It was still a novel introduction for Antigone, and she darted a quick glance to Pyrrhus and gave his hand a last squeeze. Turning to Neoptolemus, she smiled and offered her hand, which the young man took in his own and then bowed.

"It is my pleasure to welcome you to Epirus, my lady. I hope you will look upon it as your home."

"I am sure I shall, Neoptolemus. It is good of you to provide such a welcome."

"Allow me to present my officers." Neoptolemus led the way toward a group of men in splendid dress armor. "Gentlemen, it is my pleasure to present my cousin, King Pyrrhus, to you." The soldiers nodded to Pyrrhus, their faces showing a mixture of pleasure, hope, and dread. They had heard much that was good about their new king, and all believed that a good colleague could be the only way of improving Neoptolemus's skills and tastes.

The element of dread was the concern that Pyrrhus could be just as bad as the king they already had, and, like Neoptolemus, it would be difficult to get rid of him short of civil war. Hope struggled with fear, and, in these men, hope was to carry the day. The oldest and most distinguished of the officers anticipated the introduction and approached Pyrrhus.

"Sire, my name is Abantes, and I have the honor to be the king's chief of staff. I also had the honor of being presented to you in the palace, before your exile. You will not remember it of course . . ."

"I remember it very well, my friend. It was the same night that I danced with the prettiest girl in Epirus. I was hoping that we would meet again today."

Pyrrhus shook Abantes's hand, looked into his eye, and gave him one of his irresistible smiles, on this occasion, quite genuinely. Inwardly, as he was presented to Neoptolemus's other officers, Pyrrhus said to himself, *Thank God, I now have one friend in Epirus.*

As Neoptolemus led Pyrrhus past his officers and effected the introductions, he looked toward the dock and saw, with some consternation, the continuing disembarkation of the finest and best equipped infantry he had ever seen. His sense of insecurity was intensified by the thought of the cavalry that would no doubt accompany them. Summoning up his remaining reserves of courage, he continued the presentation of his officers and finally returned to the official platform, where he introduced Pyrrhus and Antigone to his prime minister, Meriones.

Pyrrhus shook the politician's hand and received his bow. He then said to him, "It is a happy coincidence, my friend, that this is the third time since I left Epirus where I have met namesakes of the great heroes of Homer's *Iliad*. My companions, Diomedes and Menestheus, are as fine men as I could wish to meet, and you, sir, I am sure will do honor to the memory of the son of Molus and the squire of the great Idomeneus."

As always, Pyrrhus's manner and greatness of spirit made a powerful impression on this new acquaintance, and Meriones responded with a formal response and a deep bow that signaled his allegiance to his new king. Pyrrhus stepped back from Meriones and returned to Neoptomemus's side. He thought to himself, with two friends in Epirus, he may survive longer than one month.

Neoptolemus led the party back to where the litters were parked to return them to the nearby village, where the kings of Epirus kept a large country house and where a banquet was prepared for the royal party. They would rest there for the remainder of the day and begin their journey to the Epirote capital, Ambracia, tomorrow. There, Pyrrhus and Antigone would be officially invested as the king and queen of Epirus, to join Neoptolemus and Iphis.

Antigone's stomach had well tolerated her morning sickness up until now, and she had survived the passage of the Mediterranean with only the occasional vomit out the leeward window of the captain's cabin. But now she could not bear the prospect of lunch. So far, she had only experienced mild twinges of nausea, but she was sure that her good luck was about to end. She applied all her will to think of something else and found many things to see and understand. She had arrived in her new home, with the love of her life, and was determined to remain calm, despite the cold sweat beading on her forehead. As the litters made their way toward the palace, she found excitement in looking at the countryside of Epirus. It was a hard land, some of it quite barren. All the areas that were suitable for grazing and the planting of crops were utilized to their full extent, and each farmer had erected a small shrine on the side of the road where travelers could find shelter and make their own prayers to the gods.

It had brought sadness to Pyrrhus in his travels to hear of Epirus spoken of by many Greeks as a barbaric land, with nothing to contribute to the greater Greek world. He had spoken to Antigone of this sadness, and she now took in her first impressions of her new home. It was indeed a poor country, if this village was at all representative of the whole, but she was sure that with Pyrrhus's energy and devotion, as well as her own, the land could be made to blossom. The greatest challenge of her life was about to begin.

Epirus had had two kings who tried to bring the country into the mainstream Greek world. Alexander, who was tragically killed in Italy, when he went there with his army to help the Tarentines in their struggle against the Lucanians. Secondly, there was Tharypas, who had made Greek script the official written language of Epirus, and who had beautified many of the cities and towns of Epirus.

Tharypas's successors did not continue his good work, and it would now be the task of Pyrrhus and Antigone to continue the blossoming of Epirote culture.

After the party had reached the palace, Pyrrhus was given two extremely important messages, both whispered into his ear before they made their way into the reception hall. The first was from Antigone, who said that her only hope of making it through the banquet was if she could be given a small bowl of clear soup and a glass of water. The second was from Cineas, who took advantage of this last moment of privacy. "You are safe for the moment, Sire, but at all times from now, you must have trusted men with you, including those who will guard your door at night." Pyrrhus nodded and replied to Cineas, "I am in your hands my friend. Speak to Menestheus, and I will go along with whatever you two think is best."

Pyrrhus then sought out Meriones before they entered the hall. "Meriones, I must ask a kindness from you, as I believe that you are the man who could help me."

"I will do all in my power, Sire," replied Meriones.

"My wife, Antigone, is in the very early stage of her first pregnancy and has up until now been extremely well. Her stomach is beginning to trouble her, and she tells me that her only hope of not being overcome with nausea is to be presented with nothing but a small bowl of clear soup and a glass of water at the banquet. It may be prudent to pour her a glass of wine that could sit in front of her and give the appearance that she was taking part in the meal."

Meriones had had a similar experience during his own wife's pregnancies many years ago and said into Pyrrhus's ear, "I thank you for the confidence that you have shown in me, Sire. I will speak to the servants as soon as we enter the banquet room. I see that your general has now joined us. I will bring him over to you before I arrange the queen's lunch."

There would be many things for Pyrrhus to adapt to in this new life, and he had just been presented with two, the title of queen for Antigone, and general for Menestheus. He was hoping there could be other surprises that were as pleasant. Meriones approached Menestheus as he entered the reception hall and introduced himself. The two men had a brief but clearly pleasant conversation and then they walked over to join Pyrrhus and Antigone. Meriones said to Pyrrhus, "I will leave you in the care of Menestheus, Sire. We are ready to take our seats for the banquet now, and these servants will show you to your places. I will return shortly. Please call on me for anything you may need, at any time." Meriones then bowed to Pyrrhus and Antigone, smiled at Menestheus, and made his way to the kitchen.

Antigone took Pyrrhus's arm and said to him, "You are very good, my love. Shall we make our way in now?" Pyrrhus smiled at her and replied, "Of course. Come with me, my lady." The new king and queen entered the banquet hall, followed by Cineas and Menestheus. Neoptolemus's chamberlain greeted them as they entered. "Welcome, Sire, my name is Actor. The king and his party have already taken their places. If you will follow me, I will take you to join them."

Actor lead the way to the head of the table, and, as Pyrrhus walked through the banquet room, all those who were already at the table stood up and smiled at him. Pyrrhus and his group took their seats, and, as they did so, Abantes raised his cup of wine and said in a loud voice that all could hear, "Welcome to our new king and queen. I ask all here to join me in wishing them health and prosperity, which will in turn bring these benefits to all of us in Epirus." A cheer came up from the guests, together with loud applause. The only person who did not appear to be pleased with the situation was Neoptolemus. He did have some civil words left in him, however, and he introduced Pyrrhus and Antigone to his wife, Iphis. Once the introductions were over for the time being, Pyrrhus stood up and said to the guests, "My friends, it is a wonderful thing for a man to be able to return to his home in such happy circumstances. I look forward to getting to know my new friends and companions. I give you my solemn oath that the well-being of Epirus and its people will be the guiding principle for myself and Antigone. I give you a toast, my friends. Let us drink to the happiness and prosperity of our people." Another cheer came up from the assembled guests, then, after Pyrrhus had resumed his seat, the banquet began. It proved to be a long afternoon, but an illuminating one. Many of the guests approached Pyrrhus to introduce themselves, and it was clear that his return was looked on extremely favorably. A number of these faces were familiar to Pyrrhus from when, a lifetime ago, he had been the sole young king of Epirus. Cineas also kept himself busy and spent much time in conversation with Neoptolemus and Meriones. Menestheus, for his part, seemed to have an inexhaustible number of subjects to discuss with Abantes and his other generals.

Once the banquet finally drew to a close, Meriones approached Pyrrhus. "You and your friends must be very tired after your journey, Sire. If you wish, I would be pleased to show you to your quarters. After a good night's rest, we will journey to Ambracia tomorrow, and then you will truly be home."

As Meriones lead the party to their rooms, Antigone was almost overcome with relief. She had found that the bowl of soup provided for her had settled her stomach temporarily, but her nausea had begun to rise again toward the end of the meal. She was beginning to feel wretched and desperately needed to have some privacy and to rest. Meriones clearly understood her situation and quickly showed the royal couple their suite, explained that the servants had provided everything they were likely to need and that he could be summoned at any time to attend to them. He then left them to themselves and took Menestheus and Cineas to their rooms.

Once inside the suite, Antigone looked at Pyrrhus and said, "I will be back in a moment, my love." She then dashed into the bathroom to vomit. After washing her face and hands a number of times, brushing her teeth and combing her hair, she rejoined Pyrrhus in the bedroom and sat down on the bed. "I am so glad that did not happen in the middle of the banquet. I think I might be on clear soup for a few days."

Pyrrhus sat down next to her and took her hand. "Is there anything I can do?"

"Yes, my dear. Please hold me in your arms and tell me that you love me."

Pyrrhus did as he was asked and kept hold of Antigone while she cried for a short time. As her breathing became more regular, he stroked her hair and whispered words of love into her ear. "I will put you to bed now. I must speak to Menestheus briefly, but I will be back with you in a few moments." Antigone nodded and allowed Pyrrhus to undress her and settle her comfortably in bed. "Only a few moments, I promise."

Pyrrhus left his suite to speak to Menestheus and Cineas, whom he knew would be waiting outside his door. In a few moments they had settled the matter of posting guards outside the suite and the disposition of the soldiers so they would be able to rally together in case of treachery, and then Pyrrhus was able to return to Antigone.

He entered the bedroom quietly in case Antigone was asleep, but a voice called to him from the bed. "I am awake, my love. How do you think I could go to sleep when I knew you would be back with me soon?"

This brought a laugh of delight from Pyrrhus. "We have the whole night to ourselves, my dear. How are you feeling?"

"Much better, thank you. Will you please come to bed?"

Pyrrhus nodded, and quickly washed, and changed into a sleeping tunic. He then slipped between the sheets of the bed and took his wife into his arms. Antigone rested her head on his shoulder and placed her hand on his chest.

"Is it good to be home, Pyrrhus?"

"Yes, my love, but this is the best part of this day."

"I am glad to hear that. Could I tell you something?"

"Of course."

"Firstly, I am feeling much better, and, secondly, young ladies who are pregnant are not impossibly fragile."

Pyrrhus looked into Antigone's eyes and ran his fingers
through her hair. "I could be happy anywhere if I was with you."

Antigone smiled at Pyrrhus and blew out the candle.

Chapter XXXVII

Pyrrhus and Antigone woke the next morning when the first rays of sunshine shone through the partly open windows. Antigone had slept well and was full of hope that today could be an improvement on yesterday. She was even able to enjoy the breakfast that the servants delivered to their suite.

When they were washed and dressed, Pyrrhus said to his lady, "Are you ready for our first meeting of state?"

"Let it begin, my love."

Pyrrhus then went out to the corridor where he knew Cineas and Menestheus would be waiting for him. "Please come in, gentlemen. Antigone is feeling much better, and it is my hope that she will always join us in our meetings."

The three men made their way to the living room of the now royal suite to be greeted by Antigone, who was already excited about her new life. "Good morning, Cineas," she said as she embraced him, then greeting Menestheus in the same way.

"Good morning, my lady," they both replied. Cineas then said, "I am very glad to see you in better spirits this morning, my lady. I am afraid that yesterday was something of an ordeal for you."

"It was, Cineas, but I am sure that the worst is behind me. Perhaps there was too much excitement yesterday."

"Please sit down, gentlemen," said Pyrrhus. "Have you had breakfast? There is plenty of food and drink here if you would like it."

"That would be very welcome, Sire," said Cineas. "Menestheus and I have spent the last couple of hours with Meriones and Abantes." After Pyrrhus had made sure that his two friends had something to eat and drink, he invited them to tell him of what they had learned.

"I am glad to say that in Meriones and Abantes you have two very loyal friends, Sire. They see your return as the event that will enable Epirus to return to her former glory, and they have worked tirelessly to engage the support of the army and the nobility since they first learned that you would return to your country. As a result, you have many firm friends here, and a spirit of optimism is apparent in everyone I have spoken to. Abantes and Meriones spoke very openly to us, and it is clear that there are a number of problems in Epirus. Despite the efforts of capable men, the political system and the army are in some disarray, largely through the inconstancy and vacillation shown by Neoptolemus. He appears to be suspicious of anyone whose actions shine too brightly, which naturally leads to a great deal of caution in those about him. Also, his interference and indecision has led to much confusion. Epirus is desperate for firm and capable leadership. This is what the country wants from you."

Pyrrhus sat in his chair, digesting this information. In some ways, it was exactly what he had hoped for, that the country would both welcome and need him. The difficult thing would be to achieve his aims without obstruction or hostility from Neoptolemus.

"I am glad to hear that I am needed here, gentlemen, and that we have this much support. It will take quite a lot of tact to put things right and still keep Neoptolemus's goodwill. I will be open to all suggestions regarding how these goals can be achieved."

This statement was taken by Cineas as an invitation for him to resume his life's work. He looked at Pyrrhus with a smile, and replied, "As you can imagine, Sire, I have given these matters a great deal of thought, and I have some ideas I would like to share with you."

"You do not surprise me at all, my friend. Please continue."

"The first steps I believe you must take are to assure all the various leading men in Epirus that they have your ear and that you will work with them to try and achieve the ends which we all believe in. This has been conspicuously absent in Epirus during Neoptolemus's reign. Once the formalities of your coronation are dealt with, I would suggest that you hold a morning audience each day in the palace. You would meet with the military and civil leaders, as well as men of commerce. This will enable you to get to know the state of the country, and that knowledge will enable you to find the solutions you seek. It will take some time to speak to all the men who have something to contribute, but I would think that the most pressing issues would make themselves apparent fairly quickly. Also, it would be a good thing for you to involve yourself in matters of appeal and justice as soon as possible. As in Macedonia, the people are accustomed to having access to their king and deeply resent it if it is denied to them."

"All you have said is true, Cineas, and Neoptolemus cannot object to his colleague working for his living. There are some curious aspects to kingship in Epirus that I should acquaint you with before we settle into life in Ambracia. Although the simple description of my role is the king of Epirus, I am in fact the king of the Molossians, who are the dominant people in the Epirote Confederacy. So, there is some degree of tact required. The king is the accepted military leader of the confederacy, and as long as the various nationalities in the confederacy feel as if their interests are also being considered to an appropriate degree, then my role functionally becomes that of the king of Epirus.

"The other thing you should know about is that after the formalities of my coronation are taken care of, which will be a unique event, fairly shortly we will be presented with the annual exchanges of oaths by the king, or kings, and the people.

Theoretically, the authority of the king is renewed each year by the people after he pledges to rule justly and wisely, and the people in turn swear to respect this undertaking by giving their industry and loyalty."

"Thank you for explaining these things, Sire," replied Cineas. "I had some idea that Epirus was unique politically, but I was not clear on the details. As you say, some tact is required."

"As for Neoptolemus," continued Pyrrhus, "I will try and impress on him that I intend to do these things as his colleague rather than his rival. After that, we will have to take his reactions into account. Hopefully he will come to understand that we can achieve many things if we work together."

Cineas was about to reply when there was a knock on the door. Pyrrhus opened it to find Meriones and Abantes. "Good morning, gentlemen. Please come in."

"Thank you, Sire," replied Meriones. "I hope we do not disturb you."

"Not at all. We have just finished our breakfast. If you have not eaten yet, we would be pleased if you would join us."

Pyrrhus led the way inside, and, after the greetings had been made, Abantes said to Antigone, "I hope we see you feeling better today, my lady."

"Very much, Abantes, thank you. I am looking forward to our journey today."

"I think it may be slow going, my lady," said Meriones. "I understand the road is already lined by thousands of people hoping to see you and the king, so Abantes may not be able to take us to Ambracia at the gallop, which is his usual pace."

Antigone let out one her charming giggles at this and replied, "I am sure we will get there eventually. I know you gentlemen have already been working hard this morning. Can we offer you some breakfast?"

"If you please, my lady," said Abantes. "I was not sure when we could find time to eat."

"Please help yourselves, gentlemen," said Pyrrhus, "and then sit down and join us. Cineas has been telling us of your efforts, and

I know that the wonderful welcome we have received is largely due to you two men. I hope you will find me grateful for your friendship. And now tell me about the journey you have planned for us."

"We will be ready to leave in about an hour's time, Sire. Your men have taken it upon themselves to prepare your carriage and have been very frank about brooking no interference. They have spared no effort in the preparations so that the queen and your friends may travel in comfort. I know you would prefer to ride your horse for at least part of the way, but it would be a good thing if you and the queen rode together in the carriage when we travel the crowded parts of the road to Ambracia. This is partly due to the effect it will have on the populace, when you are seen with your beautiful queen, but it will also make my task and that of Menestheus easier. We are the ones who must ensure your safety, Sire, and we can achieve that more confidently if you are riding in the carriage."

"I am sure you are right, my friend, although traveling in a carriage does not come naturally to me. However, I am in your hands, and must take your advice." Pyrrhus turned to Antigone and took her hand. "You may have to put up with my company today, my love."

"I will try and bear it, Pyrrhus," replied Antigone, squeezing his hand and giving him one of those smiles that Pyrrhus lived for.

"Menestheus, perhaps you could tell me about the marching orders that you have given the men, and then we should all prepare for our departure."

Menestheus spent most of the night and early morning organizing his small army, and the arrangements were faultless. Pyrrhus and Antigone would travel in comfort, while their safety would be assured as much as was humanly possible. Once again, Pyrrhus felt blessed by the loyalty and friendship of these men.

These arrangements taken care of, the party made their preparations, and a short time later Pyrrhus escorted Antigone down the steps of the country house to join his waiting entourage. As they made their way down the steps, the men of Pyrrhus's Agema broke out into a cheer, which was soon taken up by the men of the

Epirote army. Pyrrhus smiled at his men and waved. "Thank you, my friends. Today will be a long day traveling, but it will be the greatest day in my life and that of my queen. Long live Epirus!"

Another cheer broke out, and the men formed up in their marching order. The men of the Agema had made it clear to their colleagues in the Epirote army that they were prepared to regard them as brothers in arms, but would not be done out of their duty as royal bodyguard. This arrangement had been argued over a substantial quantity of wine last night, and, with some prodding from their officers, the men of Epirus had agreed, on the condition that they were the ones to lead the expedition as it marched. All involved felt that natural justice had been served and felt comfortable with their individual roles.

Realizing that fate was only beginning her cruel treatment, Neoptolemus walked out of the country house with his beautiful wife, painfully aware that his presentation to the waiting escort would provoke no cheering. He smiled and waved as best he could and then approached Pyrrhus.

"I see that you are ready for our journey, cousin. Shall we make a start?"

"By all means, Neoptolemus. It is only fitting that your carriage should take precedence. I will be content to follow you."

"That is good of you, Pyrrhus. Shall we?"

The members of the royal party made themselves comfortable in the carriages, and the day's journey began. Leading the way, the cavalry of Neoptolemus's royal guard was followed by the infantry of his own Agema. Part of Pyrrhus's cavalry followed, half of the infantry marching behind them. A single column of men marched on either side of Pyrrhus's carriages, the remaining infantry and cavalry following behind. Cineas rode with Pyrrhus and Antigone in the carriage, Menestheus riding his horse alongside. Menestheus had outdone himself today. Somehow, he had managed to look resplendent in his armor and bearing despite the fact that he could not have had more than two hours' sleep last night. He chose not to wear his helmet, leaving an attendant to carry it for him. In its place, he wore the laurel that Ptolemy had presented to him at the army games, and he had decorated his horse's saddle with flowers. As they began their journey, Pyrrhus leaned out of the carriage and said to him, "You have done well, my friend. I do not know which of your two natures to be most thankful for, the soldier or the philosopher."

"You do not have to choose, Sire. Both will always be at your service."

"That is good, Menestheus," replied Pyrrhus, settling into his chair and taking Antigone's hand.

The royal party had only traveled five miles before they found the road lined by well-wishers, and, before long, both sides of the road were packed by the patient people of Epirus. Pyrrhus insisted that the driver stop the carriage a number of times so he and Antigone could alight and speak to the people. This caused Cineas and Menestheus a considerable degree of agony, aware as they were that only one assassin's dagger is needed for a dreadful deed to be accomplished. All their concerns were unnecessary on this day, however, and the only sentiments that made themselves apparent were those of hope and goodwill. Their carriage steadily filled up with gifts of flowers and local produce, and their arms ached with the constant waving.

It was indeed a long day's traveling that brought them in the end to Ambracia but an extremely gratifying one. It seemed that, for the whole day, the new king and queen were smiling and waving at the people of Epirus, and the degree of obvious goodwill was a great tonic to Pyrrhus and Antigone. Nothing can be achieved if the people of a country are reluctant to follow their leaders, but it seemed to Pyrrhus that he and Antigone could do almost anything with this amount of support.

As the cortege finally approached Ambracia, Pyrrhus felt a stirring in his breast. To enter the royal palace would be the final step in his homecoming. Ambracia was something of a rare jewel in Epirus, a handsome city where much of the architecture was inspired by the examples of Athens and Corinth. True, it could not match these two in its grandeur, but, nevertheless, it was a fine city for a king to have as his capital.

The procession slowly made its way through the crowd, and the carriages stopped in front of the palace where the dignitaries alighted. Pyrrhus and Antigone followed Neoptolemus and Iphis up the stairs, where they waved a last greeting to the crowd before entering the palace.

Careful to avoid a single moment when their king and queen were left unprotected, Cineas and Menestheus followed, with ten men of Pyrrhus's Agema. Menestheus had already made arrangements for one of the steady junior officers to liaise with Abantes about the quarters that would be provided for his men, and the roster of guard duty that would be required in the palace.

Neoptolemus turned to Pyrrhus and said to him, "I will ask Meriones to show you to your quarters, Pyrrhus. I hope you will be able to spend some time resting, and then I would like you and Antigone to join us for dinner. I will leave Meriones to take care of the arrangements."

"That would be very good, Neoptolemus. We will look forward to seeing you then."

Meriones invited Pyrrhus and Antigone to follow him to their apartments with his two advisors, who would be next door. As he walked through the palace, Pyrrhus was struck by a curious mixture of old and new. He had known this palace as his home in days past, and in some ways it seemed as if he only left it yesterday. In other ways, he felt as if he was seeing it for the first time.

It seemed inevitable that Pyrrhus's suites would be in the west wing of the palace, when those of Neoptolemus were in the east wing, the wing that traditionally held the rooms of the king and the queen. From the very start, there would be a differentiation of the two wings, and inevitably there would be assorted polarizations of loyalties. The suites that Meriones led them to were magnificently presented, however. They had originally been built to house the most distinguished visitors to Epirus, and as such were well appointed and spacious. Pyrrhus was sure that Alexander himself had slept in these quarters as a young man, when he had accompanied his mother on a visit to her family in Epirus. The thought of sleeping in the same bed as Alexander lifted Pyrrhus's spirits at this moment of turbulent thoughts and helped give him the resolve to follow his path, wherever it may lead.

Following Meriones's lead, the party came to the door of Pyrrhus's and Antigone's suite. Pyrrhus said to Meriones, "If you would kindly indulge me, Meriones, there is something I must do." Meriones bowed, indicating that he was happy to wait for as long as required. Pyrrhus opened the door of their suite and turned to Antigone. "Some rituals are holy, my love." He then picked Antigone up in his arms and carried her into their new home.

As he walked into the reception chamber of their suite, Antigone entwined her arms around his neck and nestled her head into his shoulder. This would be one of the greatest embraces that Pyrrhus would ever have, and he was determined that it should last as long as possible. He carried his love through all the different rooms, pointing out to her everything she should be familiar with. Lastly, he took her into the bedroom and reluctantly let her down so she was standing next to the bed.

Antigone took Pyrrhus's head in her hands and looked deeply into his eyes. "Thank you for the guided tour, my love. Perhaps we could do it again some time."

"I am available at any time of day for such an important duty. Shall we bring our friends in now?"

"Yes," replied Antigone, "as long as they do not stay too long. We must have some rest before dinner." Antigone then kissed Pyrrhus with an intensity of love that he had never known, which sent a shiver of fear through his soul. *What will become of me if I ever lose this woman?* he asked himself.

Antigone was aware of his shiver, and, understanding today was a day that would be overwhelming for her husband, she kissed him again. "You should feel proud and confident today, Pyrrhus. You are again king of Epirus, and the people have made it very clear that they need you to guide them. I will also stand by you, as will our sons, as long as we live."

Pyrrhus could say nothing at this moment but held his love in his arms until the fear of loss began to subside.

"I am sorry. I had a moment where I felt as if someone was walking on my grave."

"Not yet, my love," said Antigone. "I will bring our friends in now, which will make it all the sooner that you can take me to bed."

Meriones then led Cineas and Menestheus into the royal suite, following Antigone's invitation. "I hope your quarters are satisfactory, Sire," he said to Pyrrhus. "As we had considerable warning of your return, we have done the best we can."

"I could ask for no more, my friend," replied Pyrrhus. "Please join us in a glass of wine, gentlemen, and you could tell us what our decisions are regarding our immediate duties and the disposition of the troops."

Meriones was a man to whom thoroughness was a passion, and he had all his detail at hand. "Today holds little, Sire, apart from resting for the remainder of the afternoon, and dinner with Neoptolemus and Iphis tonight. Tomorrow we will all make our way to the assembly chambers, where you and Antigone will be proclaimed king and queen. Following that there will be a service of thanksgiving at the temple of Zeus. It will only be two weeks after that when the annual exchanges of oaths between the kings and the people will take place at Passeron. I hope that in those two weeks we will be able to begin your audiences with prominent men in Epirus."

"I have spoken to Meriones about our thoughts, Sire," said Cineas. "His support is vital for us to have a future here."

"I understand that, Cineas," replied Pyrrhus, "and you have my blessing. Such friends as he and Abantes are priceless. I will speak to Neoptolemus tonight about these plans, and I hope he will offer his support. Now, Menestheus, if you could tell me about the security arrangements that you have made, we will have covered the most important topics, and it will give Antigone and I a chance to rest before dinner."

CHAPTER XXXVIII

Dinner with Neoptolemus and Iphis was something of an ordeal, and both Pyrrhus and Antigone were left with an awareness of unspoken hostility. Neoptolemus had clearly proposed the joint kingship between the two of them as the last resort of his own survival.

Aware of his own shortcomings as king, he looked on Pyrrhus's proposals to involve himself in the judicial process and to hold audiences each day with his subjects as a testimony to his own inadequacies. Unable to put up a cogent argument against them, he tended to sink into a torpor of drunkenness and impotence.

It was with heavy hearts that Pyrrhus and Antigone returned to their own quarters. This was the first check they had experienced that threatened their enthusiasm and their hopes, and they lay in each other's arms during the night wondering if their dreams for Epirus would be realized.

Even these fears could not dampen their ardor for the day of the coronation, however, and the morning found them in good spirits and eager for the day's events. After giving them sufficient time to settle themselves into the new day, Cineas and

Menestheus knocked on their door and were cordially invited to enter and to take their breakfast.

"I must thank you for your consideration, Sire," said Menestheus. "Although we disturb your mornings, your invitations to breakfast are very welcome to Cineas and I, as we seem to have a number of important meetings soon after dawn."

"I know that you two are acting on my behalf, Menestheus. Also, the two of you will always have access to our door at any time. Now, help yourselves to something to eat, and you can tell me about the day ahead."

Cineas was the one to continue. "The day will progress largely as expected, Sire. Two pairs of thrones will be set up in the Hall of Assembly and Neoptolemus and Iphis will take their places early. You and your queen will join the assembly and be escorted by Meriones to your thrones where the civil ceremony of your coronation will take place. Once that has been completed, the high priest of Dodonian Zeus will take you to the temple, where the religious rites of a new king will be performed. I have been able to speak to the high priest, whose name is Oeneus, and he is potentially a firm ally. Like Meriones and Abantes, he has almost reached a state of despair regarding the fate of Epirus and has great hopes that you may be the country's salvation. I believe he is one of the few men whom Neoptolemus trusts, and he may be a valuable mediator."

"We may need such a man, my friend, as Antigone and I had a dismal night with him last night. The man appears to have no vision and no hopes for Epirus, content to merely keep himself in a comfortable position while the country languishes. He was almost offended when I told him about the audiences I plan to hold with prominent people to increase my understanding of our country."

"We will need to be on our guard against him, Sire," said Cineas. "In such a position, he could contemplate almost any action to restore his fortunes, including an attempt on your life."

"That, Cineas, I am glad to say, is your problem. I will change the destiny of Epirus. You and Menestheus will ensure that I retain my life to achieve these ends."

The day of the coronation proceeded as described by Cineas's timetable. Although Neoptolemus clearly had a dreadful headache, he managed to be civil during the proceedings, and all other aspects of the day restored Pyrrhus's and Antigone's hopes. The religious leaders, the commanders of the army, and the large crowd of his people who took a large or small part in his unusual coronation were conspicuously in his favor. Every man and woman he had looked at, with the exception of his royal cousin, favored him with a smile and a bow, and a huge number of bouquets of flowers had been laid at their feet.

The civil part of the ceremony was a noble experience for them, but the service conducted by Oeneus in the Temple of Zeus was uplifting. Oeneus was obviously a man who held great hopes for Epirus, now that Pyrrhus was able to guide her, and he made the ceremony moving as a result of his passion. This passion was what made the service memorable for Pyrrhus. He could now understand the feeling of divine light that had inspired Alexander at the oracle of Zeus-Ammon, and, after all, was Pyrrhus not being proclaimed as the instrument of Zeus's will now, just as Alexander was? This was the moment when his ambition for himself and Epirus became tangible.

Late in the evening, Pyrrhus and his queen sat once again in their quarters, drinking a glass of wine with their two counselors, discussing the events of the day.

"And now, gentlemen, if you will excuse me, I must put Antigone to bed. We have all had a very big day. I will see you for breakfast tomorrow."

"Good night, Sire," said Menestheus with a smile, "and to you my lady."

Cineas bowed to Pyrrhus, smiled to Antigone, said good night, and then he and Menestheus retired. Pyrrhus walked them to the door, and, as he returned to the living room, Antigone walked up to him and took his arm. "Must you put me to bed now?"

"I had to say something. I wanted to say that you were desperate to take my clothes off, and I had to bite my tongue at the last minute. I still live in hope, however."

Antigone squeezed Pyrrhus's arm and replied, "Come then, you can put me to bed."

After a memorable night of love, Pyrrhus gently shook his lady's shoulder as the first light of day appeared in the window.

"The first day of our new life has begun, my love. You are now the queen of Epirus, and we have work to do."

"That will be nice, Pyrrhus. But only as long as I have my king." Antigone held Pyrrhus in her arms and let her love course through him. When all she wanted was to lie down and go back to sleep in the arms of her husband, she sat up and took Pyrrhus's hand. "Come, my dear. You have to inspire me."

It was a very full day that awaited them. They met with Neoptolemus and Iphis early in the morning, and Neoptolemus's displeasure at Pyrrhus's activities was once again obvious. Pyrrhus would have to do his duty as it was clear to him and afterward try and keep the peace with his royal colleague. Antigone then left Pyrrhus to meet with Menestheus. The two of them were to interview the servants allocated to their wing of the palace to form an opinion of their loyalty and trustworthiness. Pyrrhus and Cineas made their way to the law courts to meet the magistrates with whom they would have to work.

As they arrived at the courts, Pyrrhus found the most senior of the judges waiting for him at the door to the chambers. The most influential of them approached them and greeted them as they approached.

"Good morning, Sire. My name is Tleponemus, and I would like to present my two colleagues, Lycymnius and Morys." The three men bowed, and Pyrrhus replied, "I am very pleased to meet you, gentlemen. I am hoping that you can help me to find a role in my country. I present my friend and advisor, Cineas."

Tleponemus nodded cordially to Cineas and then said, "Please follow me, Sire. We can speak in privacy in my offices."

Tleponemus led Pyrrhus and Cineas through the legal chambers to his own offices and invited them to take their seats while servants brought in refreshments. Once the servants had left, Tlepolemus and his colleagues took their seats and the judge said to Pyrrhus, "I was very pleased when you requested this audience, Sire. The legal system in Epirus has been struggling for some time without the guidance of its king. I hope that we will be able to regain some of our integrity with your help."

"That is my deepest wish, my friend. I need to be a part of my country, and this is where I believe I should start. I hope to start holding audiences as soon as possible, but I need your support and advice."

Tleponemus nodded and sat back in his chair. "We have a common cause, Sire, and I pledge our support."

"Please consider some ideas of mine, gentlemen. You and your colleagues are trained in the law and jurisprudence, where I am not. I would not contemplate interfering with your work. I see my role as something of a right of appeal, or where the issue is more philosophical than legal. In essence, as Cineas said, it is the right of my people to be able to have the ear of their king. The boundaries of my authority and influence I would like to determine with you."

Tlepolemus smiled at Pyrrhus. "Sire, my colleagues and I have prayed for this for years. I would suggest to you that you appoint a secretary whom you trust without reservation, who can receive applications for an audience with you. After discussing them with you, this secretary would then arrange for an audience. In addition to that, I would ask that we magistrates have the right to defer cases to you for your judgment. This may be because of political ramifications, or where the issue of right and wrong is not clear, and an assessment of fundamental justice is required."

"Also, as the chief magistrate of Epirus, I remind you that the king has the right to overrule the judgments of the magistrates. The only remaining point, Sire, is to pledge you our eternal loyalty, if you, as you appear to be doing, give your life and soul to Epirus."

"Then we are agreed, my friends. I will be here for two hours each morning for the next two weeks, and, after that, for the same period, on three days each week. If there are times when I have no cases to review, I will use the time to meet with additional people from the community. If you are agreeable, I will begin tomorrow, at mid-morning."

Pyrrhus left the chambers and, as they were walking back to the palace, said to Cineas, "I am afraid this will be one more duty for you, my friend. I do not know of anyone else whom I could entrust with the task of arranging audiences, apart from Menestheus, and he will have his hands full with the troops."

"I will be happy to do this, Sire. It will enable me to keep a finger on the pulse of the community."

"We are agreed then. Shall we see how Antigone and Menestheus are doing with the servants?"

Pyrrhus and Cineas walked back to the palace to join Menestheus and Antigone. They found them in the living room of the guest quarters, where they were interviewing the last of the servants. As they entered, Antigone looked up and said to her husband, "Come and join us, Pyrrhus. Menestheus and I have almost finished." She then turned to her maid, Thebe. "I understand, Thebe, that your mother and father were also servants in the palace."

"That is true, my lady. They taught both my brother and myself to be loyal to the kings and queens of Epirus. I entered the palace as a maid when I was fifteen, and my brother became a soldier in the king's army when he was eighteen. He hopes to be offered a place in the king's Agema when he is more experienced."

"That is good, Thebe. We are very pleased that you will be in our service, and I hope you will continue to be happy here."

"I am sure of that, my lady. All of us in the palace have been looking forward to the day when you and King Pyrrhus would be with us."

Thebe curtsied to Antigone and Pyrrhus and left the room to continue with her duties. Pyrrhus sat down next to Antigone and said, "What do you think of the servants?"

"Menestheus and I are agreed that we do not have any problems with the servants, Pyrrhus. They have all been in service at the palace for at least two years, and there seems to be a great deal of goodwill towards us."

"That is good. It is a relief to find that there have been no changes in the household staff since Neoptolemus first found out about our return."

"How did you get on with the magistrates?"

"Extremely well, thank you. Tleponemus was very helpful, and I will make myself available for audiences beginning tomorrow morning. I also hope to start speaking to the community leaders tomorrow. As we have no plans for the remainder of the day, would you like to go for a ride in the countryside?"

"That would be lovely, my dear, but I promised the midwives that I would not go horse riding from now on."

Pyrrhus's face began to turn grey. "Is everything all right . . . with you and our baby?"

"Yes, Pyrrhus," said his wife. "I think it is." Antigone's lower lip began to quiver, and she continued, "I have been told that if I get enough rest and avoid strenuous exercise, our baby will be well. But if I ignore their advice, complications could occur. I had some bleeding a few days ago, and a few crampy pains. They have stopped now, but they have told me that I must heed it as a warning, and be careful."

Cineas and Menestheus had become so close to these young people that they were truly family, and it was not at all surprising to any of them that Antigone chose to speak of these matters in their presence. Menestheus looked as grey as Pyrrhus, and said to his Queen, "My lady, if I had known, I would not have arranged this interview this morning."

"It is quite all right, Menestheus," replied Antigone. "I do not have to be an invalid, I just have to be a bit careful."

"You will tell me straight away, next time, I beg you," said Pyrrhus.

"Yes, my dear, I will. I had no idea what to think this time, but, thanks to the midwives, I understand what is happening, and am no longer afraid. I could not tell you about it when all I had was fear without any understanding." Antigone reached out and took Pyrrhus's hands in her own. "Our son will still join us as expected, Pyrrhus, and I will remain with you."

Pyrrhus experienced that feeling of someone walking on his grave for a second time, and the look of fear of ultimate loss on his face was unmistakable to Antigone. "Perhaps it is time for me to rest now. Pyrrhus, would you stay with me for a while?"

"Of course, my love. Gentlemen, I think we have dealt with all our issues for the time being. If you are agreeable, I will see you tomorrow morning, and we will make our way to our first appointments."

"Of course, Sire," replied Cineas. He and Menestheus then retired.

Antigone then stood up, still holding Pyrrhus's hand, and took him into the bedroom. As they lay there in each other's arms, dealing with their own fears and torments, Antigone was the first to speak. "All will be well, my love. Tell me, have you thought of a name for our son?"

"There is only one possibility. We must name him *Ptolemy,*" replied Pyrrhus, "if you agree."

"I do agree. My father will be greatly honored."

"He is more real to me than my own father, who died so long ago. I will never forget his love and kindness."

"It is decided then. Let us sleep now." Antigone rested her head on Pyrrhus's shoulder, and the two of them slept in each other's arms until the middle of the afternoon. This sleep of love was as restorative to Pyrrhus as it was to Antigone and allowed them to set aside their fears. Whatever happened in their lives, they would always have this love, and, God willing, that of their children.

CHAPTER XXXIX

Pyrrhus began his first day of official duties promptly the next morning. He spent two hours meeting a number of important figures from the Epirote community before presenting himself as promised at the law courts. His initial interviews had confirmed his view that he had the support of the people, who seemed desperate to find a king whom they could trust and who would act in the interests of their country. There was only one judicial case to review at the courts, and the preamble of the misdeeds of three young men did not endear them to him, and he was in a stern humor when the boys were admitted to the chamber.

As the boys stood in the dock, he read out to them the charge that had led to this hearing. "I am told that you three spent a large part of the evening following my coronation slandering me in a bar in the city. It says here that your comments included 'An upstart king foisted on us by Ptolemy.' The other quotes are no better. What have you got to say for yourselves?"

The oldest of the three took it upon himself to reply on behalf of the group and said, "It is true, Sire, but we would have said worse things still if we had had more wine."

Pyrrhus looked angrily at the youth for a short time but could not resist the beginnings of a smile. His reserve was quickly broken, and he began to laugh, completely charmed by the honest frankness of the reply. "You three are incorrigible. You will please me by not repeating this exercise. Off you go, and come and see me when you are prepared to do something useful."

"Thank you, Sire," replied the spokesman, and they left the audience chamber to tell their friends about their ordeal.

Pyrrhus kept himself busy with his interviews for the next two weeks and began to feel that he was beginning to understand his own country. Antigone had no more frightening episodes and seemed to be a picture of health, despite the occasional bout of desperate tiredness, which was said to be completely normal in early pregnancy.

The other crucial meeting that Pyrrhus had in this time was with the royal treasurer. Until this meeting, Pyrrhus had no idea what rights he had with regard to finance. He was pleased, however, to find that despite how incompetent Neoptolemus appeared to be, the Treasury was in good shape. Also, there was a royal account to be used at the discretion of the king, on which he now had a half claim. The general exchequer was also happily in the black. Pyrrhus now knew that his "fighting fund" to rebuild his country was sufficient for the time being. He must also look at the rates of taxation and excises. It was possible the only reason the finances were healthy was because of extortionate taxation. He may need to lessen the load on his countrymen.

The event that came at the end of his furious first two weeks as king was a very significant occasion, the annual exchanges of oaths between the king, or kings, and the people.

The hard work that led up to this event would have been exhilarating in its own way if it were not for its sinister aspects. Despite his attempts to court Neoptolemus's friendship, his royal colleague was clearly not a man of any subtlety and was also no better disposed to him than he had been at the beginning. Several rumors were about the city, in various ways saying that Neoptolemus was regarding Pyrrhus as a temporary nuisance whom he planned to deal with in his own way. Cineas and Menestheus had heard the same things, and the security in the "guest wing" of the palace was extreme. It was a somber group that presented itself at the Temple of Zeus Areius at Passeron on the day of the ceremony.

Neoptolemus, however, seemed to be in outstanding spirits, a man who has found a solution to his most pressing problems.

The ceremony wound its course through a ritual that was centuries old, and the temple resounded to the wonderful music of Epirus. Part of its nature was Greek, but part of it showed its roots in the music of the wild tribes of the hills of Epirus and the orgiastic rites of Dionysus. At the conclusion of the ceremony, the kings and their retinues made their way to the banquet that would end the day's celebrations. Before the meal began, the customary exchanges of gifts occurred. As Pyrrhus and Antigone made their way to the banqueting table, Gelon, a close friend and advisor of Neoptolemus approached them.

"It is customary, Sire, at this celebration," began Gelon, "for the king to be offered gifts on behalf of the people. It is my honor to present you with these four oxen, a gift from the people of my district. It is meant to symbolize the work that you and your queen endure on behalf of the people of Epirus."

"I thank you, Gelon," replied Pyrrhus, "for these fine oxen. I believe it is also customary for the king to acknowledge the gifts from the people and then to make a present of them to worthy people in his retinue."

"That is true, Sire. In fact, I believe your cup bearer, Myrtilus, has passed a very keen eye over them."

"Myrtilus is a fine young man, Gelon, but I must make my first acknowledgements to Abantes and Meriones. They were my first friends here in Epirus, and I will ask them to share the oxen between them as an acknowledgement of their loyalty."

Myrtilus, who had been standing right behind Pyrrhus, overheard this conversation, and was quite unable to disguise his disappointment. A custom that Pyrrhus was unaware of allowed the king's cup bearer to be the first to benefit from the king's generosity on this occasion. Myrtilus stepped back from the king and was silent while the oxen were presented to the two councilors. This disappointment did not escape the attention of Gelon, and he approached the young man after the banquet had begun. He sat down beside Myrtilus and said, "Do not trouble yourself too much, my friend. A king has much on his mind, but I know that a man such as yourself finds it hard to let an insult pass him by."

"That is true, sir. I am saddened and troubled by the king's action. I know, however, that he must take some time to become familiar with the customs of Epirus, having been away from the country for so long."

"It is good that you are so loyal and understanding. Perhaps you would like to come to dinner at my home tomorrow night, and we could discuss how an appropriate gesture could be made to salve your disappointment."

"That is very kind of you, sir. I will look forward to it." Gelon then excused himself and approached Neoptolemus. After Gelon had whispered into his ear for a short time, Neoptolemus smiled benevolently and made a reply that seemed to meet Gelon's expectations. The creature then took his own seat at the banquet table, seeming to find the wine particularly pleasing.

None of these exchanges escaped the eye of Cineas, and his level of fear and concern rose markedly. There seemed to be no doubt that Pyrrhus was in very grave danger.

The banquet ran its course, and the royal party said their goodbyes and made their way back to the palace. Pyrrhus, who had not been able to observe the undercurrents of the afternoon, was feeling rather pleased with himself, and was glad that he had been able to publicly reward the declared loyalty of Abantes and Meriones.

The next day, Myrtilus presented himself at Gelon's home just as the sun was setting. It was not often a young man from the palace was invited to the home of such a great man, and he hoped that he would be given a dinner to remember. His chagrin at the events of yesterday had left him with his night's sleep, and he was not at all sure what to expect from Gelon. Perhaps Gelon had noticed how diligently he had tried to carry out his duties? Could he possibly hope to be promoted to the chief wine bearer? Hope was running rampant in his breast as he knocked on the door. Gelon himself opened the door and invited him to come in.

"Myrtilus, you are very punctual. A quality I have always admired in you. Please come in. Dinner is almost ready and we can converse in private." Gelon took Myrtilus into the dining room, and invited his guest to take his place on a couch. They discussed many topics of current gossip as the meal progressed, and when the moment seemed right, Gelon leaned over to the young man and said to him, "I know of your disappointment yesterday, my friend. I can assure you that Neoptolemus is a king who is prepared to reward loyalty."

"Is that so, sir?" replied Myrtilus.

"Yes. It is in these difficult times that loyalty is most rewarded. I would like to suggest a way in which you could gain the perpetual favor of your true king."

Myrtilus was close to panic and felt that his only way to survive the evening was to appear to go along with these appalling suggestions.

"What is it that I could do for the king, sir?"

"With your help, I could arrange for Pyrrhus to be poisoned, and we would not have to put up with this absurd usurper any longer. Is that not an exquisite thought? You and I could be the most honored advisors to Neoptolemus. Just think of the rewards that would be bestowed on us!"

"How could we go about it, sir? King Pyrrhus is very closely guarded by his men, and Lord Cineas never takes his eyes off him for a moment."

"Leave it to me to do the planning, my lovely. Now that I have your support, I will work out the details. Perhaps you could come and dine with me again, one week from today?"

"I would be honored, sir. Perhaps I should leave now, so I do not return to the servant's quarters too late?"

"That is wise. We will meet again in one week. Be brave, and the world will be at your feet, my young friend."

Myrtilus left Gelon's house with as much calmness as he could muster, and as soon as he was out of sight of the front

door, he ran with all his speed back to the palace and sought out
the most distinguished man whom he had any right to disturb,
Alexicrates, the king's steward.

After telling Alexicrates all that had transpired this night,
the older man took him to see Meriones. After listening to the
story, Meriones took the two servants straight to Pyrrhus. When
they arrived at the king's door, he took some time to impress on
the two soldiers who guarded the royal suite that their business
was sufficiently urgent to disturb the king and queen. Halfway
through this debate, Pyrrhus opened the door and asked, "Would
one of you please tell me the reason for this noise?"

Alexicrates turned to his king and said, "I am sorry to disturb
you, Sire, but I have urgent news that must not wait."

"Come in then, my friend, and bring Myrtilus with you."

Meriones waited at the door and said to Pyrrhus, "Sire, this
news is sufficiently important that I must seek out Cineas and
Menestheus. I will bring them to you shortly."

"As you wish, Meriones. Come straight in when you return."

Alexicrates then invited Myrtilus to recount his story, and
Pyrrhus listened to it, deep in thought. After chewing on his finger for a short time, he said to Myrtilus, "I am sorry that I have
unknowingly offended you, my friend. Also, I am deeply in your
debt for bringing me this news. If you are willing, I will ask you
to help me defeat this plot, and I promise that I will never again
give you cause for disappointment."

"I will do all in my power to help you, Sire," replied Myrtilus.

"There's a good lad. When you meet with Gelon next week,
I would like you to take Alexicrates with you, ostensibly as a fellow conspirator. When this all comes to light, I must have more
than one witness who can vouch for the truth of the story."

"Yes, Sire," replied Myrtilus, deeply afraid that he was getting out of his depth.

"Until then, all you need to do is to carry on with your duties. Also, consider what I can give you as a reward for your
loyalty. You could either become Alexicrates's chief steward, or,
if you wish, you could become Menestheus's secretary in my

Agema. Menestheus needs someone to help him, and he could instruct you in your military duties before you started. Give it some thought."

"Sire, I would be honored to join your Agema."

"It is settled then. Menestheus usually begins his day by breakfasting with me and the queen. If you join us tomorrow we can discuss the matter further." Turning to Alexicrates, Pyrrhus continued, "You too have been a faithful friend, Alexicrates. Perhaps you could stay for a glass of wine, and we could discuss how I may repay your loyalty."

Pyrrhus walked Myrtilus to the door and returned to join Alexicrates. "It has been a very full day, my friend. I did not realize until a moment ago quite how momentous the day has been. Loyalty in a time of crisis is a thing to be treasured. Please tell me how I may help you."

"I am content with my lot, Sire. I am very pleased with how you have honored my young steward. I seek no other reward."

"Very good. I will insist that you become my councilor, however. Please be good enough to join Cineas and Menestheus here each morning for breakfast."

"Thank you, Sire. I will see you in the morning." Alexicrates reached forward to grasp Pyrrhus's hand and kissed it. He then made his way out of the royal chamber to his own quarters.

Soon after Alexicrates had left, Meriones returned with Cineas and Menestheus. As instructed, they gave a short knock on the door and then entered the royal suite. All this was too much for Antigone to sleep through, and she entered the living area looking ravishingly bedraggled. "Is everything all right, Pyrrhus? You seem to be throwing a party of some sort."

Pyrrhus laughed and said, "Not quite a party, my love. I am glad you are up. Please come and sit down. There is some important news to deal with."

Pyrrhus explained the news of the evening and the first step he had taken to enlist Alexicrates as a corroborative witness. Antigone began to look rather pale, and Pyrrhus took her hand. "We know about the plot, which means we can defeat it. Don't look so worried. And now, my friends. Please tell me what else you think we should do."

When Myrtilus and Alexicrates met with Gelon the following week, the sordid scheme began to take shape, and, in the week that followed, several other reports reached Pyrrhus about Neoptolemus's schemes. He seemed to have lost all caution and spoke about his plans as if there was no such thing as failure. On one such evening, he had even spoken of his plans to assassinate Pyrrhus at the dinner table. One of the servants, loyal to Pyrrhus, had overheard the conversation and reported it back to Antigone. The queen had reacted to this news with apparent quiet and inner turmoil and was on the verge of weeping as she recounted the episode to her husband. "It seems that we are close to the moment when affairs will be settled," said Pyrrhus. "There are times when a king must act in a way that seems harsh. Perhaps you should retire while I discuss matters with Cineas."

"No, my love. I know that you must defend yourself. Let us have no secrets." Antigone reached out for Pyrrhus's hand and squeezed it. She resumed her seat and said, "Send for Cineas, Pyrrhus, and I will stay with you."

Pyrrhus nodded and got up to send one of the guards to summon Cineas and Menestheus. They arrived a short time later. Pyrrhus presented each of them with a glass of wine and told them about the most recent chapter with Neoptolemus.

Cineas stared gravely into his goblet, took a deep breath, and said, "There is no alternative, Sire. The only way to deal with this matter is to assassinate Neoptolemus before he can achieve your own death."

"That is my own feeling, Cineas. Menestheus, do you have any other answer?"

"No Sire. He has left us with no option. If we sought a political solution, we would end up with the civil war that you have feared from the beginning. If you wish, I will be the assassin."

"Thank you, Menestheus, but I must be the one to do this, and it must be done soon."

The plans were made, and the councilors retired. Neoptolemus would die in three day's time. For the first time, Antigone watched Pyrrhus weep. "I will have blood on my hands very soon, my love. Can you still love me after I do this deed?"

"Yes, Pyrrhus," replied Antigone. "I had hoped that our life in Epirus would be free of the danger that besets royal families, but I know these events are not of your choosing. If it were only a case of our own lives and destinies, I would ask you to take me back to Egypt, and we would live our lives in happiness there. But everyone in Epirus knows that you are the one who will give Epirus back her soul. If the only way to achieve this is by Neotolemus's death, then fate will carry us all down this path. I will never think less of you because of this, and I will always remain with you."

"It is settled then," replied Pyrrhus, holding his wife in his arms, his tears wetting her hair.

Three days later, Pyrrhus invited Neoptolemus to dine with him. The occasion was the birthday celebration of the ancestor of the Epirote royal family, Aeacus, whose wisdom was so great that he became a judge in the Underworld, along with Minos and Rhadymanthus.

Neoptolemus arrived alone, confident in his own destiny, secretly scorning the stupidity and guilelessness of his cousin. Pyrrhus welcomed him to the dinner, seating him at his left. After pouring the wine, Pyrrhus stood up to make the customary speech of welcome. "I have asked the finest and most prominent of the citizens of Epirus to join in this celebration tonight, and in the name of my ancestors I act in the only way that will bring peace and prosperity to our country. One day, I will also ask for your forgiveness."

Neoptolemus was totally surprised by the tone of Pyrrhus's speech, and no sooner had his doubts troubled his consciousness, than he watched Pyrrhus pick up the sword that was hidden under a cushion and drive it into his breast.

Pyrrhus left the sword rest where it lay, and the lifeless body of Neoptolemus slumped into his chair. Pyrrhus then sat down and remained quiet while Cineas addressed the stunned audience. "My lords, a dreadful situation has occurred. Despite ceaseless overtures of friendship, King Pyrrhus has been faced with the certainty of his own death at the hands of Neoptolemus. There are no fewer than three direct witnesses to these plots. The only choices left to Pyrrhus, apart from allowing himself to die, were to fight a bloody civil war with the adherents of his faithless cousin or to deal with the situation as he has done. You know yourselves that Pyrrhus was cheated of his birthright and that the country has suffered at the hands of this man who knew no right apart from his own comfort. I ask you now to support your rightful king. If any of you choose to oppose him, you must first make your way past me."

The relief in the room was tangible. Pyrrhus had not been the only one to hear of the plots of Neoptolemus against his life, and every man in the room felt that this harsh justice was the only solution to the dilemma that Epirus found herself in. The first to speak was Hippoclitus, a prominent and well-respected merchant in Ambracia. "We acknowledge your right to defend yourself, Sire. No one here will speak against you." Hippoclitus sat down, and all the remaining men at the banquet stood up and cried out, "Long live King Pyrrhus. Long live Epirus."

CHAPTER XXXX

As the smoke from Neoptolemus's funeral pyre made its way toward the heavens, a collective sigh of relief went up from Ambracia. The dark ages of the country were over, and hope could be entertained for the future of Epirus. Iphis, the royal widow, attended the funeral, and then gathered her children with her to begin her journey to her native Thessaly, where she could live in peace, without fear. Either from her husband or from his enemies.

After the funeral, Pyrrhus spent two hours with Oeneus in the temple of Zeus in Ambracia. Oeneus had agreed to be his confessor and listened to the story of regicide with a grave face.

"I am a man of peace, Sire. This death troubles me greatly. I must accept, however, that a royal death was inevitable, and the current outcome is the only one which would allow any of us to have some hope. I will plead your case with the gods, and I offer you my own forgiveness and my eternal friendship."

"Thank you, Oeneus. I can ask for no more."

Pyrrhus made his way out of the temple, to find Antigone waiting for him in the gardens. "Thank you for waiting, my love. I am exhausted. Will you please come home with me and sleep for a while?"

Antigone took his arm, and they walked slowly back to the palace. Pyrrhus was deep in thought for a time and finally said, "I believe that now is the time for a gesture of confidence in the future. I have an idea which I hope you will approve of. Epirus would greatly benefit from the foundation of a new port city. The mouth of the Gulf of Ambracia would be the ideal site. I would like to start on the plans as soon as possible, and I would like to name the city after your mother."

"That is a wonderful idea, Pyrrhus. My mother would be honored, and I am sure it would meet with approval from the Assembly."

"I hope so. I must find some way to breathe new life into Epirus."

Pyrrhus and Antigone slept for the afternoon and then invited all of their councilors to dine with them. As well as Cineas and Menestheus, Meriones and Abantes were there, as were Alexicrates and Myrtilus. Alexicrates had been provided with the tunic of a member of the Epirote Assembly, and Myrtilus with that of a member of the royal Agema. Both were feeling resplendent in their new robes, Myrtilus particularly. He had also been provided with a fine panoply of battle armor, along with a field cloak, spear, sword, and helmet. Over the last few days, the armor and weapons had been polished to a degree more usual with jewelry, and he had had training sessions with Menestheus to receive instruction in military theory and practice as well as in his own immediate duties as a general's secretary. Menestheus was pleased to have this young man as his helper and was delighted at his enthusiasm. Myrtilus's face was bright with wonder when Menestheus told him about the career of Eumenes, who had accompanied Alexander to Persia as his royal secretary and who, after several small military commands, had became one of the finest of Alexander's younger generals, becoming the trusted lieutenant of Perdiccas after the death of Alexander.

When all the guests had been settled and had been provided with a goblet of wine, Pyrrhus said to them. "Gentlemen, Antigone and I are pleased to welcome you here tonight. After wrestling with our own demons, I hope that all of us will now be able to look forward to the future with some confidence. Our new life here will keep us all busy, and there are two projects that I would like to tell you about. First, I plan to found a new city, to be named after Antigone's mother, Berenice, which will, I hope, become the principal port of Epirus. Secondly, I propose to take up the pen and write a treatise on military theory."

Antigone was accustomed to the occasional surprise from her husband, but this one was totally unexpected, and she turned around and gave Pyrrhus a look of shock.

"I didn't know you had such literary aims, my dear."

"Neither did I until some weeks ago. I often think of the wisdom that your father passed on to me. Also, I still know most of his biography of Alexander by heart, and we have just survived a change of government in our own country. I have also been present at the most momentous battle of our generation. If that is not sufficient to give me some ideas for a work on tactics and strategy, then I am a poor student. Remember, my love, that the true manual of a soldier would dedicate more attention to *why* a battle is fought than *how*. I do not want to miss the opportunity of making a contribution when all of the material is there in my mind. The dedication will perhaps be the most difficult part. I must acknowledge your father, first, then Alexander, and then the Spartans. Then think of all the other great men who must claim a place. Where am I to put Themistocles and Epaminondas?"

"I am sure you will work it out, my love," replied Antigone. "After all, there is no hurry. How long did Herodotus take to write his great work?"

"A good point," said Pyrrhus. "The city is another matter. That cannot have an unlimited time for its creation. Cineas, if you are not also taken too much by surprise, perhaps you could tell me how you think we are to pay for it?"

"It is something of a surprise, Sire," replied Cineas. "There are, however, some well-established precedents that we could draw upon."

"Please continue, my friend."

"We have the mercantile communities of Epirus, Greece, Italy, Crete, and Sicily to approach, Sire. If necessary, we could go further afield to cities of Asia and the Black Sea.

"If you could picture our hypothetical city, the port area is potentially immense, and the area that this port would serve is huge. Our city would have its prime commercial real estate fronting the harbor. The avenue behind would also be desirable, and each street to the rear would have a value, which would be correspondingly less. Also, the prime residential real estate would be in the hills overlooking the port. If you were to present a plan of the proposed city to the most prominent of the Epirote merchants to consider, with an invitation to purchase their sites in advance, that would give you a basis of working capital. You could point out to them that the sites that are not taken up by local merchants would be offered to their colleagues from other cities in Greece and from other countries in the eastern Mediterranean. As well, you could suggest the creation of a trading guild, which would be joined by all of the merchants in the new city, domestic and foreign. This would give Greek merchants introductions to markets in other countries as well as their own and would provide a welcome to the foreign merchants."

Pyrrhus smiled and nodded. Cineas had taken his ideas much further than he had himself.

"Also consider, Sire," continued Cineas, clearly getting into his stride, "Corinth has made herself a great center of trade for hundreds of years because of her advantages of position. We could do the same thing, looking at Italy as our prime focus."

Why did Cineas regret the mention of Italy as soon as the words were out of his mouth? He had had the same feeling in Ptolemy's dining room when Pharaoh spoke to Pyrrhus about the importance of Italy and the great place that seemed destined for the Romans in the world. Was Italy to be important in their own lives?

Cineas was one of the least superstitious individuals of his age, but he had never been able to discount the thought that there was some greater being that toyed with the world of men, the existence of whom was largely proven by the truth of oracles and omens. All men in Greece knew the tragic truth of the words spoken by the priestess of Delphi that foretold to the Spartan priests that either Sparta would be destroyed by the Persians or the land of Lacedaemon would mourn the death of a king of the House of Heracles. The death of a Spartan king. Were the priestess's words any less accurate when she prophesied to the Athenians that the wooden wall would save them?

The wooden wall of the ships of the Athenian fleet saved not only Athens, but all of Greece. And now, there was this repeated mention of Italy. Italy, in some way, would be crucial to Pyrrhus.

Cineas was brought out of his study by Pyrrhus, who had grasped his hand.

"You are my inspiration, Cineas. As always. The first thing will be to engage architects who are equal to the task. If only we could have the services of men as fine as the architects of Alexandria."

"It may not be as difficult as you think, Sire," replied Cineas. "The architects of Alexandria would have had their students, who would have spread themselves all over the Greek world. I have no doubt that inquiries made in Thebes and Athens will lead to more expressions of interest than you can accommodate. These men are quite content to travel any distance if such a great commission is offered to them. After a number of them have submitted their drawings, you could choose the best that is offered."

"Very well then. I will arrange for draftsmen to prepare fresh and accurate maps of the area, and I will then send deputations to the guilds of architects in Thebes and Athens. So, my friends, we will soon be able to make a start. Cineas, perhaps I could leave it to you to approach the mercantile community and invite them to send expressions of interest?"

Pyrrhus was pleased that a number of practical ideas had resulted from his proposal of a new port city. From his own perspective, the idea was all very well but the execution was the difficult part. With such help as was available to him, he could leave much of the planning to Cineas and the architects, leaving himself time to devote to the economy of Epirus and his military treatise.

As he lay in his bed that night with his arms around Antigone, Pyrrhus looked at the ceiling and contemplated his new life. Breaking in on his thoughts, Antigone said to him, "Pyrrhus, will you be able to sleep at all tonight?"

"Eventually, my love. After a terribly dark time, I am finally able to believe that you and I will be able to have the lives that we have dreamed of in Epirus. I could come to love being king."

"That is how it should be, my dear. Have I told you I have felt the first movements of our baby?"

Pyrrhus sat up and placed his hand on Antigone's abdomen, his eyes open with wonder.

"No, you didn't. Does he move very often?"

"Keep your hand there for a while and we will see what happens."

Pyrrhus did as he was instructed and rested his head on his pillow. After a considerable time, as he was drifting off to sleep, he felt that wonderful movement under his hand. A new life was stirring, his son or daughter. Afraid to move, he kept his hand where it was until it seemed beyond doubt that the baby would sleep for a time. He then sat up and took Antigone's hand.

"I felt it. Soft and gentle, but I felt it. It is like a miracle."

"It is life's true miracle, Pyrrhus. You have felt our son stirring."

"Or our daughter," replied Pyrrhus.

"Our son, my love. Trust me. And now you can hold on to me." Antigone gently grasped Pyrrhus's hand and placed it on her left breast as she rolled over onto her side. It was fortunate that Pyrrhus did not have to say anything at this moment, overcome as he was by the presence of the life of their child and the love of this woman. Sometime later, Pyrrhus was able to sleep, treasuring the moment.

Pyrrhus was still in his state of grace when the sun shone through their window the following morning. The light woke him instantly, and he turned to gaze at Antigone, still asleep, lying on her left side. He turned gently, hoping not to wake his love, and settled where he could place his right hand on her shoulder and listen to her breathe. He never felt more at peace than at this moment, and he wished this moment could last forever. Eventually, Antigone could not stay asleep with the morning sun in her eyes. Instinctively, she grasped Pyrrhus's hand and rolled over to face him.

"Good morning, my love. Have you been awake for a while?"

"Long enough to remember that you have gorgeous shoulders."

"That is good," said Antigone, rolling over so that Pyrrhus could take her in his arms. "Let us stay here for a bit."

They enjoyed their twilight of waking for what seemed only a few minutes, before being disturbed by a knock at the door. "If only Menestheus would be an hour late occasionally," said Pyrrhus, getting up from the bed and putting on his gown.

"Good morning, gentlemen," said Pyrrhus. "Please come in, breakfast will be here shortly."

The now customary group of six men entered the suite, and Pyrrhus invited them to take their chairs. They waited, however, as the queen entered the living area shortly after them.

"Good morning, gentlemen," repeated Antigone. "Please sit down. Pyrrhus has something very important to tell you."

"That is true. I felt our baby move for the first time last night. Perhaps you would all care to dine with us this evening to celebrate."

The response from these largely hardened men of the world touched the young couple. The workings of palace gossip had ensured that even the humblest of the servants knew that the queen had had some difficult times in her early pregnancy, and the reassurance that the child was alive and well was wonderful news for all of them.

"We would be delighted, my lady," replied Cineas, favoring them with one of his very occasional beaming smiles. "The timing could not be better, as a ship arrived late last night from Egypt. Your parents have sent some barrels of Pharaoh's favorite wine, along with several pieces of lovely furniture, and some cuttings from Queen Berenice's favorite plants from her garden."

"Bless them," said Pyrrhus, remembering how good Ptolemy's taste in wine was. "Pharaoh and his queen have never failed us yet, and I doubt that they ever will. And now, gentlemen. What do you have for us this morning?"

"Several things, Sire," replied Cineas. "Some good, some bad. I have arranged to meet with the civic draftsmen and architects later on today, Sire, and I will meet with the city's merchants as soon as we have something to show them." Cineas's face became more grave, and he continued. "A letter arrived from Demetrius last night, Sire, sent from Thebes. As you had already retired, I took the liberty of opening it. He says in it that although the two of you are old friends, friendship must be put aside when kings make their decisions. He seems to have regained his power base in central Greece, and he respectfully asks you to bear in mind that Thessaly has traditionally been an ally of the cities in central Greece, rather that Epirus or Macedonia."

"What a load of rubbish, Cineas. The cities of mainland Greece have always snubbed Thessaly as much as Epirus when they choose to talk of barbarians, except when they need their cavalry. We must look at protecting our borders. Demetrius is the one who has dictated that friendship is to be put aside. Menestheus, please arrange to meet with me and the other generals at midday. There is not a moment to be lost." Turning to Antigone, Pyrrhus continued, "We are to stand alone, now, my love, and we will need all our wits about us."

Pyrrhus was under no illusions with regard to Demetrius. Their friendship of many years' standing was of no account now. They were both embroiled in the affairs of power and international politics, and Demetrius would pursue his aims as single-mindedly as he did when he laid siege to Rhodes. Antigone felt the pangs of sadness and remorse as keenly as Pyrrhus, but with the added element of fear for her unborn child. Would she have to watch her son thrown from the walls of Ambracia as had Andromache from the walls of Troy?

Neoptolemus, the savage son of Achilles, had killed the infant Astyanax so he could not avenge the sack of Troy. Was the same tragedy waiting for her?

Pyrrhus turned to Cineas and Menestheus. "Gentlemen, please wait a moment while I dress, and I will be with you. We three and Abantes must look at the state of the army before we meet the generals." After dressing quickly, Pyrrhus rejoined his advisors. "Come then, you can tell me what state we are in to fight a battle." Looking at Antigone, he continued, "I will be back later, my love. Do not fear for Epirus. Demetrius is not strong enough to conquer the whole world. Our task will be to merely keep him out of Thessaly. For the time being." He then kissed his lovely wife and led the way to the Council Room.

"The good news, Sire," said Menestheus, "is that the small army you brought with you from Egypt has been made very welcome here in Epirus. They and the men of the Epirote army are happy to stand alongside each other in battle."

"That is good, Menestheus. From now on, however, all our men are in the Epirote army. All the men from Neoptolemus's Agema are invited to join mine. I have no objection in principle to being guarded by an extra 500 men."

"As you wish, Sire. All together, our standing army consists of 12,000 men, in addition to the men in your bodyguard. These men could be mobilized as soon as the baggage train and the provisions are prepared. In time, the provincial levies could provide another 5,000 men. All the levies would be infantrymen. 2,000 men of the standing army are cavalrymen."

"I do not think we can wait for the levies, Sire," said Abantes. "It will take weeks to assemble them and make sure they are properly equipped. I suggest that we mobilize the professional army as soon as possible and secure Thessaly before Demetrius can do the same thing. The levies can be prepared so they will be able to support us if the fighting becomes difficult later. We must also leave some of the army here in Epirus to cover all eventualities."

"You are right, Abantes, of course," said Pyrrhus. "Assemble all your officers here this afternoon, and we will get them to work on getting the army ready to march as soon as I have spoken to the rest of the general staff. It is also clear that in the future we will need a larger standing army than is at our disposal at the moment. When this current crisis has been dealt with, I would like you to present me with your plans for expanding the army. Initially, an extra 5,000 men would be required, and then we can look at what else we can do to make ourselves more secure."

When Pyrrhus met with the general staff, he presented them with the immediate task of the mobilization of the army of Epirus. He also pored over maps with his generals. "You will remember, gentlemen, that the Pass of Thermopylae is critical. If we do not hold that, then we will not be able to keep Demetrius out of Thessaly, and our task will be much more difficult. I suggest that we send 6,000 of our infantrymen to Thermopylae and encamp all the cavalry and another 2,000 of the foot soldiers near Lamia, where they can act as a strategic reserve. Abantes, I will ask you to march the main force to Thermopylae. Menestheus and I will march with my enlarged Agema as soon as possible, to Larissa and Crannon. Thessaly is not a united country that acts with a single will, but these two cities are the political centers. I will meet with the patriarchs there and try and engage their support, or at least their neutrality. We do not need secondary military engagements to hinder our movements. It is even possible that they may contribute some of their fine cavalry to support us. I can see no reason why they would look kindly on Demetrius taking over Thessaly."

Pyrrhus looked about him to see if the other men were keeping up with his thoughts. He was pleased to observe that his audience was still with him and nodding its approval.

"After I leave Crannon," Pyrrhus said to Abantes, "Menestheus and I will join you at Thermopylae. Please be good enough to send scouts out each day to see if there is any activity on Demetrius's part. And now, my friend," he said, turning to Abantes, "the only remaining decision is to who will command the force which will encamp at Lamia."

"There is one man I could recommend without reservation, Sire. His name is Theopompous. He has been something of a protégé of mine, and he is part of the general staff that we will meet with shortly. He is still quite a young man, but he is a fine soldier, and a respected commander."

"Very well, then. I will ask Theopompous to command our reserves. And now, gentlemen, we need to look at some practical details regarding equipment and provisions for our troops."

Pyrrhus spent the entire day with his officers, and, by the time he returned to his quarters, a workable framework had been agreed upon. It came as no surprise that an officer as competent as Abantes kept a ready store of provisions that would supply most of the needs of the army. The remainder would be obtained as fresh produce over the next two days. The men's kit and weapons were also pleasingly complete, and, as a siege train would not be required, it was quite realistic for the army to be ready to march in three day's time. The nature of Greek politics had long demanded that each city or region was always prepared for a battle at short notice.

Pyrrhus's remaining task was to explain his decisions to Antigone. She was a keenly intuitive politician herself, as well as a young mother to be who had her own fears.

"The third body of troops is my bodyguard," said Pyrrhus, sitting next to Antigone in their living room, holding her hands. "Menestheus and I will go with them to meet the Thessalian leaders in Larissa and Crannon. Their support is vital. They may even look kindly at becoming part of the Epirote Confederacy if we are able to do them a service now."

"And Cineas, my dear. What will he do?"

"I have asked Cineas to go to Thermopylae with Abantes. If something happens at Thermopylae before I get there, I need him there to speak for me. Not every confrontation between two armies has to lead to a battle. Meriones will stay here and look after you and Epirus for me. He will have the remaining 2,000 soldiers of our army under his command."

"Crannon is a city with a tragic story, Pyrrhus. There was that terrible battle there a few years before I was born. Please be careful there." Antigone's fears were beginning to well up in her, and even the thought of her husband walking over the plains of a previous battlefield sent dark shivers through her breast.

"There is one more thing, my love," said Pyrrhus, taking a stronger grip of Antigone's hands. "I must leave one day before the rest of the army. I must speak to the Thessalians and explain my intentions before they see my soldiers in their country."

Antigone nodded, having understood the necessity of these decisions, but she was still unable to speak. She rested her head on Pyrrhus's shoulder and pulled his arms around her. After the initial tears had dried, she finally looked up at his face. "You must come home to me, my love."

"Nothing in the world could stop me from coming back to you. Come to bed now, you look exhausted."

Antigone smiled and replied, "I am tired. It has been a very eventful day."

CHAPTER XXXXI

Pyrrhus was sitting in the chambers of the most influential of the Thessalian statesmen in Crannon, waiting for the reply to his statement of friendship and fidelity. Menestheus, sitting at his side was no more at ease. As they sat there, ignoring the fine wine and food that had been offered them, Pyrrhus studied the face of Adrestus, who had been a leader of men since before he was born. It was the face of a wise but troubled man. After an interval that seemed interminable, he finally spoke. "I thank you for seeking me out, Sire. There will clearly be difficult times for all of us in the near future, and I do not want to speak hastily. There is a certain amount that I can do on my own authority; the remaining matters I must refer to the council of the Thessalian League. Your father and I knew each other well, and I admired him. Although we have not met before as adults, all that I have heard of you is good.

"Time is clearly of the essence at the moment, although I dearly hope that Demetrius does not force the issue. I also understand that you must make your way to Thermopylae quickly. For the moment, let me say that you have the blessing of Thessaly to help us defend our borders against Demetrius. I will send word to our various cities that you are to be treated as friends and allies, and if I can persuade my colleagues, I will send cavalry reinforcements to Thermopylae as soon as possible. As far as Thessaly acting in concert with Epirus under your leadership, I can only say that in these times everyone needs powerful friends, and I will put your case to the assembly, with my support."

Pyrrhus breathed a silent sigh of relief, and replied, "I thank you for your council, Adrestus. I sought you out because of the friendship you had with my father, and because I knew you were a man of honor who could speak on behalf of the people of Thessaly. It has been my wish that our two countries could act together, for our mutual support. As you say, all we can do today is to agree that we have a common cause, and I hope the rest will follow. My men have been instructed to behave as if they were in their own country. If my army is in Thessaly for any length of time, would you be agreeable if I invited surrounding cities to set up markets for my soldiers' provisions, to be paid for by me at standard market rates?"

"That would be entirely acceptable, Sire. Also, if I can send men from Thessaly, we will cover their costs ourselves."

"Thank you, my friend," said Pyrrhus, standing. "Menestheus and I must take our leave shortly, but first, I would like to accept the glass of wine you offered us earlier and propose a toast to the friendship of our two nations."

"Let us drink to that, Sire," replied Adrestus. The three men drank their toast and shook hands. As Pyrrhus and Menestheus were about to leave, Adrestus said to them, "I will be in touch as soon as possible, Sire, and I will report any developments of interest to us both."

"Thank you, Adrestus. You know where to find me."

One week later, Pyrrhus and his Agema joined Abantes at Thermopylae, the main body having arrived two days earlier. Pyrrhus approved thoroughly of the dispositions that had been made.

Abantes had occupied the middle gate of the pass, inspired no doubt by the decision of Leonidas in days gone by, who chose this gate to make his stand against the Persians. The camp of the army had been made carefully and with great skill. He also allocated an area of the camp for the Agema and its cavalry.

As Pyrrhus and Menestheus led their men through the west gate, they were welcomed by the advance guard of the main body, having already passed several groups of scouts. Men of the advance guard led them through to the main camp, where Cineas and Abantes were ready to receive them, and Abantes took them to his tent and called for refreshments, then invited his guests to take off their armor and wash.

"You are a very good host, Abantes. I thank you," said Pyrrhus, now comfortably seated with a goblet of wine in his hand.

"I know that you have had a long journey, Sire. My own body was aching when we finally arrived, and I was sure you would feel the same, despite your youth."

Cineas felt that Pyrrhus was ready to be questioned and said to him, "I hope you had a successful meeting in Crannon, Sire. Did the Thessalians offer us their support?"

"We had as good a meeting as I could wish for, Cineas. Adrestus, the chief magistrate, whom we met with, gave us as much help as he could on his own authority, and he was hopeful that he could persuade his colleagues to support us with their cavalry."

"That is very good news, Sire. We may need all the help that we can get, if Demetrius is planning a serious expedition to Thessaly."

"That is quite possible, Cineas, but I doubt he will be in a position to send a large force against us." Pyrrhus reached out for the wooden leg of his chair as he said this, and then continued. "He is still finding a place in Greece for himself. What I think is most likely is that he will send a small force, firstly to reconnoiter, and then to establish a base if he meets no opposition. This is what I interpreted from Abantes when he pressed us to waste no time and not to wait for the reinforcement of our provincial levies."

"Just so, Sire," said Abantes. "We would be extremely unlucky to have to face a large army now. All the same, he could send a force that would make us sweat."

"Tell me, Abantes, have your scouts encountered any enemy activity?"

"Not yet, Sire. I sent some long-range scouts out yesterday. They will report back sometime tomorrow, but the men who have been sweeping the area closer by have seen nothing."

Pyrrhus sat back with a wry smile on his face and said to his general, "In that case, my friend, we seem to have time on our side. Beginning tomorrow morning, I propose to fortify our camp. I took the liberty of bringing some carpentry tools with me, as well as rope and such things, and as much planking as I could lay my hands on in the time available."

"You do not surprise me, Sire. Menestheus has told me of the work you did at Megara. I took the liberty of sending a detail of men to begin felling trees this morning. Before we begin the work in earnest, would you like to see the memorials to the Greeks who fought the Persians here?"

"Very much. You are familiar with the pass, no doubt?"

"I have passed through here twice in the past, Sire. On both occasions, I had time to make the journey at my own pace, and I was able to view the monuments and the grave of the Spartans and the Thespians. It is a very moving experience to see the memorials and to tread the same ground as these heroes. It is not very far from our camp, if you would like to follow me."

The group of men redressed in their armor and followed Abantes out of the command tent. "It is only a short walk from here, Sire, and if we chose to stroll rather than ride, we could enjoy this wonderful twilight."

"I am in your hands, Abantes. Please lead on."

As they walked, Menestheus called Myrtilus over to his side so that he could speak with him. "We will see memorials to some of Greece's greatest heroes shortly, Myrtilus. The fame of the Spartans is well known and deserves to live forever. I am sure I do not have to tell you the story of the magnificent Leonidas, but I will tell you about the other great men, whom you may not have heard of. Firstly, I must tell you about the Thespians. Even though they were not from the Peloponnese, and they all understood that the price that would be paid for delaying the Persian army was certain death, they refused a direct order to retire with the main body of the Greek army. They fought in the front line with the Spartans and beat back every attack of the finest Persian troops, until their position was betrayed by a man named Ephialtes. This man led the Persians, by night, along a goat track known only to certain locals, and the Greeks were attacked from behind, as well as from the front. The Spartans and Thespians fought until the last man, and they all share a common grave. Even Xerxes honored them as heroes."

Menestheus collected himself for a short time, breathing deeply as they walked. When his emotions were more under control, he continued. "Many other brave men were here and through no fault of their own, survived the battle. A large contingent of Phocians guarded the pass to the east of the middle gate. To their horror, at dawn they saw the Persians marching towards them. Surprised, but prepared to fight to the death, they withdrew to nearby high ground and waited for the attack that never came. The Persians marched straight past them to engage Leonidas and his men. These men were heartbroken that they could do nothing to save the Spartans, but in their endeavor to do something useful for the Greek cause they retired to join the main body of the army and to deliver the tragic news."

Menestheus walked along, deep in thought, for a time. "The other man I must tell you about is Megistias. He was the seer of the army and clearly divined to Leonidas that he and all of his men were soon to die if they remained at Thermopylae. Leonidas, for his part, thought it unbecoming for a Spartan king to flee the pass he had been sent to guard, and when it was clear that they had been betrayed, he ordered the main body to retire. Megistias also declined to depart and save his own life. He did, however, send his only son away so he would not share the army's fate. It is to these men, Myrtilus, that the memorials we will soon view have been put in place to honor."

The group was now approaching the mound that held the memorial, which consisted of a small pyramid of stone, the large stones at the bottom showing numerous inscriptions, and to each side of which were displayed two suits of armor, now much rusted or discolored, one of which was the armor of a Greek hoplite, the other the remains of a breastplate and embroidered tunic of a soldier of Xerxes' Immortals, his elite troops.

Abantes took the lead as they approached the mound. "On the left here, Sire, is the epitaph of the Spartans, in the middle that of the Greeks in total, and the stone on the right is the memorial to Megistias. The memorial itself is above the common grave of the men who died here."

Abantes was clearly close to his limit, and Menestheus felt he must help. "If you wish, Sire, I could read the inscriptions for us all?"

"Yes, Menestheus, if you please."

"First, the epitaphs of the soldiers:

> 'Go tell the Spartans, Passerby,
> That we obeyed our orders,
> And dead, here we lie.'

"Also,

> 'Four thousand here from Pelops' land
> Against three million once did stand.'

"This last one is for Megistias,

> 'Here lies Megistias, who died
> When the Mede passed Spercheius' tide
> A prophet; yet he scorned to save
> Himself, but shared the Spartan's grave.'"

The group of men nodded in silence, gathering their thoughts. Menestheus and Myrtilus both carefully wiped the tears from their eyes. Pyrrhus was silent for a moment longer and then said, either to himself or to his fellows, "Where are we to find such inspiration?"

Cineas was one of the few men to hear Pyrrhus's question. He had placed himself close to his king, so that he could observe him at this formative moment in his life. This could be the first time when Pyrrhus would make a decision regarding peace or war, retirement or battle. Would he be prudent? Would he strive at all costs to prove his courage to himself and to others? Pyrrhus's question disturbed him greatly.

"Perhaps we should be getting back to the camp, Sire. Menestheus will want to see to his men, and we must consider our plans."

"Yes, Cineas. It is almost dark. Let us see to the men and then discuss our matters over dinner."

"Are you ready to help me fortify another camp, Menestheus?" said Pyrrhus as the servants cleared the dinner table and refilled their masters' goblets.

"I hope so, Sire," replied Menestheus, laughing. "I still remember how much my body ached last time."

"I am counting on your help, my friend,' said Pyrrhus. "And now, gentlemen, I would like you to look at the plans of the encampment at Megara. I believe we will be able to make a good approximation of our fort without stepping outside the tent."

The next morning, the work on the fortification of the camp began in earnest. Menestheus's recollections of bodily agony were not in any way exaggerated, and when the work was complete, he said to Pyrrhus, "I hope it will be some time before you ask me to fortify another camp, Sire."

"I hope so too, my friend, but just remember that we have completed the fundamental preparation of the materials, as well as setting up the camp. We will now have the materials to carry with us, so that the next time, we will not have to cut down so many trees."

"Thank God for that then," said Menestheus, before being rudely interrupted by the entrance of Myrtilus.

"Forgive the interruption, Sire," said Myrtilus, "but the remote scouts have just come in at the gallop. A large body of men has been sighted ten miles from here."

"Do you know how many, Myrtilus?"

"They thought at least two or three thousand, Sire. They were not sure."

"We must reinforce the men at the east gate, Menestheus, and post a strong guard on our walls tonight. Demetrius is too far away for a rational man to attempt a night attack, but let us be prepared, all the same. All the men who are not detailed will sleep for the night but be assembled with full weapons before dawn. Please call Abantes in, and then you and I can do our rounds of the men."

At dawn, the advance guards at the eastern and western gates, as well as the main body of the army at the camp were ready in full battle armor. The men had completed their preparations, and their breakfast, by the time the first rays of sunshine lit up the eastern sky. Lookouts had been posted at all areas of high ground, and every man was in a state of exquisite anticipation. It was certain that an army marched toward them. The strength of the force was not yet known, nor its intention. All of the men in Pyrrhus's small army were affected by the same emotions—excitement, anticipation, and fear. They were also affected by a strange sense of destiny. In this exact piece of ground, a battle had been fought by men who had been honored by the greatest gift of posterity, the esteem and admiration of their grateful countrymen. If one had to suffer a premature and violent death, what better place than this?

The silence continued for another hour, during which Pyrrhus and his commanders visited all their men. They greeted all the men whom they knew by name and spoke cheerfully to the others. Every man in the army began this day with words from his king.

The peace of the early daylight was softly broken by the distant sound of an army on the march, and a faint cloud of dust could be seen, marking its position. Another group of scouts came in, with a certain estimate that the approaching force was comprised of a maximum of 3,000 men, 500 of which were cavalry.

Pyrrhus felt confident enough to present his army and said to Abantes and Menestheus, "Gentlemen, it is time for us to form our men in battle order. The advance guard at the eastern gate will retire and join the main body. I want to leave 500 men guarding the camp. The rest of our soldiers will form up in battle order 500 paces in front of the camp. The guard at the western gate will stay where they are in case an attempt is made to turn our position from the rear. We do not want to share the same fate as the Spartans."

Abantes and Menestheus began the process of marshaling the men, leaving Pyrrhus with Cineas. "Tell me, Cineas. Do you have any comments regarding our dispositions?"

"No, Sire. We have a strong position and a superior force. It is appropriate to be bold. I dearly hope, however, that we will not have a battle on our hands today. The only thing I could add is that we place a body of archers on the slopes of the hills overlooking the eastern gate. From such an elevation, such a crossfire would be formidable."

"You are quite right, my friend," said Pyrrhus, who then called out the order to Menestheus. "And now we must wait for a while. When the men are in position, there will be time to review them before anything happens."

Well before the enemy was in sight, Pyrrhus and his companions rode through the ranks of soldiers. In the confined pass, it was clear that the cavalry would not be very useful, and they were kept behind in reserve. Some of the archers were ready on the hillsides, the remainder in front of the infantry. The infantry was formed up in the usual array with the phalangites in the center, and the hypaspists on the flanks. Once again the narrowness of the pass limited the width of the front line, but the depth of the Epirote army was most impressive. The men were aware of their numerical superiority, which gave them a great deal of confidence. Once Pyrrhus had completed his inspection, he took his place at the head of the army, together with his senior officers, and waited the approach of Demetrius's soldiers. Despite his confidence, there was still room for some anxiety when this body of fine soldiers entered the pass and continued their march toward him. They marched confidently and at a good pace, and Pyrrhus was full of admiration for them. When the front line of infantry were 300 paces from him, their commander gave the order for the halt, but he himself continued to approach Pyrrhus on his horse, together with his officers.

As they came nearer, Pyrrhus recognized Pantauchus. Demetrius had sent his best general on this expedition. Would their old acquaintance count for anything today? Probably not, since it had made so little difference with Demetrius himself. Pyrrhus felt his anticipation growing greater as every moment passed. This was his first moment in command of an army where all the decisions would be his. What were his emotions? Fear, certainly. No commander of any force can entirely rule out the possibility of the despair of defeat, no matter how strong his position. Greater, though, were exhilaration and excitement.

When Pantauchus and his officers were a stone's throw from Pyrrhus's entourage, they dismounted from their horses and approached their adversaries on foot. Pyrrhus and his men did likewise and walked to meet Pantauchus, who bowed to Pyrrhus and said to him, "Greetings, Sire. King Demetrius sends his best wishes to you and trusts that you are well."

"Please thank Demetrius for me, Pantauchus, and also deliver my own best regards. Perhaps you could tell me the purpose of your expedition."

"Demetrius is keen to unite the whole of Greece, Sire, and he has sent me to explore the possibilities of Thessaly coming under his sway."

"This is certainly no diplomatic mission that you are leading, Pantauchus. I must tell you that it is the wish of the Thessalians to ask Demetrius not to enter their country. They prefer to maintain their traditional independence. I have offered them my support, which they have accepted."

"Demetrius will not be pleased about this, Sire."

"That cannot be helped, Pantauchus. You have a fine army with you, but you are not strong enough to win the day and displace me from this pass. As no change to our current situation will be effected by a battle between us. I ask that you retire from this field and allow our men to live another day."

Pantauchus looked into Pyrrhus's face for a moment. He then stepped back and offered Pyrrhus a short bow.

"As you wish, Sire. You were right years ago when you made me fortify our camp in Megara, and you are right again today. I will retire, and we will not have a battle today. Understand that while I admire you and respect you, the gods have now made us enemies. I give you my word that the next time we meet, we will fight each other."

"As you wish, General." Pyrrhus offered Pantauchus his hand, which the older man took.

"Good-bye, Pantauchus," said Pyrrhus.

"Good-bye, Sire."

While this parley was going on, the front ranks of the two armies faced each other, ready to fight a battle if it was demanded of them. The shields of both armies were locked together, the long spears ready to be lowered for the attack. Tension increased on both sides as the commanders returned to their horses and mounted. Pyrrhus remained where he was and returned the salute offered by Pantauchus as he turned to ride back toward his own men to give the order for the army to retire.

As he watched the disciplined withdrawal of Pantauchus's soldiers, Pyrrhus felt an inner glow of victory. The glow of the finest victory of all, where one achieved the aims of a campaign without bloodshed. Even a Spartan king would have been proud of his achievement today. He then turned to his officers and said to them, "We may stand the men down, now, gentlemen. You will be good enough to redeploy the advance guard here at the eastern gate, and the rest of the men will retire to our camp. Once the men are settled, I would like you to join me for lunch, and we can discuss our plans."

Pyrrhus left his generals to deal with the retirement of the men, and he and Cineas returned to the camp. As the two of them rode through the gate, a huge cheer came up from the men guarding the camp. The significance of the withdrawal of Demetrius's army without a blow being struck had not escaped them. As well as the emotional and logical appreciation of Pyrrhus's achievement, they were also delighted that they would all live through this day, an event that was not at all certain when they took up their positions some time earlier.

Comfortably seated in his tent, Pyrrhus said to Cineas, "We have been very fortunate today, my friend. To celebrate, I would like you to join me in a glass of wine before the others join us for lunch. Then you can tell me what you think about my ideas of where we go from here."

Pyrrhus called for his servant and asked him to bring a skin of his best wine and two goblets straight away, and then to prepare lunch for the larger group in two hours time.

"As I see it, Cineas," said Pyrrhus, nursing his goblet of wine, "Demetrius is not in a position to send a sufficiently large army to displace us at the moment and probably will not be able to do so in the immediate future. I suggest we place a garrison here at Thermopylae and leave our reinforcing battalion at Lamia to support the Thessalians if trouble does arise, and then retire to Epirus with the remainder of the men."

"I agree wholeheartedly, Sire. We must of course leave some men to hold the pass, and your suggestion of leaving some of the army in Thessaly is a very good one. We must be careful, however, that we leave enough men to be militarily useful in case Demetrius does surprise us, but not such a large force that it appears that we are trying to keep Thessaly under our control as an occupied country."

"My thoughts exactly, my friend. We should be able to come to a decision as to numbers when we meet with Menestheus and the other generals. On our way back home, we should meet again with Adrestus in Crannon and present our plans to him. The approval of our actions by the Thessalians is crucial for our mutual well-being, and we may have to be a bit flexible, depending on their response."

Cineas was about to make another comment on their plans when Menestheus entered the tent, looking rather excited and pleased. "Forgive this interruption, Sire. The deployment of our men is not yet complete, but I thought I should let you know that some of our cavalrymen from the western gate are escorting a large force of Thessalian cavalry to the camp."

Pyrrhus could not have been given better news, even if he had been given days to think about the best thing that could happen to him, and then to wish for it. The presence of these soldiers meant that the Thessalians had accepted the alliance with Epirus, under his command. This alliance meant a great deal in terms of the security of Epirus and also gave him a significantly greater force to draw on if the need arose.

Menestheus withdrew to meet the commander of the Thessalian cavalry and returned sometime later to introduce him to Pyrrhus.

After making a reasonable attempt at knocking on the tent flap, Menestheus brought his guest into the tent after Pyrrhus had called out for him to enter. As the two men entered, Pyrrhus gazed in admiration at one of the tallest and handsomest men he had ever met. Menestheus said to his king, "Sire, it is my pleasure to present Meges, who is the commander of his force of 2,000 Thessalian cavalry."

Pyrrhus stood up and walked over to meet Meges. "I cannot tell you how glad I am to see you, Meges," he said, shaking the other man's hand. "I present my advisor, Cineas."

Cineas approached their guest and had his hand wrung in turn. Pyrrhus drew up a chair for Meges, invited him to sit, and gave him a goblet of wine. "I am afraid the only excitement I can offer you, Meges, is our company at lunch. A short time ago, I had a meeting with Pantauchus, who was commanding 3,000 men from Demetrius's army. He clearly stated the purpose of his mission, to bring Thessaly under Demetrius's influence. I told him of the friendship between Thessaly and Epirus, and that it was the desire of the Thessalians that Demetrius's forces not enter Thessaly. Fortunately for all of us, he chose to withdraw, as it was clear that he was not in a position to force the issue. So, my friend, it leaves us in a position to comfortably discuss the problems facing us over a good lunch."

Meges was much impressed by what Pyrrhus told him. Pantauchus was known as a fine commander and a brave man. He would not have withdrawn if he had held any hope at all of a military victory. "I am very relieved to hear your news, Sire. I have taken part in a number of battles, and I am always relieved when I can count all of my men still alive after any confrontation. If you will forgive me, I will see to my men before lunch is ready. In the meantime, perhaps you would care to read the letter that Adrestus sent with me, addressed to you."

Meges handed Pyrrhus the letter and promised to return as soon as he had made arrangements for the encampment of his men. Pyrrhus broke the seal and read:

Adrestus of Crannon to King Pyrrhus, Greetings.

> *It is my pleasure to inform you, Sire, that I have presented your case to the council of the Thessalian League, and my fellow councilors are of a like mind to me. As a result we have voted overwhelmingly both to accept an alliance with Epirus, and to regard you as the commander in chief of our combined forces if an occasion arises which requires a military response. I send this letter with our finest cavalry commander who will lead 2,000 of our men to join you at Thermopylae.*

> *May God keep you all safe.*

Pyrrhus's face broke out into a broad smile as he passed the letter over to Cineas to read. "Epirus has found a friend, Cineas. We will not have to fight the world on our own, it seems."

Cineas read the letter and was as pleased as his king by the evident goodwill of the Thessalians. "We could not receive better news, Sire." Cineas would have continued with a detailed interpretation of the current events but was cut short by the return of Meges and Menestheus, with Abantes and Myrtilus close on their heels. They were closely followed by Pyrrhus's servants, who had judged the lunch party complete and brought in a fine array of food and wine. After the meal had been laid out, and the servants dismissed, Pyrrhus said to his guests, "Please help yourselves, gentlemen. Meges, when you have found something to eat and drink, I would be pleased if you would sit next to me, so we can discuss the wisdom and understanding of your countrymen."

Meges was delighted to be given the position of honor at this informal meal and listened patiently as Pyrrhus told him of the favorable impression that Adrestus had made on him at their first meeting and also of the ideas that he hoped to present with regard to leaving a force of Epirote soldiers in Thessaly. Meges seemed in complete agreement, as none of them believed that Demetrius would regard this as his last attempt to bring Thessaly under his sway. Once Pyrrhus had dealt with the items of most immediate importance to them all, Meges said to him, "I know that the memory holds a great deal of sadness for you, Sire, but could I ask you to describe the Battle of Ipsus to me? Even in Thessaly, we have heard great tales of your exploits and how you managed to turn defeat into victory."

Pyrrhus began his tale, which seemed a rather simple one to him. Menestheus listened with all his attention, as he had not yet had a chance to see it through the eyes of a commander, despite the fact that he had been present himself. All the other men looked at Pyrrhus in something regarding awe. The story that seemed so simple to him was a revelation to the others, and the fighting withdrawal to Epirus and their subsequent escape to Greece was a tale that would amuse poets for generations to come. Even now, they were aware of an element of a poet's tragedy. The army that had just withdrawn had only declined battle because of numerical inferiority, and the king of that army was Pyrrhus's friend and companion from Ipsus, and later, in Greece. What changes of fortune lay in wait for all of them?

Chapter XXXXII

As Pyrrhus led his men back into Ambracia, he felt pleased with himself and smiled and waved to the cheering crowds, occasionally brushing flower petals off his shoulder. It was a gesture that was meant well, but they left an awkward stain on the iron discs of his armor.

His meeting with Adrestus had been extremely successful, and his Thessalian colleague had insisted that the force of 2,000 cavalry from Thessaly should stay in Lamia to reinforce the Epirote soldiers. He could now be confident in the new friendship that had been forged between the two countries and that Demetrius, for the time being at least, was unable to force his hand.

He felt an uneasiness, though, as he and Menestheus approached the balcony of the palace, where he would return the salute of the army and dismiss them to their usual quarters. He could see Antigone and Meriones on the balcony, waving at them, but there was a sadness in their faces that was not there when he left them for Thessaly.

Full of misgivings, he dismounted from his horse at the bottom of the steps, and when Cineas and Abantes had joined them, they made their way as a group up the stairs to the palace platform.

Antigone took him in her arms, saying only, "Welcome home, my poor love," before embracing her other returned friends.

Meriones bowed to Pyrrhus. He too looked as if he had just been dealt a cruel blow by fate. Pyrrhus took his friend by the hand and said to him, "I thank you for your welcome, Meriones. I had hoped that our return from our expedition would have been more a cause for happiness than sadness."

"All of Epirus will give thanks to the gods, Sire. You have returned safely to us, as have all the men in your army. Your friends are saddened, though, by news that arrived last night from Egypt. A letter came addressed to you from King Ptolemy. In your absence, I gave it to the queen to read. I must tell you that your beloved sister, Deidameia, is dead. It seems she did not recover from complications of the birth of a son for Demetrius."

"When did this happen, Meriones?"

"Three months ago, Sire."

"And the boy?"

"The child was stillborn, Sire."

Pyrrhus's face became a mask of bewilderment. The person whom he loved above all others, second only to Antigone, was dead. All he could think of at that moment was the wonderful smile with which she welcomed him back to Sotion's house after he and Menestheus had been at work on the army's camp, the loving way she herded them into their baths and patiently listened to their story of the day's work as they ate an impossibly late dinner. This wonderful woman was now dead, caught up in nature's web of deceit and disappointment. Slowly, it came to him that this was how Demetrius had been able to harden his heart toward him, a friend who had saved his life and liberty after their disastrous day at Ipsus.

Antigone took his arm now. "My love, give your salute to the army, and then you must come to bed with me. Menestheus and Cineas can take care of all the details. They are your friends, and after your splendid victory, you can rest for a while."

Pyrrhus nodded to his lady and called Menestheus to him. "Deidameia is dead, my friend. Let us give the army their due salute, and then I will leave you to deal with them."

Pyrrhus walked to the edge of the balcony, and the waiting faces of the soldiers showed their understanding that their king had been given sad news of some sort. Pyrrhus raised his right hand to motion them to silence. "My friends, my soldiers, we have returned home victorious today, and you all have my thanks. For my part, I thank the gods that all of you have returned safely from our campaign. Go now and have your well-deserved rest." Pyrrhus then embraced Menestheus and Abantes, then took Cineas's arm as he returned to Antigone's side. "I have just been told that Deidameia is dead, my friend. Antigone and I are going to retire to our chambers. I will leave you to take care of Menestheus, if you are agreeable."

"Of course, Sire. If there is anything I can do, please call on me."

Antigone held Pyrrhus in her arms as they lay in their bed. She held him tightly as he shed his tears and lightly stroked his hair after his breathing had become more regular.

Some time later, Pyrrhus said to her, "After you, she was the finest person I have ever known. It seems so unfair that she should be the one to die."

"I know, my love. There is never any way to explain such things. All we can do is to keep her alive in our memory. I never had the pleasure of meeting her, but I read her letters to us, and I think of her as a dear friend. This is all she would ask of you, and you must not let your sadness overcome you."

"You are right, of course. All I want to do now is to go to sleep in your arms. That will allow me to think that there is still some good to be had in this life."

The six members of Pyrrhus's royal council waited until mid-morning before knocking on their king's door the following day. As he opened the door, Pyrrhus felt that he had worked through the greater part of his grieving and was aware that Menestheus and Cineas must be as heartbroken as he. As they entered, he could see they were deeply troubled, and he embraced each of them before leading them into the sitting room.

"Please sit down, gentlemen," said Antigone, who was waiting to receive them. "Pyrrhus ordered a special breakfast today that he wanted to share with all of you."

As he sat down with his plate, Pyrrhus said to Menestheus, "Do you remember the look on Deidameia's face when we arrived at Sotions's house late at night from Corinth? Sotion was ready to take our heads off with his sword, and when she realized that we had only come back early to get the ships ready, she told us it was very ungracious of us to surprise them, and then had our baths prepared!"

"She did have a wonderful sense of humor, Sire. And she was always ready to accommodate us at all hours," replied Menestheus. "And how happy she looked when Demetrius was with us for those few days."

"They were good days, my friend, despite all the sadness of the events leading up to them. She was almost able to make Demetrius forget his troubles with one of her smiles."

"She will always live in our hearts, Sire," said Cineas. "I explained to the officers why you excused yourself yesterday, and they asked if they might send some flowers to the temple of Zeus in her memory."

"Thank them for me, will you Cineas? That would be a wonderful gesture. Tell me, my friend, would it be appropriate for us to hold a service for her at this late date?"

"I think it would be entirely appropriate, Sire. She was much loved here in Epirus, and it would allow the people to have their own time to celebrate her life. For the living, it would be equally important to commemorate her life with either a banquet, or athletic games. It is said that even Achilles was able to derive comfort from the games held in honor of Patroclus."

"I know she would like the idea of games, Cineas. She told me once that one of the few things that would make her consider wishing to come back to this life as a man was the pleasure of competing in athletic competitions. It was her only grievance at being born a woman. We could perhaps manage to fulfill both of your suggestions, as we should have some sort of meal together after the games are held. I will have no reservations about giving Ptolemy the credit for his inspiration, and I will use his military games as the model for Deidameia's funeral games."

It is a very useful thing for a man to be kept busy at times of extreme grief, especially if there is the belief that the departed loved one, in some unknown place, can derive some pleasure from these efforts. For Pyrrhus, the time spent in organizing the service at the temple of Zeus in Deidameia's honor, and the subsequent games was intensely therapeutic. He was able to bring himself to believe that she was somehow aware of the love that was being shown toward her, both by himself and his fellow countrymen, who had always deeply admired her. The banquet that followed the games was not one that compared with a state occasion but was a meal enjoyed by all of the people of Ambracia and the surrounding areas of Epirus who chose to attend the games. The common people, as well as Pyrrhus and his retinue, enjoyed a plain meal of bread, cheese, and cold meats along with an ample quantity of simple wine. Although it had not been his intention, Pyrrhus won the hearts of his subjects by allowing them to join him in his grief, and the celebration of her life. As he walked among them, with Antigone at his side, their tears and wishes gave him great comfort when he understood that their loss was as great as his own.

This was perhaps the definitive moment in the process of emotional bonding between Pyrrhus and his people. Up until this moment, the men and women of Epirus looked to Pyrrhus with hope, but from now they also offered their love and loyalty. They were also pleased to see Pyrrhus compete as an equal in the games. Curiously, the final results were a reproduction of those of Ptolemy's army games. Menestheus won the running race, Pyrrhus the javelin, and in the final bout of the wrestling Pyrrhus was once again laid on his back, this time by a powerful member of his Agema. The sight of this enormous man helping her husband to his feet left Antigone almost incapacitated with laughter, further endearing her to all who were close enough to witness her mirth.

After a short period of rest, Pyrrhus felt able to embark on the projects that were the most admirable of his life. He worked long and hard on the design and construction of the new city of Bereniceia, which gave Epirus a wonderful port.

The opportunities of trade gave his country the realization of creating wealth by means of commerce and intermediation, wealth that otherwise would have been denied her if she relied solely on natural gifts of pasture and fertility. This new wealth in turn enabled Pyrrhus to create schools for the children of his country and philosophical colleges for the gifted minds of his own generation. Architecture was also endowed. A new palace, known as the Pyrrheion was built on the most prominent hill of Ambracia. It included spacious offices for his civil service as well as the most successful of the city's merchants, in addition to enclosed theaters and open amphitheaters, where dramatic contests were held that were the equal of those seen in Thebes or Athens.

A personal event also occurred, enabling Pyrrhus and Antigone to finally call themselves a family, the birth of their son, Ptolemy.

Smaller achievements were also to be found. He encouraged the farmers and pastoralists to make the most of those things with which nature had endowed Epirus. A special breed of cows, known to all as "red skinned," became sought after all over Greece for the quality of their milk. He also supported the breeders of the dogs known as "Molossi," said to be the finest sheep dogs in Greece.

Over several years, Pyrrhus was able to bring Epirus into the greater Greek world. The prosperity of his country was such that their currency was favored over that of Corinth in the course of trade with Italy, and many Italian merchants chose to base their Greek operations at Bereniceia. He was also able to pursue his own personal interests, and two years after his sister's funeral, he published his literary work, *Comments on Military Theory and Practice*.

During this time, Pyrrhus achieved his greatest peace-time accomplishments, and also the greatest denial of his true desires. He was a warrior at heart, and these years of peace and happiness fulfilled only part of his soul. His life was soon to change. Evenhanded as always, fate would give him the opportunity to become embroiled once again in the struggles of the greatest powers known to the world, while it took from him the companionship of the woman whose love meant more to him than life itself.

The end of Book I .

A Pyrrhic Victory

Volume II

Destiny Unfolds

CHAPTER I

The smell of Antigone's funeral pyre still haunted Pyrrhus during his waking hours, and the loss of her embrace made his nights lonely and windswept. On this morning, as on each morning of the last sixty days, he gazed at the rising sun with an emptiness in his heart. On his lap sat the letter that had arrived two days ago from Egypt from Ptolemy and Berenice, reread so often that he could recite it by heart without any conscious effort at all.

From the Father to the Son, Greetings,

My dear Pyrrhus, it is with the greatest sadness that I acknowledge your last letter, telling us of the recent death of Antigone. The tears of Berenice and myself have spattered this parchment as I wrote this letter. Our deepest sadness is that your grief must be even more severe than our own. Please accept our most sincere wishes that you will be able to continue your life and your works, despite this tragedy. I understand how great a loss this has been to you, but please believe me when I say that your life

*may still have meaning in the future, if for no other rea-
son than it will enable you to watch your fine son grow
to manhood. I will be eternally grateful that your esteem
for me enabled you to allow your son to carry my name.*

Ptolemy

Pyrrhus continued to stare out his window over the roof-
tops of Ambracia until the morning's customary knock startled
him out of his brown study. He walked to the door to admit his
advisors and allowed himself his first smile of the day. His son,
Ptolemy, would be the first to enter his chambers and would
sit on his lap as he conducted his morning audience with his
council. The boy was now three years of age and, with the
adaptability of the young, had accepted the death of his mother
more quickly than had his father. As Pyrrhus opened the door
to his suite, his son beamed a smile at him, spread open his
arms and said, "Papa!"

Pyrrhus picked his son up and hugged him. "How is my little
soldier this morning?"

"Papa," repeated Ptolemy, holding Pyrrhus's neck with all
his strength.

"Would the young man like some breakfast?" said Pyrrhus,
unable to resist a smile.

"Breakfast!" repeated his son, happy to be carried to the table by his father.

A short time later, when Pyrrhus's tunic had been sprinkled
with a mixture of bread crumbs, butter, and saliva, he turned to
Cineas and said, "And now, my friend, what do you have for me
this morning?"

"This is no ordinary morning, Sire," replied Cineas, glad finally
to be able to offer his king some news that would ease his torment.
"A letter has arrived from Macedonia, bearing the royal seal."

"Indeed!" said Pyrrhus. "We are in exalted company this
morning. Gentlemen, please help yourselves to something to eat
while I open this epistle."

Cineas and Menestheus, along with the other members of the royal council, kept one eye on Pyrrhus as they helped themselves to food and drink. Macedonia was the greatest power in their region, and a letter with a royal seal could not be other than important.

As Pyrrhus read the letter through several times, it became obvious to Cineas that it was of great import. Pyrrhus's mouth cautiously curled at the edges to form a smile, and his eyes gave a promise of an excitement that had not been seen for many a day.

At length, Pyrrhus sat down again and passed the letter over to Cineas to read. His son took the opportunity to jump into his lap, giving the father a moment's disquiet as one of his testicles gave a loud complaint.

"You will see, my friend, that we are invited to aid Alexander, the young king of Macedonia, in his struggle against his older brother, Antipater, who has gone against the wishes of their mother and usurped his share of the kingdom. What could be more perfect?"

"A domestic dispute in a royal family is fraught with danger, Sire," replied Cineas.

"True, my friend, but it is also full of opportunity. Please show it to Menestheus and the others, and when I have cleaned this young man's face, we will have an opportunity to discuss the matter."

After their customary game of chasing around the room, Pyrrhus returned his son's face to a state fit for others to see and took his hand. "I will send you off to play with the other children now, my son. I will see you for dinner."

"Yes, Papa," replied Ptolemy. As he opened the door, the young man caught sight of his nanny, the source of many of the good things in his life. With a squeal of delight, he took her hand and walked toward the nursery, turning back to wave good-bye to his father.

Pyrrhus felt an optimism that had long been in abeyance well up in his breast as he returned to his meeting, sat down in his chair, and asked Cineas to read the letter aloud to him, so that they could all absorb it.

"And now, my friend, perhaps you could try and sift the facts from the rhetoric, and give us all a summary of how you see matters in Macedonia, and we can then discuss our response to his request."

"It is reasonably clear, Sire, and reminiscent of many such disputes within ruling houses. You will recall that after the death of Cassander two years ago, the eldest of his three sons became king of Macedonia. This young man, Philip, died some six months ago, following a fall from his horse, so the throne was once again vacant. Cassander's widow, Thessalonice, then made a decision, the like of which has often caused turmoil in such circumstances. She felt her two remaining sons should have an equal claim on the throne and decreed that they should *both* become kings of Macedonia. As a result, the country was partitioned, with Antipater, the older son, governing the eastern half of the country, while Alexander, the younger son, would govern the western half. That is the background to this drama.

"This letter is from Alexander, the younger of the two, who has been the victim of the inevitable conflict. He states that his brother has put their mother to death, and that Antipater has driven him from Macedonia and taken the whole country under his sway, proclaiming that Macedonia has always been a single nation under a single king and he has only taken what was his to claim. Alexander, as the aggrieved party, naturally raises the objection that his kingship had been decreed by their mother as regent and had the support of the Assembly of Nobles and the people. Alexander goes on to ask you to intercede for him, to reclaim his lost patrimony, adding that he is prepared to be generous to you in return for helping him to regain his rightful throne. He adds that he has also written to Demetrius in a similar vein, hoping that one of you will be able to come to his aid. He says finally that he is in hiding with those of his bodyguard who remained loyal, and the messenger who brought this letter will know how to find him."

"A very lucid summary, Cineas," said Pyrrhus. "My own first reaction is that this proposal could offer us a great deal. The only risk to us in helping this young man would be the fight we could have on our hands if the Macedonian army wholeheartedly supported Antipater."

"Exactly so, Sire," replied Cineas, "although I doubt the murder of his mother has endeared Antipater to his fellow countrymen. I suspect there would be a great deal of sympathy for Alexander in the army. It is one thing to kill a direct rival but quite another to kill one's own mother. You recall the hatred that Cassander earned for himself after he executed Olympias and the rest of the great Alexander's family."

Pyrrhus thought for a time and then looked at Menestheus. "And you, my friend, what do you think of all this?"

"I think it is an opportunity that you should interest yourself in, Sire. You would have a considerable amount of natural justice behind you, and, in the worst event, if you face an undivided Macedonian army supporting the claim of Antipater, there is no reason why you could not retire without accepting battle."

"Those are my feelings, Menestheus. Cineas, perhaps you would be kind enough to draft a letter to Alexander, offering my support. We could discuss it over dinner tonight. And now, gentlemen, I must prepare myself. I am due to review several cases at the law courts this morning."

Pyrrhus smiled to himself as he walked to the court building. He was sure the cases he would review today would be anything but pleasant, but the letter from Macedonia had stirred something deep inside him. These recent years of peace had enabled him to earn a considerable degree of self-worth, and he felt rightfully proud of how Epirus had blossomed during this time. The adventurer and soldier in him now demanded to be heard, however, and he knew he could not neglect this opportunity to be a player on the world stage. He would demand a suitable compensation for his efforts, but even if the compensation consisted only of adventure and prestige, he could not bring himself to decline this invitation.

The afternoon that Pyrrhus spent at the law courts was as difficult as he had suspected, but even that could not suppress his enthusiasm. He had two hours to himself before he was due to dine with his advisors. He had spent part of the time playing with his son, and now, lying back in his bath, he was able to contemplate his future. To accept Alexander's invitation would take him from his stable, peaceful world and return him to the turbulent arena of Hellenistic politics, the only world to which he truly belonged. There was no doubt in his mind that it would lead to conflict with Demetrius. If Pyrrhus was to become stronger, then he would naturally become a rival, which was anathema to a man like Demetrius, who had no concept of sharing power with anyone in the Greek world. There was little doubt that Demetrius was aiming at complete mastery of Greece. It was also possible he was planning to reclaim all of his father's previous dominions.

Also, there was Lysimachus to take into account. If Pyrrhus came to the aid of the young Alexander, it was likely that Antipater would turn to Lysimachus for help. What a struggle was in the making! The events leading up to Ipsus were no more charged with possibilities than this moment, and he still thought of that battle as the most formative experience in his life. For now, he could enjoy his bath. There were no doubts in his mind that he would accept this invitation, and then see where fate would lead him. All of his being cried out for the clamor of battle, and now it was certain he would hear it soon.

Two weeks later, another letter bearing the royal seal of Macedonia was brought to Pyrrhus's chambers by Cineas. Pyrrhus invited his friend to sit and gave him a goblet of wine.

"Please be so good as to open the letter, my friend, and read it to me."

Cineas did as he was bade and quickly scanned the letter before reading it aloud to his king. Cineas was also not left unmoved by the adventure that was promised them, and he could not resist a smile as he read the letter to Pyrrhus:

King Alexander to King Pyrrhus, Greetings,

> *My dear Cousin, I was very glad to read your letter, and am pleased to acknowledge your willingness to help me in this dark hour. As to the means at my disposal to*

*show my gratitude, I am pleased to offer you the districts
of Stymphaea and Paravaea, which form the western-
most part of Macedonia. These regions would be ceded
to Epirus with my gratitude for your aid. Please give me
your decision as soon as possible.*

Alexander

"He is as stingy as his father, Cineas," said Pyrrhus. "He
wants me to do all the work and offers me a few cow paddocks
for my troubles. Please draft a reply acknowledging his letter,
but point out that I also demand the territories of Ambracia,
Acarnania, and Amphilochia. If he is prepared to do this, I will
return him to his rightful place on the throne of Macedonia."

Cineas did not reply for a moment, but sat back, deep in
thought. After a moment's reflection, he smiled and said to Pyrrhus, "I agree with you, Sire. This undertaking is not to be taken
lightly, and there must be a worthy strategic objective if it is to
have any basis in logic. You realize, of course, that, even if it
does not antagonize Demetrius, then you will come into direct
opposition with Lysimachus? Apart from his natural hostility,
Antipater married Lysimachus's daughter, Euridice."

"That is clear to me, my friend, but we cannot let ourselves
become anyone's lackey, and we may even be doing Lysimachus
a favor if we prevent Demetrius from becoming more powerful."

Pyrrhus was in no doubt that his terms would be accepted by
young Alexander, and he gave Menestheus and Abantes instructions to begin to prepare the expedition immediately. It could be
two weeks before a reply was received from Macedonia, taking into
account the indecision of a weak young king, and he could have
the army prepared in that time. As patience was not one of his most
outstanding virtues, Pyrrhus was happy to use the time effectively
so he would be able to march as soon as he had his reply.

His friends were also affected by the excitement. Cineas was
pleased to return to the world of international political intrigue,
and Menestheus and Abantes were no less excited. The great

virtue of this particular situation was the great benefit it offered with so little risk. It would strengthen Epirus significantly and give his army a campaign with its supply line intact, with little likelihood of bloodshed. A situation to be savored.

Pyrrhus joined his commanders each day to discuss the preparations and visited at least part of the army every day. The accounts of his previous military exploits had grown in many retellings so that he was already being compared to the great Alexander. He did not know that this idea would spread over the coming years so that his very presence at a battle was worth a battalion of phalangites.

As the days came and went, the Epirote army reached its moment of readiness, and, just before Pyrrhus's hypothetical fortnight was up, he received his reply from Alexander. He agreed to Pyrrhus's terms and indicated that he and his retinue would watch for Pyrrhus's approach and join him on their march toward Macedonia. Despite the fact that the young man was in hiding, he clearly had sufficient resources to be aware of the events that he had set in motion.

HISTORICAL CONTEXT

The manuscript of *A Pyrrhic Victory* is fiction, but it is loyal to the known history of Pyrrhus's life.

Many of the supporting characters are also historical figures.

I have tried to be loyal to the history of these times both philosophically and factually—to the great deeds of Alexander the Great and his contemporaries, to the wonderful achievements of classical Greece, and to the Romans, who are nearing their time of greatness in the Mediterranean world.

There are a few small liberties that I have taken with fine historical detail to avoid unnecessary complexity. An example of one of these liberties is my giving the names of Lucius Cornelius Scipio and Gnaeus Fulvius as the consuls of Rome at the time of Pyrrhus's and Antigone's wedding. These two men were the consuls in 298 BC, but it is possible that they entered their time of office a short time after the wedding. I avoided speaking about the consulship of 299 BC because in that year there was an interregnum of the consulship, with the election of Military Tribunes with consular power. Such interregna occurred from time to time in Rome when there was a serious dispute between the patricians and the plebeians, at this time usually related to access to offices of power by the plebeians.

AND DEMETRIUS   <u>GREECE</u> - ANTIGONUS
<u>EGYPT</u> - PTOLEMY

THE HELLENISTIC KINGS IN 301 b.c

N

BLACK SEA

OLIA
• IPSUS

• GAUGAMELA
• ARBELA

◉ ASIA

Euphrates river

Tigris river

CYPRUS

• SIDON
• TYRE

• GAZA

BABYLON

PERSIAN GULF

RED SEA

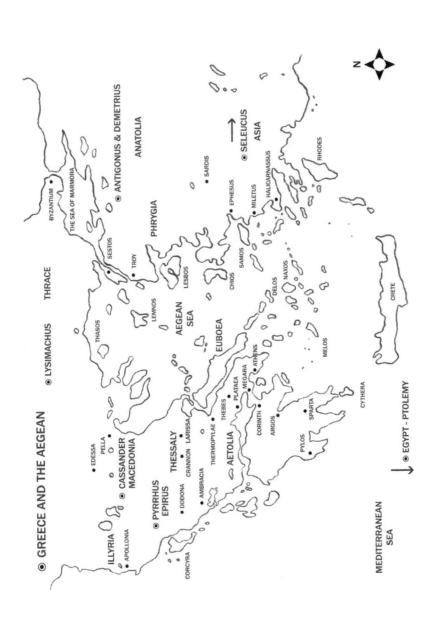

GREECE AND THE AEGEAN

BIBLIOGRAPHY

I have drawn on both ancient and modern authors and historians to try and create an image of the ancient Mediterranean world as the ancients saw it.

Among the ancient sources are, in alphabetical order:

AESCHYLUS — *The Persians.* Translated by Philip Vellacott. 1961.

ARISTOPHANES — *The Frogs.* Trans. David Barrett. 1964.

ARISTOTLE — *The Athenian Constitution.* Trans. .J.Rhodes. 1984.

ARRIAN — *The Campaigns of Alexander.* Trans. Aubrey de Selincourt. 1958.

HERODOTUS — *The Histories.* Trans. Aubrey de Selincourt. 1954.

HOMER — *The Iliad.* Trans. E.V.Rieu. 1950.

HOMER — *The Odyssey.* Trans. E.V.Rieu. 1946.

LIVY — *The History of Rome from its Foundations.* Books I– V. Trans.Aubrey de Selincourt. 1960. Books VI – X. Trans. Betty Radice. 1982. Books XI – XXX. Trans. Aubrey de Selincourt. 1965. Books XXXI – XLV. Trans. Henry Bettinson. 1976.

PLATO — *The Republic.* Trans. Desmond Lee. 1955.

PLUTARCH — *Plutarch On Sparta.* Trans. Richard Talbert. 1988.

PLUTARCH — *The Parallel Lives of the Noble Greeks and Romans.* The lives of (in chronological order): Solon, Themistocles, Pericles, Alcibiades, Lysander and Flaminius. Trans. Ian Scott Kilvert. 1960. The lives of: Agesilaus, Pelopidas, Timoleon, Demosthenes, Phocion, Alexander, Demetrius and Pyrrhus. Trans. Ian Scott Kilvert. 1973.

POLYBIUS — *The Rise of the Roman Empire.* Trans. Ian Scott Kilvert. 1979.

QUINTUS CURTIUS RUFUS — *The History of Alexander.* Trans. John Yardley. 1984.

THUCYDIDES — *The History of the Peloponnesian War.* Trans. Rex Warner. 1954.

XENOPHON — *A History of My Times.* Trans. Rex Warner. 1966.

XENOPHON — *The Persian Expedition.* Trans. Rex Warner. 1949.

The modern sources. These are the historians whom I have come to admire as my teachers. Some of their inspired teaching has made its way into the text.

In particular, I have drawn on their wisdom with regard to Alexander's goals and ideals, and the interpretation of his influence on the history of the world.

General Fuller provided the great summary regarding Alexander's legacy, drawing on the contributions of both ancient and modern historians.

BURY AND MEIGGS — *A History of Greece.* 1975.

MICHAEL CRAWFORD — *The Roman Republic.* 1992.

GENERAL J.F.C. FULLER — T*he Decisive Battles of the Western World.* 1954

GENERAL J.F.C.FULLER — *The Generalship of Alexander the Great.* 1960.

JANICE J. GEBBERT — *Antigonus Gonatus.* 1997.

EDWARD GIBBON — *The Decline and Fall of the Roman Empire*. Editor: Oliphant Smeaton. 1910.

PIERRE JOUGUET — Foreword to: *Macedonian Imperialism and the Hellenization of the East*. 1928.

J.P.MAHAFFEY — *A History of Egypt Under the Macedonian Dynasty*. 1899.

DR.W.W.TARN — *Alexander the Great and the Unity of Mankind*. 1933.

ULRICH WILCKEN — *Alexander the Great*. 1932.

F.A.WRIGHT — *Alexander the Great*. 1934.

Printed in Australia
AUHW020750130422
362261AU00002B/2